I t all happened in seconds. The air swirled in her ears and she could hear the sounds of shells exploding around her. Then the sounds quickly faded.

Twisting and turning in the air, she felt a hard snap, then a reassuring tug on her harness. She pulled on her risers, checking that she had a good canopy. She hung in the air. She saw the flashes of the ground guns firing, following the light beams as one after another they zeroed in on the plane.

Suddenly the plane exploded. The Nazi ground gunners had found their mark.

With the seconds she had left under the canopy, there was nothing to commit to memory; no prominent landmarks could be seen—everything was black. She had to find her radio transmitter.

The ground came up hard, but she made a good landing. She was at the edge of a plowed field. She quickly gathered up her canopy and raced into the forest, not stopping until she was deep in the woods.

She rolled the parachute and hid it under the brambles. Using essential moments to check her gear, she removed a button on her coat. Unscrewing the top of the button, she could see a tiny luminescent compass pointing north. *Get moving.* She moved out, heading due west.

With every step she took, Eileen tried to remember the lessons of her spycraft and what she was in Germany for. There was so much to try to remember. The first step she took was months ago, when she joined the army. Becoming a spy was the last thing she had expected.

Also by Michael Salazar

DROP ZONE
THE LUCIFER LIGHT
THE WAR ANGEL

THE
SHADOW WAR

MICHAEL SALAZAR

BANTAM BOOKS

NEW YORK   TORONTO   LONDON   SYDNEY   AUCKLAND

THE SHADOW WAR
A Bantam Book / October 2004

Published by
Bantam Dell
A Division of Random House, Inc.
New York, New York

Bantam Books and the rooster colophon are registered trademarks of
Random House, Inc.

ISBN 0-553-58632-7

Manufactured in the United States of America
Published simultaneously in Canada

OPM   10 9 8 7 6 5 4 3 2 1

DEDICATED TO EILEEN GOULD, THE REAL DEAL.

To Violy, my wife and dance partner in life.

With respect to those in the OSS Book of Honor and the unnamed stars on the wall at the CIA headquarters.

ACKNOWLEDGMENTS

Nita Taublib, John Flicker,
Carole Bidnick, Eileen Gould,
Peter Pinto, Michael Yon, Jean
and Julian Leek, Boyd Lease,
James Baarda, Charles Meador,
Hugh Mcfadden, Sonny Ruben,
Victor Davis, Dennis Whitfield,
and T. Davis Bunn.

I would like to express a special
thanks to my sister Patricia for all
her valuable help, ideas, and
suggestions.

It is always good to have a friend
willing to help place the final
pieces.

Who controls the money controls the government.
Who controls the government controls the people.

—LAW II OF THE 99 LODGE

Faust
Where art thou damned?

Mephistopheles
In hell.

Faust
How comes it that thou art out of hell?

Mephistopheles
Why, this *is* hell, nor am I out of it.

—CHRISTOPHER MARLOWE, *THE TRAGICALL HISTORY OF DOCTOR FAUSTUS*

Then I heard the voice of the Lord saying, "Whom shall I send? Who will go for us?"
"Here I am," I said, "send me!"

—ISAIAH 6:8

THE
SHADOW WAR

0230 THURSDAY / 27 MARCH 1941
THE CENTURION CASTLE / GERMANY

NINETY-NINE MEN STOOD IN LINE IN FRONT OF A copper bowl covered with diamonds. A black velvet cloth covered the bowl.

Seventy-six men had already reached into the bowl. They were watched closely by the lodge demon wearing a hooded purple robe.

Number seventy-seven held his left hand high and spoke, "The Red Fox cannot be here. *I* will draw for him."

He plunged his hand under the cloth and pulled out his fist. He turned and faced the demon. He opened his fist. A white marble was in his hand. Smiling, he passed the marble to the lodge demon.

Raising his hand once more, he paused. "I will now draw for myself."

He repeated his act again. This time a black marble lay in his scarred palm.

There were gasps of shock by some but relief by the others still standing behind him. Number seventy-seven was shocked. It couldn't be! All his astrologers had guaranteed his success at the draw. They guaranteed it! He stood mute, his mouth gaping.

The lodge demon guided the man to the base of a green marble altar.

"Priest, complete the crossover." The lodge demon stood back.

A tall man wearing a white robe came forward and stood next to the bewildered man. The priest made a few strange hand movements in front of the tabernacle at the left of the altar. Then he opened it up and took out a blue glass chalice.

Number seventy-seven tried to talk but he could not form the words. This could not be happening! It was not foretold. Someone had deceived him.

The priest drew a sharp crystal dagger from his robe.

The man recoiled. "I invoke the right of the Golden Centurion!"

There were shouts of objection and the room quickly became bedlam. The lodge demon raised his hands to silence the room. "Silence! According to our law he *does* have the right to claim this position, he *is* who he is."

There were grumbles.

"I am the demon and I interpret the law. Some here just want to see blood spilled, and you will. He drew the black marble and our law still remains. No one is above the Order, but the Order." He turned to the trembling man. "You forfeit all your assets to the Order. Half will go to your replacement and the rest will be absorbed. Before you leave you will leave your blood."

Without waiting the priest took hold of the man's left hand and held it over the glass chalice. He drew a knife and sliced his palm. Blood ran freely into the cup. The priest almost tossed his hand away, then he pointed to a man wearing a white robe. "You have been selected. Do you sell your soul to the Order and all it entails?"

The man nodded and thrust out his left hand. The priest stabbed deeply into the man's left palm. Blood spurted over the altar and into the chalice. When the priest was satisfied he nodded to the lodge demon.

The demon pulled out a rolled parchment paper from his robe. He handed it to the priest along with a quill.

Grimacing, the man then dipped the quill into the chalice and signed his name in blood. He put down the quill and picked up the chalice. At the priest's command he took a drink, then handed it to the priest. The chalice was passed from man to man.

The priest turned to his first victim. "Now go, Golden Centurion, you have forty-five days from this day and this hour to complete your crossover to the Dark Sun."

Rudolf Hess, Deputy Führer of Nazi Germany, staggered from the small room, confused and dazed. "How could this have happened? Not to me. Not to me!" He looked down at his bleeding left hand and clenched it into a fist. "Not when I have the power! I brought it here and it is over for me?" It couldn't be right. It had to be a hex. Hess stumbled into his black Mercedes and held out his hand to the ministrations of his aide. "Take me to my castle!"

He banged his right hand on the seat again and again. He would find the source of the hex and lift it; otherwise, he was a dead man. As the Golden Centurion he would have to give his life to the Order in a grand and heroic fashion. He had no intention of losing it.

CHAPTER 1

1045 WEDNESDAY / 25 FEBRUARY 2004
NEW YORK CITY

BLOOD WAS EVERYWHERE. FIVE MEN LAY ON THE floor of an abandoned warehouse. Four of them were dead. One was wounded. Blindfolded with their wrists tied behind their backs, two of them had been executed.

Glass shards flew and laser dots rained in from the smashed out windows, painting the only man standing in the room like a red Christmas tree.

"DON'T SHOOT!" Sunny Vicam yelled at the top of his lungs, holding the empty revolver over his head. It was still smoking.

"Drop the gun! Get on the floor. Get on the god-damned floor, now!"

Sunny obeyed the faceless words by pitching the gun away, then dropping to the floor.

Doors and windows of the warehouse exploded in wood-and-glass splinters as cops with guns appeared everywhere.

Sunny was jumped on by everyone; all he saw were the feet, hands, and arms that held him to the concrete. Men wearing FBI blazers handcuffed him.

"You're under arrest!" an FBI blazer yelled in his ear and started reading him his rights.

Sunny could barely hear because his ears still rang from the echoing shots that he'd fired in the open building.

"I count four dead. One wounded. Looks like he executed two of them," said an FBI guy wearing dark Ray-Ban sunglasses.

The first body, whose wrists were bound, was turned over.

"Hey, this is one of *ours*," said another FBI agent. The way he combed his jet-black hair made him look like a part-time Elvis impersonator.

The second body was checked.

"So is this one," said FBI Elvis.

FBI Elvis looked at the dead body, then jerked Sunny to his feet. "And just who the fuck are you?"

Sunny just stared at the man. "It looks like you were about a minute too late, Elvis." He had nothing more to say.

"Hold him. Hold him good." FBI Elvis backed up and kicked Sunny in the stomach.

Sunny fell to the ground gasping for breath.

THE INTERROGATION ROOM WAS SMALL, CRAMPED, AND hot. Sunny sat in a wooden chair next to a steel table. His left hand was cuffed to a bar in the wall. Two men entered the room. One wore dark Ray-Ban sunglasses. The other was FBI Elvis.

Sunny's stomach was sore. Looking from the shackle to the man who'd kicked him, he nodded. "I don't care who you are, asshole. Even like this, if you try a go at me again, I'm gonna fight back. So come on, if you think you're bad enough, Mr. FBI Elvis."

FBI Elvis's eyes lit up, his face turned red, and he tried to step forward but was quickly restrained by the other agent, who opened the door and pushed him out in one motion, slamming the door behind him.

He yanked off his sunglasses, then stalked over and

got nose to nose with Sunny. "You've already been read your rights, but you still want to play stupid and tough." He looked back at the door. "I *wanted* to let him beat you, hell I'd help. I'm old school. He's old school. But I can't. The rules even apply to you. Here in America we really do have rules of law—and my people *will* follow them, old school or not, like it or not. That's *if* you cooperate. Otherwise, I can always call him back in and leave you cuffed." He took a step back and glared down on Sunny. "Right now I got four dead bodies on my hands, and one critical. Two of my UCs are dead; executed, all killed by the same gun. Everyone witnessed that you were the one holding that smoking gun in your hand."

"I didn't kill all of them. Not your boys at least." Sunny glared at him. "And just who do you think I am?"

"That's what I'm trying to find out. Who are you?"

"Who are you?"

Mr. Ray-Ban glared at Sunny. "Rob Rose, FBI agent in charge of this op."

"Well, Mr. Rob Rose, *old school* FBI agent in charge, I'm just a working stiff with a possible blown cover."

"Oh yeah, *really?*" Rose grinned wide. "Okay. I'll play along. You're CIA, right?"

Sunny shook his head. "Mossad."

Rose grinned wider. "Ah, the Institute. Great! Even better. Now *that's* original, a terrorist mole coming from the Jews. There are a lot of legal boundaries to cross and more details to check out. So now what? Are you going to cry for a lawyer, too?"

"I just want to get the fuck out of here."

"So, are you going to talk?"

"First get a guy named Frank Delgado here."

"Delgado, who's he?" Rose asked.

"My handler. The only thing I really know about him is that his name *isn't* Frank Delgado. I would guess that you'll find him listed somewhere in your own secret yellow pages." Sunny caught Rose's eyes rolling. "Hey, I'm not crazy. Go ahead. Make the call. It'll only take a minute, right? What have you got to lose?" He looked at the manacles. "I'm sure not going anywhere at the moment."

Rose peered into Sunny's ice-cold eyes. "*Just who in the hell are you?*"

Sunny smiled and raised his eyebrows. "Look, can I get something to eat and drink, please?"

Rose stood up and walked to the door. "I'm going to check it out."

He was gone for only a few minutes, then came rushing back in the room. He uncuffed Sunny, handed him a bottle of Pepsi, and said, "Damn! The orders I got from the top are that you will remain here until Mr. Delgado gets here, and I'm to make you comfortable."

"Food." Sunny rubbed his wrist. "And some air-conditioning."

"Right."

The police station was bedlam. Cops were furious that an unannounced, uncoordinated, unsanctioned, then botched undercover FBI ops happened on their beat. The station suddenly filled with incensed federal agents who'd just lost two of their own and the arguments began. Everyone wanted a piece of the mystery man in Interrogation Room 3.

There was nothing to know or remember about Mr. Frank Delgado. He was just someone in the crowd, and the moment he walked into the police corridor, both Rose and the police commissioner hustled him into a side room.

It was over two hours later and a couple of thrown punches by lower-level players before any understandings were finally reached. Several secure phone calls to highly placed people had been made. The last one went directly to the White House. Delgado and Rose entered Interrogation Room 3 with some very shaky and tenuous understandings.

Rose looked hesitant. "Do you want to file assault charges on my second?"

Sunny looked confused. "On Elvis? For what?"

"Assault for kicking you back in the warehouse."

Sunny shook his head. "Two of yours were murdered, execution style. I'm just glad that he didn't put a few slugs in me. I would've done worse. You just tell Elvis that I said he kicks like a little girl and we're even."

Rose crossed his arms and gave a slow and satisfied nod. He knew that he was working with a kind of ally, but just what kind he intended to find out. "All right. Done. So, then, what went down back there?"

Delgado nodded to Sunny. "Go ahead, all we agreed that he has to know it too. Tell him."

Sunny looked at Rose. "First, I want to know something from you."

"Go."

"How did you guys know two of your boys were compromised?"

"A tip-off. A tip that came too late."

"I see," Sunny said to Rose, then pointed toward Delgado. "Okay. Delgado came to see me in Israel while I was working a job for Mossad and went deep cover for the Shin Bet."

"What did you do for them?" Rose asked.

Sunny sat silent.

Delgado said, "It's okay. Start to finish."

"I was a *kidon*. I took out the trash."

Rose was incredulous. "Be more clear; you mean you were an assassin?"

"Yeah, but never on American soil." Sunny wanted to laugh at how fast the color drained from Rose's face. He hadn't even seen the tip of the iceberg. "See, I've worked on and off for Delgado and his company a whole bunch of times; freelance contracting and that sort of thing. He needed someone who knew Hamas and the PLO. It was his hunch that they had a chapter in New York working out of the Islamic Society Mosque.

"At the time I'd been working undercover in Palestine for the Jews on a two-year contract. It took over a year to penetrate; first I joined the Muslim Youth Association. I just mimicked their fair-haired boys, if you can call them that. I was in. From there I was recruited by Hamas."

Rose was hooked. "What did you do for them?"

Sunny glanced at Delgado, who nodded

"I was a rat killer. You know what that is?"

"Yeah. In prisons they're inmates who kill snitches or carry out vendettas."

"And who says that the Palestinians aren't in prison? You never woke up in Palestine, huh?" Sunny let out a humorless chuckle. "It worked out perfect for Mossad; if anyone was on their hit list, it was a double bonus day for them. If their own people were on the Hamas hit list, they were tipped off before it happened." He cupped his mouth and sighed. "But in a very short time I got *totally* burnt out on the Palestinian rubble and the constant murder. Hate and revenge is the way of life over there, but I don't have to tell you all that shit."

"When I went to Mossad they let me have what was left on his contract," Delgado interjected.

"So, I jumped at the chance to get out of there and go to New York." It was Sunny's turn to level with Rose. "See, Mr. Rob Rose, like you, I'm an American, a *loyal* one. The cover story I used when I went into Hamas was as a *disgruntled* Muslim American. I learned to speak the language well enough to blend in. I did a few hit jobs for Hamas Council against the Israelis. The killings were arranged by Mossad to look genuine. The Council bought the whole act. I was golden. After talking with Delgado I went back to the Hamas Council and told them that I was burnt out. At the time I had been their primary executioner. Hey, even *they* have burnout issues. So they bought my story and sent me to New York."

Rose leaned closer. "So what's the deal here?"

"Hamas uses credit card fraud and counterfeit money to build up a giant tobacco buy. Then they take the money to a tobacco connection in Raleigh and buy over-produced and unstamped brands of cigarettes from a crooked source producer.

"See, with the countless tons of tobacco they process

twenty-four hours a day, all that the tobacco foreman has to do is let the machines run for an extra ten minutes longer than scheduled. Do you know how many cigarettes ten minutes can give you?"

"No." Rose shook his head.

"Millions of dollars' worth. Then they'd truck the loads and sell them to the Russian Mafia in New Jersey, tax-free. I know you've seen the kids on the street with their black trash bags full of cigarette cartons. They sell them for less than half of retail.

"With the genuine currency from the deal, Hamas then funnels the rest to secret accounts. They buy guns and munitions and bankroll their nasty activities. You'd be amazed at the weapons and munitions that can be bought online these days. It's starting to give arms dealers a bad name.

"Anyway, my sponsor here in New York is named Mustafa al Habib. It's his *real* name." Sunny eyed Rose. "He's the guy I wounded. See, I made my bones in Palestine and Mustafa treated me like his own brother. He put me in charge of the delivery of the cigarettes.

"So that's me for a couple of months, then today Mustafa picks me up and says that he had a list of rats in the organization. I ask him where, and he says in his head. Then he pulls out a .38 revolver and says that I'm the one that's going to put them out of action. It was back to rat killing.

"We got into a heavy argument because rat killing is exactly what I came to the mosque to get away from. I told him I would do it, but then I'd be going to the Council with a grievance.

"He backed off because he knew that he was overstepping his bounds. He said he'd do it, but I'd have to be a witness to it. I said okay. What else *could* I say?

"Your boys were already tied up and blindfolded when we got to the warehouse. They were ready to go, on their knees with two goons holding them there. I had no idea who they were. *No one* clued me in to a tandem operation. Nothing!

"Now here's the deal. A mock-execution isn't beyond these guys. I've seen them do it before. I've even been involved in them. It's used to test loyalty. Hell, the Mossad even does the same thing. Old school, right?"

Sunny looked at the floor. "It all happened so fast. We walk in, Mustafa puts the gun to one guy's head, pulls back the hammer, says to me that he's FBI. Bang! Brains and blood fly. As fast as that, he pops the second guy. I think, 'This guy's going to pop more of *our* guys,' and me too. So, forget the undercover; I got to stop this guy, you know?

"As soon as he turned toward me, I chopped him in his throat and grabbed the gun. I put a bullet in his leg and nailed the other two guys in the head." Sunny looked at Delgado, then Rose, and pursed his lips. "There. That's it. The next moment you guys were there, all over, about to nail me with the gun in my hand." He gave Rose a level look. "So how is it that you got to your guys too late?"

Rose looked sheepish. "We *would've* made it but . . ."

"But what?" Sunny got instantly pissed.

"We went to the wrong warehouse first."

"Figures. Well, I gave you Habib. I could've killed him. Now it's up to *you* to get the rest of the hit list out of him with your *old school* ways before any more of your guys go down. And unless you keep him on ice, my cover's blown—I'm dead. But at least your guys will be safe."

"You got anything else for us?" Delgado asked Rose.

Rose shook his head. "Yeah, everything he's said just raises more questions."

"Look. We already talked." Delgado's words were cold and precise. "*Everyone's* talked and it's all arranged. Don't you even try to pull some bullshit crap on me. He's outta here."

"I need to know how to contact you guys."

"You go through the official channels." Delgado said as he opened the door for Sunny. "Let's go home."

"Not with you." Sunny pushed past Delgado and Rose,

then made a hasty retreat from the police station and out onto the busy New York streets.

Frank Delgado caught up with him in seconds. "Come on, Sunny. At least let me give you a ride."

Sunny stopped and looked down at Delgado. "Why didn't you tell me the FBI was working the case?"

"I swear to God that I didn't know," Delgado answered.

"You didn't know? How is that possible? Listening to your rap I tried to do something right, or close to it, and it fucking backfired on me. So, now I'm outta here!" He waved down a cab.

It slowed to a stop and Sunny opened the door.

"Where are you going?"

"What do you care? I thought I could help. Now two of the good guys are dead. I wanted something really simple, less stress. Relax a while. I really didn't need this kinda shit when you came to me back then, and I sure don't need it now. So I'm dropping off everyone's radar screen. Frank, you just better forget about me for a while."

"Look, Sunny, we can work this out. You just can't walk out on me now. Not now."

"Oh, no? Watch me. I got no contract with you. That was your mistake, not mine. It means I can walk and you know it."

Sunny started to get into the cab but Delgado stopped him.

"Hold on. Hear me out. With as far as we've gotten, the way I've got it figured, with your sponsor out of the way, this could get you in deeper with the Hamas."

Sunny grabbed Delgado by his shirt collar so hard he ripped it. "Damn you! I said I'm *out*. Can't you understand that?" Realizing his social error, he immediately let Delgado go. "I was on Mossad's dime, but the contract was up weeks ago. Buddy, I'm a free man. Besides, before this thing started I told you to fill me in on all the details, *all* the details. I told you not to leave me hanging, and you *did*." He was about to get into the cab again but turned around. "I owe you nothing. I want my life back, and I'm taking it."

Sunny got into the cab and disappeared into the New York traffic.

CHAPTER 2

EILEEN WEISS KNOCKED HARD ONCE ON THE THICK mahogany door just the way the drill instructors had taught. It hurt her knuckles.

"Enter," a muffled voice commanded from the other side.

Opening the door, then closing it behind her, she did her best facing movements until she was in front of a big wooden desk. The man in the Army uniform sitting behind the desk held a folder in front of his face. She couldn't see who he was.

Standing at attention, Eileen saluted and held it. She had learned how to recognize ranks just a few days earlier. She saw the silver eagles of a colonel pinned to his epaulets. An Army Nurse Corps recruit, she had to be in some real trouble to be standing in front of a full bird colonel.

She fidgeted as she stood there at attention, holding her salute in front of a folder. There was no way she was going to drop it before he recognized her by returning a salute. The folder didn't move down even a fraction of an inch.

Now she had an attitude. She'd been questioning her decision to join the Army since she first raised her right hand to swear in. First they took away her comfortable overalls and put her in a girdle, bra, and stockings, all two sizes too large; then they put her in a scratchy khaki uniform. "Starch and shine, hillbilly," they said. She had never even been in the hills.

As she stood in an ill-fitting uniform, holding a salute, her home in Virginia Beach, Virginia, seemed a lifetime away. A Depression-raised child from a family with more social pretensions and mean-spiritedness than assets, she had made up her mind to get away from her threadbare existence at the first opportunity. She just didn't know how she would ever make it happen.

Her father had emigrated from Germany after World War I. He had run a prosperous private school in Bremen, Germany, for the children of European aristocracy and international diplomats. He had used his American connections to buy a tobacco brokerage in Virginia.

Eileen was born in Virginia in 1919. They lived well and prospered, traveling to and from Germany on first-class liner passage. Then came the Depression. The family was suddenly broke. Eileen was in Germany at the time, left there with her mother's parents while her father and mother looked for work in America while blaming the president for all their troubles and the defeat of Germany.

When she was fifteen, Eileen's grandfather grew tired of his daughter never paying for Eileen's support. Her father's parents wanted nothing to do with a child who was not *pure* Aryan, so Eileen was sent packing back home in third-class steerage on an old, leaky, rusty ocean liner. It was a miracle that they made the crossing.

Back in Virginia, her bitter mother treated her like an unwanted stepchild, always there to put Eileen down and make sure that she would never measure up, ever. Eileen's only use was as a house servant. Her mother continually harped upon her own mistake of ever marrying Eileen's father and having a worthless child.

Worthless? Even when she did bring money to the house her mother continued to say that she was worthless.

Her father, ever the alcoholic disciplinarian headmaster, was as mean as he was proper. Expecting all courtesies, he whipped Eileen with his belt for almost any infraction, such as using incorrect grammar. How she hated the sound of the belt as he yanked it off his pants.

Too busy keeping up appearances, her constantly socializing mother did nothing to stop his verbal and physical abuse. Hers was worse—she seemed to live for grinding away at Eileen's spirit.

They held her spirit but not her will. She wanted to be free, but what could she do? There weren't a lot of opportunities in life for a girl from the wrong side of the tracks.

When she first spoke to her parents about joining the military her father acted as if she spoke heresy—he was part of the National German American Bund. For his participation at meetings he received a few staples and moonshine whiskey. He drank, waiting for the day that the American Reich would take its proper place as the new masters of the country.

"America will be called New Germany," he asserted. When Hitler ruled, her father said that he would control the American tobacco market. Negroes and other minorities would provide the slave labor. It was already agreed on by the Bund. Then he would prove to his wife and her family that his blood was even more German than German. It would be a rich new day for the American Nazis' when Hitler ruled.

"Hitler will *never* go to war with America. And if it happened, no daughter of mine would ever support such a war. Ever! You will never speak of this again." He raged, and threw things within his grasp; but he did not strike her. He instinctively knew that she would fight back.

Her mother laughed hysterically at her, then made an

offhand remark that she was too small to join. "They would never take you. You could never measure up."

Mother. Her words became a challenge and a dare.

So Eileen signed up, barely making the five-foot height limit and one-hundred-pound minimum.

"You're really not who we're looking for," the Virginia Army recruiter had said.

It didn't matter that the recruiter wanted only men, or that he said the pay was bad, or that training for women wasn't totally organized, or anything else that came out of his mouth. It didn't matter in the least that the only job opened to her was as a scrub nurse; she would've dug ditches.

Back at home she said not a word until it was time to ship out. She couldn't imagine how her life could possibly get any worse, but it did. Her parents treated her as a traitor; but they still made sure she kept bringing in the money that put her life at risk. Eileen would have to endure the abuse for only a short time longer.

When the reporting date arrived her parents were shocked as they never had been. Her father said that she was no longer his daughter. Her mother raged and wailed—for her it wasn't Eileen's leaving, as much as it was losing the power of control over another's life. Their worst tragedy hit when they suddenly realized there would be no more cash coming from their daughter. At 21, she was an adult of legal age so there was nothing they could do to try to stop her when she left.

Basic training had been hard, but not overly tough. She was surprised at the less-than-enthusiastic attitude most of the drill instructors showed. Not a man there seemed to think that women belonged in the Army. She endured the jeers and taunts other male recruits directed at the women recruits for wanting to be like men.

The other female recruits who thought that an undersized recruit was an easy target to haze were quickly put in their places. The drill instructors even tended to back away when they saw the "I'll do it or die," attitude she showed when challenged. But it wasn't all of their drama that bothered her, it was the "yes, sir, no, sir," that she had to answer to every person in authority that got to her the most. Eileen had her fill of that with her father years ago. They were men who expected respect just because they had a little authority.

There were a couple of places that she had wrangled to compete with the men. The rifle range turned out to be a place that she felt she did well—it was a place that women just didn't belong. Women were not allowed in combat.

One morning her troop had been marching by the firing range. A jeer from an instructor about women with weapons became a dare. The dare became a challenge to a shooting match. Only Eileen had raised her hand to meet the challenge After she had a few basic instructions in rifle shooting, the men couldn't match her scores or even come close.

Being such a great marksman made her an excellent candidate for early-morning guard duty, another place that women weren't allowed. The other girls were just as surprised as she was when her name first showed up on the guard duty roster. But it was just fine with her; it kept her off kitchen duty and the other mundane jobs to which the women were relegated. Guard duty was peaceful, there was no one yelling at her to keep in step while marching. Still, it left her wondering when they would seriously start training her in the medical areas.

Guarding a converted college didn't seem to be too glamorous or necessary. But it did give her a chance to be alone with her thoughts. Out of the darkness a weaving car with the lights out drove up, then screeched to a stop just inches from the barrier.

Eileen had her rifle at the ready.

"Yo, you there, open the gate! Now!" A male's gruff voice yelled out from the car.

Seeing Eileen hesitate, he yelled, "Hey, you, stupid, get over here!"

Eileen cautiously approached the car. The man stuck

his head out of the driver's window and saw that he was facing a woman. He then began to browbeat her, trying to intimidate her into raising the barrier and let "a real man" onto the post.

Reeking of alcohol, the man wore a wrinkled dark gray suit, stained white shirt, and a blue polka-dotted tie. He looked just like another self-important, drunk bureaucrat. She'd seen them before at the social gatherings her mother sometimes hosted. Using up most of the money Eileen had brought into the house to buy illegal moonshine, her mother gave it freely to any man she thought might improve her social position. The other male passenger looked to be passed out with an empty Jack Daniel's whiskey bottle on his lap.

The driver was unrelenting in his insults about women in the military. Eileen might've raised the barrier, but the man's foul mouth and condescending behavior got her mad. "You got a permit, or some form of ID?"

"No. I don't need one. And you *will* call me 'sir.' " He slurred, gunning his motor as if he intended to ram right through the barrier if she didn't move it.

In an instant Eileen raised her rifle and took direct aim at the man's head. Finger on the trigger of her weapon, she narrowed her eyes. "You even move this car an inch, and you will be dead, *sir.* Now shut off the car."

The man, seeing her finger on the trigger of her weapon quickly killed the engine. He instinctively raised his hands from the steering wheel, knowing that he had suddenly wound up somewhere he was unaccustomed to being—the wrong end of a gun.

"Now toss out the keys, and *only* the keys. And do it *very* carefully, sir." She didn't want any trouble from anybody. Since her arrival she quickly learned that unknown and unseen was the best way to get through boot camp. But right there a drunken fool and his passenger were about to run her checkpoint—it wasn't going to happen.

He reached down and obediently tossed out the keys

at her feet, not blinking once at the barrel of the rifle pointed between his eyes.

Eileen didn't bend to pick them up but kept the muzzle of her rifle dead even with the man's eyes. "You will not move from that car and you will keep your hands in plain sight at all times. I'm calling my watch commander, *sir*."

"You can't do this to me! Don't you know who I am?"

"I asked if you had a permit to get on this camp? Well, do you, *sir*?"

"No, I don't, but..."

"Then I don't care *who* you are, sir. Now you stay put." Keeping the rifle leveled on the man at all times, she backed into the guard shack and then called the watch commander, who arrived at the gate in seconds.

Seeing the deadly situation, the officer quickly got between the rifle and the car. He held out his hands to Eileen in a cautioning manner. "Recruit Weiss, stand down," he ordered the moment he recognized the driver of the car.

Rifle reluctantly lowered, the officer sighed and turned to the driver of the car. "I'm so sorry, sir, she's just a recruit," he said, as if that explained it all. "I will ride with you and direct you to the base commandant's office." He quickly climbed into the backseat and frantically motioned for Eileen to raise the barrier.

"Young lady, come here," said the driver.

Rifle back at the ready, she approached the man. The passenger was wide-awake now and watching the whole scene with great interest.

"Can I have my keys back?" The driver seemed to have suddenly and completely sobered up.

She picked up the keys off the ground and put them back into his hands. Was this a test or something?

"Would you have really shot me?"

"Yes, sir." She leaned over a little, trying to get a good look at the passenger. "And you too." Stepping to the counterweight, she raised the barrier and gave a textbook salute to the very nervous captain as the car passed.

HER ARM WAS TOTALLY NUMB. IT FELT LIKE THE BLOOD had drained from it. *Say something!* "Basic Recruit Eileen Weiss reporting as ordered, sir."

The colonel slowly lowered the folder and her body turned to ice. The colonel in front of her was the very passenger who had been in the car the previous evening. *I am really in for it now.*

He returned the salute and Eileen gratefully dropped her lifeless arm.

He looked at her and gave her a cold smile. "I'm glad Mr. Donovan didn't try and run your guard mount. Would you really have shot me too?"

Eileen nodded slowly but firmly.

"The records show that you're a dead shot, the best marksman here. Where did you learn to shoot like that?"

"In the Army, sir."

"You mean *here?*"

She nodded. "Yes, sir. I'd never shot a gun before coming here."

"Oh? Excuse my manners. Please, sit down."

Eileen settled in the wooden seat next to her. The cold black vinyl seat squeaked and groaned. "Yes, sir." Just what was going on?

"So you like to shoot?"

"Yes, sir. I like to shoot but I actually don't care much for what the guns can do." She felt like she was back in front of her father.

"Then how do you explain the perfect scores that you receive?"

"I focus, sir." She did not want to tell him that she did it because the drill instructors said that a woman couldn't shoot. Some said that a woman couldn't even *lift* a rifle.

Prone in her "starched and shining" uniform they

wagered money on her to bull's-eye the target with every shot. She did and won plenty for her instructors.

"Where'd you learn to focus like that?"

"Catching rattlesnakes, sir."

"*What?*"

"Back home in Virginia Beach where I'm from they're worth two dollars apiece to the college there. They'd milk them for antivenin. I could catch maybe four a day."

"Really?"

She unintentionally huffed. What could the scrubbed and polished officer in front of her possibly know about doing anything hard to make a few dollars in order to eat for the week? Sure, she'd go after any viper on the open dunes, sometimes even in the pine roots of her home. It was good money. After catching the fast movers in a gunnysack, Eileen would add them to a barrel that she had in the backyard. Every Friday the snake man from the college would stop, count the number as he picked them up, then give the money to her father. Her dad never gave her a penny for her work, but it did mean that there might be food on the table the following week if a party didn't happen first.

"It also says here that you got a perfect score in Morse code."

"Yes, sir."

"Do you have previous experience in codes?"

"No, sir."

"Tell me how you got a perfect score on your record."

"I like the sounds, sir." Again, that was the short answer. The long answer was that it was more than the code. Long after every other recruit had tossed down their headsets in failure, she sat there with her eyes closed; she loved the noise.

Her mother would get the creeps when she came in Eileen's room and found her sitting in front of her radio. The radio would be on, full blast, just pulses of noise and static blaring. One day her mother poured a jug of water over the radio and ruined it.

That was the day Eileen finally decided it was time to stop wasting her life with parents who didn't even love her. *That* was the longer answer.

The officer was beginning to annoy her.

"Your father belongs to the German American Bund."

"Yes, sir. He does. I don't."

"He is being watched by the FBI."

"Well, unless they like to watch drunks, let 'em have a go at it, sir."

"So you don't agree with his beliefs?"

"No, I don't, sir. I was born *here*. I am an American. My family has disowned me for joining the Army."

"Yes, I see. Tell me about your relatives in Germany. I understand that you know Germany well, Recruit Weiss."

"Colonel . . . just having Nazi sympathizers for parents, or having relatives living in Germany doesn't make *me* a Nazi, does it? I was *born* here. The records prove it." What was going on? Did they think that she was a spy or something? That was it! It had to be. How much did they know about her family in America and Germany anyway? What were they doing over there? She was sure she was headed straight from the Army and into the stockade.

"Recruit Weiss, I'm not here to accuse you of anything. Quite to the contrary, I would just like to ask you some questions."

"If you don't mind, who are you, sir?"

"My name's not important, Recruit Weiss." He pulled out a pack of Chesterfields and offered a cigarette to her.

"No thank you, sir. It'll stunt your growth," she sarcastically replied.

"I see." He grinned through a clean set of teeth. "Can you speak German?"

"Like a local native."

"I'd like to have you tested, if you don't mind."

"I do mind. Why am I here, sir? Can you tell me that?"

The man lit a cigarette and blew the smoke over his head. "Have you heard from any of your German relatives, mail or wire?"

"No. Not in months, and I am *very* worried about them."

"Recruit Eileen Weiss, how much do you love your country?"

"I love America, yes, but compared to what?" A nervous laugh escaped her. What was he searching for? The man's stone face made her stop laughing. She thought for a moment; then countered. "Sir, let me ask you; how much do you love *your* country?"

"I'll do anything for it. I'll even die for it."

"Oh."

"And you? With this coming war, and it *is* coming, is this just a game for you, a woman? Are you here just to meet a man and get married? Or are you really a patriot? Recruit Eileen Weiss, how much do you love your country? *Are you willing to die for it?*"

Eileen sat, stunned. Her original motivation to join the Army was just to get away from home. Now she sat in a chair across from some unknown man she would've shot the night before who was asking her something she hadn't really thought about until that moment. Was this real? What to do? It suddenly hit her and why she was there. *Tell the truth.* "You're damn straight I love my country! My own family's disowned me because I do. I'm here to try to make a difference. I'm here to fight the damned Nazis however I can! If it's fighting them, then I'm on board with whatever you want me to do."

The man drew heavily on his cigarette and exhaled the smoke through his nose. "Good. Good. It looks like the nursing corps is going to have to get along on one less scrub nurse." He stubbed out the smoke in an ashtray and folded his hands on top of the big mahogany desk. "Private Eileen Weiss, you will go back to your training unit and act as if this meeting never happened. Next week, you will get travel orders to Texas. A car will be waiting for you the moment you graduate. It will take you to your next assignment, but it will *not* be Texas. If anyone in your barracks asks you what happened here, tell them that they called in the wrong person."

Without another word the man stood. Eileen came out of the chair, came to attention, and saluted. The officer casually saluted back and left the room.

Hand at her temple Eileen stood astonished at what had just transpired. She slowly dropped the salute and exited the room.

Outside headquarters the uniform was hot and big, but she wasn't sweating as much anymore. The girdle still fit like a straitjacket and the stocking seams still ran like zigzags down her legs. But if she had heard it right, the colonel acted as if it was already a done deal and had even promoted her!

She'd changed her mind about quitting. Someone was actually interested in *her* for a change. She would see how far she could go.

CHAPTER 3

1710 WEDNESDAY / 25 FEBRUARY 2004

THE LEGROOM IN COACH WAS NOT DESIGNED FOR A guy six-three who weighed in at 235 pounds. The only bonus, though, was that he had a row of three seats to himself. He ordered a couple of Stoly miniatures. He wasn't surprised to find that he only had a twenty left in his wallet. The change wouldn't cover a cab ride home to Melbourne, but it would get him to his dojo in Winter Garden—with no tip.

He poured one of the bottles over the ice in the plastic cup, reclined his seat to the max three inches, then stretched out as best he could. He took a sip while pondering over how he had wound up sitting where he was.

Damn! I think I'm actually a lot farther behind than where I started. Now how'd that happen?

Abandoned by his mother at twelve in 1982, he had lived on the streets of Los Angeles, doing anything to survive. He did things for money that he would never tell anyone. Ever. The worst creeps and perverts loved to get their hands on young blue-eyed, blond-haired boys. Sometimes he ate out of trash cans and stole whatever he could to survive.

Early experience and common sense made him avoid

gangs like Rockwood, or the Eighteenth Street West Side gangs at all costs—they loved to beat up on poor, unaffiliated white guys.

The black and Mexican gangs taught him to fight back fast and lethal, then run like hell at the first opening. The neo-Nazi gangs were even worse. Watching too many friends wind up in jail or dead because of their associations with gangs and drugs gave him the wisdom to try it alone. As long as he paid the street taxes from time to time, and didn't diss whoever the gang de jour's ruling parties were, everyone pretty much left him alone.

His only dream in life came from a television movie he once watched on a TV in a storefront window. *Follow That Dream*. Elvis moves to Florida, and after a little struggle, lives the good life forever. He knew that the good life didn't happen to people like him without a fight, so he took what he could get and did whatever it took to get off the streets.

At thirteen he looked like he was twenty, but he still had the mind of a kid. At fifteen he had seen a lifetime of the wrong things.

He got busted selling a hundred blotter paper tabs of LSD to a narcotics agent who put him in the holding tank at the Wilshire Police Station. But rather than turn him into the Youth Authority System he saw something a little different in the young man than the usual street hoodlum. So he turned him over to an LA truant officer named Isabelle Del La Torre.

Sunny thought he was getting off easy, but he had made a big, big mistake. Officer Del La Torre made a drill instructor look like a basket-weaving teacher.

She legally took control of Sunny's education in one day. Guardianship papers in hand, they pulled up in front of the Fairfax Continuation School. Officer Del La Torre gave him an ultimatum.

"Look, kid, you can't bullshit me. And there's no sob story you can hand me that I haven't heard. So I'm going to give you a choice—it's jail or me."

"I don't want to go to jail." The holding tank had

been bad enough. Sunny knew of guys like him who'd been raped in the first hour they were in the general population. "Look. I'll do anything you want."

"Then you're coming in with me." She uncuffed him and took him straight to the registrar's office. "This is school for the bad boys and girls. You will be here during school hours, and you will be locked down. While you are here you will go to classes and I'll see to it that you get lunch for free. You can read?"

Sunny nodded. She then put him through a third degree that made the Inquisition look like a Cub Scout meeting. She was as tough as any street gangster he'd ever met. No. Tougher.

She finally backed off an inch. "You can write?"

Sunny nodded again.

"You know math? I bet you can figure out how many ounces are in a kilo of pot in less than a second, right?"

He nodded again.

"Well, it's a start. Now we can get you registered."

"But I don't have an address."

"You know how many times I've heard that one. So? What do you want from me? I'm not your mother or father. In this town I'm your truant officer." She grabbed him by his hair. "Do you understand? Anyone your age has to be in school and you happen to be in a town that has *me* as that truant officer.

"If you don't like it, then you can run away and you better keep on running. Or you can get with this program and change your situation in life. You *will*, as long as you are in my district, be in school at the appointed time when it's in session."

Hard as steel, there was nothing nice or warm about her. Whatever she was, she was the real deal.

Sunny wanted to put on an attitude, but he instinctively knew that this woman with flaming red hair and wearing a perfume that could peel paint could unload hell. So he signed the attendance contract and planned on just shinning her on until he was out of her sight.

He shivered, remembering when she got nose to nose

with him back out on the street. She had read his mind. "I know what you're thinking. You've missed me for fifteen years, so you think you can just hide from me after this is over. Well, boy, if you miss one day of school, one hour, one minute, one second, you better be dead because I'm going to hunt you down wherever you are. It's my job and I'm the best." Her smile came straight from hell. "You're under *my* watch now."

He never missed a day of school after that. She left him alone as long as he showed up for classes. But she became a constant and haunting specter in his life. Sunny got an education under duress. But at least the lunch was free. He even behaved and did well enough with his grades to get out of Fairfax and Officer Del La Torre enrolled him in Los Angeles Public High School. He even got honors classes. Go figure.

Sunny took another sip of Stoly. He might've stayed in LA and really made it a home. But at seventeen he screwed up again and it was Truant Officer Del La Torre who saved his ass by getting him out of town and into the United States Army.

It turned out to be the spark he had been looking for in his wasted and empty life. His spirit and drive earned him a place in the Seventh Special Forces Group at Fort Bragg outside Fayetteville, North Carolina—he had nowhere else to go.

He found the guns and sanctioned violence to his liking—dealing with the anger of others helped him hide from his own issues. The world suddenly became a hop and a skip from one operation to the next. Sunny didn't care. He was having fun.

Back in the US, the training was never-ending and he loved it that way. He discovered aikido and a host of other martial arts that served him well as a hand-to-hand combat instructor for the group.

Sunny wasn't a cruel or an evil man, just one who grew up without love. A loner, he was used to his own company. He never went looking for a fight in downtown "Fayettenam," and walked away from many when there was no point to make.

Affection was alien to him. Maybe that was why he couldn't keep a woman or any really close friends. It wasn't that he was cold and emotionless; a life without ever receiving any affection made him very wary of anything that involved too much human kindness. But the Army wasn't looking for sensitive trigger pullers, just good ones, and Sunny was exceptional.

He was trained by snipers from the former Phoenix Program in Vietnam, then sent to Colombia in 1993 on loan to the DEA, where he took out five key narcoterrorists, bringing down an entire cocaine circuit.

A few weeks later he was tasked to do a simple photographic recon mission with a young Marine spotter named Joe. A certain Colombian general was suspected of trying to establish another drug circuit to the US—Sunny had eliminated the competition for him and his CIA backer with his accurate sniping.

Pictures taken, they made it back to the pickup point, but the only people waiting for them were the bad guys. Captured, he was tortured for three weeks. They had no real plans of ransoming Sunny; they just had to keep him out of action while the Colombian general consolidated his hold on the cocaine trade in the region.

He finally escaped and it took him more than forty days to make his way back to Panama. Left arm swollen and paralyzed, almost naked, and thirty pounds lighter, he penetrated Howard Air Force Base, then walked into the back door of the Seventy-first Special Operations Squadron. He got out of the country on an Air Force MC-130 Hercules headed for Fort Bragg the next morning.

He would've stayed in the Army if not for breaking the CIA case officer's jaw during the debriefing back at Bragg. The case officer took it personally and wanted to throw Sunny in the stockade for life. But the case officer suddenly disappeared. Instead Sunny was given a 10 percent disability pension and discharged with a meager severance. It was that or the stockade. At twenty-nine Sunny was homeless once again.

Following the high-security route other "former operators" had taken, he served a few stints in protective service for the Saudi royal family, and a five-year hitch as a manufacturer's representative for the arms maker, Heckler & Koch.

Working for the big arms conglomerate, he saw big money moving and changing hands, fast. Sunny wanted a taste of it, so—with the help of a colleague—he ventured into the world of underground arms and munitions dealing.

The money was great but the dirt that came with it wasn't. It was a step *below* drug dealing. That realization and morals acquired along the way told him enough to know that he'd made a big mistake trying to make it as a death merchant. He lost all his capital when his supposed partner burned him on a big gun deal by disappearing at the delivery. It was a costly lesson. Sunny had put up everything he had as collateral. He hadn't counted on the greed factor. He got out of the business and was broke and homeless once more.

By then all of his experiences put him in a unique position to do certain things for certain people. Israel's Mossad was interested in utilizing his knowledge and talents and paid him well. He went to work again for the Saudi royal family security organization. Mossad now knew where important Saudis were at any time of the day. The royal family also paid well. Sunny was doubledipping so now he had a few more bucks. Things were looking good, real good. His future in the intel and security world looked very promising.

With his own investment money he finally got to Florida; but Elvis wasn't there. So Sunny bought a threestory beachside house on Melbourne Beach and an older sixty-foot motor yacht. He then set up shop by buying into a martial arts studio in Orlando. He put the word out to the intelligence and security world that he was available. They could contact him discreetly through the dojo. The good life was calling to him from right around the corner.

Vetted and holding top-secret clearances, Sunny started getting calls from different intelligence agencies to do covert work. In the intelligence and security world he became a freelance contractor. *Gun for hire. Wire Sunny.*

IT WASN'T THAT HE FELT A CALLING TO THE DARK SIDE— he just sort of wound up there. Things like that can happen in life. He was in a high-risk profession.

Sunny finished the drink and poured the second one. Then came 9/11 and the good life had to go on hold. Above it all, in spite of everything bad in his life, the homeless street kid from Los Angeles was a staunch patriot. Sunny would do what he could for his country. A guy named Frank Delgado came calling, and Sunny's life was no longer his.

Away from the action, all at once the killing suddenly hit him harder than a right cross to the chin. In the name of revenge, too much hate was generated and too much blood was being spilled. How many times had he sheltered in the dark as an assassin on the orders of others who used religious hate for the mass murder of innocent people? The burnout was never a ruse. The shadow war was a dirty, nasty mess, conceived by perverts of the most horrible kind.

They sometimes ordered him to leave a calling card, like a black ice pick handle sticking out of an eye, an ear, or any other appendage removed for delivery to the opponent. Sunny did his job and was paid well for his deeds, from both sides—it was their world, not his. But only a paranoid psychopath could live like that, day in, day out, checking his back every other step for a counterkiller. He had to get out of there and find a friendlier place to operate. Anywhere was better than where he was, or so he'd thought.

Delgado had suckered him into the ops without any

real understanding or objective. Without a written agreement he paid Sunny the equivalent of what is termed a NOC, no official cover. He was high-risk cheap labor.

"Produce results. Do it now," was Delgado's mantra. He had a fire lit under his ass by the top levels.

Sunny downed his drink in one gulp. It burned his throat and stomach, but he liked that. Now what kind of orders were those? People could get killed on ops without a clear strategy, it happened all the time.

"We want to identify the organization's heads and its money, then take them out."

Sure. That said a lot. It said everything. Isn't that what the president, or one of his cabinet members had said? It was a lot of words with no bite; no *real* bite.

For a couple of months it looked as if the lettered agencies were actually going to work together. But too much history, bad blood, and an overabundance of arrogance were too damn hard to get over. While goodwill was touted to the media, the Good Ol' Boy program pressed forward and nothing really changed.

Sunny knew what was what—that's why he left the country when Mossad came calling. Terrorist blood was spilled for greenbacks, murder in the back streets, in the dark, for both sides.

Sunny was smart and knew his way around on the block. The problem was that he wasn't smart enough to know how to get *off* the block.

Headed back to Orlando without any solutions, there was no one sitting near, so he tried to best assess his situation in a few sentences.

"Let's see," Sunny said, taking a deep breath. "I thought I had it wired but good guys got wasted. So I had to kill some bad guys and probably blew my cover. Okay, how 'bout the good life I was headed for?" He talked to his empty plastic cup. "Assets."

He had the big house on the beach in Melbourne he could no longer afford. Hell, he hadn't even seen it for almost two years. He hoped that Julian Leek, the caretaker, would float him again for another six months.

There was a sixty-foot yacht berthed in a slip at the Melbourne Yacht harbor. But he was three months in arrears and the boat was probably ready to sink from nonuse. The Q45 Infiniti was sitting in the repair shop with a blown engine. No stocks, bonds, IRA's or 401(k)s. His savings were just about tapped out.

He wished he had more money for another drink, but was glad that he didn't—he wanted to be sober and honest while assessing his situation. At thirty-five it was time to take stock of everything in his strange and dangerous life. He'd been in the knuckle-dragging side of the intelligence business for fifteen years, then a contract operator for five. The life of a contract secret operator held little glamour and a *lot* of dirt. He wasn't James Bond—nowhere close. Bond lived a rich, elite lifestyle. Hell, Sunny had tried it once, and that was how he wound up in debt way over his head!

The descent announcement was made and a flight attendant came around to make everyone ready for landing at Orlando International Airport. The flight attendants came up the aisles collecting the trash. Sunny tossed his little plastic cup into the bag and put the seat back into its cramped landing position.

A revelation made him sit up even straighter than he was; for far too long he'd been looking after everyone else's concerns and not his own. He made a vow to start concentrating on his own interests for a while.

THUNDER AND RAIN POUNDED ORLANDO AS SUNNY rode in a cab from the airport to his dojo. He would sleep on the couch in his office, then borrow a car and go home in the morning. Entering his office through a side door, he could see through the one-way mirror that a class was in session. It was a full class. Great! He was more than gratified to see that the school was doing so well without him. His partners had good ideas and ways of teaching a host of martial arts—aikido, karate, escrema, jujitsu, and others. Gone as much as he was, maybe it would be better to deed the place over to them. It really didn't seem like the dojo was his anymore. It was just his front.

Pan Jhandi, his top instructor, walked into the room and was astonished to see his sensei sitting behind his desk. Pan gave a short, formal bow. "Sensei, I didn't know you here."

Sunny nodded. "I'm not, so please keep my arrival quiet."

"Yes, sensei. It's good to see you anyway." Pan smiled.

Once again Sunny was stunned by Pan's feminine beauty.

One afternoon, five years earlier, Pan Jhandi had walked into the dojo. He was fresh off a plane from the Philippines. The whole aikido class stopped in awe of his alluring and exotic features.

Sunny knew the Far East well. The natural beauty of some of the Asian men surpassed the looks of even their own women. Often, johns searching for easy sex on Rojas Boulevard in Manila or Angeles City would often find themselves in the loving embrace of a tawny lady-boy for days and not even know it.

Small and thin, the soft-spoken exotic man formally presented his certificates and claimed that he was an es-crema master. Sunny was in a mood to entertain his students. He'd trained enough in the fast game of trying to whack an opponent with rattan sticks to be intrigued by the pretty bantamweight standing in front of him. Pan agreed to an on-the-spot match as an "on-the-job inter-view."

It was a farce. Pan *whipped* Sunny's ass. The little man was an unstoppable demon with heavyweight impact. It was a very embarrassing, but enlightening experience for Sunny. After class the welts all over Sunny's body confirmed the lithe man's phenomenal talents. Pan then cemented his place in the regime by giving Sunny a massage that gave him the idea to open a true deep tissue therapy massage parlor, something that could heal both the spirit and body. Pan jumped at the opportunity to join the dojo.

Pan said that he felt that he had an almost spiritual calling to spread his fighting and relaxing techniques around the world. Once hired, he stayed to himself and never spoke of his home or past. To keep him Sunny also offered him free board at the studio. Quiet but firm, Pan was the real reason the students came to the dojo. Pan also took care of the studio's upkeep and finances, another *big* reason it stayed open and thrived.

"A man come here looking for you couple day ago," Pan said.

"Yeah? Who was he?"

"He not say. He sound, *rich*."

"Did he say what he wanted?"

"He want to talk to you."

"Pan, lots of people want to talk to me. What makes this guy so different?"

"I know, just the way he ask for you. You gonna see. You okay?"

"Yeah, just tired."

"You hungry, want something to eat? I cook for you."

"No thank you, Pan. I just need some privacy." Sunny pulled out a calculator and the financial records in his desk.

Pan gave a short bow, then closed the door behind him.

IT WAS TWO HOURS LATER BEFORE SUNNY WAS FINISHED updating his financial records. Things didn't look good, not good at all—creditors didn't give patriotism grace periods. If anyone else, like the IRS, wanted to take a deeper look at his records, they might start questioning him as to where he got the money for his big house and yacht. If they took an interest in him, there were questions he'd rather not answer.

How was it that he had gotten so deeply in debt? Getting burned in an illegal deal was one thing. Not being around to handle finances was another. Not facing either was yet a third. "What to do?" He could start selling off some of his possessions, but what were they really worth? Then what? And what about the dojo? He had to trust somebody with his personal affairs. Sunny seriously pondered asking Pan to consider taking over his personal finances.

A knock on his office door diverted his attention.

"Yeah? Come in."

Sunny immediately knew it was the man that Pan had spoken of. He had jet-black hair and looked to be thirty-something. He wore a suit that cost at least a thousand dollars, wore nice shoes, and carried a black briefcase. Sunny took a fast look at the briefcase that he held, making sure it wasn't an H&K briefcase—the one with a machine gun in it.

"Can I help you?"

"Mr. Sunny Vicam." He stood in front of Sunny's desk and held out his hand. "My name is James Lambert. I represent just one client. My client would very much like to meet with you."

Sunny leaned over and shook the man's hand. Firm grip. It was a *real* nice pin-striped blue suit and purple tie. His shiny black shoes looked to be of the expensive, soft leather, handmade Italian kind. "No card?"

"No. As I said, I have only one client."

"You a lawyer?"

"Yes, Mr. Vicam."

"Please sit down, Mr. Lambert." Sunny braced for some trumped-up lawsuit by some weirdo.

Lambert sat on a chair, opened the case on his lap, reached into it, and held out a white envelope to Sunny.

Sunny opened the envelope. It was full of hundreds— ten thousand dollars 'worth. "What's this for?" He was on guard, watchful, and wary.

"A consultation." Lambert was expressionless.

"A consultation? For what?" Sunny was alert for any compromising words that would make Mr. Lambert suddenly flash a treasury or IRS badge. Sunny didn't put Frank Delgado above blackmailing him back to work.

"A consultation."

"*Really?* And where's your client, Mr. Lambert?"

For a younger man Lambert looked soft, out of shape, but his eyes were sharp. He wasn't an easy read. Maybe he was wired and there was a camera in his case. But a prospective client could pay anything for a meeting; it was his cash. That was legal.

"Not here. I have a private jet waiting for us at the Sanford Airport."

"You want me to go with you, now?"

Alarms should've rung in his head, but he had his hands on *cash*. Sunny could use it. He hadn't broken any laws by taking the money, so far.

"Yes, sir, and the sooner the better. I have a car and driver waiting outside."

"Where? How long will we be gone?"

"Virginia. We'll fly there by a private jet. If your meeting is not successful, you'll be back by morning."

What else have I got going on? Besides, I got no other checks coming in at the moment. "Mr. Lambert, will there be a screener for weapons?"

"Not for us."

"Good. Do you mind waiting outside while I tie up a couple of loose ends. I'll be out to your car in a few minutes."

"Very good. I'll let my client know that we are on the way." Lambert smiled, got up, and left the room.

Sunny pressed the intercom. "Pan? Please come here."

Pan was in the room in seconds. Sunny counted out the money and split it in two neat stacks. "Pan, drop half of this in my savings account." He leaned back in his chair and eyed his instructor. "I need help with my bills. You've made this dojo into what it is not only by your teaching, but by handling the finances in a way I never could." He pushed his bills into a small pile and gave Pan a weak-assed smile. "Think you want to have a crack at my personal finances?"

"If it would help you, then yes."

"Great! Then take my record books and pay out with this until it's gone." He pointed to the other stack of bills.

"You will leave with the man?"

Sunny nodded. "Don't know when I'll be back." He unlocked a drawer, pulled out a pistol, checked the magazine, then stuffed the gun into his waistband.

"The usual arrangements then?"

"Yeah." If Sunny hadn't called Pan or e-mailed him within two weeks, then Pan would call a few numbers to start a search by whoever answered the phone. It was just a security measure—people like Sunny always ran the risk of disappearing involuntarily.

Sunny couldn't keep the grin off of his face when the chauffeur opened the door of the Cadillac limousine for him. Memories of guarding the Saudi royal family came back to him, except that this time *he* was the principal.

They rode in silence. Lambert shuffled through papers in his briefcase. Sunny sat back and sipped on a drink while listening to the soft music.

Money in hand always seemed to brighten up a situation. It certainly distracted him from his problems.

They passed through the access gate unchallenged and pulled up next to a Learjet. They went from the car directly to the jet. Sunny and Lambert climbed aboard the jet and the copilot closed the door.

Sunny was very surprised to see that the pilots were in United States Air Force uniforms. "Mr. Lambert, is this a military jet?"

"Yes, it is."

"Is this a classified mission or something?"

"I'm sorry, but I can't answer any question about what we are doing, Mr. Vicam, not until you have had your consultation."

Lambert seemed nice and polite enough, professional. Sunny appreciated the confidential nature of the situation.

The Learjet was small but plush and well stocked

with liquor. Sunny had to refrain from overindulging in the vodka. As badly as he wanted to tie one on and forget about everything, he had to be sharp to meet the mystery client. One thing for sure, the client had connections and probably lived the good life.

As fine as it all looked, he knew the good life *wasn't* calling for him to join.

CHAPTER 4

1730 / MONDAY / 2 DECEMBER 1940

THE DARK OLIVE DRAB 1940 PACKARD CLIPPER slowed as it approached the Canadian border. The driver and sole passenger sitting on the rear seat never got a second look from any of the guards as they passed. They traveled on the frozen Toronto–Kingston highway for what seemed like endless hours, making one stop in Toronto for gas and food before they came to a bleak location on Lake Ontario.

Eileen was stretched out in an exhausted daze on the backseat. The young Asian driver hadn't introduced himself nor spoken one word from the time he picked her up. Every time she tried to strike up a conversation he would shake his head and say, "Orders." She wondered if *orders* was the only English word he knew. He wore a black, close-fitting uniform. A Thompson machine gun was attached vertically to the dashboard for quick release. She couldn't wait to fire one.

For the past year, her favorite radio program had been the Green Hornet. Locked in her room, she could hardly wait for the familiar sounds of, "The Green Hornet. He hunts the biggest game of all; public enemies who try to destroy America."

Until her mother ruined it, she would sit next to the RCA Victor radio, her only true possession, and listen intently, visualizing the Green Hornet battling crime with his trusted aid, Kato. They would ride in the Black Beauty, the supercharged rolling armed fortress Kato wheeled through the night. She became the hero and the enemy was a dark force that at the time looked an awful lot liker her mother. Now the Green Hornet was valiantly moving on to face the next challenge.

She passed some of her time on the long, but comfortable ride trying to imagine how the Green Hornet might fight the Nazis. She knew her fantasy could never match the reality of what lay ahead, but for a while she could still be silly enough to pretend that she was the courageous and fearless Green Hornet instead of a young woman alone in a man's army.

Basic training was the first time she had literally been out of her own backyard, and yet there she was being driven to a top-secret camp somewhere north, in Canada. No one back home really would know where she was, what she was doing, or the type of people that she'd meet.

She'd prewritten a year's worth of homey letters to her despised mother and a few friends that would be posted every month at Fort Hood—a post in the middle of the Texas desert. The letters were generic in nature, and said absolutely nothing. In the letters she said that she didn't make it into the nurse corps but was a supply clerk instead—a bench warrior. Her mother would like that twist.

It didn't matter that the letters would probably go unread and unanswered. A traceable and plausible paper trail had to be established to blur the lines of reality to cover her movements. All she really knew at that moment was that she had agreed to a phantom wearing a colonel's uniform to fight the Nazis however she could.

She had been the last one left in the empty barracks; everyone else had been bussed to their next duty locations. While she was sitting on her bunk bed with her duffel bag of uniforms, the phantom officer showed up to see her off. He carried with him two small suitcases. She helped him carry one from the barracks. It was heavy.

He led her to her own "Black Beauty" and they put the suitcases and her duffel bag into the trunk. Only then did it occur to her how heavy the suitcase really was. Her own duffel bag of uniforms was bigger but lighter.

FROM THE HIGHWAY THEY TURNED ONTO A SIDE ROAD and drove for less than an hour before coming to the first checkpoint. It was not much more than a shack manned by a Royal Canadian Mounted Policeman. He nodded at the driver, then peered inside at Eileen, then stepped back and let the car proceed.

The next stop was a lot more substantial. A chain fence topped with barbed wire ran along a forest edge and disappeared into the distance. Two armed guards thoroughly inspected the papers the driver handed over before opening the gate. They drove a very short distance before the car stopped in front of a small, one-story building. She watched as three men came from the building and approached the car. Without speaking a word, one man opened the door for her as the other two men opened the trunk and took out the suitcases. They then dropped Eileen's duffel bag in front of her and walked off. Kato and the Black Beauty roared away.

"Hello, and welcome to Project J, also known as Camp X, among other things. I am Captain Peter Fleming. I have been assigned as your liaison officer to help you through your training while you are here. Please follow me." He picked up the bag and tossed it over his shoulder.

Although Eileen was not attracted to him or the pipe that he smoked, he had an easygoing and engaging manner as he spoke. In a faded gray tweed suit, with handsome looks and ash blond hair, he looked like the typical Hollywood Englishman. They stepped inside a small room. Peter propped the bag against a wall, then he motioned for her to sit on a simple wooden chair. He had manners enough to tap out his pipe in an ashtray before speaking.

"The first thing you must always remember while you are here, and wherever you go, is never to reveal your identity to anyone. *Anyone.* I am the only one who will know your real name. As of right now, and whenever asked, you are Number 26. Your number assignment is not an insult. It is exactly the opposite—the number identifies the type of training you will receive. Number 26, do you understand?"

Eileen nodded. Excited, she no longer was a name, but a number. She was very much enjoying the cloak-and-dagger approach. *I'm a number.* It already surpassed all the scenarios she had played in her mind on the long journey. And sure beat the hell of actually having to live in the middle of the Texas desert changing dirty bedsheets and emptying bedpans.

"Concentrate only on the essentials and forget about the technicalities of everything else. Keep it simple and moving forward. You will learn things that even I will not know about. My job is to make sure that Number 26 will be ready to do a special mission. There's nothing to sign." Peter held out his hands. "Nothing. Do you understand?"

Eileen nodded.

"Yes." Peter nodded back. "You may come to find this place rather dreary, I do anyway. But then a lot of effort was made to make it look that way. We would like to attract no attention." Peter said, "This is as far away from the Jerries as we could get to put together an unsavory sort of people and ideas to train people like you to strike back at them. This is our Dirty Tricks Training Camp.

"You will discover that this is not a traditional camp with all the British formality and stuffiness. Many languages are spoken as people from all over the world are here. Most left their homes and fled the Nazis. They want their land back and have bitter scores to settle.

You will not see too many uniformed people; instead, we have forgers, safecrackers, assassins." Peter leaned close. "You are going to have a rather large bag of dirty tricks learned by the time you leave here."

Eileen asked, "And when am I leaving here, *where am I going?*"

Peter smiled. "Ah, you think that I may know something of your mission. At this time I can assure you that I know nothing; it's designed that way. This camp is made to teach you everything you need to know about appearing to know nothing, while seeing *everything*."

She understood. "Don't ask questions and don't listen to answers."

"Yes, exactly! That's the concept."

So began Eileen's training at Camp X. Between training sessions she read the international news clippings and listened to the radio. The Nazis were on the march to global domination and seemed unstoppable.

She was a native-born second-generation German-American. Had it not been for deadbeat parents, she'd probably be in a Nazi uniform doing something for Hitler. What did she know of world affairs, a hick kid? All she knew was that she was going to be ready for the challenge whenever it came. Whatever she did would be done in the name of world freedom. That was all she knew. Number 26 would be ready when the call came.

The training was constant, at all hours—she loved it.

In classrooms she learned how to make explosives with common household materials, assassination techniques, hand-to-hand combat, and firearms—she was especially, and proficiently, schooled in firearms.

Stage magicians and convicted pickpockets showed her how to misdirect attention in order to lift almost anything from a mark. Hollywood directors and actors taught her how to develop and put on a character quickly and convincingly to enact a scene and act any role at a moment's notice.

Then she went out into the field and practiced what she had learned. The woods came first. Compass and map, Eileen ventured out into the Canadian wild, first with an instructor, and then on her own. With minimum supplies, she always made her checkpoints on time.

She finally got about all that she could handle during interrogation training. This was the chance for the trainers to trim her cockiness. The drama came to blows, but Eileen got so mad that she struck back and put her interrogator on the floor. She would have failed the course had she not agreed to "remedial" training. There was nothing like hanging upside down naked in a cold room to show what bad manners could bring—Eileen got the point.

There were so many weapons to fire that she never asked *what* she fired, just *how* it fired. "The bullet for the weapon looks like this. This is how to chamber it, put it on fire, and pull the trigger." Once demonstrated, give her a gun and she'd have it fired and field-stripped for cleaning in record time. Her instructors gave Number 26 their own code name for her, Annie, after the famous American trick-shot artist, Annie Oakley. Soon she was showing *them* special ways to squeeze the trigger.

They started her with a sniper scope rifle, then moved her to a large-caliber handgun. Getting closer to the target, she learned close combat with various arms that fired small-caliber bullets. Eileen mastered close killing with the stiletto, needle, and spike. She was outstanding in all phases.

In small buildings she drank at inns made to look like German beer garden establishments. She spoke fluent German with others; playing whatever role they gave her while learning how to feign drunkenness and only pretending to consume great quantities of alcohol. Then her trainers really got her drunk and tested her ability to hold secrets.

They schooled her on the art of seduction. Still a virgin, she had a terrific time learning the lines, come-ons, and other endless sexual traps that men always fell for. A tomboy most of her life, she was shocked one evening to see herself for the first time in a full-length mirror after a real Hollywood makeover.

Like Narcissus, she could have stood in front of the mirror forever admiring her reflection. A movie screen makeup artist put her in a red nightgown that blended perfectly with her auburn hair. Lavender mascara dramatized her green eyes.

She finally understood the mysterious power of female sex appeal at the "set up" social gatherings in Toronto. "Oh, so social." She mimicked her mother's mindless blather, saying nothing, agreeing with everyone, and flattering the self-centered egoholics with whatever they wanted to hear. She had no trouble finding and making her marks, picking their pockets with a casual ease.

With the war, men were at a premium and knew it. Many held court like potentates selecting, then basking in their harems. Even the homeliest man allowed himself to be fondled and pampered, as women vied for his attention.

Getting close to her mark, she would palm requested items in exactly the way the stage magicians had taught her. Sometimes she would slip up, but each and every time the marks were willing to trade secrets for a tussle between the sheets with a cute young American.

She kept her honor and virginity intact though, not because she wanted to, but because having made the marks, none of them were ever interesting enough or clever enough for her to go beyond the mission.

How much longer? she would ask herself again and again. Eileen thrived, but she was lonely. Because of her status, a number was always isolated from other trainees. She had a small hut to herself. In some ways she felt like a caged animal, brought out only for training and feeding. She felt like she was slowly and surely loosing her identity.

It was during the surveillance and tailing phase of her training that she recovered a piece of herself again. Shaking her tail had been just about impossible. She'd followed all the procedures; but he was still there; worse, she knew other ghost tails were near. Looking for a way to lose him she saw the most amazing thing she could possibly imagine. On the marquee of the Avalon Theater was an advertisement for *One Million B.C.* starring Victor Mature and Carole Landis, but that was not what stunned her. In smaller letters beneath the headliner, the first of the Green Hornet matinee serials was advertised.

Could it be possible that her beloved hero was now on the silver screen? With a speed and stealth that she never thought possible she ran up Danforth Street and lost her tail in a maze of stores, triple-backtracked, then lost all exposed tails in the wind, and finally, bought a ticket to the movie.

Unchecked by any surveillance team, she sat anonymous in the dark, enraptured as her visions came alive. Britt Reid, walking, talking, and fighting his way through a host of villains, while Kato, the brilliant inventor, chopped and hacked at notorious bad guys. As soon as the film was over, she appeared on the street to the astonished wonderment of the surveillance trainers.

After that, anytime that they needed a rabbit for surveillance training she was always the first to volunteer. Even Major Victor Davis, the chief instructor, couldn't flush her out. No one had any idea that she was actually catching the latest installment of the action chapter in the Avalon Theater.

In radio coding she excelled beyond anyone's expectations. Her trainers discovered that she had such a close affinity with the radio transceiver that it almost seemed she worked magic. The radio section was the temple of Camp X, and the radiomen were its high priests. They treated the subject of radio energy as if it were mystical. Words like *pulsed induction, magnetic fields, light, sound, heat,* and *frequencies* referred to all-powerful concepts that only the truly committed, or gifted, could grasp. Eileen became a disciple of the sacred noise.

There was a sign above the blackboard in the classroom that read:

**To look is not to see,
To listen is not to hear,
To learn is not to understand.**

During wireless training relays she had to learn the different time zones in various parts of the world in order to synchronize her watch to broadcasts and receptions. It was dots and dashes, and a lot of noise. To Eileen, it wasn't a cacophony; it was a symphony. She was a natural scratch master, hearing the codes through her headset and writing them down on a pad. Deciphering in record time, she'd pass the message to her trainer, always letter-perfect. No errors. She never knew if what she had handled was training or an operational message.

Alone for hours in front of her station she listened for what the trainers called "from drums to light;"—frequency waves in patterns, any and all noise, static or pulsed amplifications. On open channels she listened, transcribed, decoded, then answered back in kind. Sometimes the messages made no sense whatsoever, other times they were poems right out of the training manual. She had no idea where in the world the transceiver operators were located, but she had to admit that actually communicating with someone "out there" was great fun. The best.

When it was her turn to play "pianist," what the radio operator in the field was called, she discovered what was in the suitcases that had accompanied her to Camp X. One of the suitcases was hers. They were prototype "suitcase radios." In it was an HF transceiver, power supply, hand-cranked generator, antenna, and extra tubes and crystals. The headset and tap key fit in a small pouch.

Once familiar with the new setup, she sent out coded lines to a designated time and frequency. She hid the messages of prearranged code in lines from her favorite Green Hornet programs. Decoded—whoever the decoder was on the other side was sharp, very sharp—they even sometimes came back with the next lines of the program in code.

It got to the point that Eileen dreamed in codes. In casual conversation she listened on different levels, looking for any hidden codes or meanings in anything anyone said.

She would only occasionally see Peter. Every time she did the opening conversation always went something like:

"Peter, hasn't Number 26 completed her training yet?"

Peter always replied, "Not until your bag of dirty tricks is full, Number 26, not until it's full."

She liked Peter, but he never talked about himself. He kept everything general, never personal. And the more "dirty tricks" that Eileen learned the more remote it made her feel from "civilians" like Peter. She'd been in camp so long it was becoming difficult to understand the lines between honesty and deception in normal life. With every word that she traded, she looked for the angle, code, or lies that could be wrapped in casual conversation.

CHAPTER **5**

THURSDAY / 26 FEBRUARY 2004

SUNNY GLANCED AT HIS WATCH WHEN THEY touched down. It read 1:40 A.M. He must have dozed off in the plush velvet seat. "Where are we?"

"Virginia."

"Oh." Outside the cabin window, it was all black. There was nothing to see. They weren't at any major airport. Lambert explained that they were on a private estate. Sunny wasn't worried but ready for anything. The H&K P7 pistol in his waistband had a chambered 9mm silver-tipped round.

They taxied until they reached a small apron and the jet cut its engines to idle. The copilot got out of his seat, opened the door, and let them out, then closed the door. In only seconds the jet was back in the air.

It was quiet and dark.

"I thought you said I could go back home if I didn't like this deal."

"Yes I did. It's all right, Mr. Vicam. My client can call on them anytime for their services. Please, this way."

Lambert led Sunny to a parked van. He started it up as Sunny climbed into the passenger seat. They drove over a ridge and Sunny was astonished to see that the road led directly to a huge mansion. The only size perspective he could relate it to was to the palaces of some of the Saudi royal family. It was a castle.

Still, it was very dark, and shadows and size were all Sunny could discern. He followed Lambert from the van through a foyer somewhat reminiscent of Hearst's Castle, except that this one was bigger, and into the great hall, which was gigantic. Even though the place was filled to capacity with antique furnishings, including a grand piano, he had the sensation that no one was there; it was more like being in a museum.

Lambert led Sunny to a two-story marble fireplace. The mantel had to be at least twelve feet high. The rest of the room, like the mansion itself, was out of a *big* budget Hollywood movie. The room was at least fifty feet in any direction. Four huge chandeliers lit the room. Intricately carved dark wood panels rose forty feet and blended into amber fan tracery. Chippendale furniture made of burled wood stood on big, beautiful hand-tied Oriental carpets, which lay on marble floors.

"Please, sit here." Lambert motioned to an overstuffed leather couch. "I will leave you here, for now." He walked away, his footsteps echoing in the distance.

Sunny was tired, but very intrigued. Whoever requested his presence had to be wealthy beyond his limited imagination. Fatigue started to overcome him. He stared at the roaring fire, mesmerized by the colors and crackling sounds of the burning wood. It was warm, comforting. He was falling asleep.

"Sunny Vicam," the fire called to him.

Sunny sat up. Wait. Was he dreaming? Did the fire really talk?

Suddenly the pyre exploded into a ball of smoke. When it cleared a wide-awake Sunny was on his feet in a fighting position and looking at a small old woman standing in front of the fireplace. She started giggling when she saw the look on his face and clapped her hands.

Sunny lowered his guard, still ready for anything.

"Oh good, it still works!" She used a cane to walk

over to a wing-backed chair and slowly sat down. A satisfied look was on her face. "Donald, my late husband, used to do that trick for new visitors. It's quite easy to do, actually. The fireplace is so big that you can stand inside of it, off to the side. I'm an old lady, but I still can test a prospective investigator." She waved her hands to close the trick, then clasped them together. "Please forgive an old woman her secret ways of bringing you here, but I will tell you why I did so in a short while."

Sunny scratched his head and smiled, beguiled by the old woman's alert eyes and charm. She had the presence, charm, and attitude of a Katharine Hepburn.

She held out her hand. "I'm Sally Fine. My husband was Lieutenant General Donald Fine. Do you know who he was?"

Sunny walked over and took her hand. It was warm. She had a strong grip. "I'm sorry, ma'am. No."

She let go of his hand. "That's okay. You sit down on the couch over there. Relax. You've come a long way, and I'm very grateful for that. I've got a story to tell you, but it's not too long."

Sunny took a seat on the soft leather couch. Out of the darkness an elderly butler rolled out a pastry and coffee cart, then quietly left.

"Sunny," she beamed, "Donald always disapproved of my sweet tooth, but at ninety I can indulge myself anything. Please, help yourself." She reached out and took several chocolates and stuffed them with glee into a little pink linen purse. "I used to hide my chocolates from him in this purse." She smiled. Her green eyes twinkled. "I think that he knew though."

"Mrs. Fine," Sunny started to say, trying to be businesslike. He instinctively liked Sally; which made him instantly cautious—liking people was always costly.

"Oh, please, call me Sally."

"Okay, ma'am, Sally, why am I here? You're not paying for me to watch parlor tricks and sit here eating pastries with you."

"I'm not?" She raised her eyebrows. "Oh no, of

course not. But I do want to ask you a couple of questions first."

"Sure."

"Do you know much about World War II?"

"Some. I guess as much as anybody else."

"How about after it was over and something called the Marshal Plan?"

"Sure, a little, in high school history class. It was the plan for the reconstruction of Europe. Right?"

"Do you know anything about it, how it worked?"

"Nothing at all."

"Then I will tell you some things about it. After the war my late husband worked for General Marshal throughout Europe to help implement the plan."

"I see."

"I was with him as a contracts officer." She glowed for a moment and smiled. "We first met over his refusal to sanction a 30-million-dollar oil buy from Iran for Greece. He pointed out that the deal wasn't legal because of previous Soviet agreements. I supported his stance. He was under pressure but stuck to his guns and was 'promoted' out of his position. The oil suddenly became Romanian oil and the deal turned Soviet. It cost him, but I admired his honesty. He was a fighter and rewarded loyalty. He asked me to be a part of his staff. We made a good team, for fifty-six years."

The smile left her. "But there's a dark side to it all. The crime boss, Lucky Luciano, with the full approval of the US government, had collaborated with the Italian Mafia to create the Italian underground resistance, and prepare Italy for the Allied invasion. Once the war stopped they were given a free hand to make any reconstruction deal to their advantage. The Swiss still had untold gold, diamonds, and tons of currency to launder. The Nazis had to move their plunder out of Germany. There was a lot of it to hide. But that is not real news, is it?"

She looked weary. "In reality, through no fault of my husband's and other honest people's, the plan we tried to remain faithful to turned out to be one of the biggest money-laundering operations in history, still is. Donald was an honest man. He, we, saw what was happening, but he had the 'Plan' to administer. He didn't get involved in the crime, graft, and racketeering. He didn't need to. He was already wealthy. We are old, old money. He did an impossible job—the best that he could. For what he did, he was given certain privileges when he retired; access to government VIP travel was one of them. He made sure I'd still have those privileges after he died."

"Follow me." She got up from her chair and tottered to an end table and opened a drawer and pulled out a faded green folder and an old, yellowed book. She laid them on the table. "This is the dossier and diary he kept. Please, look at them. I cannot let you take them, so you will be a guest in my home until you've finished reading the material and consulted with me."

Sunny picked up the diary, thumbed through it, and saw beautifully handwritten words. Each section had times, dates, and places entered. "Have you read this?" Some of the pages were missing.

"Oh yes, several times."

"Ma'am, I don't really think you got the right guy. I'll be straight. I'm not a financial investigator. Hell, I can't even balance my own checkbook. You should get someone versed in international finance."

"No. I'm looking just for you, and only you."

"I see. How did you hear of me?"

She shook her head, then ran her fingers through her thin, graying hair. "You are not the first man I've contacted about this. The first man gave your name should anything happen to him, and I think that something has happened. He's gone missing in Zurich. That's why I called you."

"What's his name?"

"Corey Brichner."

Sunny's heart jumped and he caught his breath.

"You know him."

"I do." *Corey Brichner*. The rotten things he could tell her about him.

He didn't know whether to stay or leave. Corey Brichner was an intelligence informant, opportunistic gun dealer, con man, pirate, enemy, and sometime friend. The last time he'd seen Brichner, or hadn't seen him, was when he didn't show up with half a million dollars to close an underground gun transaction. First he had to talk his way out of getting killed, then he had to put up everything he had to cover it. It broke Sunny. "Sally, I'm more than curious. Why would he name me as a recovery backstop, me of all people?"

"I wouldn't know, but I'm very worried about him. He's such a nice boy."

Sunny held back a laugh. Corey had a long list of descriptions, but a nice boy wasn't one of them.

"If I can ask, how is it that Mr. Brichner is working for you?"

"He was a personal recommendation. Mr. Brichner should have called me by now. If you take this case, finding him will be your first priority."

Sally walked slowly to the big window that overlooked huge low-lit lawns and terraces. "I think that you're going to find the diary *very* interesting reading, but most of the improprieties you will read are past most legal statutes of limitations. But I think that there are parts of my husband's story that still apply, and could be worth billions, more, *trillions*. Do you think that there are people who would harm Mr. Brichner if they caught him looking into these matters?"

He gathered up the material, walked back to the couch, and sat down. "I don't know about this, Sally. I've never dealt with international banking. I'd be a fish out of water." Sunny propped his shoes on a footstool and lay back into the overstuffed couch. What had he just stepped into? Just hours ago he'd lain spread-eagled on the floor of a warehouse, swearing that he would start taking care of his own interests first; instead he was sitting in a massive mansion listening to an old woman's *very* strange tale. But she said the proof was in his hands and the dossier.

Sally turned from the window. "I am going to bed now. I'm very tired, as you must be, also."

Walking toward Sunny, she stopped just a few feet from him. An almost frightened look came over her face. It was as if she didn't want to get too close to him and his world. "I did not intend to have anyone hurt or killed in this matter. Now I'm afraid that the opposite may be true. Above all this, I am much more interested in finding Mr. Brichner safe than a penny of the money."

Tapping her cane, she shuffled into the elevator. "Tom, my butler, will show you to your room when you are ready. There will be someone to see to your needs at all times while you are here. Good night, Mr. Vicam."

For a while Sunny sat mesmerized at the size, opulence, and elegance of the dark mansion. So this was how the elite rich lived. He wondered if Sally could relate to a guy like him, from the streets. But Sally seemed genuinely down-to-earth. He liked her. He wanted to help her. But what would it cost him? Why? Was getting involved a mistake?

Sunny had made enough mistakes very early in life in trying to read people. One error had almost cost him his life at an early age. What a world of difference from where he sat, to when it happened. Had eighteen years actually passed since that night? It was a repressed memory just waiting to burst.

He had been just a couple of weeks from graduating high school. He was a homeless seventeen-year-old kid living on the streets of Los Angeles. Sleeping in alleys, abandoned buildings, or wherever he could. He woke every morning to the sight of the **Hollywood** sign over him—the good life. It was a school night. And final tests for graduation were coming up the next morning.

One thing was for sure: Officer Del La Torre would be checking the ADA (Average Daily Attendance) to make sure that he was on the list. He'd die before missing class. Besides, his grades had been excellent and he was actually looking forward to the final examinations. Officer Del La Torre had told him that there was no excuse for an uneducated kid on her beat, homeless or not.

Sunny was hungry, but not hungry enough to eat out of trash cans that night, or to wait in line at the soup kitchen, or wash dishes so he could eat the leftovers in the bus trays. He needed some easy money and didn't want to take the time to panhandle enough for a meal.

Cruising Santa Monica Boulevard in Hollywood or "Boy's Town" as it's known to the locals, was just blocks from the alley he normally slept in. All the other boys were out strolling and the action was brisk—chicken hawks looking for fresh chickens. Sunny wasn't gay and didn't turn tricks, but he did take offers of kindness from strangers. He started strutting up the neon bright street to walk on the wild side.

No unaffiliated person ever contested turf with Sunny's quick fists. He paid his "taxes" to the gangs in one way or another, running this errand or that and at times carrying a message to a rival gang. That way he was recognized as neutral. The only turf Sunny politely asked to cross belonged to the black transvestites. He'd seen them in action. No one could stop them. Most were former prison bitches, *killer* prison bitches. They thought Sunny was cute and always let him wander past.

It only took a few blocks and about five drive-by propositions before Sunny decided he'd rather eat leftover scraps than turn a trick. He turned off Santa Monica and headed for Sunset Boulevard. He'd wash a few loads of dishes at Denny's, get a few bucks from the waitresses, then go and sneak into Grauman's Chinese Theater to get some sleep before classes started.

In the alley he cut through a silver Porsche pulled up next to him and stopped. The passenger's mirrored window slid down. A chicken hawk smiled at him. "I'm looking for a date."

Sunny looked at the john and grunted. "Forget it, I'm not working."

"Come on, pretty boy. You're trade. You know it and

I know it. You trade boys are *always* working, aren't you? Twenty bucks?"

Sunny coldly grinned. "I'd rather suck King Kong's cock."

"Mine's not quite that big. Look, here's fifty if you just ride with me." He reached into his wallet and pulled out a wad of bills, then picked up a Polaroid camera. "Look, I just want to take some pictures of you, that's all. I'll throw dinner in too."

Sizing up the man, Sunny thought he could take him.

"Your call," the man said.

The night had suddenly changed. Sunny jumped into the passenger seat with a Sizzler's steak bought right off the menu on his mind.

The passenger seat was covered with a plastic wrap. Before Sunny's alerts went up the man handed him a fifty-dollar bill. Money was money wherever it came from, even a freak.

"Yeah, baby, you just smile your pretty-boy smile for me." The man held up the camera and pushed the button.

The bright light was blinding. Before Sunny could move the man was on him. Instinct made him grab the man's hand. The man held a stiletto switchblade with a pearl red handle.

Sunny was just about overpowered and there was little room to fight back. This was the man's car. Sunny struggled for his life. How he did it, he never could say, a miracle maybe, but the knife wound up in the man's chest. Sunny was so frightened and enraged that he stuck him a few more times. Blood flew everywhere. He tried to get out but the passenger door release was missing.

He sat in shock and watched the man shake, then die. Regaining emotional control, Sunny reached down and picked up the wad of cash. All he wanted to do was get the hell out of there. He reached over the dead man, opened his door, and pushed him out.

As the man fell to the ground, several Polaroid pictures fell from his coat.

Sunny jumped out of the car and carefully picked up one of the pictures by the edges. It was of a young black boy. His throat had been cut. The other pictures scattered on the ground were of more young boys, all dead. Sunny dropped the picture and slipped into the shadows. No one had witnessed the event.

He raced back to his own alley and then sat in shock for what seemed like hours. When he came to his senses he counted the money—$7542.00. Now he was *really* scared. Still a kid, he had seen dead people many times; it was the first time he had killed a man. He'd badly misjudged the man and almost paid for it with his life.

The next day after the tests he planned on turning himself in to Officer Del La Torre. But he got cold feet and was glad that he did; there wasn't a mention of the murder anywhere in the news. Sunny figured that the Hollywood police didn't want to draw attention to a rich serial murderer killed by a potential victim in their town.

One morning a couple weeks after his graduation, Officer Del La Torre came busting through the motel door where he was staying. There were no smiles; she wasn't there to congratulate him on getting his diploma. No. She wanted to know where an eighteen-year-old had gotten the money to suddenly start living large—she knew.

There was never any lying to her. Ever. It was impossible. He broke down and cried, telling her the whole ordeal. Rather than cuff him, she took him straight to the Army recruiter and signed him up. She never asked him for the money he had taken. She never mentioned it. She was there at the downtown Greyhound bus terminal the day he left for basic training. She locked eyes with him moments before he boarded.

Officer Isabelle Del La Torre never wavered. She poked him hard on his shoulder. "Don't you *ever* tell anyone about that night. It wasn't your fault. You did what you had to do and he paid for it." She put her hands on her hips, narrowed her eyes at him, and said, "Now the world is out there. I don't want to see your ass back here on these streets again unless you legitimately *own* what they're built on, understand? Now get on the bus."

There were no good-bye hugs and kisses; there never were. But when the bus pulled away from the station he did get a last look at Officer Del La Torre. She was wiping the tears from her eyes with a handkerchief.

A warm breeze from the fireplace brought Sunny back to reality. "Officer Del La Torre," he said, "if you only knew how bad I've been." How he missed her ass-kicking no-nonsense support. It was the only time in his life that someone was there for him. Tough love was at least love.

He got up as the ancient black butler appeared and wordlessly showed him to his room for the night.

"Excuse me? Excuse me?" It took a few more tries, but the old man turned around. "What is your name?"

"You can call me Old Tom, everyone else does."

Old Tom's face was so wrinkled that Sunny couldn't tell if he was smiling or what. "Thank you."

Old Tom turned and continued walking into the darkness. Sunny stood in the hallway and marveled at its length. If he fired his gun, he wasn't sure if the bullet could even reach the other end. He couldn't wait to go exploring in the morning, but work came first. Again it was odd that no security measures were obvious.

Sunny walked back into his room and locked the heavy oak door and sat down at a reading table for twenty. Exhausted as he was his mind became caught up in General Donald Fine's diary of sordid double, triple, and quadruple dealings. It was one man's attempt to keep the dirty deeds straight. Like Sally had said, tanker-loads of Iranian oil magically turned into Romanian oil bound for Greece, and only the dirty players made millions off the deal. The same thing happened for coal, steel, and any other commodity needed to rebuild a war-torn continent. It was nation rebuilding and everyone who was "connected" had it made. General Fine did a great job of making the connections. But did they still exist? The players had to be old or dead. But to whom did they leave the vast fortunes? What were they worth today—enough to kill for? Again he noticed that pages were missing from the diary.

The corporation charters were impossible to read. He couldn't even get past the first two lines in most of them. Lambert was undoubtedly aware of what they said. At the end of the legal agreements it was possible to read a few signatures. A few names appeared time and again. He made a short list to look into later.

The general had made a detailed list of questionable bank accounts and banking cartels investing in programs that would've made any carpetbagger proud. In summary, it was the general's opinion that certain deals were made to divert the repayments of the Marshal Plan into shadowy and questionable Swiss holding accounts. They would have been sitting for over fifty years, collecting gazillions in interest. Who held the accounts? *Somebody* was cheating, but who? He read on and on. He reflected on what he had been reading. There was still so much more to digest. He had to continue—Sally paid big cash and would expect his full attention.

Story told—it was fascinating, international trade and finances gone underground. They were things he never had any dealings with. Investments? Sunny couldn't even invest in a good suit. He was *way* out of his element. Busting down doors and general mayhem he understood. He definitely wasn't the guy to be consulting with, but the only thing that kept him in play was Corey Brichner. Should he stay missing? If Sunny let it go, he would miss an opportunity to find out why Corey burned him.

Corey would be worth going after just to try to get his money back. If Corey wasn't dead when he found him, he could buy him a drink, find out where his money was at, then maybe kill him. As long as he pressed forward, money from somewhere was going to come in. *What else is going on in my life?* With that thought, he finally drifted off.

A SOFT KNOCK ON THE DOOR BROUGHT SUNNY OUT OF his deep sleep. Luxury. The king-sized colonial four-poster bed and down comforter could've eased him back to slumber, but he was working. The soft, thin, silk Persian rug caressed his feet as he padded across the room to open the door and check the hallway.

Old Tom was shuffling away up the hall. Breakfast was on a cart. It was a feast—it had everything. It had enough fat and carbohydrates to kill any diabetic. "Thank you," Sunny called out, but the old man acted as if he hadn't heard a word. Sunny rolled the cart to his bed and dived into it. "Ah, breakfast in bed!" The food was delicious. He could really get used to the good life.

After he ate he got out of bed and took a long, hot shower, then got into his only change of clothes. Still tired from only a few hours of sleep, he left the room and wandered the halls until he came to a study. He saw no one the whole time. Entering the room, Sunny immediately surmised that it was the general's "I love me room." And what a room it was. Pictorially, the walls were a history lesson.

Sunny got a good look at the black-and-white official photos of General Donald Fine. Tall and thin, a crew cut of gray hair, his even stare came from a lifetime of command. He looked like every stereotypical American general who'd been on the battle line since the Revolutionary War.

Countless other pictures in the room showed the general photographed with everyone—Roosevelt, Churchill, Stalin—hundreds of old pictures. Accolades, citations, and awards also filled the room.

A gold-plated Thompson submachine gun stood on a stand under glass. Sunny walked over, lifted the lid, and picked it up. It was gorgeous. A picture of Fine holding the weapon with General George Marshal was affixed to the stand over a bronze plaque. Reading the plaque on the stand, Sunny read that it was a gift from Marshal himself. It looked fully operational. He'd never fired a tommy gun. It was a lot heavier than most automatic weapons.

Sunny stood in front of a gigantic plate-glass window cradling the weapon in his arms. The window overlooked a green, lush valley that seemed to roll on into forever. He tried to imagine what it would be like to see this every day.

"It works. Donald had me shoot it once. He was very proud if it."

Sunny turned at the sound of Sally's voice. "I'm sorry. I've never held one before." He quickly returned the weapon to its stand. "I bet that they're great guns to shoot."

"I expect my husband would've taken you outside to fire it if he were here. I'm sure that there are some bullets around. Fire it at your leisure. Donald has a rifle range just over the hill." Sally sat in an armchair. "Was everything to your satisfaction? Did you have breakfast?"

Sunny nodded. "Yes to both." He paused a moment, then walked over and stood next to her. "So, Sally, I've read most of the material. There are some missing pages in your husband's diary. Do you know why that is?"

"No." Sally quickly shook her head.

"Now what?"

"I was hoping that you might have an idea of what's next."

"I *would* say to find yourself another man, a lawyer with a degree in international finance. Why doesn't Mr. Lambert handle it?"

Sally almost jumped. "No! He's a good boy, he won't..."

"Pull a trigger?"

"Yes, that's it."

"Well, Sally, I don't do these kinds of financial investigations. I never have. I don't know where to start.

But." He hesitated and paced the length of the long window, then stopped and came to a realization. "Corey's gone missing," he said to no one. "And can *stay* missing—he's got no family. Now I know why he used my name—we're carved from the same bone. I'm the only recovery he's got." Caught in a tight jam, a friendless guy like Corey just might call on Sunny for help no matter how badly he had burned him.

"I believe Mr. Brichner was a good man." Sally looked hopeful. "So you are going to take this case?"

There were threads everywhere in the general's material and someone was needed to piece the missing pieces of the puzzle and reveal the true picture. "Well, *someone* has to find Corey." *Or lose my money,* he wanted to add. "This finance thing isn't my bag. Whatever he might've said, I don't think Corey knew any more about what you have than I do." He crossed his arms. "Again, how did you first contact him?"

"I got his name from someone who once worked for Donald."

"If I take this case, I'll do what I can. But I can't make any guarantees." If Sally wanted to pay for him to go to Zurich, it was her money. "What were the contract terms you gave to Brichner?"

"We signed a contract that James drew up. Five thousand a week, plus expenses, eight weeks guaranteed. And if things pan out, 3 percent gross of whatever he might turn up."

"Life and health insurance?"

"Yes. Full coverage."

"I'll take the same deal."

"So you're in?" She held out her hand.

Sunny shook her hand. "I'm in. I need to finish reading all the material and make notes from the records, do some research, you know, maybe make a few calls, then design a game plan and time line."

Sally beamed. "I'll have James draw up another contract. You'll find everything and more in the library—computers, printers, faxes. You can call anywhere in the world on our satellite phone line. Donald made sure that we had all the latest gadgets. My home is your home. Any travel on my dime is first-class."

"Then I'll get to work now."

"Yes. Oh good, very good!" She suppressed her joy for a moment, then said, "Mr. Vicam, if for even a second it becomes too dangerous, you will drop everything you're doing and get the hell out of there. No heroics, please. It's just not worth it."

"You can bet on that. And if you want me to call you Sally, then you gotta call me Sunny. Fair?"

She nodded.

"Sally, I've been meaning to ask, what security measures do you have here?"

"I have a security company subscription."

Oh, boy. "And house guards?"

"None. Do you think I need them?"

"You might. You definitely might."

CHAPTER 6

0145 / FRIDAY / 17 JANUARY 1941

THEY LEFT CAMP X IN THE BLACK BEAUTY. KATO was back at the wheel. They got on the Toronto–Kingston highway headed south. And as before there was no reason given why she should just get in the car and leave training. She had just finished making her third parachute jump. She was having fun!

The Black Beauty pulled up on the drop zone, Kato got out, and wordlessly opened the door. Everyone else acted as if Number 26 had suddenly disappeared. Nonplussed, she climbed out of her jump harness and into the car.

Huddled in the backseat, Eileen had a chance to think over the training she had been receiving. She could pick locks, shake and pin tails in an instant, secretly open mail, write secret letters in code, kill in a number of different ways, and listen to, decrypt, and send codes around the world through a transceiver.

She could outshoot anyone at Camp X. It didn't matter what weapon they fired, Eileen could shoot it, clean it, and have it ready for service in record times. The shooting helped her maintain a sense of balance while she learned the lessons of mayhem. She found the crack of the bullets fast, reassuring, unerring, her answer to the deadly gibberish that she listened to in training.

IT WAS PITCH-BLACK BY THE TIME THEY DROVE ACROSS the Canadian border, unchecked, and rode for an hour on twisting back roads before the car came to a stop. Eileen had no idea where she was, or why they had stopped.

"You will please get out here, ma'am. I will pick you up when it's over."

"Well, Kato, you *can* talk. So tell me, when what's over?"

Kato got out and opened her door. Silent again, he waited until she was out, then got behind the wheel and peeled away, Black Beauty's red taillights disappearing in the dust. Eileen found herself standing in blackness. The short hairs on her neck rose. She had no idea what, why, or where she was. All she could hear were the sounds of the creatures of night—crickets, screech owls—and wind rustling through the trees. It was so black that she could barely see her hand in front of her face. Pockets empty, she was nervous and unarmed. She *really* missed the feel of a big Colt .45-caliber pistol in her small hands, or a stiletto strapped to her forearm. It was too dark to go looking for something to fashion into a weapon.

There had to be a good reason why she was there, unarmed. It had to be another endless test. "But what if this is a trick of some sort?" she asked aloud.

Slowly feeling around with her feet, she found a steel track in front of her. She stepped over the track, then knelt and felt for the other rail. It was there, and began to vibrate.

Looking up, a small pinpoint of light began growing. She hopped back over the track and watched the light grow as the ground started rumbling. In seconds a locomotive at full speed whistled past her. Sound, smoke, and wind whooshed all around, then the locomotive was gone, leaving just settling dust.

Eileen realized that she hadn't let out her breath during the entire scene. A long sigh escaped her. "What was that all about?"

It was okay, though, she was still ready for anything. The Brits were at war, and she wanted to be in the fight. She had loved to fight, even when she was a little girl. She didn't fight to be mean, she just loved the challenge of beating the odds.

A distant sound caught her attention. Cupping her ears, she heard a chugging sound. It sounded like a slow-moving train. A few minutes later the unmistakable presence of another elephantine locomotive slowly rolled by. It wheezed and huffed. Coupled to the locomotive were a few cars and a low-lit Pullman car at the end, which was dimly illuminated by a red-and-green light.

The locomotive hissed to a stop with the Pullman right in front of her. The back door opened. She carefully climbed the stairs and entered. The door shut automatically behind her. A small light at the end of a corridor gave her just enough light to inch cautiously down the passageway. All the compartment doors were closed. Anyone could jump out at her, but she was ready for anything.

Chronically exhausted from the constant training, she was tired of always having to be on her guard. After nearly two months, the exertion was taking its toll. There was a heavy smoke haze that hung like a fog, cloaking everything in the car. She discovered that the only light source came from a small Tiffany spider lamp on a round table in the middle of the room. A chair was next to it.

"Welcome aboard the *Roald Amundsen*, Number 26. Please sit down," a deep warm voice said.

A hand holding a cigarette set in a dark-stained ivory cigarette holder came into the light and gestured to an empty chair next to the table. "Sit next to me, please. We have a lot to talk about. I understand you've excelled in your training. The gentlemen of the Club and I wanted to meet with you."

Eileen sat silent in the chair. Slight movement made her aware that the train had started moving. Her eyes were already adjusted to the dark. She looked around and counted five shadowy men in the room. She couldn't see their faces—they hid behind their smoke. Another man used an ivory cigarette holder. Someone smoked a pipe; the pipe looked familiar. They all wore suits but it was so dark that she still couldn't discern any particular details or colors.

A hand reached out from the darkness and held out a pack of cigarettes.

"No thank you." As it was, she could barely breathe through the smoky haze.

"Would you like something to drink?" another voice said.

"What are you drinking?" she asked.

"Ah, a fine and rare bourbon."

"Water will be fine, thank you." She thought she knew the voice from the radio, but it couldn't be who she thought it was. Could it?

The water was brought to her in a crystal glass. She caught the profile of Peter Fleming and his pipe as he set the water in front of her, then stepped back into the shadows.

The man across the table began a long talk on the attributes of drinking pure water.

The moment he paused, Eileen interjected, "Okay, sir, that's all very interesting, so why am I here?"

There were a few short laughs followed by a long silence. The man sitting across from her pulled out the butt from his ivory holder, stubbed it out, set in another cigarette, then lit it. She caught the unmistakable features of President Franklin Delano Roosevelt in the light from the match.

"You know the northeastern area of Germany well? Well, do you, Number 26?" An intimidating voice from the dark asked, puffing up a cloud of cigar smoke.

Eileen cringed for a moment. The voice belonged to the man she almost shot on guard duty, William Donovan. "My mother and father are from there, sir. I spent time there as a young girl, until I was fifteen, sir."

"You speak the language well?" Donovan asked.

His presence was almost overwhelming.

"Of course, sir, even most of the regional dialects." She waved away the haze in front of her.

"So you have an *intimate* knowledge of the area?" the president asked.

"Yes, sir. That's right," she clipped and sat up straight in her chair. *Best manners, young lady.* She wasn't intimidated by these powerful men. "So, what do you gentlemen want exactly from me, if I may ask?"

The president pushed back from the table and rolled the custom-made wheelchair he sat in closer to Eileen. He put his hands on hers, and said, "I am going to do something my colleagues will find totally out of my character and be completely straight with you. Hitler and his Nazis are intent on world domination. That is a fact. Holland, Denmark, and Poland have fallen and are under their domination and terror. Britain is now fighting for her survival. But I don't need to tell you all that.

"What you don't know is that *I* will not put up with Hitler's goals. I will stand in his way. I have every intention of getting into this fight and beating the damned Nazis into oblivion!" He banged the little table with his fist.

He sat back and kneaded his hands. He tried to calm himself, but became pensive. "It is just a matter of time until we are up to our eyeballs in this war. It will be one incident. I don't know where it will come from, but it *will* come." He sighed and patted his legs. "Right now there are forces in this country who would try to impeach me if they heard what I've just told you. I've secretly been putting those things in place that will have us ready for this fight. But I need to do more.

"The Brits are at war with Hitler, and Churchill vows to set Europe ablaze. It has been *suggested* that I do something to demonstrate to Prime Minister Winston Churchill that our intentions are not just political and material, but deeper—something that shows that we are in this thing together, allies in this effort.

"I will tell you this much about the mission that is being considered. We know that the Nazis have perfected almost unbelievable methods of secret communication. It is *essential* that we be able to read their mail before we enter the coming war. We need someone with an intimate and thorough knowledge of Germany to carry out our mission."

"Me." Now she knew the reason behind her selection and training.

Roosevelt looked around the room, then back at Eileen. "I didn't say that. Let me continue. This agent will not get the final piece of his mission until a few days before he actually goes into Germany. This mission is extremely sensitive to my position. For that reason, should anything happen to that person, such as capture, then that person is completely on his own. If asked, I would say that I know nothing of that person or any events that he is involved in."

No one spoke.

Eileen couldn't stand it. She wanted to say, *"What? Are you crazy?"* Instead she said, "And you're looking for a volunteer?"

"Yes, we are," answered the president.

A slow smile bloomed on her face. "Back in training they said *never* volunteer for anything."

She heard a couple of gasps. All the men in the car started fidgeting—except the president.

Eileen knew what she was going to say, but kept silent. She wanted to enjoy the feeling and a moment of having the most powerful man in the world wait on her.

Ever since she was a little girl she'd never had a thing in her life that made her feel important. If only her mother and father could see their little girl now. For one moment in her life she was equal to anyone. Even if she failed in her mission, she would have dared greatness.

"Yes, Mr. President. I'll volunteer. There's no one who could keep me out of it, whatever *it* is!"

She heard a collective sigh of relief. The president remained calm and just held his caring eyes on her. If her parents had looked at her only once in her life that way, she would have died for them.

The train had come to a stop. Roosevelt put his cigarette holder into an ashtray and reached over the table and took Eileen's hands in both of his. "There's another reason I wanted to meet you. I wanted to meet one of America's first secret agents who's about to carry the fight back to our enemy. You see, I've often wondered what it was like for George Washington to secretly send patriots directly into the den of the lion on missions that we'll never know about. And I've wondered what those fine Americans must have looked like." He squeezed her hands tightly. "Now I know."

He picked up his cigarette and took a puff, then wistfully blew the smoke over her head. "Then Number 26, this is good-bye for now. I wish you the grace of God and all the luck in the world. When you come back I will insist that you personally tell me the whole story."

"Yes, Mr. President." She made her way back through the smoke haze, out the car door, and down to the tracks.

The train slowly wheezed and hissed away.

Car lights came on and the Black Beauty rolled next to her. She got in, not sure if what had just happened really had. "That was *some* train."

"What train? I didn't see a train."

"You're right. Let's roll, Kato."

CHAPTER 7

I T HAD TAKEN TWO DAYS OF NONSTOP WORK IN THE finest surroundings imaginable, and two wonderful hours firing the general's machine gun, but finally Sunny was itching to get into action. He gave some idle thought to telling Sally that it would take at least twenty years to get ready, of course living the good life in the meanwhile.

To familiarize himself with the grounds Sally told him to use any car in the garage. What a choice to make! The garage was its own building. There were six vehicles to choose from, all classic and luxurious vehicles. He drove a white 1964 Rolls Royce Silver Cloud around the massive estate.

He knew the opulent wealth of the Saudi royal family, had flown on their private airlines, and experienced world-class luxury on every continent. But that was only as an armed servant. This time he was the man in charge.

He pulled over to the private dock on the river. A fifteen-foot fishing boat hung in a sling next to the dock. It looked like Sally was vulnerable and an easy mark. She had a very small and old staff, a lady cook, gardener, three elderly maids, and Old Tom, the butler who doubled as a chauffeur. Sunny made a mental note never to have Old Tom do any driving for him. Other than Jim Lambert, the closest one to sixty was the gardener. To whom would the estate go once Sally was gone?

Corey the Con Man had to have seen the opportunity to milk Sally for a plush ride. He figured that Corey would hang around, behave, and eventually get in Sally's good graces for a piece of her will. Sunny gave some thought to doing the same thing but couldn't justify doing it to a nice old lady. He was there for the money at the moment, but the case looked *very* intriguing.

He gave more thought to some of the things he might be facing. Maybe there were outside consultants to talk to about Swiss financing, but whom could he trust not to go nuts with greed if it all panned out? He would have to trust his own instincts, bad as they were. The clouds looked heavy with rain, promising to ruin a great ride. He decided to turn around and get another look at the general's material back in his room.

Papers lay out in neat stacks all over the room. Having the basic working idea of what General Fine had recorded, Sunny felt a little like an actor trying to assume an unrehearsed role. "Hell, I'm a knuckle dragger. I don't even have the first real clue of what to look for."

He knew the basic facts and would just have to dazzle whoever was on the other end with some very brilliant bullshit. Still, he felt as if the general was trying to convey a deeper, possibly hidden message.

He was about to wrap up all the material, and was idly flipping through the last stack of pages of the general's handwritten penciled notes, when he noticed that one of the yellowed onionskin papers was just a hair thicker than the others.

He inspected the paper and it really was thicker. Holding the paper up to the light he could see that there was something typed behind the pencil notes. It was two papers stuck together.

Very carefully, peeling apart the sheets, he was astonished to see that the second paper was a carbon copy of something. Reading it again and again, he realized that he was holding a copy of a Golden Century Profit Share D that he'd read about the night before. The names of the shareholders were blanked out, but most importantly, there was a serial number on the copy.

"Jackpot!" The damned thing did exist!

Somehow the general had gotten one of the copies of the shares and stuck it to a list of meandering notes meant to stay buried. It was almost as if the general was calling from the other side. Creepy. Or had he foreseen the day when someone would find the hidden document and search out its origin. Well, the man probably hadn't imagined a guy like Sunny Vicam picking up the trail.

The hair rose on the back of his neck.

He read and studied, trying to decipher the Golden Century Profit Share D. The copy listed the name of a well-known Swiss bank as the guarantor of the share. It was rated for 130 million dollars. Sunny whistled. "If the D share really exists, at today's rate it'd be worth a *hell* of a lot more."

Armed with a real find, it was a place to start. It was time to go into action.

Back in the great hall he sketched out a simple plan to Sally, not telling her about what he had found, and giving her only enough information to feel secure with his actions. He would book a flight to Zurich using a fake name and passport. He planned on being there for a week and would call only if he had any hard information.

If he found Corey he would find out where his money was, and if he didn't kill him first, help him with his investigation and even possibly extend his own stay if things played out. Damn Brichner, he was clever; who else to better call for help than someone who stood to lose a big investment if he didn't respond?

Swiss obsession for financial secrecy stepped over the line to the incredibly paranoid. He had once used that very paranoia for Mossad to pull a very clever caper in

Zurich, illegal as hell, but it worked and he got away clean. He had bought his yacht with the money that they paid him. The right people in Zurich could be very helpful, and he knew one; but those that thrived on concealment could make his search for Corey and his quest impossible.

Sally didn't need to know everything he did. She was paying him just to do some checking, that's all. There would be no reason to explain cut outs, spookies, dead drops, or intelligence sources.

He'd genuinely come to believe in Sally's desire to find her man. She seemed not to care as much for the hidden money as for the safety of Corey. She'd only known Corey for a short time and was already committed to his safety. Sunny hoped that she would be as concerned if something happened to him. She offered the use of a military jet, but Sunny reluctantly refused. If anything went wrong, he didn't want any trail to lead back to a nice rich old lady—client confidentiality and protection always came first.

The vow he made to take care of his own concerns first once again would have to go on hold. He was on the clock and Zurich would be his first stop.

CHAPTER 8

EILEEN ARRIVED BACK AT CAMP X IN CANADA IN another world. In her cramped quarters she tried to recall every word and detail of what had happened and what was said on the train. Was it *really* the president of the United States, Franklin Delano Roosevelt, who had spoken to her?

No. It had to be an act. It had to be. "Why me?" she asked the walls.

Questions filled her mind. Why would they entrust her with such a crazy mission? Why would they tell her now? When would the mission begin? Did it even have a name?

One thing that she was sure of was that there was no reason for the president to entrust some backward kid with getting into a war that was close to being declared. It had to be another game. It'd been fun, exciting, but now there were just too many games to play.

Weary, she was too tired to start even a little fire so she crawled into her bed, thankful for the down blanket Peter had given her. At any time she expected the door to fly open and "enemy" agents to take her away for a long, long interrogation. She would need the sleep.

"Number 26. Wake up, Number 26."

Eileen rubbed her eyes. Peter was knocking at her door. "Oh, Peter, when is my bag of dirty tricks going to be full?" Eileen asked groggily.

"Now."

"*It is?*" She leapt from her bed and ripped open the door. "You better not be kidding me, Peter." She shielded her eyes from the sun. It was bright and sunny for a change.

"Yes, you must ready yourself. Pack your kit and go to the mess hall to get something to eat, the sooner the better, dear. We're about to take a long trip."

She was out the door in minutes and trotting over to the mess hall. She almost forgot that there was a thing called the sun. It made her excited.

She ate well, wolfing down ham, real eggs, potatoes, and toast. She drank about a gallon of coffee. The Americans had supplied most of the food. Through the window she saw Peter pull up in the Black Beauty. Kato was at the wheel.

She grabbed a huge lunch bag from the cook and raced out to the car. Peter got out and opened the door. He closed the door after she got in.

"Peter, aren't you coming? I've got a million questions to ask you."

"No, dear, that's precisely why you must travel alone again."

"Damn! Not again? Where am I going?"

"I'm sorry. You'll know when you get there."

Eileen could only fume. "Damn you, Peter, I was just beginning to like you. And I bet Kato won't breathe a word to me either."

"That's right. I will share with you one bit of news. The battle grows ever more desperate. It is time for you to leave this tea party and join forces with the real Mad Hatter." He handed her a stack of folders. "This is some more study material for the ride." Peter smiled and backed away from the car. "Have a pleasant drive, Number 26. Reminisce on all you learned and those

things you have in your bag of dirty tricks." He nodded
to Kato and the car roared away.

EILEEN SNACKED ON ALMONDS AS SHE READ THE FILE
that Peter left her. There wasn't all that much more to
learn. She knew how to operate the microfilm cameras,
how to transmit and receive, and how to kill someone in
countless, sometimes clever and seemingly simple ways.
The rest of the deadly material was mostly theory at the
moment and almost put her to sleep.

Even though she was back on the road as the Green
Hornet, it wasn't anywhere near as much fun as the first
time. The fun was almost gone—one had to *work* at being a secret operative. Nevertheless, she was on the road
to wherever the next stop was, a stop that was just that
much closer to real danger, and real death. She wasn't a
storybook Alice falling into the rabbit hole. It was time
to put the childish games away and grow up.

CHAPTER 9

0730 MONDAY / 1 MARCH 2004
KLOTEN INTERNATIONAL AIRPORT
ZURICH / SWITZERLAND

THE SWISSAIR PLANE TOUCHED DOWN AT THE Kloten International Airport. The American passport Sunny used to clear customs bore the name John Carrillo. Having only one carry-on and a suit bag, he walked down to the train terminal and took the first train leaving for the short ride downtown.

There was a light snow falling. Skis were mounted to racks on cars; ski season was in full swing. He checked into the Ambassador Hotel, the same hotel as Corey, who'd checked in under his own name. *Idiot!*

Sunny thought that it was a big mistake using one's own name, but Corey was more con man than spook. Corey *always* wanted people to know his name. He liked to drop *Who's Who* names in the first minute of meeting people. He might've looked at the trip as a paid skiing vacation where he'd do a little investigation, concentrating mostly on his next scam.

Checking her computer, then making a phone call to housekeeping, the desk clerk said that apparently Mr. Brichner had not been in his room for at least a week.

"He's paid up until tomorrow, Mr. Carrillo. Perhaps he's skiing. I don't know, sir, he was a private booking."

Sunny glanced at the computer screen and caught Corey's room number.

Dropping his bag in his room, he took the elevator to the third floor and meandered around the halls until he saw the room. Empty hall, Corey's door was open in seconds.

A small black gym bag was on a nightstand and an open suitcase was on the bed. Sunny carefully and quietly inspected the messy contents. Nothing unusual, a shaving kit, a windbreaker, and a pair of dirty socks, no definite scents anywhere. No trail anywhere except a note on the nightstand with the name of the Credit Suisse Bank written on it in Corey's handwriting. It looked as if Corey expected to return to his room at any time.

He held the paper up to the light looking for any other messages. It was written on the Ambassador letterhead paper. There was nothing added to it. It was clean.

The rest of the room he didn't know about. He didn't have an electronic sweeper for bugs so he *had* to assume that it was bugged. Corey was out on point alone without any backup. A simple research investigation for a rich old lady, it might have looked like a vanilla job and easy money for Corey. Sunny might've taken the same casual steps. But Sunny's instincts told him that something was up. Beating the bushes was his only option. His next stop would be the bank whose name Corey had written down.

THE CREDIT SUISSE BANK WAS AS IMPRESSIVE AS IT WAS old. Dressed in a silk three-piece black suit, Sunny was able to get the immediate attention of a cockeyed bank agent. Older, balding, small, and rotund, the man seemed friendly enough. Sunny tried to make eye contact by focusing on the good eye through his thick glasses.

"My name is John Carrillo."

"How may I help you, Mr. Carrillo?" the man asked in heavily accented English.

"I'm trying to locate a man. His name is Corey Brichner. He might've come here last week." Sunny then went on to describe Corey.

"No, I've no recollection of a man like that."

The man looked annoyed not to be discussing bank business.

Sunny shook his head. The man acted as if he smelled a bad wind. It was time to go fishing. "I think that he was here looking for evidence of a Golden Century Profit Share D plan," he lied. Corey could not have possibly seen the paper he pried apart in the general's files.

The banker looked confused. "A what?"

"A Golden Century Profit Share D plan," Sunny answered, enunciating each syllable.

"I've never heard of that. What is it?" The man's lip began to sweat.

Sunny saw the look of a shrewd banker used to lying through a smile. He stood to leave. "Well, if you don't know, then you don't know." He pulled a piece of paper from his pocket and handed it to the fat little banker.

The banker looked at a sixteen-digit code. Sunny saw the man pale. "What is this?" Beads of sweat began forming on his forehead.

"Something that might interest others here in this bank. Check it out. Show it to your higher-ups. I'm staying at the Ambassador Hotel up the street. I'll be looking for my client's man or any information on that code."

"Have you tried the local authorities?" He nervously looked about as if he were trying to get the attention of someone.

"The police? Not yet, but they are next on my list." He grasped the old man's sweaty hand. "Thanks for seeing me."

Wide-eyed, the man acted as if he couldn't wait for

Sunny to leave. The man even came out on the street to see which way he was walking.

Sunny's next stop was at a local tailor shop. He left the place with a new wool coat and a Walther P22 pistol and noise suppresser neatly concealed inside—the coat was also lined with Class III body armor. The nervous look in the old banker's eyes told Sunny that he'd better do something about personal protection; one could never be sure who one's friends were. The tailor shop was run by a *sayanim,* a Jewish sympathizer working for Mossad. To keep from raising any alarms Sunny told the tailor to let Mossad know that he was in the area working on a private contract and just borrowing the equipment.

After walking back to the hotel Sunny made a local phone call, then left his room and took a long walk about the lake area. Looking like any other tourist with a high-tech video camera to the casual observer, he reconnoitered his surroundings, taking video of likely hide sites, trying to spot any tails, then he checked various entrances and exits for quick retreat routes. Confident he hadn't been tailed, a walk in a nearby park allowed him to plant his "spooky," a slim pouch with cash and another phony ID that he could use if things got hairy and he needed a quick getaway.

He finally walked into a coffee shop that he knew well. The last time he was there he had been involved in running an operation that converted worthless Jewish shekel coins into valuable Swiss currency. A minute reduction in the size of the coin made it a perfect fit for exchanging them in the ubiquitous coin machines in Switzerland. Over the period of a couple of weeks the coins, almost valueless coins were put in the machines and came out in Swiss marks, which were then laundered for millions of dollars.

A freethinking Mossad agent conceived the caper to augment their black operations. It drove the Swiss authorities crazy and netted some fifteen million dollars.

Sunny ran the operation so smoothly that only one person from Interpol ever caught on to the scheme. That Interpol agent kept quiet about what he knew.

A heavyset man sat at a small table with his back against the coffeehouse wall smoking a cigarette and sipping coffee. He was old and gray. He chose his words carefully before he spoke. "Sunny, it's always good to see you, as long as you do not have too many loose Jewish coins in your pocket, or any of your friend's pockets that you might want to change for Swiss marks. The exchange rate is *still* not in our favor." The old man slowly stood up and gave Sunny a bear hug before they both sat down. He poured Sunny a cup of coffee from his coffeepot.

Sunny wordlessly lifted his cup to Melton and took a small sip. "And it's always good to see you." He had known Interpol inspector, Thorsen Melton, for years. Even though they sometimes worked opposite sides of the streets, they had a fond and grudging respect for each other's abilities. They were both good for their word. Sunny had done many favors for the inspector, who had reciprocated in kind.

Melton never said anything about Sunny's caper; he felt that the Swiss still owed the Jews for some of the underhanded things they did and failed to do during the war. The books were a little more balanced now, in his own estimation.

"So what brings you back here to my streets?" Melton took a last drag on his cigarette, then stubbed it out.

"I'm working for a private client. Have you seen Corey Brichner? I'm looking for him. He's here on his own name."

"What's he in trouble for this time?"

"Nothing." Sunny corrected. "Well, not much. I'm here on behalf of a client."

"Yes, I see. I saw him last week. We had coffee right here. He said that he was here for a client looking for evidence of a secret money-laundering scheme. He made me laugh, him looking for a money-laundering scheme right in the middle of the biggest money-laundering mat in the world. I told him to take his pick." Melton gave Sunny a sidelong glance. "I would guess that you are working for the same client, yes?"

Sunny continued sipping at his coffee. "Melton, do you know where he is?"

"He was staying at the Ambassador Hotel."

"I know. He's still registered there, but they haven't seen him lately. I think something's happened to him."

"Do you want to file a missing persons report? I can take care of most of the paperwork. You think he's met with foul play?"

"I do think that there's definitely that possibility." Sunny could see Melton's bushy eyebrows rise and fall as he started making mental calculations.

"Then I'll have it looked into. But Corey's a resourceful, slippery man. Like you, he seems to have the ability to disappear and reappear at will." He gave Sunny a piercing look. "Tell me, why are you really here?"

"Trust me, Melton, it's no scam this time. Corey owes me money too. So I'm straight up looking for him, plus looking into a couple of things he might've missed."

"Yeah? What kind of things?"

"Listen, you were here during World War II. You must've seen a lot of strange things go down right after it was over, right?"

"That was a long, long time ago. Everything was strange during, and after, the war."

"What can you tell me about the Marshal Plan?"

"What do you want to know about it?"

"I read some pretty interesting material about the Plan the other day, material you don't find in any history books. Basically the material says that, theoretically, up to now, and including interest, there's been some 2 *quadrillion* dollars paid to the Allied nations for the war reparations. But if the repayments just sat in locked bank accounts, then interest alone would be worth trillions today. Anyway, I haven't made any phone calls directly to the Treasury Department, but I'm sure Germany or any other Axis country hasn't written them a quadrillion-dollar check lately."

Melton whistled. "Okay, I follow you so far. What's your point?"

"If payments are being made, then where's all the money going?"

Melton laughed. "Oh, that would a *very* big question indeed. It's like the Nazi gold; everyone would like the answers to that one, including me." Melton then thought about what Sunny had said. "If what you say has merit, then there would be people who would like to keep that information secret. What do you need from me?"

"First help me find Corey."

"I'll see what I can do. Where are you staying?"

"The Ambassador, same as Corey."

Sunny stood to leave, but Melton grabbed his wrist.

"Sunny, be careful. This isn't the old Zurich you once had fun running a scam in. Things are changing rapidly. Sure, the money is dirty but with the world as it is the players have become meaner. Old allies are no more, and our enemy doesn't look for profit anymore, just blood. Maybe Corey found this out. Be very, very, careful of the game that you play. The gnomes of Zurich are *not* friendly."

SUNNY SAT ON THE EDGE OF A COLD PARK BENCH OVER-looking the cold Zurich River. Snow blanketed the city. The call had come to his room in the middle of the night.

"Twelve-thirty. Be sitting on any bench in front of the river." The phone went dead.

Even armed, he felt naked before God and everyone else. He was right in the middle of a park in the middle of the day. Anybody could be in the forest line or the buildings in the area. As far as he knew, he wasn't expecting any danger. But that was the worst assumption to take in an unknown scenario. If any enemy—known or unknown—knew where he was at that moment, then they had a clean shot.

The snow was falling heavier. It had already carpeted the field white.

A figure in black emerged from the tree line and slowly made his way across the white field. Behind him Sunny could see some people darting through the trees. At least two people led dogs on leashes.

"Oh fuck me," Sunny whispered. The only exit he had was the Zurich River. And that would be a cold swim. He instinctively and unconsciously began to plot out the shots that he might have to make with his pistol if things went sour.

Sunny could hear the crunch of the man's boots. He involuntarily stood up and reached for the gun in his coat. The man came to a stop in front of him, coolly smiled, and held out his hand.

"You don't need your gun here, Mr. Sunny Vicam. I am unarmed. I am Nathan Happa." He held up his hand for a brief moment in mock surrender. "Look around. Those you see with me are here for *our* protection." He smiled, but the commanding coldness in his ice-blue eyes could even freeze hell. There was something vaguely familiar about him. He held out his left hand. There was a deep diagonal scar across his palm.

About six feet five inches, Nathan Happa was tall, but rail thin. He wore a black leather trench coat and a slouch hat in a rakish manner that covered part of his gel-slicked platinum blond hair. All he needed was the Nazi swastika on his arm to complete the total Gestapo effect. Sunny wondered if he wore one beneath the trench coat.

They were fast. *They've already made me.*

There was no denying Happa had a presence. Sunny knew his kind well, whoever he was. His eyes darted around as if he possessed great secrets. Sunny slowly let go of the butt of the gun, then reached out and took Happa's left hand.

The cold shock made him try to pull his hand back

but he couldn't. It felt like he was gripping a dead man's hand—he couldn't move. Stopped in time, it wasn't that Happa was looking *at* him, as much as *into* him.

His thin, angular face was pure white. Sunny could see veins pulsing blue beneath his skin. Sunny wasn't about to lose control of the situation. "And just who are you?"

Nathan let go of Sunny's hand. For all the silent power that Happa emanated, Sunny felt that he could drop the man in an instant, but knew better than to make snap judgments about people.

"I'm a bank security specialist. Please excuse having you meet me this way, but it makes it easy for me to just move on if you don't check out, Mr. Vicam. Anyone traveling on a false passport is *always* subject to suspicion."

"Sure, Nate." This wasn't going well. He could be a target in anyone's scope.

It was difficult to break away from the man's unblinking, penetrating stare.

"I prefer we keep the names professional for the moment, Mr. Vicam. I have agreed to meet with you for my own reasons. I hope that you can understand, every year countless thousands of people approach the Swiss banking system with claims that they feel are founded to gain open access to our private bank accounts. Some claims are outlandish, others, intriguing. If I may ask, where did you get the account number?"

"It's a private matter."

Happa smiled. "The Swiss are nothing if not private. How long are you staying here?"

Push buttons. Someone had thought enough of his efforts to bring out a foil to test him. "As long as it takes. Say, I don't hear a German accent. You sound like you're from New Jersey or somewhere like that." Sunny saw the surprise in Happa's face.

"I'm not here to discuss my English or where I'm from." Happa bristled. "What is it exactly that you're looking for, Mr. Vicam? *Whom* are you representing?"

"That's two questions. First, my client remains private unless I'm told otherwise. Second, I'm looking for somebody. Look, you help me out and I'll help you out."

"Who is it that you are looking for?"

"A guy named Corey Brichner."

"And who is this man?"

"A colleague."

"I see." Nathan slowly turned to face the entrance of the park and nodded.

At least twenty people stepped out from concealment. Sunny could hear the attack dogs howl and snarl.

"A lost friend." Happa pursed his lips. "Yes, I can understand that. I will do what I can to help locate your *colleague*. I don't guarantee anything. But if I do this favor for you what do I get in return?"

"So the Golden Century Profit D shares *are* valid?"

"No. The life of all the shares has run out. But how it came to be is very interesting. To be honest, it's actually a hobby of mine. *That* is why I agreed to meet with you." He turned back and faced Sunny with his ice-blue eyes and smiled. "You see, it is the account matrix that fascinates me."

"Oh yeah?" Happa almost seemed half-convincing. Sunny tried to look interested.

"Maybe it turns out that you can actually help me. I've been interested in some of the parties that were involved. The Golden Century is old legend stuff among the financiers here, but it still holds quite an appeal for me." He put his thin white hand on Sunny's shoulder. "Mr. Vicam, Sunny, do you really know about the share plan?"

"Look. I'm a novice, a rank amateur. But I do have a basic understanding of how it existed." Sunny felt as if he was out on the thin ice floating down the river.

"I would like to see if you know, or can learn any more than I can. If you like, I do know of a place where you can do more research to find out exactly which cartels put it together. It is a private investments research center near where you are staying. If you like, I can have a driver take you there or have someone there to help you."

"When?"

"Tomorrow. Would that be fine?"

"When?" Happa was holding all the cards at that moment.

"How about ten in the morning? I'll send a car for you at the Ambassador. If you like we can have dinner afterward and you can tell me what you learned. And I will then tell you what I've learned of your Mr. Brichner."

"Sure. Ten. I'll be ready."

Again Nathan held out his left hand. "Then good day, Mr. Vicam." He turned and retraced his steps in the snow.

Cars started and screeched away. Everyone faded away.

Heart now racing a mile a second, Sunny was ready for a whammy or anything, but it didn't happen. Sunny bundled himself tighter against the shivers. "Now what the hell was *that* all about? He was a cold fish one moment, then my best buddy the next." Nathan Happa was as strange a person as he'd ever seen, using the left hand for shaking hands. But he was also extremely elegant, alluring, walking in another world.

If Happa was the enemy, then Sunny knew he had stumbled right into the Big League of crime. He was no match against a cult army. The best thing to do was bug out, right then and there, take Sally's money, and then call it a day. But he knew he couldn't do it. For him to have generated the response that he did, something *had* to be happening. Besides, there was a little matter of half a million dollars of his own money to recover.

CHAPTER 10

EILEEN AND PETER STOOD ON THE EASTERN FORTI-fications of the Halifax Citadel in Nova Scotia, huddling together against a cold and bitter wind as they looked down on Halifax Harbor. Freezing winds blew off the ocean, whipping up the water below into whitecaps and foam. The wind whooshed off the water, up through the Halifax streets, and over the rise where the citadel stood. The wind chilled Eileen to the bone.

Peter looked through his binoculars. "There, down there, you can see her three masts. She's under full sail."

"I can see it," replied Eileen.

"Take a closer look." He handed her his binoculars.

It took her a few moments to make adjustments and focus the glasses, but when she did she caught her breath. "I can't make out any name."

"It's called the *Illusion*."

"I'm sorry, Peter, but I don't know much about ships, but I can see it's beautiful."

"I don't either. Yes, she's magnificent, isn't she? I understand that it's called a three-masted rum schooner. One hundred and fifty feet long, it also has engines and a propeller. I'm sure there are a million and one other details, but the captain can tell you all of them."

"Who's the captain?"

"He's an American chap named John Lee. I've never met him."

"Peter, why are you telling me this?" She adjusted the binoculars until she could clearly see several people manning the line to let the wind out of the sails. Suddenly all the forward speed ceased and the ship slowed to a choppy stop.

Eileen had a bad feeling in her gut.

Standing behind her, Peter put his hand on her shoulder and whispered in her ear. "The *Illusion* is here just long enough to load some supplies, then she will leave on the outgoing tide in a few hours. Oh, and she'll be carrying one very secret passenger."

Eileen whipped around. "Hold on! Peter, I don't really like being on boats." Her mind flashed back to when she was a third-class passenger in steerage on a steamer from Europe. She was freezing, hungry, and sick the entire winter voyage. The prospect of making a return trip in similar conditions filled her with dread.

Peter remained quiet, holding a sanguine look on his face.

"Oh, you ass. You actually expect me to go aboard that boat, in that cold water." She pointed to the bleak horizon. "Out there in the frigid North Atlantic, where ships can—and do—sink; I do know *that* much about them, Peter."

"Dear, you really have no alternative." Peter bent low, eye to eye with Eileen. He took a quick look around, then said, "This is the only way that we can get you where you need to go and keep your mission secret. You can't tell me that you would come this far just to turn around?"

"I didn't say that."

"Are you scared? Don't think you can do it?" He scowled.

"Oh yeah, I can do it, even if the damned barge does

sink, thank you. It's just that I hate the idea of being in the middle of the cold ocean in *that*. I'm not looking forward to it, that's all."

Peter acted as if he hadn't hear a word and they climbed back into the Black Beauty, plunging down the steep streets to the base of the wharf. The moment they came to a stop and got out of the car the sun disappeared behind the black clouds. Eileen didn't care for the omen one bit.

"Anything that you need has already been provisioned on the ship. The captain and crew do not know who you are, or anything about your mission. You are still Number 26 to us. To them you are a woman without a history to discuss with anyone. Anyone. Only the captain knows of your destination." Peter let out a deep sigh. "I guess . . ."

"You're acting as if you're the one who's going on this secret voyage." A thought came to her mind. "Peter, are you going to actually miss me?"

"I am, Number 26. I've never met a Yank with your pluck."

"Well, as long as it holds out I'll be game. See you on the other side."

They shook hands. While they liked each other immensely, both knew that their worlds would never touch more than beyond a handshake. But they might become friends.

A dinghy could be seen rowing from the *Illusion*.

Eileen turned and waved to her driver. "Bye, Kato." She would have liked to have gotten to know him better, but he followed the rules.

The driver got out of the car and waved. "Number 26, ma'am?"

"Yes?"

"How did you know?"

"How did I know what?"

"That my name is Kato, it's Sawa Kato."

Eileen threw a couple of imagined chops into the air and started laughing but said nothing. She climbed down a slippery ladder to the dinghy floating on the choppy water. Bumping down on the plank seat, she was astonished to see that the man rowing the boat was actually standing; he was a small person.

"Billy Klinke, ma'am." He grinned. His hands continually manned the oars to hold the skiff as steady as he could while Eileen's suitcase radio and duffel bag were lowered into the boat.

Billy was bald and wore gold earrings in both ears. He looked like a tiny pirate. But slight as he was, he was finely sculpted. He stood steady and was lithe on his feet while the boat tipped and yawed on the rough water. It was like he was dancing to music only he understood.

"And just who are you, miss?"

"Call me Annie."

"Nice to meet you, Annie. The skipper had me come fetch you. Are you ready for your voyage?"

"I hope so." She turned and waved to Peter.

Billy went into a furious, but fluid motion.

The wind howled and blew foam across the little boat. Eileen was already becoming dizzy and soaked. She looked back and the wharf was only a small specter, the black outline of the Packard Clipper getting smaller with every stroke Billy took. *Good-bye Black Beauty.*

"Where are we going?" Eileen asked.

"I won't know until we are well under way. We're taking on enough provisions and fuel to last a world voyage. It could be anywhere, only the skipper knows. And his lips are tighter than the ship 'e runs. Are you okay?"

The constant motion of the ocean was already getting to her. "No. I don't think so." She was queasy and wet from the frozen sea spray.

" 'S'all right, Annie, you'll get worse. This time of year, with the seas the way they is, I don't think it'll be a smooth voyage to anywhere. I'll get ya something dry to wear and something to settle your stomach once we're aboard the *Illusion*."

Eileen didn't realize how big the *Illusion* was until

they were under her stern. The crew lowered block and tackle, then hoisted the dinghy securely onto the boat.

The deck was rolling and pitching as Eileen stepped aboard. A yaw in the stern almost took her off her feet, but Billy caught her and quickly steered her below to a tiny cabin. He was back in a minute with a woolen coat and long johns.

"They'll fit big, but they're clean. We'll be gettin' under way as soon as the skipper squares away a few more things." Billy looked up at Eileen. "Annie, you're looking a little *too* green. I'll be back with something for you in a moment." He closed the door behind him.

Changed and dry, the clothing was big, but at least it was warmer. There was nothing to the cabin but a small berth. The cabin walls creaked and moaned. Boxes filled the rest of the cabin. Reading the stencils on the boxes, she realized that they were ammunition crates, crates and crates of bullets. All it would take was a random incendiary round through the wooden hull to set everything all off. She could barely move so she sat on the berth and felt her stomach lurch. Lying down seemed to be her only recourse. Things only got worse as she watched the cabin go up and down, up and down.

Billy returned with a metal bucket. He put it next to her berth. "Getting your sea legs starts with addressing the bucket." He put a drink next to her and patted her hands. "Don't drink this after until you've done yer puking. It'll help settle the stomach. I'll check on you later."

Through her nausea she heard Billy's booming voice calling out commands and people yelling affirmations.

"Full-rig, boys, let these Newfies know the *Illusion* could outrun any Nazi sub on her tail! Let 'em all out, out!"

It sounded like someone sang above the sea noise. She thought that they only did that in the movies. Soon she felt the ship move, then hum. The water slapped the sides of the boat and the cabin began to pitch up and down violently. That was it. She grabbed the bucket and lost her breakfast. She rolled over on her back and wondered how long she would be on the ship with its ever-moving gyrations. "Now I know why I never joined the Navy."

There was nothing that she could do but endure the beating. She sipped at the bitter drink until it was gone. It was a struggle to keep the concoction down, but she did. It made her feel drowsy. Everything began to fade.

SHE WASN'T SURE IF SHE'D SLEPT, OR HOW MUCH TIME had passed, but one thing was sure, she knew where she was at—on a damned-cold heaving ship! She dropped her feet over the side of the berth and tried to stand up. Light-headed, she felt as if she had taken a few drinks but things were a little better. She opened the cabin door and stepped out into the breezeway, then climbed the companionway to the top deck.

There was nothing decorative or ornate about the ship, no polished brass fixtures, no fancy, shiny nautical hardware. No luxury liner, this was a *working* ship. It smelled like old wood and pitch. Every inch of space was filled with cartons, crates, and bags. Hammocks were strung wherever there was an open space. Upon closer inspection of some of the cargo Eileen read that they were more guns, explosives, and mines. It was obvious the skipper was gunrunning a *big* load. She wondered what kind of men were willing to chance the Nazi submarines that were sinking any ship sailing east, bound for England.

She opened a door and walked in on a raucous gathering. The men all stopped what they were doing and stared at their new passenger.

Eileen thought herself fearless, but looking at the crew, she felt fear. These were some rough-looking guys. She was glad that she had some sea legs or she was sure she would have collapsed from the constant motion.

"Where's yer manners, boys?" Billy jumped up on a

stool. "This here's Annie, remember that. So you be thinking polite thoughts when you address her."

The crew muttered among themselves. The door opened and she saw a big man enter. The crew became quiet as church mice. Eileen guessed him to be the skipper.

He was bundled up in a peacoat and Eileen could not see his face. He silently walked to the coffeepot and poured a cup. He walked about the cabin, eyeing each man and nodding to some. He paused in front of her, but only for a moment. It was impossible to get a read off of him.

Eileen was surprised when she saw his face. He looked younger than most of the men. But still, even the roughest-looking crewman deferred to him.

"Billy, all our papers look in order. How's the ship look?"

"She's in fine shape, skipper."

The captain took a sip of coffee. "Then, gentlemen, there's still duty to do. Check your schedules."

It was a casual comment, but the men scrambled as if a shot had been fired. The cabin was clear in seconds. He took a few more sips, then turned around and faced Eileen.

Eileen decided that he did not look much like a leading man Hollywood sea captain, but more like a blond Viking. His blue eyes smoldered at her. "Please follow me."

The captain's quarters might as well have been just another berth. It wasn't any different from hers but for the fact it was a little bigger and had a washbasin.

"You got a name?" he asked. "Something that I can call ya by."

"I told Mr. Billy that Annie would do."

"Annie. I like that name. You look like an Annie. Mine's John Lee. I got a few rules while you're aboard. Number One is to stay away from the men. There's nothing like a shipboard romance to sink the crew. I've seen it happen. Other than that you'll pretty much be left to your own devices. Stay off the deck when the weather's rough, which promises to be most of the time. I won't bother you, but when I tell you to do something, you do it."

Eileen could not guess his age. He looked young, but his eyes were steady, with a control that only those who have had a lifetime of hard experience could understand.

"Where are we headed, and how long will it take us to get there?"

John looked surprised. "No one told you?"

"No one's told me much at all, I'm afraid."

"Well, Annie, we're headed for England. It should take us no more than six days, weather and U-boats permitting."

"Thanks." It was refreshing not to play mind games with John. Six days or more, weather *and* U-boats permitting. If her stomach could hold out, then so could she. There wouldn't be a lot to do but try to stay warm, eat, and sleep. "I'm told that this is a rum schooner. What exactly is that?"

John smiled and Eileen suddenly realized that being a virgin no longer mattered to her, if it ever had. She also realized that countless women around the world had probably fallen, heels up, to that smile. Smiling, John Lee was a *very* handsome and alluring man.

"Me 'n most of the men are from Virginia. From what I've been told we are related to good old General Robert E. Lee. But I would bet that our bloodline ain't *that* blue. See, I come from a long family of rum smugglers that goes all the way back to the Revolutionary War. There are those who uphold the law and others who love their country but don't agree with the politics; we're still both American. Right? Anyways, I crewed the *Illusion* with my father as a boy before and during Prohibition. We ran loads of sugar all over the West Indies. Then we bought rum from the Jamaicans in the Caribbean and whiskey from the Canadians. When we had a fleetload we anchored off New York and sold our loads to whoever tied off alongside.

"The *Illusion* was made by my family in Virginia to carry cases and barrels of Demon Rum, lots of it." He smiled at the memories. "I worked my way up from cabin boy to captain."

He smiled again and Eileen felt her heart jump. He had a beautiful smile beneath his golden beard, perfect white teeth.

"But now you carry guns."

John's smile vanished. "That's right. Like you, I'm carrying them for 'our friends.' "

"*Our* friends?"

"Just because I don't believe in paying liquor taxes don't mean I ain't American. Hell, this country was started by my kind. I love my freedom out here. No one tells me what to do, especially not some damned Nazis!"

John's fiery eyes excited Eileen. He was a man in full control, used to control. The idea of being on the open ocean was no longer a concern. She was in good hands. Now she knew why the crew put their trust in him.

"Vincent Astor, a personal friend of the president, came to me with a negotiable idea. See, a lot of our people were rottin' in jail, caught and convicted during Prohibition. If they signed on with his deal, then they could get out, with presidential secret amnesty and be part of a flotilla of rebels like me. To seal the deal he convinced us that running guns to England could be *very* profitable. It is. I've run a lot of loads already, and he was right; the Brits need as many weapons as they can get, plus a few cases of rum. It pays great money for everyone involved. From his cut Astor's making an incredible fortune.

"When Astor told me about it, it sounded like the good ol' days when sailing was all about running the blockades. Money's money, but I won't work for the Americans who want to remain neutral. Shit! We all might end up speaking German if we listen to the pro-Nazis. My boys might be a little rough around the edges, but when cut, every one of 'em bastards bleeds good American blood."

"And me?"

John smiled again. "Astor was asked by some *big* skipper to find transport for you. The run's been good. I owe him for the profits I've made, so I volunteered."

Eileen sighed. "War is profitable for everyone but the losers."

"That might be true but if there were no profit in war, then who would want to make war?" He got up and opened the cabin door. "Well, Annie, I have a ship to monitor. I trust you can find your way around. Don't fall off."

Eileen liked John's rough demeanor. With his ship and crew he was free as they came. True, his politics were just to the left of Al Capone, but he had the attitude of a John Paul Jones *and* a Confederate rebel. She looked forward to the coming days, once her stomach finally settled down. But she was no longer sure now if the feeling in her stomach came from the movement of the sea, or the smile of John Lee.

CHAPTER 11

THE MATERIAL AND DOCUMENTS SUNNY LOOKED over at the Executive Business Center didn't present anything new. If anything, they looked intentionally muddled to mislead a researcher or investigator away from what amounted to a simple security investment plan.

The Golden Century was a German investment firm formed in 1923. It held together during World War II and became a brokerage house after the war before being disbanded in 1953. There were no new revelations. Again, it was vanilla work. If Happa had wanted to reveal anything, it sure wouldn't have been at a private investment research center. It didn't seem right.

But it didn't matter; Sunny was just going through the motions—it was Happa's ball. He had to play the game, but paranoia began to put an edge on everything. Were the clerks moving in a way to keep him in sight at all times? The security cameras felt as if they were zooming in, looking over his shoulders. He was sure that someone was monitoring the computer he was on. This was wasted time. He had to get out of there and really check things out.

Back out on the streets things still looked the same, compressed, cosmopolitan, but he trusted his instincts. Acting the American tourist, he took a very slow and methodical walk back to his room. There weren't enough things to videotape or snap digital pictures with his combination camera. Back in his room he rewound the video camera to the moment he exited the research center. The camera had done its job.

The tail had tried to be less than conspicuous, but he couldn't have been more obvious to an experienced shadow as Sunny crisscrossed streets, doubled back, then ran across the street and into the Ambassador Hotel.

"I made you, and you know it, and whoever put you out there knows it."

Young and bald, wearing a black tanker jacket, his faded blue jeans and black Doc Martens boots made him stand out like a flag: neo-Nazi. A few years ago he would have been out of place on the conservative Zurich streets, but neo-Nazism was on the rise. His tail eventually became so obvious that Sunny wondered just what the man's orders were.

Closer observation of the skinhead's moves revealed that there were at least two, or possibly three more ghost tails. They appeared to have the same, almost military movements. But whoever they were they were smoother, much less obvious than the neo-Nazi.

The thug was stupid or he was meant to be a warning. Sunny got up and walked around, examining his room. They would have already been through his travel bag, but it would've revealed nothing. He had to believe that the room was bugged—there was no way he'd try to contact Sally.

He peeked out the window overlooking the street and wondered where the observation post was. How big of a watcher team was out there? Which vehicles carried the rolling surveillance? Once again it felt as if an enemy was out there lying in wait for him to screw up.

He found himself rubbing his left hand and then took a closer look at it. The two middle knuckles were fused together. The index knuckle was almost twisted totally around. Stress always made him rub his left hand. Painful memories were always the hardest to forget, impossible to forget, with him every moment of his life.

It was 1989. He was in Colombia. The orders were just to confirm that a certain Colombian officer was doing business with a major player from the Cali Cartel. Once confirmed, the termination order of the officer would shortly follow.

Sunny and Joe, his young Marine spotter, had been choppered into the Colombian jungle by a ubiquitous green Huey. They located the "hidden" coke lab, then just waited for their mark to show.

The mark, a respected antidrug Colombian general, showed as expected, and the only thing Sunny shot were telephoto pictures of the congenial meeting. The general drank with the drug producer, snorted coke and smoked dope with the gang. The pictures would show that the CIA-backed general was *very* cozy with the cocaine cartel people.

When they made it to the extraction point on time, the only reception waiting for them was a committee of armed thugs. They tried to evade, and Sunny hid the camera in the underbrush before being captured. Blindfolded, they were taken to a right-wing, cocaine-rich, Revolutionary Armed Forces of Colombia (FARC) camp.

For two weeks they beat and tortured him and Joe. They accused them of being CIA spies. For weeks Sunny refused to talk or even give his name. Their leader, a young man called *el Cucui,* didn't seem to want information as much as he wanted to cause pain. *El Cucui* seemed to take great pleasure in torturing "gringos."

After being beaten to the point of death, Sunny explained that they were just contract workers for the State Department. It didn't mean a thing to the sadist. Chained in a small box, abandoned by the government, Sunny resigned himself to the possibility that he was going to die if he didn't give up the camera. They finally got the camera when they put a pistol in Joe's mouth. It was the camera or Joe. Sunny led them to the camera.

They killed Joe anyway. One morning *el Cucui* walked into their cell box and pulled out a pistol. He waited until Joe opened his eyes, waited for the surprised look, then pulled the trigger. He had his band chop up the young Marine's body in front of Sunny, then they fed his remains to the piranhas in the river. *El Cuci* then had Sunny, who was starving and dying of thirst, sign his name to a bogus confession and realized that his prisoner was left-handed.

Sunny would never forget how they tied his left wrist to a thick tree branch. Then they took turns bashing it with their rifle butts, rocks, and clubs. But the creeps got too high one night celebrating the delivery of the camera and left him tied to the tree. Then they all wound up passed out in a drunken stupor.

There were ten dead bandits and one escaped prisoner that morning. The commander of the FARC in that region found the body of *el Cucui* minus a left arm. Furious, the FARC scoured the countryside looking for Sunny.

Sunny didn't know that while he evaded his way to Panama a war of vengeance in his name had been launched on the cartel by someone on his side. Secret agreements and handshakes made behind closed doors by the schemers and manipulators of the drug war went down the tubes. With Sunny and his spotter missing, his DEA handler suddenly went nuts and smashed the surface tension that usually kept the drug world running relatively smoothly.

DEA Agent Ricky Talon, put together a group of seasoned assassins from the right-wing death squads called *los Pepes* and went looking for his men. Talon had lost both his top man, a spotter, and his mind in that jungle. With all the drug-induced violence in Colombia, nothing before could compare to Talon's savagery—the FARC had to call on the CIA to take the man away or risk an all-out civil war.

Flexing his left hand the best he could, Sunny thought about the physical and mental scars he'd taken in the name of patriotism. On his own he had to learn how to adjust and compensate—suppress the rage. Over the years he learned to become right-handed, and fashioned his left hand into a daggerlike weapon. He could drive it through three planks of wood with his fingertips and with one chop could snap two unsupported bricks in half. Suppressed rage gave him the power to do so.

He wasn't about to let himself be caught and tortured again. Ever.

Stuffing his hand into his pocket, Sunny silently chastised himself for not making finding Corey his first concern. Questions. Had Corey gone through the same scenario he had? Where did they take him? Did they directly come at him, and with what? Did he fight back? What had he found that made him such a target? What secrets did he give up or take with him? Did they torture him to make him talk? Where was he? "Brichner, where's my fucking money?"

Happa must already have everything on Sunny's background. Had Corey given him away, or were Happa's sources of intelligence that good? Happa acted as if he still wanted the connection to Sally Fine. There was no way he was going to try to contact her. Lambert, her attorney, played the "cutout" part well. Sally was clean. Undetected. Sally had smarts. But she hadn't told him the whole story. Why?

It didn't matter at the moment. It was time to take off the investigator hat and put on his fighter hat.

Pulling out the P22 pistol, he checked it for operation, chambered a round, then pocketed a second clip. Twenty bullets. "Ah, damn." Recently, working in Palestine, close up to an opponent, he got used to shooting a small-caliber bullet—one-on-one. If it came to shooting multiple opponents with .22 bullets, he couldn't afford to miss even one shot.

Sunny didn't like to make mistakes, and he was certain he already had made several too many. He wondered which one might punch his ticket. He was working the high wire without a net, backup, or recovery. "Three times stupid," he muttered. He walked to the picture window and peeked out the curtain.

The streets looked cold. The snowcapped Alps and low clouds made him feel trapped by the mountain walls. Lake Zurich was flat and black. Somewhere below they were watching him, waiting, but for what? How could an old financial program make these people even more secretive and suspicious than normal? There was only one way to find out.

The weakest link in his armor was his size. He was too big. It was always easy to make a smaller man larger and countless options for disguises. Tailing and countertailing on the streets sometimes took on ridiculous dimensions. Trying to be a stealthy big man on the almost empty streets of Zurich wouldn't work. That option was out.

He would meet with Happa head-on, walk right into his web, and hope that he would be able to walk out.

CHAPTER 12

IT HAD TAKEN VERY LITTLE TIME TO ADJUST TO THE constant movement of the ship. But, other than adding more layers of clothes, there was little she could do to get any warmer. Her biggest wonder about the *Illusion* was how it stayed together at all. Rising above the ocean swells, it would come crashing down to the ocean trough and send shivers and vibrations throughout the whole ship. Did wooden ships get better as they aged, or was this one on its last voyage?

The crew knew the sounds and moods of the *Illusion* and Billy kept the men in constant action, stowing lines, trimming sails, caulking the ever-present leaks that seemed to spring at the worst moments.

With nothing to do, she asked Billy for something to do. In between running the crew he showed her, stern to stem how the ship operated and sailed. In no time she learned enough to recognize the difference between a flying jib and spanker, standing and running line—a line was not necessarily a rope, it could be the shape of a ship.

Looking from the stern to the bow, port was on the

left side and starboard was on the right. There was a certain way to tie off a line to the jib. Soon enough she became a part of the deck crew and even stood watches. The crew mistook her work for enthusiasm and readily accepted her. They didn't know that she was just playing at one of many roles to come. A spy just practicing her craft, there would be no telling when she might find herself at sea again.

Between watches she sometimes took coffee with John in his cabin, as he'd check and recheck his nautical charts. She had never been in love and was sure that that wasn't what she felt. But whatever it was it sure bothered the hell out of her. It made her itch. Whatever it was she enjoyed listening to his tales of travel.

He had been everywhere. She could only imagine what it would be like to a salty sailor in a strange foreign port. "John, how old are you?"

"I'm twenty-five."

She was astonished. How could such a young man be in control of such a big ship and tough crew? "Aren't you a little young to be here?"

John smirked. "Aren't you a little young to be a spy?"

Eileen huffed. "I have my skills." She wanted to try to impress him but knew that she couldn't reveal anything about herself.

"And so do I. Age can determine our position in life, but it's our experience and grit that puts us where we are. I happen to be in a position to command this vessel because I've earned it, no more."

"So how do you keep your crew in line? They all look just like pirates to me."

John threw back his head and laughed. "Fear."

"Fear?"

"I told you we all come from the same area. We're *family,* at least the core of the crew is. Even pirates can have a lineage. If there were a mutiny on the *Illusion* the family would know. There would be no place on earth they could hide from the family. I know; my father's first ship was mutinied by a mercenary crew. It took years, but the crew was tracked down one by one. I helped. The family, we took back our ship." John looked at Eileen through steely eyes. He didn't have to elaborate on the mutineers' fate. "And you, Annie, don't you know fear?"

Up until that point she had never thought about it. Trying to trap a coiled rattler had to have some sort of fear associated with it, but the idea that catching it represented food on the table drove her fear into a box that she never looked at.

She'd been brought up not valuing her daring actions. Her parents never warned her against life's dangers. None. Most of her life had been conducted on dares, dares she never turned down no matter how dangerous they were. She had never been seriously hurt. The cuts and bleeding from scrapes and falls never left any lasting damage, not to her body. The hurts to her heart and soul were another matter.

Jumping out of airplanes and hand-to-hand combat were exciting. Handling explosives and subterfuge produced violent and intense results but no fear.

Take into account that no one ever really cared for her, so there was nothing to be afraid of. Fear? Being lonely could be fearful, but lonely was her way of life.

"No," was all that she could say. Then she told the truth. "I don't have anything to lose."

"I'm scared every day of my life."

Eileen laughed. "Oh no, not you, John Lee, that's impossible. I think that you generate fear instead."

John took a drink of coffee as he scanned the charts. "You say that you have nothing to lose. I have a lot to lose every moment that I'm out here on the ocean."

"You have a lot to gain too."

"There you go, the gain and loss create the fear for me."

"And you have a wife and children, aren't they afraid while you're out here?"

It was strange. Here he was convincing her of her fearlessness, but now she feared his answers.

John smiled. "I think I'm still a little too young for that."

"So then you have a woman in every port."

"Some of my boys do. Billy has several *everywhere*. I don't have that luxury."

She tried to take some of the poses the Hollywood directors taught her. *Ugh!* What did she think that she was doing? This was only a short voyage. There was no way a girl like her could charm a man like him. Nothing could ever come of it. But still, she remembered to casually brush back her hanging forelock with just the back of her right wrist.

John finished making notes in his logbook, drank the rest of his coffee, and sat back in his captain's chair. He took a deep breath and ran his hands over his face and hair. "You know, I don't really sleep on these voyages as much as I stay in sort of a trance for the entire time. I can feel every mood of the ship, then just try to finesse her over the sea. Sometimes I think that it's the fear that keeps everything on course."

CHAPTER 13

1920 TUESDAY / 2 MARCH 2004
ZURICH / SWITZERLAND

SUNNY LEFT THE HOTEL BY THE FRONT EN-
trance. The neo-Nazi stood in the open across the
street. Wearing a leather bomber jacket and black
Doc Martens bootheels echoing, he almost goose-
stepped in pace with Sunny. Sunny felt like pulling out
his pistol and nailing the creep dead in the head at fifty
feet with one shot.

It was a short stroll from the hotel to the Handi
Indian restaurant. Sunny walked in and stood near the
headwaiter. The place was quiet, prim, and elegant. The
pungent smells of curry and rich spices assailed his nose.
The clientele looked just like the surroundings. He knew
Happa had people everywhere.

Nathan waved Sunny over to his table. It was already
covered with plates of steaming food. "Not knowing if
you are familiar with Indian fare, I've already ordered
for us. I have a penchant for Eastern food. I hope that
you don't mind curry, or have an allergy to shellfish."

"Not me." Sunny was famished and dived into the
curried king crab legs. There was food everywhere. Large
chunks of lamb lay atop piles of saffron-yellowed rice.

Bowls of curries and chutney spiced up the fare, and mint leaves dressed the tangy yogurt bowls. Two waiters hovered around the table trying to anticipate their every need.

"This is great," Sunny got out in between almost inhaling mouthfuls of his food.

"I'm so glad that you enjoy this."

Sunny noticed that Happa ate little, mostly drinking out of a peculiar-looking bowl. It was ivory-colored and intricately carved with blue rune designs. He held it in his left hand by his thumb, forefinger, and little finger. His two middle fingers were folded into his palm.

When Nathan drained his bowl, a waiter immediately poured more amber liquid from a crystal decanter. Happa held the bowl out to Sunny.

"No thank you." It smelled strong.

"You won't drink Chivas from my bowl?" Happa narrowed his eyes, chugged the drink, and set down the bowl.

"No. I don't like to drink whiskey."

"I think that your client was on the wrong track," Happa said.

"That may be true, but I've looked a little deeper into the certificates at the research center. All kinds of certificates were used to finance the rebuilding of Europe. Golden Century was just another financial cartel. Their Golden Century Profit A through E certificates exist, but strangely there's nothing to find on the D shares. The A, B, C, and E shares are all accounted for. They were simple bonds that matured at different rates. They are all cashed. It was those pesky D's that seemed to have disappeared that kept up my interest. I made a few calls but couldn't turn up anything more. It's my hunch any public materials on them are erased. I even made a few calls to some sources of mine who confirm my hunch."

"Mossad may be effective in their ways, but their understanding of our banking matters is entirely insufficient. It always has been that way for them."

Sunny stopped eating. "I never said anything about Mossad."

"No, that is right, you didn't."

Sunny didn't argue the point. "So I figure that the Profit Share D certificates do still exist. Someone still owns them, and they're worth a mint. But who owns them?"

Nathan methodically worked at a morsel of his food, concentrating on the act while at the same time nodding and speaking to Sunny.

"This is a fine old building, hundreds of years old. It never suffered under American bombs. The Swiss were smart to stay neutral. I will tell you a story." Happa picked up his bowl, waited for it to be filled, then took a drink of whiskey. "It begins just after World War I and years before World War II started. There were groups of influential men with like minds. Even though they lived as communists, capitalists, monarchists, and, of course, Nazis, they all shared a common idea—oneness of interest. Have you ever heard of the term?"

Sunny shook his head.

"It's a common term that held this group's secret ideas together. They would get together every five years and compare notes. At that gathering one member would be removed and a new member initiated. Fifty percent of the old member's assets would go to the new member and the group would absorb the rest. It was a way of keeping the blood fresh and powerful. Right now there are some very influential men, rich, and powerful men who still share those ideas."

"What's the big idea?"

"Ah, that's *my* secret."

Suddenly Happa lost the friendliness in his voice. "You tell me who you are working for and I'll tell you what you want to know."

Sunny wiped his face with his right hand and let it drop into his coat. He gripped the butt of the P22. "No. I told you before that I can't do that. I don't really know you. Look, I think I'm gonna go right now and don't try to stop me."

Happa frowned for a moment, then raised his almost platinum eyebrows. "Okay. Well, Mr. Vicam at least let me finish telling you this story, or aren't you interested in your Mr. Brichner?"

Sunny hesitated. His body was starting to feel odd. He could see and hear just fine, but his reason and reaction responses were feeling out of sync.

Happa continued. "As I was saying, the men behind the original idea were neither capitalists nor communists. They believed that only the influential families should control the world trade and economy, very select bloodlines per se."

Sunny was tired of the games. "So why are you telling me all of this? What have you turned up on Brichner?"

"Oh yes, him. I'll show you." At his motion the waiters cleared away the table, leaving only Happa's bowl on the table. "Now leave us."

The waiters were gone.

Nathan reached into the briefcase beside him and pulled out a small, black portable DVD player, then set it in front of Sunny and lifted the screen. "I've turned off the sound to keep from attracting any attention from the other diners. Watch. You will see why in a moment."

At first Sunny couldn't figure out what was going on so he just sat and watched a blank screen. It then flickered to life and Sunny was watching the back of a man wearing a hooded purple robe standing inside of a circle.

Some sort of ceremony or ritual was taking place. Blurry, the camera caught naked bodies swaying in a circle. What was it? Sunny wanted to turn away, but he was becoming transfixed by a weird tape with satanic pornographic overtones. It was something he really didn't want to view. Happa had to be some sort of pervert. What in the hell was going on?

The camera panned back and he could see a naked man calmly standing in front of the hooded man, oblivious to everything going on around him. *Oh my God.*

Happa poured more whiskey into his bowl and took a sip. He ran his finger over the designs on the bowl. "You see, Sunny, that's your first investigator, Corey Brichner. I told him the same secrets I just told you. It's better that way—you become a Keeper of the Secret into the beyond.

Something was wrong. Sunny couldn't blink. He tried, but he could only stare at the screen in front of him. Try as he might he couldn't close his eyes. The man's hooded robe dropped away. It was Nathan Happa. In his hand he held a black dagger. The people began to sway faster and faster. Soon they were frantically jumping to unheard music.

Something was very, very wrong. He couldn't move. It felt as if he was watching himself in a movie. "Wha', wha', what's going on?"

Nathan moved close to Sunny. "I see that the potion that I put in your drink and food is taking effect. Good. What you have coursing in your system right now is a derivative neurotoxin made from the green-ringed octopus of northern Australia." His smile was triumphant. "You drank the ultimate zombie juice."

All Sunny could do was have the scene unfolding on the screen burned into his brain. Happa raised Corey's chin. Throat exposed and unbound Corey didn't fight or resist but continued to stare blankly into the camera. Happa plunged the dagger deep into Corey's throat. For a moment he looked surprised, then shock and pain registered as the blade cut out his larynx.

The blood spurted over Happa as the crowd jumped or fell on the ground in orgasmic ecstasy.

Sunny was losing feeling throughout his body. "Wh', why?" was all he could gasp and wheeze.

Happa shut the lid on the DVD and quickly dropped it back into his briefcase.

A haughty look flashed over Happa. "Because you wouldn't give me the name of your client, that's why, and I have no time to waste." A look of regret then crossed

Happa's face. "It's a shame I have to leave Zurich so soon. It's a shame. I would like to take my time with you before you cross over." He smiled and got close to Sunny's ear.

Sunny could feel every nerve on his neck and ear recoil from Happa, but nothing happened. He couldn't move. *Oh my God, don't let this be happening to me!*

Happa whispered, "I would deliver to you personal truth through blinding pain. The violence I share is taken directly from Nazi torture manuals. They are the bibles of pain, you know. I have a complete, original volume."

Sunny was aware of the world around him, but there was nothing he could do to react to it. It felt as if he was trapped inside of a glass jar. He tried to pull his gun, but could only make his arm quiver, and even that was beginning not to register.

"Whoever sent you can send another investigator, and another." Happa leaned back in his seat and snapped his fingers. "Just like cockroaches, I will snuff all of them out. Eventually I'll get to the source of this problem." He reached over and tapped Sunny's head. "Besides my many other duties, I'm an exterminator, and I'm pretty good at staying well ahead of your type." Happa leaned closer and inspected his prey. "You're quite handsome, you know, blond hair, pretty blue eyes, a perfect Aryan specimen. I might just have to delay my departure before I send you over to the other side. Yes, and after that I'm going to take some souvenirs off of you, your heart maybe." He caressed Sunny's blond hair. "No. Maybe more, like your whole head."

Trapped, Sunny wanted to shrivel up and die, but he couldn't even do that. He actually had to will himself to breathe. Panic and adrenaline coursed through his body, but in his state they felt more like syrup.

Nathan spoke loud enough to be overheard. "My friend, I think that you have had a little too much to drink. We should go before you lose your meal in an unpleasant manner. Here, let me help you."

The sensations and fog were more than Sunny could deal with. He knew that he was walking and being guided but he couldn't lift a finger or plant a foot to stop it.

A black limo pulled up, then stopped in front of the restaurant. The rear passenger door opened.

Sunny's mind was crystal clear and that's what terrified him most—he had no control over the situation he was in.

Someone helped him into the car. Before the door shut, Sunny saw the neo-Nazi on the other side of the street. He gave Sunny a cold smile, then came to attention, clicked his heels together, and threw a Nazi salute.

Sitting on the seat, Nathan calmly reached into Sunny's coat and pulled out his pistol.

"*Nice.*" Nathan studied the weapon and figured out how to eject the magazine. "Only a .22-caliber? I thought your kind carried heavier firepower." He frowned. "Now I'm even more curious about you, Mr. Vicam. Who are you really?"

Happa put the magazine back into the gun. He put the muzzle against Sunny's head and cocked the trigger.

"It's a small caliber, but this is how it's used properly, I know. This is an *assassin's* gun." He reached into Sunny's coat and pulled out the noise suppressor. "See. I was right."

Sunny heard the appreciative alcohol-scented gasps of people around him. He had no idea how many people were in the vehicle besides Happa and him.

"Sweet," someone said.

Happa screwed the silencer to the gun. Holding it at Sunny's head for a moment, he leveled it just inches above Sunny's left shoulder and fired the gun twice into the seat upholstery. It sounded like car doors slamming.

The women in the limo squealed with delight and clapped.

Nathan dropped the gun in Sunny's lap.

"Go ahead, pick it up and shoot me in the head."

Happa leaned forward and closed his eyes for a moment, then fell back into his seat.

He would have gladly emptied the clip into Happa's head, but as much as he tried, Sunny could only fidget.

Nathan picked up the gun, then fired another silenced round through the car's roof. "A big strong man like you, I figured you for the .357, or .40 type. You know, a Dirty Harry, busting down doors, bang, bang and all that sort of messy work. You're an assassin, are you not? I think so. Did you come here to kill me? Now *that* is exciting; the executioner becomes the executed. But I will not execute you." He pointed and touched his finger to Sunny's forehead. "Not execute. Yours is a free will sacrifice, and your sacrifice will bring me exquisite power." Happa crossed his arms. "But first I must offer you a chance to refuse your fate. Go ahead," he said, holding the gun butt first and nodding at the pistol. "Take it and go, or come with us and offer all you have to the group in oneness of interest."

Sunny was a zombie with no will.

Happa grabbed the gun, unscrewed the silencer, then pocketed the gun. Suddenly he was all business, holding the silencer like a baton. "For the record, your silence is your consent. Get him ready for the ceremony. We do it as soon as we get to the château."

Sunny was aware that others in the car were doing something to him, but he could not turn his head to look at them. He couldn't blink, and tears clouded his vision. Hands moved him, removing all of his clothing. There were possibly five people in the car. One had to be a woman. For what they were doing to him, the conversation was casual. He could hear perfectly.

"Nathan," the feminine voice said. "This one has a *gorgeous* body; it would be such a waste for you to share him with us few. Shouldn't we save him for the Grand Jubilee? He would make a *wonderful* sex zombie."

"My dear, I totally agree with you, he is a quality catch, to be sure; but for my business it's best that he go now. His spirit is too uncontrollable. Besides, I've the jet to take to India in only a few hours and I can't drag his body all over the world. He would be ruined by then. I'll tell you what, you get to film everything tonight."

Sunny heard a squeal of delight.

A yellow paint was applied to Sunny's body and a green sheet was wrapped around him.

"I normally take my time and condition my selections, but I think it's important that I send your client a message, again." Nathan got close enough to stare into Sunny's vacant blue eyes and caressed his flaxen hair. "You got *way* too close to something that will never be found. Ever."

Happa leaned back in his seat. "You know, I got a copy of your intelligence jacket yesterday. You have a lot of blood on your hands, don't you? I am very surprised we did not approach you to do contract work before. If your blood were pure, you might even have *been* one of us. It's not going to be too hard to make your demise look as if someone had a grudge against you. Only your client will understand why you're dead. You should have left us alone."

They rode on in silence. Sunny, painted yellow, naked, and unbound, wasn't able to move a single muscle. He was doing his best just to breathe. He should have known better than to think he could outmaneuver a skinny, perverted banker. But Nathan wasn't a banker. What was he? *Who* was he?

The car slowed to a crawl crossing a bridge in bumper-to-bumper traffic.

With enough concentration to burst his brain, Sunny moved the little finger on his left hand. Something cracked in his mental shackles. It was all the motivation he needed. He reached over and opened his door and rolled out.

Like a stumbling drunk, he pulled himself to a stone rail and looked back. Through the hypnotic state he was in he clearly saw that the black Mercedes limo had stopped and several people were running toward him.

Aware that he was on a bridge over water, he had no idea how long the fall was, or how deep and cold the water was, but it was his only option for escape.

With all his effort, he leaned over the rail until he was floating in the air. It was his last conscious thought.

CHAPTER 14

1755 / SATURDAY / 25 JANUARY 1941
NORTH ATLANTIC OCEAN

THE WIND WAS AT GALE-FORCE INTENSITY. THE
Illusion climbed and crashed over the dark green
waves, which now looked like a sea of undulat-
ing skyscrapers. The sails were trimmed for the gale and
the engines were running hard, trying to keep her on
course.

Eileen, safely tied to the deck rails, braced herself
against the bottom rail with her rubber boots. The icy
sea spray thrown by the bow stung her face like needles.
Bundled in her duffel coat and mittens, she watched the
endless churning power around her. She was amazed at
the ability of the crew to maintain an organized calm in
the middle of the maelstrom. Anyone who went over the
side was surely lost.

John Lee stood at the helm, calmly reading the wind
and waves. He was young but looked at the fury before
him as a challenge he had faced many times. Eileen
watched as the cold sea spray, thrown by the bow crashing through the waves, slapped her landlubber face. The
Illusion shivered and groaned as she cut through the
ocean. In the middle of the maelstrom and on the edge

of potential disaster, Eileen was thrilled by the natural violence. She at last understood why men like John Lee sailed the seas.

Only the intrepid and the foolish would dare this furious ocean crossing. The Lee family had salt water in their blood. John looked at the sky and ocean as one, pointing out to Eileen the finer aspects of where the *Illusion* was, and needed to be. Billy would call out, whistle, or give hell to the crew to do those things to keep the ship on a safe course.

Billy pulled on John's hand and pointed to something Eileen couldn't see. He grabbed a pair of binoculars and hung them around his neck. He then nimbly climbed the ratlines to the crow's nest. He smiled and waved down to Eileen, then looked back at the ocean through the binoculars.

She wasn't frightened anymore; she was exhilarated. Out in the middle of the wild and raging ocean the ship and crew *thrived*. The *Illusion* wasn't just a collection of wood and cloth; it was an ageless leviathan put together by the men who cut her from the Virginia woods. At that moment if John had offered to steal her away for a whirlwind adventure around the world she would've foolishly jumped into his arms and said yes.

"Annie, over there, on the port bow," John yelled over the shrieking wind and pointed north toward the dark sky.

Eileen nodded.

"That's a bad North Atlantic gale," he yelled. "We'll be skirting it for at least another day before we reach England. It's going to be a very rough passage."

"We got company, skipper," Billy cried down from the crow's nest. "A submarine on the surface, ten points to starboard. It don't look good. Yeah! It's flying a Nazi flag. The boat's diving."

"Annie, go below. Billy, get down here and break out our Nazi flag," John screamed over the gale. "Run it up. Quick!"

John barked out several commands as he turned the

Illusion to run with the wind. The day crew was all over the deck, letting out sail as the rest of the crew scurried from below.

John set the engines to full throttle.

Giant sea waves rolled under a black sky.

John scanned through his binoculars. The sub was right on his tail. It was going to be a race to reach the maelstrom for a modicum of protection. Their salvation could also spell their doom. Suddenly an idea struck him.

"Billy, take the helm!" He frantically spoke into Billy's ear for a moment.

Billy grabbed the wheel as John went forward.

Eileen hadn't moved from her spot watching the drama as it played out.

John looked as if he was taking measurements, constantly looking back, trying to get a position on the submerged sub's periscope. Billy looked at nothing but the captain's hand movements. He looked small, almost insignificant holding the big wheel. Even through the cold Eileen could see sweat running down his face.

Suddenly John threw his hands in the air to the port side and came running back toward Billy.

Billy started to pull the wheel. Hand over hand, his rippling muscles worked to bring the ship around as John screamed out commands to the crew manning the sails.

John jumped at the wheel and helped Billy. The *Illusion* almost heeled over as it came about. In almost no time it was heading straight toward the sub's periscope.

"Oh my God!" Eileen cried.

John looked surprised at hearing her voice. "Annie, damm it, I told you to go below. Get in my cabin, now!"

The cold look in John's eyes was colder than the ocean below. She jumped up and scooted toward the hatch as the crew began passing up machine guns and other small arms. Instead of going below she joined the line to pass out weapons.

All the fine seafaring notions she'd had were gone in an instant. Instead, visualizations of a torpedo exploding through the hull overrode her thoughts. She almost came out of her skin as a loud, high-pitched grating sound raked the entire ship.

"Annie, I ordered you below!" John bellowed.

He sounded like her father, and she suddenly changed her mind about going below. "No, not when I can help. What just happened?"

Billy was frantically spinning the wheel in the other direction as the crew trimmed the sails to the rudder. They were headed directly into the storm!

"We just ran over their periscope," John yelled. "They have to surface if they want us, and if they do, we'll be ready." He nodded toward the several machine guns his crew held. "We might not be able to sink them, but we sure can keep their heads down!"

"I want to help," Eileen yelled.

"No. You're too valuable to expose you like this."

"What? If they sink us, they sink *all* of us. John, I know the guns we carry. I can shoot the hell out of them better than your boys." Her throat burned from salt water, emotion, and stress.

"Right then. Help Saunders over there amidships, he has never fired the gun before."

With a death grip on the slippery rails she made her way amidships port side to a scrawny man fumbling with a Browning .50-caliber machine gun.

Pushing the man out of the way she set the gun securely to the top rail and was ready to fire. Taking a deep breath, she listened to the men calling out the sightings and position of the sub. They had seasoned eyes— she couldn't see shit.

She let out a deep, nervous sigh; it would be the first time that she fired a weapon against the enemy.

The second mate reported to the skipper that all the hatches were sealed and that everyone and everything was battle-ready. Rafts were positioned and tied to the deck, ready for deployment if they were sunk.

John was suddenly next to Eileen and speaking directly into her ear. "The Nazi sub is on our tail, but without their periscope. They have to stay surfaced if they want a chance to get us. They'll try. They'll use the deck guns. We're running about twelve knots. They can run at eighteen, but not in this gale. I've leveled the playing field a bit, and I'm betting that we'll get deep into the storm before the sub can get any good shots at us. Once we're in it we might even lose them." He chuckled over the roaring wind. "Or we might get sunk by the damn storm itself!"

She put her lips against his ear. She wanted to kiss it. "What can I do?"

"Be ready to fire on them from your position if they get within distance. Keep your life jacket on and stay tethered to the deck. If for any reason we start going down, cut the tether, make it to the stern, and get into the lifeboat. But be careful, you could get swept overboard and you'll be dead in minutes in the freezing water. This could get real nasty. If they get just one lucky shot, with all the explosives we carry we'll be gone in a flash."

Shivering, Eileen nodded.

"Oh, one more thing. This is just in case something happens and we don't make it and we don't see each other again." He grabbed her and kissed her hard.

Eyes wide with fear, Eileen could see the sub was trying to move to a port position. "Looks like they didn't buy the flag trick."

John and the crew made a great living secretly ferrying war material to England. While subs wreaked havoc on the shipping lanes, he'd been able to elude Nazi E- and U-boats by using charts and passageways drawn by American privateers during the War of 1812.

"How do you think they found us?" he yelled to Billy over the noise of the wind.

"Not one of the boys went ashore."

"I wouldn't have suspected them anyways. It probably

was a Nazi agent perched on a hill overlooking Halifax. But it doesn't matter now. Look."

The sub was well to port and looked to be angling for a deck gun shot. They could see men scrambling on the deck to pass shells to the deck gunner.

"What do we do now, skipper?" Billy asked.

"We keep tacking and wait until they do something."

They didn't have to wait long. Six-inch shells fired by the sub's gun crew flew both high and low. There was so much noise and smoke that no one could really tell how close to the mark the gunner was getting.

Eileen felt sick to her stomach and had let loose on the wet and slippery deck. The ship groaned and strained under the wind. Suddenly she was thrown to the deck as the railing seemed to come apart.

She saw Saunders fly through the air and roll off the other side of the ship. "Man overboard," she tried to yell, but was slapped to the deck by a wall of water.

Dazed and soaked, she realized that a shell had found its mark. She weakly got to her knees. The gun was still ready, but Saunders was gone.

Her head still swam when she felt something warm on her face. She wiped her forehead and her hand came away covered with blood. She pulled out her ascot and tightly wrapped it around her head; she would check for damage later. At that moment she had a gun to man. She was mad, terrified, bloody, and ready to fight back.

"Skipper, they're putting a fish in the water!" someone cried out.

John looked through his binoculars, and sure enough, a torpedo was headed for them.

"It's a wild shot."

John yelled out commands and made signals to the crew. The *Illusion* tacked and at times almost heeled over as she evaded the Nazi U-boat.

Eileen held on to the machine gun for her life, shivering so hard that she thought she would lose her grip on the gun, but didn't. The big hole shot in the ship's railing next to her was just waiting for her to slip off at the right moment—Neptune would welcome her into his embrace.

The Nazi sub was getting desperate. It wasn't designed to ride the gigantic waves like an oceangoing vessel like the *Illusion*. Without a periscope their captain hadn't been able to get a target solution on the *Illusion* and was instead trying to get a dead-reckoning shot. A few more missed shots and he would lose her.

The crew of the *Illusion* fired wild, hopelessly trying to hit the sub with small arms. Their only real defenses were hope and a raging storm.

The sub was now closing; it was obvious that it intended to ram the wooden hull. It was all the crew of the *Illusion* could do to fight the storm and keep distance from the sub and be ready to shoot back.

The *Illusion* was under the anvil of the storm. Lightning cracked all around. Freezing sheets of icy water began pounding onto the deck, making any kind of movement a sure slide into the ocean. The giant waves were coming from every direction. Still the sub dogged the ship.

The *Illusion* crested a giant swell, and then pitched over the edge of an immeasurable crest. The prow of the ship reared high out of the water and, after an eternity, came smashing down the face of the wave.

Eileen felt herself go weightless, then it felt as if the ship was on an endless slide. She wrapped her legs around the anchored gun. She heard a massive crack, then a ripping and tearing sound. Shrieking, snaps, and pops made her close her eyes. When she opened them she couldn't believe what she saw. The forward mast had snapped. Lines began falling all around her. If that wasn't bad enough, the most amazing thing of all happened.

The Nazi sub punched through the crest of the wave. Like a giant whale, it dived from the face of the wave and came hurtling out of the water. The nose of the sub smacked the water just yards from the ship. Guns blazed from the Nazi conning tower as the *Illusion*'s own guns fired back.

Eileen could see the sub's gunner just yards away. She could see his young face. He was firing over the ship and was trying to correct for it.

She squeezed the trigger and the gunner was thrown back by the impact of the bullets. Gun still roaring, she traced the fire line to the conning tower.

The momentum of the sub carried the conning tower closer. Any closer and the loose ropes from the *Illusion* threatened to tie the vessels together. They were in real danger of both going down together

"Oh shit!" Eileen cried. She was out of ammunition. It seemed hopeless.

Suddenly a colossal bang startled her above all the chaos that surrounded her. A hole was blown into the side of the sub's conning tower as it dived beneath the *Illusion*.

Eileen looked aft and saw Billy holding a bazooka over his head. He pumped it up and down in triumph. He had made the shot.

One battle was over but the other was not.

"Annie!" John cried. He made his way over to her and grabbed her. "You're bleeding. Where are you hurt?"

"I don't really know." She grabbed him and wouldn't let go. She was grateful for the gale because he couldn't see the tears that she cried.

He guided her to the wheelhouse and the companionway. "You get below. And this time I mean it! Go to my cabin. I'll have Billy look at you as soon as we get outta the mess we are still in. The foremast is in the water and the sails are acting like sea anchors. We got to cut them away. Now." He gave her a quick squeeze. "You did great, Annie. I'd ship with you anytime. Now get below."

"ANNIE. WAKE UP, ANNIE!"

A firm hand pulled her from a deep sleep. "Wha', what?" She sat up and banged her head on the overhead beam. She saw stars and fell back on the bunk. "Oh damn!" Her head really hurt.

"I'm so sorry," a voice spoke through the stars in her brain.

She opened her eyes and saw the concerned face of Billy.

"I didn't mean to startle you, but the skipper asked me to look in on you. I'm the unofficial ship's doctor. Can I have a look at yer head?" Billy opened a first-aid kit.

"Yes. But Billy, how is everyone else?"

He looked pained. "We lost three men overboard. Three more are wounded, but they'll survive."

"Was Saunders one of the men lost?"

"Yeah he was."

"He was killed when the gun hit us and got blown off the other side."

"Well, at least we know how it happened. Be quiet and let me finish looking at you."

"But Billy, tell me about how you hit that sub? What a surprise."

"I couldn't miss!" Billy grinned. "I remembered we had ten crates of bazookas in the forward sheet locker. I brought them aboard myself. I had the boys bring one up. I had no idea how to do it so I said a quick prayer to God and loaded it. I didn't even know how to aim it. When it went off I was just as surprised as everyone else." He then leaned over and kissed her gently on the cheek. "It was you that kept their heads down long enough for me to get off the shot." He jumped back down to the deck and opened the door. "There's still nonstop work. The skipper will be down when he can. You're lucky, Annie, it's a superficial head cut, bleedin' always looks worse than it is. You stay here, sleep."

"But I'm sure that I can help."

"Oh no you don't. The skipper says that he'll keel-haul me if he sees you back on deck, so promise me you'll stay here until he comes to see you."

"I promise, really." She was totally exhausted and couldn't hold her eyes open any longer.

CHAPTER 15

H IS CONSCIOUSNESS CAME BACK IN STAGES. THERE was a sensation of light, then sounds, and finally violent shivering brought him to his first complete thought.

"Holy Christ, I'm cold!" Lying on a shallow bank, he climbed from the river, stood, and looked around; his body shivered so hard that his legs gave out from cramping. Grimacing in pain, he massaged his legs while trying to get his bearings. At the same time he kept a sharp eye for any searchers.

He was freezing and had to get warm, fast. He crawled from the cold lake and stood naked on the bank. It was getting lighter and he saw a row of cars parked along the road opposite a row of houses. Few lights were in the windows.

Peering into the cars, he saw an older Volvo with a coat laying on the backseat. He took a deep breath and sharply banged the port window. It shattered and there was no car alarm. He jumped in and put on the coat. It was a black woolen trench coat. It was about five sizes too small. It would have to do.

It took time, but Sunny warmed enough to start
thinking about his next move. He searched thoroughly
and found no money or potential weapon in the car. The
car clock said 6:00 A.M. Lights were coming on in windows. People were rising for work. He couldn't stay
where he was.

There was no question that Happa's people were out
looking for him, but who were they, and how many were
there? He vigorously rubbed his arms and legs until he
had established some feeling. He had to get moving. It
was only a matter of time until they found him. Hyper-
ventilating until his lungs felt strong, he left the car.
"God, this sucks!" His bare feet almost froze to the
ground.

Going to Mossad or Interpol was out of the question—at that moment he couldn't trust anyone. They
were sure to have his hotel staked out. Walking along
the river, he was amazed he'd made it out of the cold water at all. He'd floated around the Zurich River all night
without being spotted. It must've been his instincts and
training that kept him from drowning. The zombie juice
that Happa had slipped him probably saved him from
going hypothermic while he was in the water. He said
the zombie juice was made from the green-ringed octopus.

Raising the collar of his stolen coat, he tried to look
anonymous, but it was impossible. It was a freezing gray
morning and a few intrepid joggers were already on the
road. Some gave him odd looks as they passed. *Pervert*.
He felt like a flasher just waiting to expose himself.

It seemed as if every passerby on foot or in a car was
slowing to get a look at him. One positive ID would be
all that was needed for Happa's people to recapture, and
then kill him. Nathan's bodyguard, Mr. Skinhead, was
probably leading the search, goose-stepping somewhere
along the nearby river. He had to get off the street, fast,
so he started to jog and he suddenly could be mistaken
for a jogger, albeit a barefoot one in a trench coat.

The city was on the other side of the river. The area

he jogged through was starting to look familiar. A quick plan began forming in his head.

Hiding behind a black BMW, Sunny tried to massage life back into his cold feet. There was a crunching sound in the snow. Sunny peeked over the back of the car. Thorsen Melton had stepped from his small, white house and was walking toward the car.

Thorsen was about to get in his car when he heard a voice from behind.

"Don't turn around, Melton. And keep your hands empty."

Melton remained motionless while his pistol was pulled from the holster in his waistband by unseen hands. "Sunny, why? What's wrong?"

"Get in the car. Now."

He did as he was told and sat in the driver's seat until Sunny climbed into the backseat.

"Now drive. And turn on your heater, full blast!"

Melton felt the muzzle of his own weapon against his neck. He looked in the rearview mirror and saw Sunny's haunted eyes and disheveled face. "Sunny! What in the world is this all about? What is happening? Tell me."

"Maybe you can tell *me*. I meet a supposed banker last night and he drugs me then tries to kill me."

"Who?"

"His name is Nathan Happa."

"Never heard of him. Sunny, I am not your enemy. Take away the gun."

Sunny instinctively knew Melton was telling the truth. He dropped the gun into his lap.

"Listen," Melton said, "I've got to tell you something. I've found Corey."

"Where is he?"

INSTITUTE OF FORENSIC RESEARCH / ZURICH

No one dared stop the Interpol inspector or the bum behind him as they descended to the basement.

The attendant opened the steel door, pulled out the slab, and unzipped the white body bag.

Exhausted and miserable as he was, Sunny suddenly felt a lot worse. *I ain't getting my money.*

Corey Brichner lay on the slab. Throat sliced open and eyes wide like he'd seen hell. He looked a lot smaller on the slab, waxlike. He *was* smaller. His head was bandaged and it looked like the top of his head was flat. What had happened to him after Happa murdered him?

"His body was found floating in the river a few days ago. He's under a John Doe right now. I found him here yesterday." Melton wouldn't make eye contact with Sunny. "They..."

"They what?" Sunny wanted to shake the shit out of Melton.

"Take a closer look at his head."

Sunny pulled back the all plastic that covered Corey's head. The bandage fell off. Sunny froze. The entire top of his head was gone. There was only an empty hole where his brain once was. "Oh, *shit*." Now he knew what the bowl that Happa drank from was made out of.

Melton touched Sunny's shoulder and Sunny jumped. "His brains, liver, and heart have been cut out. I've ordered a full autopsy. Preliminaries indicate that he was ritually murdered."

"I know. Happa filmed it." Sunny felt sick to his stomach.

"You will bear witness to this?"

"Bullshit. I'm bearing witness to nothing. I'm outta here." Sunny couldn't go back to the hotel. He'd found Corey and stirred up a hornet's nest. He could stay and let Melton start an investigation, but Happa would be long gone and his people might go to ground, or kill him—it was their turf.

What had he stepped into? Gazing at Corey's corpse, one thing was evident; there was no more reason to stay in Zurich. He gave a suspicious look at Melton.

Melton caught the look. "Sunny, I don't know what has happened, or how deeply you're involved in all this, but I want to know about what has gone down as much as you do. More. These things can't happen here. Not in *my* backyard."

"Melton, I ain't staying around for an investigation, hell no. I'm not fucking around. I need some clothes, and a way out of here, right now. I'm a dead man if I stay here. You know that."

Melton nodded. "You might be right. But this will be difficult; I have a body with a few missing personal items. Where do I start?"

"Try the Credit Suisse bank. Look for a fat little cockeyed banker wearing bottle glasses. I didn't get his name."

BACK IN ZURICH, MELTON GAVE SUNNY AN OVERSIZED jogging suit and a pair of running shoes from his gym bag and retrieved Sunny's spooky from the park. They then drove north until they reached the coal trains headed into Germany. They parted company as allies. Sunny jumped a coal car and was gone.

The nonstop flight to New York from Frankfurt, Germany, was uneventful. He'd beaten any tails to the airport and was on the first plane out.

NEW YORK CITY

There was no sign of Happa's people, so far. Clearing customs as David Marfin, he caught a cab to Broadway. He entered the subway and rode to West Eighteenth Street. He walked into an alley and entered the back door of the New York Akikai Aikido studio. No one took notice of him as he opened the combination lock on locker 15. He grabbed the small bag that was in it and locked himself in the small bathroom.

Inside the bag was a Heckler & Koch P7 pistol. Sixteen silver-tipped, hollow-point nine-millimeter bullets filled two magazines. Ten hundred-dollar bills were

in a black leather wallet along with Sunny's next ID—
Tom Godbold. Other useful items filled the bag, including colored chalk and a nightscope. He put on the simple
hat, glasses, and mustache disguise and left the dojo.

He was familiar with the street smells, the grit, the
sounds. The streets were trashy compared to Zurich. He
had a permit to carry his gun concealed. He was on
home ground and ready to go on the offensive.

He walked up toward Times Square and breathed a
little easier for once. He might've been big, but that was
fine. Hell, he could even be Frankenstein's monster and
not stand out.

Out on the street in broad daylight, the only people
he had to keep an eye out for were the Hamas or the
FBI. He chuckled at the irony—home and *still* hiding.
But New York was a great place to hide, the greatest.
There were a thousand and one theaters to hide in. Take
your pick. He chose an artsy cinema playing a Steve
McQueen marathon, then walked to a familiar corner.

He stopped on the corner and pulled out some change
from his pocket. A few of the coins fell so he bent down,
picked them up, then continued across the streets. No
one had seen him grind with his heel a piece of purple
chalk into the cement. He did almost the same thing a
couple of blocks later, but this time the chalk was yellow.

The triple check for tails looked good; there were
none. So he went back to the theater and paid for a
ticket. He was in the back row of the almost empty bal-
cony. No one could approach him without being obvious. Gun strategically propped under his coat, he would
get a few hours of precious, undisturbed sleep until the
night came.

TWO BOOTS PIONEER THEATER / NEW YORK CITY

Sunny checked his watch: 3:20. He was early, glad that
the alarm on the watch had woken him in the theater.
He took the subway to Brooklyn to the meeting spot. It

sure wasn't his choice. He hated abandoned buildings. Suddenly there was a noise. Sunny raised his pistol. Ready to fire, he had never been in the huge abandoned courthouse in Brooklyn.

Sunny looked through the night scope. He'd preset infrared chemical lights so he had a pretty good field of vision. It felt silly and dangerous to be where he was, but that was the way it had to be.

"Only those doing evil, and the ones fighting it are out at this hour," a voice called from the dark.

Sunny groaned, then sighed. "We must be vigilant, for evil strikes at all hours."

From out of the darkness a shadow emerged. Cape dramatically flowing, it looked like Batman wearing night-vision goggles. He looked like something one would expect to see on a Halloween night, but Sunny knew a few things about the man in front of him. One was that the stolen cape he wore was worth over 30 million dollars and he could do unbelievable things with it, like disappear.

"You left the signal."

Sunny got to his feet and made a formal salute with his right fist across his chest. "Yes, Talon. I need your help." Sunny wanted to get this part over with, but it had to be done.

The man in front of him was crazy as hell, sure, but he could never be held in a mental institution.

Once a Drug Enforcement operative, he did too much, saw too much, then sold his soul one too many times. It wasn't that he had snapped as much as he had embraced the madness. And Sunny knew why.

Sunny was loaned to the DEA to work in Colombia as a sniper. DEA Station Chief Ricky Talon had a heavy turf beef with the CIA case agent in charge of the Colombia station. Sunny got caught in their cross fire and was taken prisoner by the FARC.

Talon went on a rampage in Colombia trying to retrieve Sunny and his spotter. Talon's retaliation stepped way over the line to butchery and mayhem. He saved face, but lost his mind and then became another casualty of the war on drugs. He was taken back to a certain VA hospital in Virginia and put under a psychiatric watch designed to keep anyone from asking embarrassing questions.

Strapped to a hospital bed, after organizing the hunting and killing on the orders of others, in Talon's schizophrenic mind there were no longer any *real* crime fighters but him. He believed that the pharmaceuticals they injected him with were designed to fry his brain. So he cut himself free and walked out of the VA hospital. He took a multimillion-dollar prototype camouflage system he knew about in Maryland, then disappeared. The following week the CIA man whose jaw Sunny broke also disappeared.

In New York, Talon became his own superhero. Working as a photo shop manager during the day, he donned a mask and his cape at night and targeted street crime.

It would've been a sad and bizarre story except for the fact that Talon was a trained, skilled killer and a textbook paranoid sociopath. The chemicals they used on him probably had fried his brain. Chances were better than ever that no one would catch him. He didn't seek notoriety or publicity, exactly the opposite. Creeping through dark alleys, hiding under a cape that could blend into any environment, he kept his violent vigilante actions quiet and always covered his tracks. Most of his brutal acts were written off as drug deals gone bad. He knew that he couldn't take on the entire drug empire, but he himself could chop at it one root at a time; he'd done it before.

Talon was definitely not someone to meet in an abandoned courthouse building in Brooklyn. The only reason Sunny was there was that Talon was Sunny's "papermill." The nut in front of him was a forger supreme, an artist. All Sunny's fake IDs and passports came from Talon's photography store.

Suddenly an idea hit him. "Talon, I have something

very important to tell you. You remember how we first met?"

"I do." He said it with authority and put his fists on his hips.

When they finally crossed paths, they were both in Panama and on their way out of the mainstream intelligence and law enforcement; Sunny to the streets and Talon to a nut ward. Talon's paranoia was already evident.

"Remember those people you talked about?"

"Yes, the *hidden* ones."

"I told you that you were nuts."

"And I asked you, 'What the fuck do you know about anything?' Sewer rats like us exist only to eat the shit that they feed us in the dark."

"They're after me."

"See, I told you. I knew it!" Talon's eyes flew open. "Where are they?"

"I'm going on the trail of one of them. I expect them to try to bird-dog my trail. It might lead directly to you."

"Not if you've used my paper properly."

"I have. Barry Foster, remember?"

Talon smiled. "That one leads directly to a grave in Arlington Cemetery. I knew him, actually. I took his identity before he got cold."

Oh God. He's way gone. But then again, it would give Talon a purpose to his warped existence. He might just be the foil Sunny was looking for. "I need at least three fronts. When can I have them?"

"Passports too?"

Sunny nodded.

Talon did some mental calculations. "It'll cost you five grand in Liberty dollars, but they'll have a righteous legend portfolio too. The visas already have genuine embarkation stamps in them."

Talon might've been crazy, but even he still had bills to pay. "It's solid stuff, but I don't have to sell you on my paper. You know that already, ol' buddy."

Sunny knew it well, which is what made Talon the

best in the papermill business. Real names and identities were used. Their identities were not stolen so much as borrowed.

Using a solid legend, unknowingly a person's money could quickly come and go on credit cards, bank accounts, and money wires. Paid off instantly, if any red flags popped up the real cardholder usually reasoned it out to a computer error—they weren't out any money. In some cases when the legend was abandoned, the unsuspecting person even made some cash.

Talon stepped nose to nose with Sunny. "Who's their leader?"

Talon could be the buffer he was looking for. "The only name I know him as is Nathan Happa, and he looks like a real tall and skinny and spacey like David Bowie, but I don't think he's their main leader. He's more of a front man, like a high priest. And this guy's a freak. If I can find him, I think that I might be able to expose the guys behind him. The guys *you* want."

"Do they got a name?"

"I don't know. Not yet, just him, Nathan Happa. The Golden Century Group might be one of their names." Sunny couldn't believe that he was actually standing there rationally discussing an insane situation with a certifiable nut.

"The Golden Century Group?" Talon put his hands on his hips. "Why are you interested in revealing them?"

"They killed Corey Brichner and made a try on me."

"Really?" Talon peered close into Sunny's eyes for the least lie. Satisfied, he took a few steps back and folded his arms across his chest. "Then let them come! I'll be ready."

"Will my stuff be ready too?"

"If you follow the usual deal."

"Right." Talon didn't deal in Federal Reserve notes. He vowed never to do so if he could help it. Instead Sunny would buy the alternate American money called the Liberty dollar. Sunny would anonymously do a transaction and drop five thousand of Federal Reserve money into a certain Liberty account. In three days he'd check the dead drop for confirmation of a certain color of chalk on the same corner. Finally he'd pick up the IDs in a certain spot they both knew.

"Then, if that is all, there's crime to battle."

"Um-hum."

Talon was gone. So was Sunny, to his check on his next mark.

THE MEET WAS MORE PUBLIC BUT NO LESS COMPLICATED. Sunny walked onto the subway train, waiting by the door, then slipped out the moment the door began sliding closed. No tails. He walked up to Central Park East. He scanned the area, spotted his target, and stealthily walked up behind him.

"Frank, don't make any sudden moves."

Frank Delgado continued walking without looking behind. "I saw your mark. I'm glad to hear from you again. You ready to go back to work? I could use you. I've been authorized to offer you a two-year contract at GM-14 wages."

"I'm not here for that. I'm working a private contract."

"Oh yeah, for who?"

"I'm not saying."

Delgado almost stopped and turned, but kept walking. "Then why'd you call me?"

"Corey Brichner was murdered. You know anything about it?"

This time Delgado did stop, almost stumbling, but then kept moving. "No. How'd it go down?"

"Get ahold of Thorsen Melton on a secure line for that. It's his case, Corey's under a John Doe. Melton is getting the autopsy done. Frank, they cut out Corey's brains, liver, and heart."

"No!"

Sunny filled Delgado in on all the details.

"So what do you want from me?"

"I want to know who Nathan Happa is. I'm going to go after him for trying to take me out. I believe that he's connected to a group called the Golden Century or some derivative."

"Oh damn, Sunny, where have I heard this one before? See, again, that's just the kind of thing that screws up your files. It makes it hard for me to justify the pay with the Company when your files show you as a loose cannon."

"Hey, how many times have I told you I don't give a shit about your 'government pay'?"

Delgado stopped again. "And how many times have I told you it's not about the money? It's about the government *benefits*. Retirement. I keep telling you that it's best to have something left on the burner when it's all over."

Taking the lead, Sunny stepped ahead of Delgado, chuckling and shaking his head at the same time. Delgado had two years left before he got his full government retirement and pension. *The good life*. He glanced back at Frank Delgado, an American spymaster and one of the few who tried to stay straight in a crooked game. "Frank, I have to be careful about who watches my back, especially when it's been stabbed a few times already, you know. So if you want me back, then you'll watch my back on this thing I'm on until it's done. What do you say?"

Delgado was intrigued. "Okay. Yeah. What do you want from me?"

Sunny was relieved to have a pro on his team. "I want to know if there's an antitoxin for the venom of a green-ringed octopus of northern Australia."

"A green what?"

"You heard me. If there is, and you can get ahold of it, I needed it yesterday."

"Okay. Now what else can you tell me about what went down in Zurich? You said that this Happa was going somewhere. Where was he going?"

Sunny thought hard for a moment. "India, yeah, India. He has his own jet."

"Good, that at least gives me a point to start with."

"Then it's the same drop in three days. Watch your back. See ya."

"Where are you going?" Frank looked over his shoulder but Sunny was gone.

CHAPTER 16

**1200 / MONDAY / 27 JANUARY 1941
NORTH ATLANTIC OCEAN**

THE RISING AND FALLING OF THE SHIP WAS CON-
tinuous; but it was soothing, comforting, and
healing in its own way. But through Eileen's bliss-
ful slumber she knew that something had gone on and it
was horrible.

Eileen's eyes flew open and she tried to sit up fast but
a hand gently restrained her.

"Easy, you might hit your head on the beam."

It was John's voice. The sounds of both diesel engines
could be heard and felt throughout the ship.

"Thanks. I already did."

She knew where she was and all that had happened,
when?

"How long have I been sleeping?"

"At least ten hours. That's how long it took to get out
of the gale, cut away all the debris, and make enough repairs to keep under way. I doubt very much if we'll see
the same U-boat again. We'll be on engines the rest of
the way. We have enough fuel to make it to port, so
we're gonna be all right." He opened a cupboard and

pulled out a cup and bottle. He poured a cup and held it out to Eileen. "It's whiskey."

"No thanks." She would rather have water.

He shrugged and drained it, then poured himself another one. "I have to tell you, Annie, you did one hell of a job. I can't think of any woman I've ever known who could do what you did." He sat on the bunk and put his hand on her leg. He leaned over and gave her a kiss.

Eileen was surprised at his building passion as his hand slipped between her legs. What was going on? Sure, she wanted him, but she had yet to come to grips with what had gone on. His intensity was as alluring as it was frightening. How could she say yes and no at the same time? "Wait!"

"Huh?" John shook himself back to reality.

"John, I just killed I don't know how many men, and a young boy. I'm bandaged like a mummy, we smell awful. So I'm sorry to tell you that your beautiful smile alone won't get you a tumble."

John was up and off the berth in an instant. "Annie, I don't know how that happened. I would have whipped any of my crew for what I tried to do. Please forgive me."

"John, *please*, it's just that this is not the time or place. You can see that, right?"

"So you don't take offense at me?"

She laughed until her head hurt again. She slowly got up and tenderly hugged John. Then she opened his cabin door and made her way back to her own bunk.

Out of her damp clothes and bundled in her bunk she felt confident in John's words. *We're gonna be all right.* She told herself that if she had any real smarts she would get up and go right back into John's arms, deliciously smelly as they were.

0830 / FRIDAY / 31 JANUARY 1941

The coastline of England was clear. A time-honored tradition was going on in the galley. The fierce, piratical rum smugglers were celebrating their safe arrival while formally remembering the crewmates and family they had just lost at sea.

Eileen was caught in the center of the occasion. Billy presented her with a small picture of the *Illusion*. Written on it was "From a grateful crew, thanks Annie, for your sharpshooting."

Everyone couldn't have been nicer, but John seemed a little distant. Eileen wondered if it was from the little scene in his cabin the night before. But she rationalized that he probably had more on his mind than a roll with a passenger. He was about to give tribute to those that wouldn't come home.

John lifted his cup. "To those who sleep in Neptune's deep. They were our brothers and will be sorely missed. May they drop anchor in the Lord's safe harbor."

The *Illusion* limped into Southampton. Several lorries lined the dock. The moment all the mooring lines were tied the hatches on the *Illusion* came off. An army of men scrambled over her deck to unload the weapons and munitions.

Eileen was well rested and amazed at how much cargo the Illusion could hold. She saw John warmly greet a gray bearded man in overalls. The man carried a suitcase with him. They went below.

"It's payday, Annie," Billy said.

Eileen looked up and Billy came sliding down a rope.

There was no one waiting for Eileen when the main lines tied the *Illusion* to the dock. It was very odd. She expected to see Peter.

Eileen was more than grateful to finally step onto firm land. But the moment she did her body started moving to the roll of the ocean. "Oh no!"

John laughed. "It'll take a day or two to adjust, maybe less."

A black car pulled up to the dock. Half hoping to see Kato, she saw instead a young freckled driver. An old man in a gray tweed suit and wearing a black bowler hat stepped from the car and climbed the gangway. Without waiting for permission, he boarded and walked straight to Eileen.

"I will have a look at your papers, miss." He looked them over and shook his head. "These papers are not in good order. Are you a part of this crew or are you a passenger?" He looked down at her as if he was talking to rubbish.

Still expecting Peter to show at the last second, she was surprised and perplexed. It vexed her that with all the special training she had, they still kept her in the dark on so many other things, like her mission objective, like now.

Where in the hell was Peter? Who was this man? There were no code words to trade with him. Was this some sort of training scenario? Because if it was, she had had enough of it! These were supposed to be the good guys. She had come on behalf of President Roosevelt to help. She crossed her arms and remained silent.

"Oh? It's like that then," the man said. "I'll just inspect your baggage." He opened the suitcase and gasped. He reached inside his coat, pulled out a pair of handcuffs, and tried to cuff her but he was so shaky and nervous he wound up dropping them. He fell to his knees and growled, "You don't move. You'll be comin' with us. Home Office orders." He had landed a big fish, a *spy!* From his knees he fumbled but finally had her cuffed.

He was about to stand but suddenly found himself face-to-face with Billy.

"Beggin' your pardon, mister," Billy said, "but if you don't take those cuffs off of my mate, you're goin' over the side, right now." He stood nose to nose with the man.

The man snorted, stood, and looked down his nose at Billy. "Pipsqueak, do you think you can?"

"I know I can." Billy put his fists on his hips and sneered, then growled at the man.

His eyes grew wide with fear. He wasn't looking at Billy anymore, but the rest of the crew behind him closing in.

"N-Now just, just a minute, I am an official debarkation agent of His Majesty's government. This woman's papers are not in order. Under the law I must take her in. If you try to stop me I have the authority to impound this ship, its contents, and all its proceeds."

"Not with her wearing handcuffs you don't." John went eye to eye with the frightened man. "Now take them off her. Now take them off her this second or I *will* let Bill send you over the side right now."

Billy, small as he was, had pumped himself into a rage. He hollered and screamed, ready to attack. Even the crew gave him space by backing up a few paces.

The manacles were off in seconds.

"I ask you again. Is she a part of the crew?" He looked around at his situation, trying desperately to gain back some shred of authority. "Everything will stop. I, I, I will call the regulars and shut down the whole operation."

"No. I'm not a crew member. I was a stowaway." Eileen was fuming but saw that this wasn't a game. Something had gone wrong and she needed to defuse everything. Where in the damned hell was Peter? He hadn't clued her in to what to expect on her arrival. This was the last reception she'd expected.

He looked at John. "Did you have a look at what is in her suitcase?"

"No."

He huffed at getting the upper hand. "Then I suspect her to be a spy. She's coming with us." He pointed to two of the crew. "You and you. Get her bags and come with me." He was back in his role and itching badly to get out of there.

What in the world was happening? Eileen was stunned. Was it supposed to be this way by design? Was someone not talking to someone else on purpose?

John stood in front of Eileen. "She ain't goin' nowhere until I finish talking to her. And no one will help you unless I say so. So you go back to your car and wait there." He faced the crew. "You got a ship to unload. Go."

The crew grumbled and departed, leaving Eileen and John together.

"You don't have to go with that man you know. You can stay with me."

Once again Eileen was savoring a moment she never thought she would. "Thank you, John, but I can't. But you don't know how much what you just said means to me."

John nodded again. "Well then, here." He handed her an envelope.

"What's this?"

"Your share of the take. The crew voted you as one of the hands. *See*, you really are a part of the crew. Take it. You sure as hell earned it."

She looked at the envelope and handed it back. "Thank the crew, but I really don't need it where I'm going. You keep it for me instead. One day I'll collect it back from you, with interest."

"If that's what you want." For the first time since the voyage there was an unsure look in his eyes. "Annie, I'm sorry I came on to you the way I did, because I had no right to do that."

"I know, John, but there's nothing to forgive." She hugged him tight. "If there's ever a next time, you're the one who better watch out."

The hug turned into a passionate kiss.

Her radio suitcase and duffel were put in the trunk by two of the crew. They eyed the agent in the car as they passed.

"Hurt her and I'll cut your dick off," one of them said.

The rear door of the car opened.

Eileen turned to wave. Everyone cheered her from the ship. She felt like crying—it was the first time in her life that she felt as if she were parting with something special. Her heart cracked. Was that what love was supposed to feel like?

She climbed into the car.

The man wearing the bowler hat almost sneered at

her. He had her. "We're on to you, you know. The only
question is *whom* do you work for, so you better come
clean or you will find yourself packed away in the Tower
of London."

Eileen laughed. "*Really?* Now that's right out of a
Hollywood movie I saw a couple of weeks ago. A Nazi
interrogator said, 'Come clean. We have ways of making you talk.' I forgot who played the part. Do you remember?"

There was no Peter, no Camp X, and no American
Army coming to her rescue, just a cold jail cell. It
amazed her how easy it was to slip into a role and play it
just as the Hollywood actors had taught her.

She put her hands on her hips and took the pose of a
Hollywood gun moll. "Look, copper, I ain't sayin' nothing!" She leaned close to the man. "And if you again say
'we have ways of making you talk,' so help me, I'll have
that crew back there keelhaul you!"

She fell back against the seat as the car roared off.
The last sight of the *Illusion* and the crew was of Billy
being surrounded by three girls.

She had to trust that things would work themselves
out. She was on friendly grounds even though the creep
next to her wasn't her friend.

"We were tipped that someone like you was coming.
But no one clued us as to *why* you're coming. Perhaps
you could give us a clue, miss . . . ?"

His variations on the question seemed endless. He
didn't know anything. He was immigration, not intelligence. It was obviously his first *big* catch and he was
making the most of it before he turned her over to the
higher authorities.

Where in the hell is Peter?

The fool was nowhere as skilled as the interrogators
of Camp X. All too quickly the man lost his insincere demeanor. "Look, miss, when MI6 gets their hands on
you, you will have wished that you told me everything
first. The cells in the Tower smell very, very unpleasant.

It can take your breath away and make you vomit." He leaned close to her. "I can help you avoid all that."

Eileen idly thought about killing the man. It was only a passing thought, but too much longer and immigration just might wind up with one less agent. "Look, Mr. Bowler Hat, I'm going to shut up now. If you ask me any more questions, when I get the chance I'm going to make a call to my little friend Billy. And Billy is not going to be happy to hear what I'll tell him."

The man glowered and found much more interest in his worn, wing-tipped brown shoes than any more questions.

It was quiet along the countryside. There was no question that it was a land at war. Barbed wire and towers dominated the structures along the green rolling hills. There were the odd craters and covered structures made to keep the craters off target.

They came to London. Barrage balloons were in the air, attached by steel cables that could shear through any Luftwaffe plane trying a low, precision attack. She had no idea where they were; all the direction signs had been taken down. But she knew instantly where they were when she saw the silhouette of Big Ben.

Eileen had never seen war. The city of London was a city that looked like it was on the losing end of war. There was no way she could have prepared herself for the devastation she saw. The black-and-white pictures she had seen of London didn't compare to the reality of what passed by her car window. The smell of everything burned assailed her nose and made her eyes water.

Where man's architecture and building prowess once testified to form, culture, and sophistication stood piles of smoldering and burning rubble created from bigotry, hate, and ignorance. She grew cold. If this was what the Nazis did to a nation that wouldn't submit, what would happen to America when the war came to her country?

They drove through the prison's gate, where she was taken straight to an interrogation room.

"There." Mr. Bowler Hat pointed to a wooden chair

in the center of the room. He left, making sure that he slammed the steel door shut.

The solid stone walls were covered with mold. Mr. Bowler hat was right; it was everything that she could do to keep from throwing up.

Hungry and angry, there was nothing to say, any names to mention, or sanctuary to claim. Technically she had arrived illegally in England. Was it another endless test to see how she would react? She expected to be treated as a spy, but not executed by the Brits as one.

There was a clanking and creaking noise at the door as a key opened the lock. The door opened and a slim man in a black tweed suit entered. He looked at a stack of folders as he walked into the cold stone room. "Hello, Number 26. I am Ian, Peter's brother. Perhaps he has spoken of me."

"I don't know who you're talking about."

"Yes, that's the right answer." Ian placed the folders on a wooden bench and pulled out a pack of cigarettes. He offered her one.

Eileen shook her head.

He reached in his coat and took out an ivory cigarette holder, put in a cigarette, then lit it. "It seems that the Broadway people have failed to inform some in MI5 or MI6 that a most secret mission is being launched from our territory. They are not very pleased at all, not at all. I thought it best that we retire from this situation before it becomes intolerable."

"Who's Broadway or those other letters?"

Ian rolled his eyes.

"Okay, you want a story? There I was in Shanghai, drinking with some crazy pirates. They got me drunk, held me prisoner, and here I am. All I want to do is get back home. Can you get me outta here?" It was the best lame cover story that she could come up with at the moment.

"And the radio?"

She gave him a coy, pandering smile. "It's not mine."

"Number 26, *really*, there's no need to continue your

charade. Peter could not meet you because he is stuck in Iceland until the poor weather clears." He inhaled deeply on his cigarette, and then let out the smoke. "I know who you are, Number 26."

"Oh yeah, who am I?"

"The Green Hornet."

Eileen's jaw dropped. How could he know her thoughts?

There was a bemused smile on Ian's face. "Would you rather stay here and endure a very embarrassing and malodorous situation with that *bureaucrat* who believes that he could rattle some *very* important cages, or would you like to come with me?"

Now she remembered where she'd seen the ivory cigarette holder. Two people used them in the Pullman car. President Roosevelt had one; Ian had to have held the other that night. Eileen was at the door and opened it for Ian. "After you."

"Oh no, that would be rude." He held the door. "After you, I insist. I'll collect your kit."

His voice sounded a lot like Peter's. Walking out of the prison she enjoyed the look of befuddlement, astonishment, and pure anger on Mr. Bowler Hat's wrinkled face. "Bye." She waved. "Ta-ta, I have to go. It's been *awfully* nice, the time we had."

She quickly followed Ian out to a waiting black Buick parked in front of the Newgate Press Yard. A young, red-haired woman sitting on the backseat smiled warmly and took her hand.

"Hello, Number 26. I'm your decoder. My name is Sybil Leek." Her eyes twinkled. "I follow the Green Hornet programs too." She opened up the sack that was next to her. It was filled with cheese, dried meats, and breads.

"You!" So this was the person who was sending her secret messages. Eileen felt like she found a long lost sister. In moments they were discussing the radio program. *Finally* she was in the company of someone like her. Eileen knew the techniques to keep things social without

giving up any real information. This time she actually
wanted to make a friend, a girlfriend.

Eileen and Sybil spent hours on the drive chatting
about everything and nothing. As they conversed Eileen
caught hidden conversational messages coming from
Sybil that she could understand. She tried out a couple
on her own.

It worked!

Ian looked flustered to be left out of the cryptic conversation. "Number 26, aren't you interested in where
we are going?"

Eileen looked at Sybil. "Should I be?"

"You're safe for the moment," Sybil answered.

"Nobody's told me anything so far. As long as there's
more food and a place to sleep I'll be fine."

"You Brits sure got it rough." She quickly ignored
Ian and resumed her conversation with Sybil as if he
weren't there.

They drove northeast for over six hours. They came
to a place Sybil called the New Forest, her familial
home.

"How new is New Forest?" Eileen asked.

Sybil chuckled. "Too, it's very ancient, filled with the
magical and mystical."

Ian groaned.

They passed though a small village and stopped in the
grand entrance to a country estate. It was a majestic
English manor complete with ivy-covered stone walls.

"Is this your family home?" Eileen asked as she
stepped from the car.

Sybil laughed. "Oh no, we do live close by, but our
whole home would probably fit inside the smallest loo
here. There are many grand estates here in the New
Forest. Most of the owners who have left their homes in
England are allowing them to be occupied by the war
effort. This particular estate has over one hundred
rooms."

They entered the mansion and Eileen gasped. After
all the makeshift quarters and her own sorry family

home, this was the first time she had ever encountered such grandeur. "This is something," was all she was able to get out.

"Oh yes it is. It also happened to be Nazi German. Now it is the property of His Majesty."

"What? I don't understand."

"This is, or rather was, the home of Karl Kruse, a German aristocrat, but Ian clipped him." Sybil looked at Ian, who suddenly turned on his heels down a hall, and was gone.

Sybil watched until he was gone. "Uncle Karl, that's what I called him, came here about ten years before the war started. He made good friends with my father. They had much in common."

Eileen followed Sybil, mouth wide-open at the grandeur and opulence, tried to concentrate on what Sybil was saying.

"I came to live here and be a companion to his daughter, Margarita. Many people came and went at all times and all hours. Before the war this was a place where Aryans, both German and British, gathered. As a child my father taught me to cast astrology charts and my charts quickly became favorites of everyone. Uncle Karl had me do charts for Hitler, Rudolf Hess, and many others in his bund. I understand that they were influential in their own way.

"Now, as those nasty winds of war blew our way, what no one knew was that the estate came under MI6 surveillance. Enter Mr. Ian Fleming from the Royal Navy. He was dashing. There I am, a young girl, impressionable, meeting blueblood royalty, spinning their astrology charts, acting the medium, and loving the attention. Ian with all his charms, *sweeps* me off my feet and makes me feel as if I was the answer to England's prayers." Sybil chuckled over the memory then became cross.

"The bloody sod tricked me! From me he got the names of every person who came and went from here. One evening we were raided by an army of MI6 agents and every last person, but me, was taken away. Uncle Karl is being held in the Tower of London as a German spy. His lovely wife and Margarita, my best friend, are imprisoned on the Isle of Man.

"He tried to apologize for using me that way, but I socked him right in the jaw. Too, he made the core of counterespionage from the German agents he caught that night. It was only after the war started that I actually understood what had happened and why. My uncle Karl, a nice, wonderful man *was* a German agent."

"For the Nazis?"

"Not quite."

They came to a wide hallway. Sybil opened the door that led into a massive library. The two-story-high walls were filled with books. Sybil led Eileen to a sofa near a woodstove.

"Eileen, I'm personally glad that we have this chance to meet like this because there's a few things I want to tell you before you leave England." Sybil glanced around the room and lowered her voice. "Has anyone actually spoken to you of the kind of people the Nazis really are?"

"Not fully, but I know that they are animals."

"They are worse than that, dear. You lived there when you were young so you might assume that the German people are just misguided by Hitler."

"Yes, that's right."

"Truth be known, it's not Hitler guiding the Nazis."

"No?" This was the first time Eileen had actually discussed Nazi politics in depth. She'd learned the hierarchy matrix of the Nazis, their military strategy, and the tactics they used. Other than race supremacy, the whole time during her training no one ever expressed what they actually thought, or their philosophies.

"No, not at all. The Nazis as the world knows them, are actually the political arm of a secret society called the Thules. I know this because of two people, my father, Edward, and Alistair Crowley. Before their rise to power both my father and Alistair had been invited to the Thule bunds in Germany to receive instructions. They were so enthralled with what they learned that they established a bund here in England for further instructions. Too, they did it right here. I'll show you the place later."

"Instructions in what?" Eileen asked.

"Why, in magic, my dear."

"Magic? Like illusions and stage tricks?"

"Religious magic, ceremonial magic, dear, that's what it's called. My family has practiced the Old Religion for a long, long time. Years ago my father and the family were hounded from Russia for their beliefs. They were accused of *witchcraft*." Sybil rested her hand on Eileen's arm. "There are still witch laws in effect here. It's something we will never be able to avoid. There are those who search out my father for what they think is hidden knowledge."

"And do you have this hidden knowledge?"

Sybil chuckled. "No dear, there *are* no big secrets, or hidden knowledge. Whilst others look for the quick road to power, ours is a wisdom gained through countless years of experience, hit or miss. For some reason people just like to think there's an easy incantation that works, especially those who want ultimate power, like the Thules. But the Thules are after *black* magic." She became somber. "My father would teach anyone with a genuine heart. Alistair, on the other hand, the left hand to be exact, was only after black hearts."

"And the Thules have that black heart?"

"The blackest! They would send their sorcerers around the world in search of mystical power. We didn't know this at first. Uncle Karl practiced our Ceremonial Magic in our way. Too, he was not a bad man. He had his family and opened his home to us. That is why we accepted him. But he was only a front for those behind him. My father quickly spotted the ones behind him for what they really were; sex magicians."

"What?"

"They practice the most perverted acts imaginable.

They took what they learned and incorporated ritual murder rites into their acts." A black look crossed her face. "One bugger kept pestering me to use me in one of his rituals; a *very* disgusting one that violated every social taboo imaginable."

"No!" Just what was this woman talking about? Why was she telling her these strange things?

"After my father met with the Thules a number of times he knew how great a threat they posed to Britain. He went to the authorities but they scoffed at him. They ridiculed him, all except Ian. My father did his best to keep me ignorant of what was happening, but Ian and I had other ideas."

Sybil grew cold for a moment, stood up, and walked around the room feeling the walls. "Yes, and this was one place where evil tried to invade my homeland. I was young then, but that was just yesterday. At the time I did not really understand the extent of the evil that exists in the Nazis. Ian still does not believe the extent to which the Thules and their black arts rule the Nazis."

The door opened and Ian entered almost on cue. "That is true, but that does not mean we can't use every means to fight back—every means."

Eileen's head spun. "And why are you telling me all this? What does this have to do with me?" Was this the mission objective?

"Evidence," Ian muttered. He walked across the room and sat in a leather wing chair opposite them and lit up a Senior Service cigarette. He gave it to Sybil, then lit one for himself and put it in his ivory holder. "We do not know the actual specifics of your mission, only the general location, but . . . You tell her, dear."

Sybil nodded. "Ian, in his job, has heard of rumors of entire villages and families being moved to forced labor camps for slave labor and that the Jews and any 'undesirables' are being experimented on in the northern reaches of Germany. There is no actual proof of this. Whatever your assignment is, we would like you, if you can, to document and relay to us any evidence of this happening, and a bit more."

Eileen couldn't move. "Go on."

Sybil gripped Eileen's hand. "We are already and completely out of protocol. Peter would be incensed if he finds out that his younger brother and another office tried to horn in on his operation. But Number 26, if we can uncover and locate the real spiritual center of the Nazis, the Thules, and their inner circle, then we have a chance to mount an operation to stab them right in the soul, if you follow me.

"What we are asking is that you keep your eyes open to everything, that's all. I will be on the other end of a wireless. I want to teach you a simple rhyme. In it are the codes by which we can communicate, if you are willing."

"Willing? I'm waiting on you."

A tall man stepped into the room. "Number 26, welcome. I am Sir John. We've been expecting you. We are terribly sorry about the row that brought you here."

He was as distinguished an English gentleman as Eileen could ever imagine. He looked down his nose at her. She didn't like that. "Sir John, if I don't see my handler soon, there's a boat I'll be shipping out on as soon as repairs are made." She didn't give a damn about good English manners.

"Yes. He will be here soon. Please follow me."

Now Sir John's nose was not only stuck up, it was out of joint. Eileen hid her smile behind her face as she followed him.

The room was small and cramped. "Nothing new."

A small knock at the door brought her around.

"Peter! Where in the hell have you been?"

Peter looked as if he had been out riding a windstorm. "I am *terribly* sorry, Number 26. The weather in Keflavik, Iceland, was fierce for several days. I was able to send my brother a message to meet you if we couldn't lift off until the weather cleared."

"Sure, I understand. I was sailing *in* that mess, thank you. I am not sure I want to go on." She detailed her harrowing voyage and her first encounter with war and death.

"Well we're all here and that's all that matters. Things will go smoother, you'll see."

"Right, shove that 'good sport' business. I have to tell you that I'm sick and tired of all the unknowns. When does the game begin?"

Peter looked surprised. "Number 26, the game has never stopped. How do you Yanks put it? Oh yes. You are up to bat." He looked over at Sir John idly sitting by a fireplace and whispered, "Sir John is the Home Director for your mission."

The room's only light came from the fireplace and a candle burning on the coffee table next to Sir John. It was difficult to see clearly through the dancing lights and shadows. Peter directed Eileen's attention to a desk and a paper lying atop it.

"Look at it carefully. Tell me what you see."

She picked up the blank paper and studied it. "A blank piece of paper."

"Look at it closer." He handed her a magnifying glass.

It took a while but she thought that she saw something. It wasn't blank. "I see a dot."

"*Exactly*," Peter said.

"There's enough light for you to see," Sir John said. "Do you know how to use this magnifying viewer?"

"I think so." It took her a few attempts, but she finally brought the dot into view. It was a page from her Army records, the words were a little blurry, but she could read most of them.

"Microfilm," Sir John remarked. "Everyone has it. It's not new. What's new is that we highly suspect that the Nazis have perfected this technique. They call it a *Mekrat*, a microdot with ten times the information of the size of a period on that typed sheet of paper in front of you. But we don't have a sample, nor do we know the process that they would use to achieve their clarity. Of course we have a theory, but no hard proof. We have no evidence, just reports.

"All we have been able to ascertain is that the possible source of the developer is in northeastern Germany." Sir John continued. "Your mission is to infiltrate into that area and locate the processing laboratory. Once you have the files, you will verify, copy the process, and return to England."

Eileen sat quiet for a minute. "That's it? I don't have to blow anything up, kill anyone, or run a resistance cell?"

"Are those some things you want to do while you are there?" Peter asked.

"No. It just seems that after all this training and time, stealing something not much bigger than a head of a pin seems minor."

"Minor?" Sir John looked truly shaken. "My dear, do you really understand the importance of this process? If you do not pull the trigger of a gun the whole time you are there, then consider yourself lucky, even blessed. Young lady, you are not going into an organized resistance cell; there *is* no resistance in Germany—Hitler is a god there. You are going directly into the viper's pit." He looked at Peter. "I am not at all sure that we have the right person for the job, not at all."

Eileen had enough of Sir John's imperious behavior. "Sir John, I don't remember you having anything to do with my selection. I'm the one going in and unless you have someone who knows the lay of the land better, then I'd appreciate it if you would try looking me in the eye once in a while without talking down to me."

"Right!" Peter was out of his chair and tried to pull Eileen out of hers. "Thank you, Sir John, we know the mission and we will be ready for it."

Eileen pulled away from Peter. "Wait. When do I leave?" She leaned over Sir John's desk and placed her fist on the desk. He was at her mercy now and she loved the uncertain look in his eyes.

"In less than two weeks," he answered. He wasn't used to his authority being challenged. The little woman in front of him was not proper, not proper at all.

CHAPTER 17

2115 SATURDAY / 6 MARCH 2004
ORLANDO / FLORIDA

PAN JHANDI WALKED OVER TO HIS BLACK J30 IN-
finiti parked behind the dojo. He was about to
get in when he heard a sound behind him.

"Pan, don't turn around. You know my voice. Has
anyone been here looking for me?"

"No, sensei."

"Good, then please act like you forgot something. Go
back into the dojo and leave a note that you have a family emergency and have to go back to the Philippines."

Pan was in and out of the dojo in minutes. He got in
his car and released the door locks. The right rear door
opened and shut in an instant. He saw a blur in his
rearview mirror.

"Just drive like all's well, then get on Interstate 4 and
head north. Adjust your rearview mirror so I can see if
anyone's following."

Pan put the car in gear and did as he was told.
"Sensei, is something wrong?"

"Very. And am I ever glad to see you! Are you sure
that no one's come looking for me?" Sunny kept his eyes
on the mirror, watching traffic behind them, scanning for

any cars that might be following. The trouble was that it was rush-hour traffic and *everyone* was following.

"No."

"I have to tell you, it'll be a while before either of us sees the studio again."

"What?"

"I'll explain later. Right now I want you to do a few driving maneuvers for me."

Taking Sunny's direction, Pan got off the highway, then got back on and headed south for a ways. He got off the highway and made some bizarre turns on Orlando's surface streets before they wound up on I-95 and headed north.

Sunny climbed into the front passenger seat, satisfied that they weren't being followed. He reclined the seat and closed his eyes. "Pan, have you ever killed anyone?"

"Why, no. Never."

"Could you?"

Pan was quiet for a while before he spoke. "I would never *willingly* take a life."

"But you would if you had to."

"If it had to be so, yes. Why you ask? You are in trouble."

"Yeah, but that's nothing new. Right now I'm trying to erase my tracks before someone else does. Unfortunately, you got caught in the path of some nasty people." He looked over at Pan and saw him turn absolutely white, so he reassuringly patted Pan on his shoulder. "Look, you talked to the guy who started me on this adventure. If the people looking for me tie you to this, you might have disappeared, too, for good. Now I got to find a place to hide you."

Pan digested Sunny's words, then came to a decision with a resolute nod, and said, "I understand. I want to help. I'm in all the way. *All* the way."

"Great. I have a little story to tell you." He filled Pan in on all that he had been through. When he was done he noticed that Pan's hands trembled slightly and that he looked to be in a world of his own, not speaking for some time.

"Where we go from here?" Pan finally said.

"Virginia." He curled up in the seat. "Wake me when we cross the state line."

SUNNY SILENTLY USED THE NIGHT AND SHADOWS AS cover to cross the wide lawns leading to the main house. The glass house garden doors leading to the house were unlocked. Drawing his pistol, Sunny was frustrated to see that overt security measures were still not in place. He crept silently through the halls until he saw Sally Fine sitting at her writing desk. He watched her for a minute, then released the safety catch on the handle of his P7 pistol. It gave with a snap loud enough to make Sally jump. Lowering his gun, he said, "Brichner's dead."

Frightened until she saw Sunny emerge from shadows, Sally began to cry softly. "Oh no. I sent him to his death." She slowly stood and walked over to Sunny and hugged him. "Did you do what I told you to do and leave? Why didn't you call me? Was it bad?"

Sunny nodded. "Bad enough. Sally, why is your house so exposed?"

"Who in the world would want to harm an old lady?" She shrugged her shoulders.

"The same people who killed Corey and tried to kill me. Sally, they're after us."

"No!" Sally let go of Sunny and gasped. "It's unthinkable! How could such old papers do this? I only wanted to find out some of the things my husband wrote about. I didn't know. I think burning the material is the best thing that we can do." She tottered over to her chair and sat. "I didn't know."

"No. Burning it is the last thing we should do." Sunny pocketed his gun and looked around. "Who's here?"

"Only a few people, my houseman, his wife, the gardener. That's it."

Sitting next to Sally, he took her hands. "Because I trusted you, I went there and poked my nose into a hornet's nest." He squeezed her hands harder. "You haven't been totally straight with me, have you?"

The look in her eyes showed that he had hit pay dirt. "You know who these people are. You know that they kill to keep their secrets. You come clean with me, or I'm out of here." He wasn't sure if the pain in her eyes was from him squeezing her hands so he let go.

"I met Donald just after the war was over. He had been in charge of building the Liberty ships, then he was personally asked by General Marshal to help administer his plan.

"He had been in Europe for a short time and fell in love with a gypsy girl just liberated from a death camp. Donald kept her with him wherever he went, quietly of course. He knew it would never work out. Since he came from a blue-blooded family, there was no way he would ever marry her and finally he let her go just before I came into the picture."

Sally quit speaking.

"I never knew about her, or their son until just recently."

"What?"

She looked up at Sunny. "Sunny, my husband was an honest man. He treated me like a queen. But when he was dying from pneumonia he told me to burn his diary and records. I told him I did, but didn't." She pulled out the torn pages of the general's diary.

"Her name was Marie." She looked down at the papers. "He knew how crooked the dealings were and was going to go directly to George Marshal but then someone stopped him. They pointed out a car on the street. In it was Marie and Donald's only son. He had only seen him once. He was told that if he ever went to the authorities with his discoveries, his son would be killed.

"The night he passed away he told me that there were people who would kill to get their hands on the materials. They are called the Golden Century. He wanted them destroyed; but it wasn't for my safety, it was to keep the son he barely knew alive."

"Why didn't you tell me this before?"

"I'm sorry, but after over fifty years of marriage, it's very hard for me to come to grips with the fact that Donald had a son with another woman while we never could. Do you understand?"

Sunny nodded in sympathy. He had to get back to business. "Did you tell this to Corey?"

"No, but poor Mr. Brichner knew there was danger. But I think that the potential gain kept him going. He wanted 30 percent of whatever he could recover."

"He must've gotten too greedy, then careless. Do you know a man named Nathan Happa?"

"No."

Sunny took a short breath and got up, then walked over to the big picture window and made a wide, waving motion. From the tree line a lithe figure emerged. He turned to Sally. "Well, now what?"

"I was hoping you would tell me."

"First, I want you to call Lambert and get him here, now. Next we got to fortify this place."

Sally looked surprised. "Do you think that they will come here?"

"I'm pretty sure that they would if they knew where you were."

Pan appeared at the door and entered. Sunny introduced him to Sally. "This man will be your bodyguard for a while." He followed Pan's eyes appreciating the opulent environment. Pan caught himself, turned to Sally, and gave a graceful bow.

"I am at your service."

FOUR PEOPLE SAT AT A TABLE THAT SEATED THIRTY IN the massive dinning hall. A pistol lay on the table in front of Sunny. The only other weapons in the mansion were the gold-plated machine gun and a silver-plated World War II Colt .45 pistol.

It wasn't the type of planning operation Sunny was used to. An old woman, young lawyer, and martial artist didn't amount to a wealth of undercover experience.

"Do we bring Mr. Brichner's body home?" Sally asked.

"For what? He has no family," answered Sunny.

"We could bury him here," she offered.

I should be so lucky. "Well, not right now. You'd be bringing them right to your doorstep. Corey's on ice and should stay that way for now." He straightened up in his chair. "So here it is: I've been fighting hard-to-find enemies for a long time. I thought I'd dealt with all kinds in one way or another. I've put my life on the line against the jihad, narcoterrorism, even the good ol' Mafia and all-American crime. But I think that what went on over there with me is diabolical and connected to this thing."

"Diabolical?" Sally asked.

"Yeah." The thoughts that had been brewing in his mind finally jelled and surfaced. "We all know that there are people who do evil and cruel things just to do them; they are inherently evil. There are clergy who wield great power whose main function is to minister to the good. They do unquestionable good. Then there are the ones who are spiritually and financially guiding the terrorists. The al-Qaeda is an example of that. The power of terror that they wield is incredible. So here's my question. Who ministers to the organized evil?

"With the proper resources are they not capable of being just as powerful as those who do good? Are there people out there who live not just for doing evil, but are out to institutionalize it? Think Nazis. Well, I'm sure there are people out there who wonder if people like me really exist.

"I thought that working for Sally here would open new territory for me, investigative work. Money recovery. Instead, I stepped on something I know I shouldn't be tackling, but it's too late to bail." He looked at Sally. "Eventually, they are going to find us if we don't go get them first."

Sunny looked at Lambert. He was young. "You made a good cutout in Florida."

"Cutout?"

"You don't understand?" Amateurs were trying to take on pros.

"I instructed him on what to do," Sally interjected.

Sunny folded his hands. "So, there's *someone* who wants to keep Sally's material a secret. Corey Brichner was murdered and ritually mutilated by Happa for whatever he might've uncovered. But knowing Corey, he might've just hit a bad nerve with this guy, who knows? I made the whole situation only worse by overplaying my hand and I stirred up a hornet's nest. They know me but haven't figured out whom I was representing, yet. Intuition tells me that Corey talked before he died and now they know we have things that they want."

"Sensei, just who are *they*?" Pan asked.

"I don't know who they are. I just know of Nathan Happa. I still don't know who they are either. Sally? Why don't you enlighten us? Don't hold back now, it's *way* too late for that."

She was pensive at first, but then answered, "I know them from long ago as the investment group, the Golden Century. I don't know how they are organized. Donald became obsessed with them. He said someone had been manipulating the world economy for some time. I figured that he was talking about the Rockefellers, the Rothschild's, and other wealthy families. I'm pretty sure now that it was the Golden Century he spoke of. But now I know that it is far more involved than just the money." She looked helplessly at Sunny. "You know why?"

Lambert spoke. "Is it? Is the money their power base? If it is, then they can be anywhere using any number of fronts. Like the drug dealers, they would be almost impossible to trace. We need to locate their real power base before we can hurt them."

"What do you mean?" Sunny asked.

"Take for example the DeBeerses."

•"The who?"

"They're a trillion-dollar conglomerate that deals in the diamond industry. Naturally their power source is not the money, the stones are. Their power source is in South Africa where they control every aspect of the process—mining, cutting, sorting, pricing. Find another, more plentiful source or cut off the source and they soon will be hurting. Many have tried but they remain on top. Like any conglomerate they do the things necessary to stay on their game."

"Even murder?" Pan asked.

Lambert didn't answer the obvious but kept speaking. "Sunny, the way you explain it, if I understand it right, this Happa guy is like their evil corporate chaplain. Find his power source and you may find everything else."

Sunny nodded. "I agree, but that takes us back to square one, looking at a windblown curtain. We have to get behind it one way or another," Sunny said. "I think that it's just a matter of time before they figure out my ties and come right here, and then waste everything. Everything. That can't happen."

Sally pulled out a lace handkerchief and patted the perspiration on her lip.

"How do we get help against a speculation?" Lambert questioned.

"There are a few guys that I can call. I know of an outfit that can be here by tomorrow. It'll cost a bundle, but that still won't stop Happa's people from getting to Sally."

"Should we go public with what we have?" she asked.

"With what, old documents, account numbers that are just numbers? It adds up to nothing more than paranoid conspiracies. We've got nothing, except that there are those willing to kill to keep it at nothing."

"Maybe we should just *give* them the papers," Sally offered. "Negotiate."

"No, it's a bad move. You've heard that the best defense is a good offense. If I can get to Happa first, I can answer a lot of questions." *That's if I don't kill him first.* Sunny had been replaying his encounters over and over; only one piece of information that stood out. "Has anyone ever heard of 'oneness of interest'?"

Pan nodded. "In the Hindu religion it means that the reason behind your devotion is *oneness of interest.* Eventually, you come to the same plane as God, Shiva.

"What you give, you get back. Your interests are same. God is you. You are God with His understandings."

"What would that have to do with Happa's people?" Lambert asked.

"There's no telling who Happa's people are, or what sort of philosophies they embrace. I can only assume that whoever Happa is with, they have to have very sophisticated levels of organizational security. Happa may also have his own branch of followers and his own security. I believe that Happa always follows some sort of religious ritual before he kills. He painted me yellow and made sure that I wouldn't refuse the offer of being a sacrificial killing. Pan, which Hindu sects do that?" Sunny saw Pan shudder.

Eyes wide, Pan's hands trembled. "Tantric. There is an extremist sect of Hindus called the Aghoris. Things they do, I only hear about. These things I will not talk about."

"How do you know all these things?" Sunny asked.

Pan's features turned dark. "Where I come from is not like here. It is, how you say it? An *Eastern* thing."

"Gotcha." Sunny knew that Pan wasn't being totally honest. *Why?* He wanted to get him alone and find out.

"So where are we?" Sally asked.

"Research. Sally, have your staff bring out everything you have on the Marshal Plan, news clips, anything and everything. We will all go through it right here. Nothing gets hidden. We copy the most valuable and important information, then I'll hide the originals. If anything happens to all of us, I know someone who'll pick up the trail.

"Next, we go back over everything again and glean anything we might've missed. What we find may tell me where I'll be headed. In the meantime we beef up security around here. We get back together before I leave."

"And when is that?" Lambert asked.

"Soon." A battle plan was forming in his mind. Weak as it might turn out, Sunny felt a little better.

PILES OF NEWS ARTICLES, TAPES, DVDS, AND DOCUMENTS yellowed with age covered Sunny's bed. While there were tons of material on grand gatherings, there was nothing specific, and no pictures of Happa. Oneness of interest turned up little. India was a big country to show up in and expect to find one man. The door was open and Pan came rushing in.

"You maybe watch this. It's a documentary on the Aghoris of India. I know about it and Mr. Lambert, he get it for me. It just arrived by UPS."

The moment the film started Sunny knew he was on a deadly trail.

Sunny pegged it the moment he saw the bowl the naked sadhu carried in his hand. "My God, Pan, Happa killed Corey, then took off the top of his skull to use it as a bowl."

A million and one ideas fired off in Sunny's mind as he watched the documentary. Now he had a start, a first step. Either Happa had to have patterned his murders on the more extreme aspects of Hinduism, or he himself was an Aghori practitioner. If he was, then someone had to have taught him.

When the tape finished Sunny had a destination in India; Varanasi, the place where they gathered to do their deeds, crematory grounds along the Ganges River in India. He was in a place that held many secrets and people that were centered on them. Still, there were matters that he either couldn't see or understand. "Pan, tell me, what is this I have just seen?"

"Magic, sensei."

"What kind of magic?"

"It can be black or white, depends on the person."

Sunny laughed. "But if I understand this right, there's necrophilia and cannibalism involved, right?"

"Yes, that is very true."

"Then how on God's good earth can this religion be a *good* thing?"

"That is something you must answer for yourself."

Sunny sat lost in disquieting thought for a long time. He was uncomfortable thinking about this voodoo crap. "Pan, what's the purpose of magic?"

"Power."

"What kind of person do you think Nathan Happa is?"

Pan looked worried. "In my country of the Philippines we got the *aswang*. To many they are a myth, a story to frighten little children. The *aswang*, they say, have powers to change their shape, fly . . ."

"Ah yes, we have the same thing, witches."

Pan held up his hand. "Witches? Close. These are not good people, they are very *evil* people; they drink blood and eat human meat. They use poisons on people, then kill them."

"Well, aren't witches supposed to do all that?"

Pan huffed and clipped Sunny on his forehead. "Sensei, you not listen well. In this matter you are novice."

"You got my full attention. Please continue."

"The *aswang* use what you Americans call black magic."

"Do the *aswang* exist?"

A strange look came over Pan's face for a moment; it was almost frozen in pain, then he looked bittersweet. "Yes, they do."

"How do you know?"

"When you tell me there is sickness in my family, I feel like I die. You see, the reason I am here in this country is because of an *aswang*, a man who practice black magic." Pan's eyes were almost hypnotic. "You asked how I know about these things. I not tell you true what I know."

"Pan, you got me. What happened to your family in the Philippines? Why don't you ever talk about them?"

"Sensei, you are right; there are evil people who do evil things for evil's sake. You ask who ministers to them." Pan got up and closed the bedroom door, then returned to his seat. "I don't talk this with anyone else but you. They are the ones who walk the left-handed path. I know." Pan shivered. He could see it again. "I come from big, big family in Visaya, island far south of Luzon. We a fishing family, happy, you know?

"My grandfather teaches us all escrema. We all good! It is our passion. As young men we travel everywhere to compete. I do good. I'm older, in my midtwenties and life is good, sensei. I even start thinking it is time for my own family." Pan let out a deep sigh. "Then it all changed. On the island is a man called Iblas Osoy. He a very, very powerful man. He got high political connections all the way to the Malacayang Palace in Manila. One day a car come and man from Iblas spoke to my father. My father not say anything to us, and he very, very sad man for a long time. Before he tell us why he so sad, he cry. "Iblas Osoy had seen me at the Manila Escrema Nationals and want me, you know what I mean?"

Nodding, Sunny unconsciously grabbed his chest and realized that he was sweating and holding his breath; things were starting to sound too familiar.

"The man say that if I do not show at Osoy's estate by one month, my family members would start to get sick and die. Then I know for sure Iblas Osoy is *aswang*."

"What did you do?"

"What I do? I go." Pan propped his knees close to his chest and wrapped his arms around his knees, staring at the fire in the fireplace. "*Aswang* think because they frighten and kill, they have *magic*. He wanted me for, for things I have never done. I kill myself before I do the things he wanted me to! He put me in a cage in his lair to force me to change my mind. From there I see how depraved this animal is.

"Sensei, I never understand how people live just to do evil. He know the things he do against God is repulsive, but he love it! He is a sex maniac. He do it with *every-thing*—the diseases he must have. And the rituals, I starving and mad from what I saw. Today I still not sure if all I saw real, or make by my starving condition." Pan shivered. "I finally tell him I ready to submit. He had me brought to him like I some sort of prize. But by then he not want me sexually; he say he want my *essence*.

"He start a strange ritual like the Catholic ritual. Then I understand the *aswang* are Catholic-influenced. He drug me and ties me to a rattan chair; the armrest was broken. When he got close enough to cut my throat I rip off the armchair handle and began to beat him with it. I try to kill him but his devotees jump on me in seconds. I beat them back with the chair handle and took off. Nobody could catch Pan, I ran from that hell!

"I never go home. Next morning I take all the money I have left in bank and leave the Philippines and buy my way here. I never been home since then." He gave Sunny a sad smile. "Now you know my whole story."

They sat in silence, Sunny marveling at Pan's ordeal. Now he understood how Pan could put such power into his strikes—they were meant for a man who once had control over every part of his life.

Until now he didn't know the agony that Pan was suffering. It wasn't a calling that Pan had to the martial arts. It was all he had to hold on to to be close to his family.

Pan spoke. "Sensei, while in the cage I see some foreigners come and go. I believe they Indian and they shared similar perverted beliefs with Osoy. One carried a skull bowl. His name Kina Baba. They speak in English. They thought I passed out from hunger and spoke freely. Like professional, they trade secrets, crazy talk. It scary. This man the Hindu, he same like Osoy."

"Pan, why are you telling me this?"

"Now you have a name and place to start. You offer

Osoy something that he want, he give you introduction to Agora guru of Happa."

"What could I possibly offer to a guy like Iblas?"

"Me."

"What? Are you crazy? You would go there with me?"

Pan gave Sunny a brilliant smile. "No. But you tell him you know where I am, say California, he believe you because you a professional liar, the best."

Pan's comment stung Sunny even if it wasn't intended.

"He give you intro and you go to India find your man."

"You got this all figured out?"

"No, sensei, but what better plan you got? I tell you how find him and all to know about him. I play sleeping most of the time, but I watch and learn how he live and work." He suddenly looked ashen. "He lie to you and tell you truth at same time. He use any trick to try to kill you."

Sunny hissed a little. "Not if I kill him first. So just exactly how do you kill a sorcerer?"

A SECURE CALL TO FRANK DELGADO GOT A FIFTY-MAN security team from Johnson Controls on the estate in less than twenty-four hours. Sunny met with Vito Scaletti, the team leader. Sunny knew the man from previous training exercises. Vito was a good man to know. He gave Sunny a CD disc of the personnel files of each man.

Sunny took hours to check carefully the records and bona fides of each man, then inspected the arsenal they brought. It wasn't enough, so he had Vito make a call to double the arms and munitions—Sunny wanted enough firepower to start World War III.

He made it clear to all involved that Pan was in charge while he was gone. Even though Pan had no operational experience, he offered a sensible and spiritual base that Sunny knew he would come to depend on.

Sunny had made his own profile of Nathan Happa. But the profile remained blank.

Who was he? Where was he from? He had to start somewhere—banker, guru, magician, sorcerer, he could be anyone.

Sunny was spending a ton of Sally's money on shadowy opponents loose somewhere in the world, but where?

He reflected on Pan's experience with the sorcerer. Until that day he had never shared his personal hell with anyone. Now, because of Sunny's own torture, there was a shared bond of blood. Pan was no longer alone; he had a friend and brother. Sunny told himself that one day he would tell Pan about his own time in hell, but for the moment he had to concentrate first on getting Happa, then what?

There was nothing more to do. It was time to leave. He found Sally in the study. She continued to apologize for involving him and for what she had unwittingly unleashed.

"I never wanted it to happen like this. I'm an old woman who is near the end of her life. I have no children and I'm one of the last of my family line. Who knows whatever happened to Donald's son? I'm not sure if I will live through this. I should have burned the papers as Donald told me. He knew. He knew what could happen and wanted to end it. Now this situation may destroy many lives and cause harm to innocent people."

Sunny nodded. "Well, there's no walking away from it now. There's no turning back, Sally, even if we wanted to. We have to see this through to the finish and pray that our team is better than theirs." Sunny wasn't truly convinced that they wouldn't all end up dead but kept those thoughts to himself.

"Sunny, my husband and I have been fighting one thing or another all our lives, and to think that there are those who've made all our gains trivial is deplorable. Awful!" She stood to face Sunny. "So we fight. Sunny, you find your man. You expose the people behind him. You do these things, and everything I have will be at

your disposal. I have made Jim draw up a fund to keep
you going in case anything happens to me."

BOUGHT FROM A PRIVATE SELLER FOR CASH UNDER AN-
other assumed name, the BMW motorcycle was built for
speed and maneuverability—Sunny had a lot of stops on
his way to New York before the hunt began.

CHAPTER 18

THE PLANE CROSSED THE NORTH SEA AND WAS about to penetrate Nazi air defenses. The pilot headed directly for the nasty weather ahead. It was a bad storm that wreaked havoc on the ground, but it was much worse to be caught flying through it. The Marquis aircraft pressed on. The lightning illuminated the thunderheads, further adding to the foreboding the crew felt—there was no turning around.

"We're going to die. I know it," Eileen whispered as she put a death grip on her canvas seat. The airplane climbed and dived like a wild stallion. Lightning cracked everywhere. Hail pelted the fuselage. A strange hiss sounded throughout the plane, then it fell two hundred feet in less than a second. At any moment Eileen expected the wings to snap off. Green with nausea, there was nothing that she could do until they reached the drop zone.

"I can do this, I can, I *can*," she murmured like a mantra and huddled against the cold in her woolen jumpsuit.

Terrifying as it could get, the aircrew could not turn

around until they had delivered their "package" over the target.

"God, I swear I'll be good forever if you just don't let me die here!" Eileen closed her eyes as the unrelenting lightning burst and fired around her. She was small. Her biggest fear wasn't just the situation that she was in; if all the loose boxes in the cargo compartment fell on her, she'd be crushed, or suffocate.

The rough ride suddenly smoothed out and the wings leveled. They were out of the clouds and in clear air—exposed air. The pilot dived toward the ground to avoid Nazi night fighters guided by radar.

The pushmaster quickly opened the drop door in the cargo compartment and positioned a box by the door. He then hooked up the box's static line to a ring next to the door. The pushmaster waved at Eileen to get her attention, then pointed toward the ground. "Get ready and hook up, miss," he yelled. "You jump right after your radio."

Eileen stood, moved toward the drop door, and peered out a port window. She could see nothing. She watched as the pushmaster counted down, then pushed the box out.

He pointed to the ring and yelled back, "Now you, mum. Quickly! Quickly!"

Thrilled and scared to death, this was going to be her fourth jump, but the first one from a plane on an operational mission—right smack in the middle of enemy territory, Germany. The plane suddenly pitched up, then back, violently throwing her back into the cargo compartment. A piece of the wall spit shrapnel everywhere. They were being hit by ground fire!

Searchlights illuminating the plane got Eileen's attention. Seconds later more bursts of antiaircraft flak exploded around the plane.

There was no way she was going to stay in the damn plane. She knew that she had to get out or she was going to die. She crawled back to the drop door and hooked up the static line. Slapping the pushmaster's arm, she

yelled, "You can turn around
Eileen jumped out of the plan

It all happened in seconds
and she could hear the s
around her. Then the sound

Twisting and turning in
then a reassuring tug on h
pulled on her risers che
canopy. She hung in the
ground guns firing following th
another, they zeroed in on the plane.

Suddenly the plane exploded. The Nazi ground gun
ners had found their mark.

"Oh no," she gasped. The mission hadn't even begun
and good people were dying. "God, please take them."
She positioned for a blind landing.

With the seconds she had left under the canopy, there
was nothing to commit to memory, no prominent landmarks could be seen—everything was black. She had to
find her radio transmitter.

The ground came up hard, but she made a good landing. She was at the edge of a plowed field. She quickly
gathered up her canopy and raced into the forest, not
stopping until she was deep in the woods.

She was frightened, but not of the woods. She had
spent summers with her grandfather in the area. The
night creatures prowled the woods. She rolled the parachute and hid it under the brambles. Using essential moments to check her gear, she removed a button on her
coat. Unscrewing the top of the button, she could see a
tiny luminescent compass pointed north. *Get moving.*
She moved out, heading due west.

With every step that she took Eileen tried to remember the lessons of her spycraft and what she was in
Germany for. There was so much to try to remember.
The first step she took was months ago when she joined
the Army. Becoming a spy was the last thing she expected.

It was like groping her way around in a dark closet. It

t was going to explode from her chest.
owls in the distance. It had to be dogs,
ng and hunting dogs! Luger in hand, she
esitate to use it. "Oh boy," Eileen muttered.
I volunteered for this, but now that I'm here,
was it that I'm supposed to do, *exactly?*" She was
er own. Whatever happened, it was all up to her.

She had to find the radio first. If the Nazis found it
before she did, they would know that a spy was working
in their territory; worse, they could catch her and torture her into using her radio for them.

Never did she feel smaller or more fearful of what lay
before her, each step bringing her that much closer to
her peril.

CHAPTER 19

UNNY SPOTTED DELGADO WALKING OFF THE packed escalator—it would be almost impossible to spot any tails or surveillance. He fell into the mass body rush for the subways and home. He came up behind Delgado. "How's work?"

Delgado gave Sunny a quick glance. "I sure could use you. Are Vito's boys working out?"

"We'll see when I get back. If they never have to pull a trigger, then things will have worked out just fine."

"You know I gave Vito the referral in good faith. I don't know what in the world you are doing."

Sunny laughed for the first time he could remember. "And that must bug the shit out of you."

"It bugs me that one of my key players is out running *his* own ops when he hasn't finished *mine*."

"Not my fault, remember? Look at the bright side, the guy I wounded for you was a prize, wasn't he? Besides, I'm not here to argue."

Delgado's mood brightened. "Yeah, you're right. He's a coordinator, not a martyr. He's a good catch. I might be able to turn him."

"Don't believe that for one second. Hamas has probably already issued a contract on him, and me too. He probably knows he's already a dead man. I'd bet he'd jump at a witness security program. So who's Nathan Happa and the Golden Century?"

"Still don't know. They don't exist."

"Hey, don't give me that bullshit."

"Unless you have some pictures or latent prints, something, anything, I can't help you. The cartel was something before, but quit operating in 1953."

"Tell me something new. What about the toxicology reports on Brichner?"

"He did have that zombie juice you talked about in his system, but that's not what killed him."

"I know. I saw the DVD of Happa killing him."

"That's not all he did to him."

"I don't follow you."

"There's evidence Corey was sodomized after he was dead."

Sunny didn't blink an eye. "Then you have Happa's DNA."

"No, just the signs of forcible entry in his rectum of something *after* he was dead."

"What does Melton say?"

Delgado just kept walking.

"Well?"

"He's missing."

"Oh no."

"What?" Delgado looked back at Sunny with anxiety.

"I called Melton on the phone from my room in Zurich when I first got there. They could've traced it and caught on to him. Oh no, I think I *really* fucked up this time." Speaking on a nonsecure phone line might have cost Melton his life. Sunny silently cursed. Most of the mistakes made in Zurich belonged to him.

Delgado was gone. Sunny raced up the subway steps and raced across the street. He slid to a stop and looked back, no one was following. He continued to the second mark. This time Delgado found him.

"Melton and I talked two days ago on a secure line, then he secure-faxed me the autopsy report. That was the last I heard from him. He never made it home. He's disappeared. Interpol is freaking out."

"Did you give them Happa's name as a possible perpetrator?"

"On what, a ghost? Forget it. I didn't give up Brichner, not yet. He's still a John Doe. Any bets that he's Happa's bait?"

"It's a sucker bet. But if they have the capability to monitor secure lines, then they could come after *you* too."

Delgado stopped and faced Sunny. "Okay, Sunny, so just what the fuck is going on? Who are these people? Why are you giving *me* your cooties?"

At that moment Sunny didn't care who was watching and listening, and was hoping that they were. "I don't know, Frank. But those cooties are killing any– and everyone around them to keep things quiet. Frank, two of *our* kind have been murdered, and they made a play for me. I can't help but take this one personally. I'm going to find Nathan Happa first and kill him." He started walking again. "Now you can go on with your ops, but I'm warning you, they *are* going to show up. And when they do, you got two options, either cooperate with them, or get greased and wind up like Corey and Melton."

"That's not all the options I have."

"Oh yeah?"

He patted the big .357 Smith & Wesson Magnum under his coat. Frank Delgado gave Sunny a rare smile. "So what are your plans? I had a secure contact in the FAA run some private jet flight plans coming out of Zurich. One had a destination to New Delhi, India."

"Yeah? When did it arrive?"

"A few days ago. I got my FAA man tracking it."

"It could be Happa. How about security cameras that might've gotten shots of the passengers?"

"Still workin' on it. So what're your plans?"

"It's best that I keep them to myself for now. I'll be

contacting you in the usual ways." Sunny looked around, trying to find the right words. "Look, I'm sorry that things got so out of hand between you and me. I just got tired of all the blood being spilled."

Delgado reached into his coat. "Here." He handed Sunny a small plastic case.

Sunny opened it and found a hypodermic needle and a small vial of clear fluid.

"It's the antitoxin you asked for." Delgado looked at the case. "From what the liaison from the CDC told me, you just fill it up and ram it home in your gut. Use it right when you've been dosed, or at least one hour before." He handed Sunny a familiar little black package.

"Thanks," Sunny said. "Let's hope that Happa doesn't like to change his poisons." He would make good use of the antitoxin if he had to, and the other package. The other package contained a vial of Ditran; the CIA's own version of zombie juice.

"Where are you headed?"

"I can't tell you. You watch your back, okay?" He passed a 3.5-inch disk to Delgado.

"I'll say the same to you. Just keep me informed of your progress." Delgado pocketed it.

The disk was a series of random pictures. Contained in the pictures was a program to encrypt messages too small to detect. Wherever Sunny was in the world he could send Delgado a picture with a secret encrypted e-mail message forwarded through a third party. Only the other person could descramble the message. "Sunny, be careful."

"I know, Frank, and I'm grateful for all the help you've given me." He took a step closer. "Don't get turned by these bad guys, Frank. I'd hate to have to kill you too."

Delgado stayed cool. "Sunny, don't you know? There aren't any bad guys, just good crooks and bad crooks. Remember, I'm no *bow tie* guy. If they were to turn me, you'd never see me coming." He held out his hand. "Good luck."

They grasped hands.

"I'll remember that."

THE FLIGHT TO HAWAII WAS UNEVENTFUL. SO WAS THE DI-rect flight to Manila. Sunny had plenty of time to read and study the material on the *aswang* and Aghoris of the Far East. He made notes on similarities in their myths and rituals.

Pan had schooled him and Delgado showed him the road. It was a path he had never even thought of traveling. This was the twenty-first century. There were no magic spells and wizards. But here he was reading papers and articles on superstitions others took for reality. He read on, looking for the key question. *How do you kill a sorcerer?*

Clearing customs and the change to the plane bound for the Visayan Islands went quickly. He never had to leave the terminal. Two hours later he had landed at a city called Cebu, near his destination.

It was hot, Hot, HOT! Sunny shielded his eyes from the blazing Philippine sun. It was pure chaos as he stepped from the passenger terminal. Horns blared. Brakes squealed and everyone spoke at a yell. "Oh my God, nothing's changed." Although Sunny had never been to Visaya, he'd done some military time on the Island of Luzon almost twenty years ago. It was crazy back then and it was chaos now. It was as if time had frozen and all the same old hustles still applied.

He stood head and shoulders above the crowd, making him an obvious mark for anyone on the make. He put his wallet in his front pocket and began to wade through the press of tightly packed bodies.

There were several modes of transportation. Jeepnies were handmade replicas of World War II jeeps. The bed of the jeep was extended to carry no fewer than a hundred people, or so it looked. Long Rabbit and Victory busses owned the road. Zipping in between all the traffic were the ubiquitous trikes. Trikes were small Japanese motor-cycles with covered side carriages. Like the Jeepnies, they all were colorful individual expressions of the Filipino people and their extended beliefs.

A trike pulled up in front of him. A Filipino boy grinned. "Ride, parre? I take you for number one blow jobs. You want for weed? I got *good* smoke. You want to change your money to pesos? I got good rate, best rate. We go play cards. You gamble? You like to play cards, parre?"

The boy rocked back and almost fell as another trike pulled up and bumped him hard.

"Hey, you get the fuck outta here!"

Sunny watched with amusement as the new driver crowded out the first driver.

He had a very nice trike, green and black with lots of chrome. The cart bench was made of overstuffed leather. A Bruce Lee picture wearing a black mask glared at the world from the nose of the cart.

The trike driver jutted his chin toward the departing driver. "He get you in trouble. If you want trouble, I call him back."

"No, no, that's all right. And who are you?"

He beamed a perfect white smile. "Ruping Abenales. I'm one of the good guys."

"How old are you, Ruping?"

"Twenty-two."

"So, you say that you're one of the good guys?"

Ruping then smiled shyly and nodded.

"Do you know a guy named Iblas Osoy?"

Ruping's eyes flew wide open. He crossed himself. "You crazy, man? You don't want to see the guy. Girls, yeah, I know them all. Good girls. Clean girls. No VD. No AIDS. I take you to see them, not *him*."

"Why not?"

Ruping looked around, frowning, trying to put the right words together, then his eyes lit up and he squinted. "He one real bad motherfucker."

Sunny started laughing. "Yeah, then that's the guy I'm looking for. You afraid of him?"

Ruping nodded vigorously and suddenly looked as if he wanted to leave. "Parre, I think maybe I call back the other trike driver."

"Osoy's an *aswang*, isn't he?"

"How you know? You not one, are you? A *white aswang*."

Sunny laughed again. "Oh no, not me, Ruping. As a matter of fact, is there anyone here who is against our boy Osoy?"

Ruping nodded. "Oh sure, Father Reynaldo."

"Then he's the guy I want to see first. By the way, what are you doing for the next few days? I'm looking for a good-guy driver and good hotel."

Ruping suddenly snapped to attention and saluted. "That's me, parre."

FATHER REYNALDO WAS MUCH YOUNGER THAN SUNNY expected and was astonished when Sunny said he was going to see Osoy. The little priest was intimidated by Sunny's size and manner.

"Look, Father, I'm not going there to do or learn evil deeds—the exact opposite. I need to know a lot more about this guy so I don't get hurt."

"You should not go see him. He *is* the devil. What do you want with a man like that?"

Sunny put his hand on the man's shoulder. "That is my business. Look, Father, I'm going anyway. I want to know what to look out for." He squeezed the shoulder until the priest winced. "So are you going to help me or not?"

THEY PULLED IN FRONT OF AN ANCIENT-LOOKING AND rickety three-story building. Sunny got out of the trike and walked toward the building. A guard stood up and walked toward him. He carried a machine gun that

Sunny couldn't identify. He wore a threadbare green uniform and wore flip-flops. There was no read behind his knockoff Ray-Bans.

"Iblas Osoy?"

The guard stepped back and looked Sunny up, then down. He twitched his head and turned his back on Sunny. Up three flights of rickety mahogany stairs and Sunny found himself in a long line of people waiting their turn to be called behind a solid metal door. Sunny was reminded of the reinforced crack doors drug dealers used in some of the New York tenements.

The guard motioned Sunny to an empty seat near the door, then he scratched on the door and went in.

The Filipinos waiting on line gave Sunny curious looks, some looked hostile—they didn't like foreigners jumping line. The door opened and the guard did an underhand motion to Sunny.

The room Sunny entered was very small, tiny. It was also dark and smoky. The walls were made of dark mahogany plywood. A shabby black-and-rust steel desk took up most of the room. On the desk was a little lamp that offered the only light in the room. The light highlighted a large silhouette of a man behind the desk. The silhouette hung up the phone and turned around in his chair.

Osoy was morbidly obese. The smoke coming from the stubby cigar in his mouth made him continually squint. But while he was as heavy as a person could possibly be, he was immaculately dressed. A cocked .45-caliber Colt lay to the side of his desk. Sunny knew better than to go with a first impression. Osoy's eyes were quick, taking in every move Sunny made—and looking steps ahead. The guy had probably been a professional sumo wrestler at some time in his life.

The Ray-Ban guard sat on a small stool behind the empty plastic chair in front of the desk. He casually propped his weapon in his lap, muzzle of his weapon pointed toward the plastic chair.

A poster of the Virgin Mary was tacked to the warped wall behind the giant.

There was an odd and strange resemblance to Happa in his manner and bearing. It was like he carried a certain amount of aristocracy.

"My name is Steve Marks." Sunny reached out his left hand.

Osoy's grip was weak and soft. His veiled, coal-black eyes revealed nothing. He sat on a dais so that he could look down on everyone. He held private court. "Sit."

"I bring you a gift." Sunny put a bottle of Johnnie Walker Black Label on the table. A business card lay in front of it.

Osoy grinned wide. All his teeth were capped in silver.

The guard got out of his chair, then reached over Sunny and took the card and handed it to Osoy. He then picked up the bottle and opened it. Pouring a little of the whiskey into a shot glass, he swallowed. He gasped, choked a little, then smiled.

"*Oh-oh. Masarap.*"

Osoy, still grinning, opened up the drawer in front of him and pulled out an ivory-looking bowl. He held it in his left hand the same way Happa did.

Sunny felt his scalp crawl.

The guard poured a healthy splash into the bowl and Osoy gulped it down. He held the cup out for more, then offered it to Sunny.

Sunny smiled and pulled out his own small ivory cup. "My traveling cup."

Osoy nodded with satisfaction, and the guard filled Sunny's cup.

"To your health." Sunny sipped his drink.

Osoy read the business card. "What brings you here to my table from so far away, Mr. Marx?"

"Mr. Osoy, I deal in information and goods of all kinds. I'm on my way to somewhere nearby and I've made a side stop especially to meet you."

"I myself deal in information, among other things."

Sunny sipped at his drink. "I hear that you are looking for a man."

"Oh, I am? Just who is it I am looking for?"

"He escaped from your power about five years ago."

Osoy's eyes flashed for just a fraction of a second. It was enough to put Sunny on alert.

"I've been told that you will give much to recapture this man."

"You seem to know much about my affairs. Tell me, Mr. Marx, how is it that you know these things?"

"Those who walk similar paths hear the same sounds and see the same signs."

"And what path is that?"

"Why, *don* Osoy, the left-handed one, of course."

"Yes, that is correct." He had already gone through a few cups of whiskey and was becoming more gregarious. "It is not an easy thing to administer these barrios and stay true to the old ways."

Sunny nodded sympathetically.

"There are those who do not understand the balance, or oneness of interest."

Sunny froze. Pan's caution returned: *He will lie to you and tell you the truth at the same time.* He just knowingly smiled and stood to leave. "*Don* Osoy, I can see that you are busy. I'll be here for another day. I apologize. In oneness of interest, I may have misread the signs."

Osoy held up his hand. "No, Mr. Marx, you may be reading them right, which makes me *very* interested in how you came to know these things. Do you have any proof of this man you say that I am after?"

Without saying a word Sunny reached into his back pocket and pulled out a Polaroid picture. He leaned over the desk and flashed it like a badge in front of Osoy's face. He quickly put the picture back in his pocket.

Osoy's eyes became narrow and intense. His chair moaned and screamed under the weight as he moved to shift his fat to the edge of his chair. "May I see that picture again?"

Sunny shook his head. "We talk first."

Osoy oozed back onto his chair. "Mr. Marx, there's nothing I would rather do than talk with you, but as you can see many are waiting for me. I am having a little gathering at my home tonight. You *must* come. I will send my car for you."

"I have my own transportation, thanks."

"Everyone knows where I live. There we can talk in private."

"That sounds fine with me. What time?"

"Anytime after the sun goes down."

They shook left hands and this time Osoy's grip was just a little firmer. He leaned closer and smiled. Sunny could see the teeth better. They were all capped to fine sharp points.

THE RIDE THROUGH THE PHILIPPINE COUNTRYSIDE AT sunset was beautiful. It looked just like a Vietnam-era war movie. Ruping looked nervous as he pulled up to an old, huge mansion to drop off Sunny. The young man couldn't get a gun so he lent Sunny his butterfly knife instead. It was fast-opening and sharp. Sunny could only hope that he wouldn't need it. Maybe he could actually negotiate with Osoy.

Osoy lived like a potentate. In a country of the haves and have-nots, Osoy was a big-time have. Beautifully dressed men and women strolled around as servants circulated with trays full of every delight.

In no time several exotic raven-haired beauties surrounded him. These were world-class gorgeous women. They spoke perfect English and soon Sunny felt like he was the only man in the world. He let them lead him to a huge veranda overlooking a courtyard. He sat on a couch among four women who gave him their full attention. Even though they pampered him, he was careful to not eat or drink anything that they put in front of him.

Instead, he pleaded a restricted diet and drank from his own flask.

The guard wearing the dark-mirrored glasses suddenly appeared in the hallway. He sneered at Sunny and motioned with his machine gun to follow. Reluctantly Sunny got up and left the glamorous harem.

In the dark study Sunny held out the Polaroid picture of Pan across the table.

In seconds Osoy's face went through several stages of anger, finally settling on smoldering. "How did you get this picture?"

"I took it."

"And, Mr. Marx, where is this man now?" His voice trembled as he spoke.

Sunny smiled and crossed his arms. "Mr. Osoy, we may be believers in the old ways, but first we negotiate. The picture ain't free." Sunny knew that the man could call on his armed goons at any time. He had to trust that Osoy's desire to locate Pan outweighed his desire to do him harm at the moment.

Suddenly two skinny men armed with machine guns stepped out of the shadows.

"Are you having a nice time here, Mr. Marx? Don't you find our women, food, or drink desirable?"

"Very much. If I had more time, I'm sure I would have found their company enjoyable."

"You leave too soon. We must now finish our negotiations."

"Go ahead, you got the ball in your court."

"Do you know the name of this man in your picture?"

"He goes by the name of Norbig Albing," Sunny lied.

"What do you want for the location of this man?"

Go for it. "The name and location of a white Aghori I know by the name of Nathan Happa."

Osoy held out his hands. "How would I know this thing?"

"Well, then I guess I'm at the wrong place."

"Mr. Marx, before we go any farther, I must insist on knowing who your master is."

"There is none." *Play it straight.* "Look, pal, I said all that mystical bullshit to get me right here; so no more games. Now do you want this guy or not? Because I'm outta here if you're not going to deal with me." Sunny stood up ready for a fight. "The name and location of a white Aghori."

"You know that he is a man who does not exist."

"He doesn't?"

The Ray-Ban guard pointed the barrel of his weapon at Sunny.

"Now give me the picture. Take it out of your coat, slowly."

Sunny reached into his pocket and took out the picture but held on to it.

Osoy looked exasperated. "The guru of the white Aghori is in the Uttar Pradesh province of India. Now let me see the picture!" He held out his left hand.

Sunny put the picture facedown on the table and slowly pushed it with his fingertips toward Osoy's greedy hands, then turned it over. Sunny saw a look in Osoy's eyes the moment he saw the face on the picture. The same look was on Nathan Happa's face when he had him as a sacrifice victim.

From the corner of his eye Sunny caught a blowpipe being raised.

From nowhere a butterfly knife appeared and was jammed through Osoy's hand, pinning it to the mahogany desk. Sunny then rolled across the table and kicked the barrel of the gun as it went off. Osoy's screams could be heard above the roar of the machine gun. Sunny directed the muzzle flash to the other guard with the blowpipe and blew his head off.

Struggling to keep the barrel off him, Sunny tried to pick up the .45 on the table but missed, instead sending it skidding off the desk. There was more deafening gunfire. The barrel burned his hand but he would not let go.

The guard was off-balance. One hand on the guard's

throat and the other trying to get ahold of the gun, they teetered back and forth. In one move, Sunny let go of the man's throat and beat Osoy's grab for the knife pinning his hand. Then Sunny pulled out the knife and plunged it up to the hilt through the glasses and into the guard's brain.

Sunny suddenly felt himself propelled through the air and was slammed against the far wall. He wasn't sure if it was his bones or the wall cracking that he heard. He was being crushed. He couldn't breathe as he faced the wall. He was held fast in Osoy's bear hug. He was amazingly strong for a fat man.

Osoy's putrid breath was in his ear. He was saying something and snapping his silver-pointed teeth. He was saying an incantation of some sort while trying to get a bite. Trying to look over his shoulder, Sunny moved his head away every time Osoy bit for his throat.

Wrapped in the anaconda embrace, Sunny was starting to lose consciousness. Then the tension slipped for an instant, allowing Sunny to get a lifesaving gasp of air, then Osoy slipped again. Sunny wiggled his head free and he was able to get a look behind him. The pistol was on the floor, and with Osoy's full weight and girth pinning him to the wall there was no way he could get to it.

Sunny looked down at Osoy's hands. He couldn't get a good grasp anymore because of his bleeding hand. Sunny was able to work his elbow down to the wounded hand and started banging it.

Osoy howled in rage, almost deafening Sunny.

It felt like eternity, but Sunny finally worked his way around to face Osoy.

Sunny jammed his thumb into Osoy's left eye socket. Osoy screamed and released his grip. In that instant Sunny brought up his left hand and speared Osoy through the throat. The moment the fight went out of Osoy, Sunny gripped his head and, with all his might, twisted Osoy's head around until he heard it snap.

Osoy fell to the ground gasping and spitting up

blood. His body writhed spastically on the ground. It was over.

Sunny checked himself and found he was none the worse for the fight—bruises maybe.

It was silent. Sunny threw back the barrier of the rusted steel door. He opened it wide then threw out the bodies of the two guards. "Iblas Osoy is fucking dead! I jinxed him. I killed him and I will kill anyone pointing any goddamned thing at me when I come out this door."

He cautiously stepped through the door. He saw everyone rooted to where they stood, eyes wide and jaws open. Not a sound could be heard. Even the night creatures were silent. "Ruping!"

Ruping came crashing through the courtyard on his trike. "Right here, parre." He jumped off the bike and stood in front of Sunny like a soldier.

"You know how to shoot this thing?"

Ruping nodded.

"Here." He handed Ruping the handmade Filipino machine gun. "Shoot the first fucker that moves," he said loud enough for everyone to hear.

Sunny went back into Osoy's office and, with a ton of effort, stripped the body naked, then pulled his body out of the room and into the center courtyard.

Gasps and screams could be heard.

Ruping fired a burst from the machine gun into the air. No one spoke.

Sunny walked over to the dead guard with glasses and pulled out the butterfly knife sticking from his eye. He walked back to Osoy's body and took the hand he'd stabbed. Body facing down and palms facing up, Sunny stuck the knife back through the left hand and into the dirt.

"You got another butterfly knife?"

Without taking his eyes from the crowd, Ruping reached into his back pocket with his left hand, pulled out a knife, and flipped it open.

Sunny took it and stretched out Osoy's right hand away from his body. Holding the knife high over his head he punched it through Osoy's hand and staked it to the dirt.

Sunny stood back and admired his work. The gross, naked body of Iblas Osoy lay in the dirt butt up, with his head looking backward to God for mercy. Blood oozed from his wounds.

"The question I had coming into this thing was how you kill a sorcerer." Sunny turned to face the crowd. They were in almost every stage of shock. He turned back to Osoy's body and looked on with satisfaction; the priest had not lied. "*That*, my friends, is how you kill one. But wait!" An inspiration hit him.

He ran back into the room and came out with the bottle of Johnnie Walker Black Label. He poured the rest of the contents over the body, then lit it. The body burst into flames. "See, that's even better." He faced the crowd. "Now, who's next?"

The Catholic priest had given him the ritual, but Mossad taught him how to get the most dramatic effect. "Now get outta here!"

Ruping fired the weapon into the air.

Screaming and pandemonium filled the air as everyone raced to get away from the crazy white man. It was a stampede to get out. No one wanted to be caught by the wrath of a maniac. In seconds Sunny and Ruping were alone.

"Ruping, I hate to ask any more of you, but can you cover for me while I look around?"

Relaxed and even smiling a little, Ruping nodded.

"From the long ride out here, I don't think we'll be seeing the authorities very soon. If I hear any gunfire, that will be my exit cue."

Sunny went back into Osoy's study, opened drawers and rummaged through papers, and looked behind anything that might hide something or hold any significance. Knocking on the walls in Osoy's office he wasn't surprised to hear a hollow sound from the wall behind his desk.

A flimsy latch held a spring-loaded panel. It released

and the panel opened, revealing a short staircase leading to an entire underground wing. Sunny quickly walked back into the courtyard and took the machine gun off the second dead guard and went to explore the hidden vault.

The moment he stepped into the wing and saw an iron cage he shuddered; this was where Pan had been held captive. He was in a temple or some such thing. The cage looked as if it were ready for him. Sunny's heart froze. It looked just like something out of the Dark Ages. It stood about four feet high and was a couple of feet wide. It hung from the ceiling by a heavy chain. It was empty and Sunny had no doubt who the next occupant was to be.

There was a white altar at the far end of the room. Sunny had no desire to go poking around there but felt compelled to. It looked to be a replica of the sort that the Catholics would use. Instead of a cross, upside down or otherwise, there was a small gold triangle at the center of the altar sitting on a red cinnabar case. Dried blood was caked all over the white marble. Inside the red case was a crystal dagger—a tool of the trade.

A small room off to the side with the door opened caught his eye. A small writing desk and chair occupied the room. Opening the drawer he saw a stack of envelopes.

The letters were in English. He scooped up the bundle and left the room, hurrying through the place of sacrifice and back out to the courtyard. "Ruping, do you know the town of Wright?"

"It's about twenty miles from here."

"Then let's get going." He took a last look at Osoy's body as he left.

THEY ARRIVED IN THE TOWN OF WRIGHT AND RUPING had to ask directions only once to the Jhandi home.

The house was the typical bamboo home. So close to the ocean, it was on stilts to withstand the seasonal floods that came with the monsoons. Sunny climbed the steps chopped from a mahogany tree.

There was no door. A kerosene lamp lit the floor. Several people were chattering at once.

Sunny knocked on the doorframe.

He did his best not to look too imposing to the little folk. "Hello, is Mr. Jhandi home?"

"Come in," said a man sitting on a woven palm mat. He was smoking a huge hand-rolled cigarette. "I am Jhandi."

Sunny stepped carefully into the room. The rattan flooring creaked and heaved under his weight. He worried that he would end up crashing through the floor.

Mr. Jhandi had the same exotic features of his son. Jet-black hair, he looked to be about twenty when in fact he had to be more like sixty. Sunny smiled and squatted as best he could. "I brought you something that you want to see." He pulled out the Polaroid picture from his jacket and passed it to the man.

Mr. Jhandi stared at the picture for what seemed an eternity, then his eyes welled up with tears. He passed the picture to his wife and soon the entire house was wailing. It was an eerie, mournful conjoining of voices.

"You don't understand," Sunny said, "he's *alive*."

Pan's father was quiet forever, then remorsefully said, "*Aswang* has his soul."

"*Really?*"

"Yes."

"Iblas Osoy?"

Everyone looked stunned. Some crossed themselves.

"Iblas Osoy is dead. The only soul he has now is his own, and it's in hell at this moment. I know because I put him there."

The house erupted in loud shouts of relief. Someone brought a flimsy rattan chair from the outside into the room for Sunny to sit on, which he politely refused.

"Is it true?" the little man asked. "Is he really dead?"

"The last time I saw him he was looking up to God for salvation because he sure didn't get it from me."

"And, *Pan?*"

He said his son's name with a reverence given only to the dead.

"He's fine. Just fine. He's free to come home whenever he wants, which should be soon."

Sunny left the barrio with people spreading the news of the witch's death faster than Ruping could drive. Scanning the letters, Sunny had learned of a post office box in India, Varanasi to be exact.

"Okay, Ruping, take me to the airport before anyone connects me to all this shit." Sunny was in a great mood. He left the village actually feeling good about killing someone. He felt as if he finally had done something good for a change.

They pulled up to the Cebu airport and Ruping shut off the engine.

"Ruping, my friend, how much do I owe you?"

Ruping smiled and crossed his arms. "I don't know, parre. Is a hundred dollars too much?"

"You know, there will be people who will know that you were with me. I'll be gone. It could go very bad for you in the worst possible way."

Ruping shook his head. "No. You not understand. Nobody can kill Iblas Osoy. *Nobody.* He hold evil power over the island." Ruping puffed up and stuck his right thumb to his chest. "*I* help you. You are killerman of evil. *I* am help you. Good people will keep me safe."

"Driving a trike? Ruping, a Rabbit bus would make short work of you."

Ruping looked wistful. "One day I will have my own Jeepnie. Then I will be a man."

Sunny grasped the young man's shoulder. "Ruping, you already *are* a man."

Ruping nodded. "Right, but with a Jeepnie I become an *eligible* one."

Sunny chuckled. "How much are they?"

"When I have three thousand dollars more I will have it."

Sunny pulled out his money belt and counted out a

wad of cash. "Here's four grand. You get that Jeepnie right now, today, and quit driving this death trap."

Ruping could barely breathe, holding the fortune in his hands. Sunny had to slap him on the back to keep him from going into shock.

"See. You really are a good guy."

Sunny waved his arms over his head. "Score one for the good guys!"

CHAPTER 20

THE RADIO WAS GONE. SO WAS THE MISSION COMpromised? Without a radio she couldn't let her handlers know that she had survived. It was her call. She would press on, but she would have to be creative and rely on her training and take what she could get. It was the hunger that she couldn't take. There were plenty of springs and a river from which she drank fresh water. But there was very little game in the German forest.

She shot a small boar in the head with her Luger. So deep in the forest she didn't take too many extra precautions other than hiding in a tree while it roasted over the fire. She could cover her food from any other animal that might have smelled the aroma.

No other predator came close. Eileen was famished. The pork was a succulent but tough and gamey delight. She took the stringy meat down to the bone and packed away what she could not finish in an old blouse. The meat would last a few days longer as she quietly followed the Weser River and made her way back to her German home.

She had decided to travel north toward the North Sea and get out somehow. But she had to stop first and see what had become of her relatives.

From an alleyway she reconnoitered the hometown of her German relatives—it was no longer a vibrant settlement. Where she once remembered the streets a fun and lively place to be, even in the winter, now they looked cold and very scary. People scurried from corner to corner like rats. The only people who walked tall were the Nazis in their striking uniforms. It was the first time she got a look at the enemy.

They had impressive black uniforms and acted like masters of the land. They walked their own land like the conquerors they were. The townsfolk, rather than embrace them as their own kindred, would stop on the street and let the Nazis pass, nodding and bowing like servants.

She watched and learned the fine nuances of the "commoner toady" given to the new masters of the world. She stepped into the street and walked a familiar route, being sure to bow and toady exactly the right way to any German in uniform she passed.

It was not that strange of a sensation to be looked through and not at—this was how her parents saw life. Where she had been afraid of discovery as a spy, she took comfort at suddenly being a nonperson. No one in training taught her how to be a nonperson. The funny thing was how easily she fell into the role—her parents had taught her well.

The house of her younger years looked cold. Windows were broken and all the curtains were drawn tight. The front door was locked. A notice on the door emboldened with the German swastika decreed that the home was now a property of the Third Reich. She knocked on the door and called out a few times before she thought about someone unwanted listening. She went around to the back of the house to a small garden. Everything was dead or overgrown. No one had tended

the garden in a long time. The house key was still under
the old green pot.

Eileen opened the back door and quietly stepped in.
The old house was silent and musty. Pistol drawn, she
went from room to room. Everything had been ransacked. Anything of value was gone.

Good and bad memories flashed in her mind. There
were the times of frolicking with her cousins, sitting in
the bedroom, giggling and talking of boys and future
plans. The country was still recovering from the last
war. No one could imagine then that another war would
tear their fantasies apart.

She remembered how her grandfather railed at the
New Germany and his worthless son, her father. Like
her father, he took out his impotencies and failures on
the rest of the family. She could never forget how one
day he took her on a short train ride to Bremen and put
her on a steamer to the United States. He told her that he
could no longer afford her in his family and her mother's
family refused even to see her—she wasn't *pure* Aryan.
She could cause serious problems for everyone by having been born in America. She never got to say good-bye
to her cousins or grandmother.

In the last room she searched she found her grandmother sitting next to a cold fireplace.

Eileen gasped and rushed over, thinking that she was
dead. She was lifeless but for a very faint wisp of a
breath.

"Grandmother," Eileen said as she gently but firmly
shook her grandmother's shoulder.

It seemed like forever before she slowly opened her
eyes. Her stare was vacant, unfocused, and listless. She
looked confused. "Ingrid? Is that you? How did you get
away? Did anyone else get away?"

She thought Eileen was her cousin.

"Grandmother, where is everyone?" She didn't want
to confuse her more so she said nothing about not being
her cousin.

"Gone." She closed her eyes and spoke softly. Her

voice was tired. She spoke to no one. It was more of a last confession than anything else. "They called themselves the Werewolves. They came in the night in closed trucks. First they came for the Jews. The mayor said that everything was all right. 'Hitler wants only the Jews,' he said. We heard the trucks every night. They would call out the names, people and families I knew. No one dared look out the windows. We closed our ears to screams and gunshots. They were always gone in the morning. We grew to fear the night.

"Then they came for the gypsies of the forest. They set starving wolves and mad dogs on those who tried to escape deeper into the forest. The mayor then said that our village was not pure."

Her sad, rheumy eyes looked up at Eileen, but she was not looking at her. "We were not racially pure. My mutti was from, from Slovakia. Then, in the night they came for my family."

"Where did they go?"

"To the labor camps."

Shocked to her core, Eileen stood and looked at the tiny old woman in the oversized chair. How long had she been like that? When was the last time she ate? She got a ripe whiff of her grandmother and realized that she must have been there for days.

The first thing was to get her grandmother warm and clean. Several trips to the almost depleted woodpile and a fire was roaring in the fireplace. Eileen didn't care who saw the smoke from the chimney; she had to save her grandmother.

After the water was warm she used a washcloth and soap to clean her, then put her into a warm nightgown. She put her on a mattress in front of the fire. Her grandmother's eyes remained vacant and dim—she was looking at another world.

There wasn't a scrap of food anywhere in the ransacked house. Going into the dark cellar she felt her way around, using a burning twig for light until she came to a far wall. Feeling around where uncle had shown her years ago, there was a kerosene lamp. She lit the lamp and pulled away one of the boards. Behind the board was a stash of supplies, dried ham, venison, and more. It was still there.

Eileen massaged her grandmother, trying to make her regain the present. But even through Eileen's insistence, she refused to eat.

"I will eat no more. The Nazis, they called me a 'useless eater.' They took my children and left me here to die. They will kill all who are not *pure*. They have destroyed my life." She grasped Eileen's wrist. "Ingrid, you cannot stay here. The Werewolves will come back and find you. You cannot stay!"

"No, I must stay to look after you," Eileen pleaded.

"No, *meinchen*, I will not be here much longer. I have nothing to live for."

"Grandmother, don't you say that." But she knew better. Her grandmother's breath had the smell of rotten decay. Things were already dead inside of her.

"You must flee deep into the forest." A small smile escaped her. "I told all the children stories of the evil forest to keep them away from the gypsies. But now the evil is in our homes. We opened the door and the vile evil walked right in and took my family away." She stared into the fire. "All gone. They are all gone. The forest. Go, go escape into the forest."

Exhausted, Eileen fell asleep where she lay.

Light from the windows played across Eileen's face. She woke up shivering. The fire was just dying embers.

She looked at her grandmother, who seemed sound asleep, but she knew better. Getting up from the floor, she touched the neck of the old woman to feel for a pulse but instead she felt cold, cold waxy skin.

Wrapped in a frayed quilt, Eileen dug a shallow grave and buried her grandmother in it. She didn't have a deep love for the old woman who had been strict with her as a very young child, even abusive. Eileen now had a better understanding of her own mother's cold and unfeeling nature.

Eileen wondered how her own mother would have reacted to her daughter's burying her grandmother. She had a feeling that her mother would have saved her own skin at the expense of her mother and just left her there. *Bitch*. Eileen felt that the simple act of burying the old woman made her the better person, yet the humane act seemed to further distance her from her parents' way of life. She threw the last shovelful of dirt on the grave and laid her grandmother's rosary on top of the mound. It was time to move on and try to make it out of Germany without being caught.

THE MOON WAS FULL BUT THE FOREST WAS AS BLACK and foreboding as the chilling tales she heard from her grandmother as a little girl. Very little light penetrated the ancient forest canopy. The only weapons she carried were a sharp kitchen knife and her gun. How she wished that she had had the suitcase radio. Then she could get some real help.

She thought of Sybil Leek, the young red-haired woman sitting at her station listening to the ethereal void for sounds of radio scatter and noise, trying to discern one sound that was a little different from the rest. The codes wouldn't be transmitted to her anytime soon, if they ever came at all.

The moon was waxing as she made her way along the animal trails that ran throughout the forest. She followed her compass to the northeast. There was no activity of any sort. It was as if the forest creatures had taken the hint and scurried for their deepest hiding holes. It became so quiet that each step she took announced to the Third Reich that a spy on the run was tramping through their forest. Then she heard the howling.

The sounds of the howling grew louder. But there were no wolves in the forest. They were killed years ago. Could they be wild dogs? Whatever they were, they were on her trail.

Panic seized Eileen and soon she ran blindly, ever

deeper into the forest. The sounds of baying wolves were just behind her, always growing louder. She caught glimpses of creatures darting through the trees. There was nothing that she could do but keep running for her life.

She broke into a wide glade. The moon was full. Behind her she could hear the wolves on her heels. They would take her out in the open. She stopped in the center of the glade.

She shot at the fleeting shadows and emptied her gun. *Damn!* She had nothing with which to fight back but a tiny kitchen knife. It would have to do. She crouched, holding her knife at the ready.

Three wraiths burst from the trees and raced in a straight line toward her. The first wolf leapt into the air and Eileen ducked, burying her knife in the belly of the animal, losing the knife. It yelped and dropped in death spasms on top of her as the second wolf crashed into them. They rolled onto the ground in a snarling bloody mess.

Eileen heard the sounds of more wolves in her ears and gunfire at the same moment. Yelps and snarls filled the air, then the howling faded away. What happened? She untangled herself from the dead animals and slowly stood, shaking. Covered with blood, she was grateful that none of the blood was hers.

"Halt. Don't move!" a voice in German ordered. "Hands high!"

A beam of light froze her like a rabbit. She threw her hands into the air. In moments men with rifles surrounded her.

"What are you doing out here, boy?" a gravelly voice asked. "These are dangerous woods. The wolves could have swallowed you whole. You have identity papers?"

From the moonlight she saw a big apparition dressed in rough-cut leathers. He looked like a German woodsman.

Her coat was ripped open and her empty pistol and identification papers fell to the ground. She was trussed with her arms bound behind her back. She wobbled in front of the giant woodsman. He tucked her gun, now his prize, into his belt.

"I see that you took on one of the wolves by yourself, little one. Very brave." He pulled off her hat and her auburn hair fell about her shoulders.

"Oh, it is a girl that killed the wolf." He looked at her papers. "What is a young woman doing out here this night, Ingrid Weiss?"

"Mein Herr, I was being chased by those animals until I became lost in these woods."

"Lost in the woods are you?" He bowed low until he was nose to nose with her. "You are more lost than you can even imagine." He stood. "You will come with us."

Hurting from the tight bonds and breathless, she asked, "Were those really wolves?"

"They were, but you might wish that they were the ones that got you instead of us."

Taken to an open-bed Ford truck, she was thrown in the rear and taken on a long and very uncomfortable ride. It was cold and her guards looked half-asleep. The bouncing helped keep her body moving while she worked on her restraints. She finally worked her bonds loose and was ready to drop them the moment an escape presented itself. The only problem with that was her gun was gone and her knife was stuck in a dead wolf.

It was almost morning before they reached an ancient-looking castle. Eileen was thirsty and hungry but knew food and water wouldn't be coming anytime soon. They stopped in the courtyard and she was dragged inside a large room. The hunter pushed her onto a chair in the corner of a room.

"Sit there. Shut up," he ordered. He marched to an immensely fat, bald man sleeping behind a desk. He kicked the desk, which made the man jump, then fall off of his chair.

Huffing and gasping, the bald man got to his feet. A huge ring of keys made him jangle as he shook with rage. He had murder in his eyes. "Vincent, this better be good."

The hunter pointed at Eileen. "We caught her in the woods. I want my bounty or I will take it directly to Keller, or even the baron himself. *Orders.*"

The fat man sneered at him through cracked and yellowed teeth. He picked up the phone on his desk, made a quick call, mumbled a few words, then hung up. "You get paid tomorrow. Now leave." He dismissed Vincent and leaned back into his straining wooden chair, propped up his black boots on the desk and then promptly fell asleep.

She sat quietly and listened to the conversation of the security guards who came and went. Guards were everywhere. A sprint from the room, through the courtyard and into the woods would only get her shot in the back. She judged that she was not in the company of friends of the Werewolves. She had to come up with something convincing so the story that she would give would be simple and true, up to a point. She was hiding from the Werewolves, who had taken the rest of her family to a forced labor camp.

It was some time before a man in an SS uniform walked into the room. Everyone stopped what they were doing and snapped to attention. Eileen heard plenty of heels clicking together but it was curious that no one flashed him the Nazi salute. The fat man fell out of his chair again, but this time he too stood at attention.

"Dick, I am very busy! Why did you call me here?"

"Herr Borz, the baron ordered me to call you anytime we caught anyone in the woods." He pointed at Eileen.

The man looked at Eileen and became furious. "I am looking for a spy, not a peasant girl!"

Eileen could see by his actions and manners that he was under the influence of something intoxicating; she would've guessed alcohol. Still, though the eyes were bloodshot, they were still sharp.

"But, Herr Borz," Dick whined, "the baron will not be back until tomorrow. His orders were the person in charge of the castle, *you*, will investigate *anyone* captured in these woods.

"Fool! I know what the orders are." Borz huffed and rolled his eyes, then pointed to an adjoining room. A guard raced to Eileen, grabbed her, and shoved her into the room.

Even though she had been through brutal interrogation during training, nothing prepared her for what she saw next. Fear ate at the pit of her stomach. The blood on the clamps and pinchers was real. The hooks and wires on the wall for holding bodies was real. This wasn't Hollywood; the red blood on the walls was genuine. She wanted to forget the whole assignment and flee, but there was no way out. She had never felt so alone. It seemed like forever before the door finally opened.

Borz wore an immaculate brown riding habit. His black riding boots were almost glowing. But he was sloppy, as if he had been up for a few days. He carried a riding crop in his right hand. He inspected her closely as if he was buying a car or stock animal. He took her palms and studied them intently. "You have survived the wolves, *meinchen*. One must be very clever to survive in these woods. Did you know that there was an English plane that was shot down a couple of nights ago not so far from here? The constabulary is out beating the countryside looking for a spy. There is a *big* reward for captured spies. So tell me, *meinchen*, what were you doing in my woods?"

"I, I was running away from the vans."

"Yes, I know all about the *vans*. Tell me more." He didn't add that he knew a top secret; the Ford vans were actually rolling carbon monoxide gas chambers.

Encouraged, Eileen told her cover story, adding the burial of her grandmother for window dressing and verification.

Borz listened as he shuffled and plodded around the room, lovingly touching and thumbing several torture implements as he moved. When she was done speaking he stood in front of her. Even though his hands were empty, the whole effect of the torture implements around him made her wince when he spoke.

"I do not believe that you are who we are looking for. So, why should I not turn you over to the Werewolves? There is a bounty on captured runaways."

Who was this man?

"They would enjoy having their way with you, then throwing your corpse to their pets. They do that a lot, and they still pay."

Eileen remained silent, shivering, then said, "I'm strong, a hard worker. I can be of use to you, mein Herr."

"Could you now? What can you do?"

"Anything you want."

"Stand."

She saw his face turn to potential lust. He felt her body. She couldn't stop shaking. His breath was fetid. Sharp and pointed, his teeth were almost fangs. His breath reeked of alcohol and cigar smoke.

Borz laughed. "You're only a small sack of bones." He circled her, then stumbled back and caught his left hand on a knife that was on a metal table. The sight of his own blood made him frantic. In a panic he grabbed at his hand and only made it worse.

Eileen dropped her bonds and wrapped one of the ropes around the left hand and tied it. Then she tore a shred that was once a right arm sleeve and wrapped it around his hand as a bandage.

Eyes wide in shock, he pulled his hand away from her and rushed to the door "Dick," he yelled, "call Dr. Grossman. *Macht schnell!*" Tears ran down his face.

Eileen almost laughed but knew better. She'd cut herself worse and dealt with it. Borz acted as if his life was in jeopardy.

A minute later a fat man wearing a white smock came into the room. He showed no deference or compassion to Borz. He just pulled out a syringe already filled with a clear liquid and injected it into Borz's arm. Grossman then quickly tied four stitches to bind the wound. Borz looked like he had undergone major surgery.

The heavyset doctor then faced Eileen. "Is she the one we caught?"

"Yes." Borz sniveled and wiped his nose.

Grossman looked at Eileen as if she were a dog. "Take off all your clothes, everything."

Eileen complied.

Grossman then gave her a cursory probing. Grabbing her arm he stuck a hypodermic needle into her and drew a vial of blood. He stood back and looked her up and down. "No," was all he said, then walked out of the horror chamber.

Borz walked back to Eileen and grabbed her chin very hard with his right hand. "You will never speak of this to anyone." He turned his back on her and nursed his wounded hand. "While it is a sacrilege to spill *my* blood, it is my duty to spill the impure blood." Borz looked back at Eileen. "Grossman does not need you. If your blood work is negative, then I do have needs for good workers in my castle. For what you did for me you will not die too soon. Will you be a good worker if I let you live, *meinchen?*"

Eileen nodded furiously trying to break his grip on her chin. "Oh yes, mein Herr!"

A vicious blow from the riding crop caught Eileen across her face. Stunned, she fell to the ground. Through her pain she heard his voice.

"*Meinchen,* you are here to serve me." He put his boot on her head. "*Me.* Not the fucking Nazis, not the Reich, and not Hitler. Me! And to me all that you are is a Slovakian bitch! Do you understand?"

Tears streaming, she nodded through the pain and humiliation.

"Good. Then you will live for today and serve the Order. Say it. 'I will serve Gruppenführer Joachim Borz, and the Golden Centurion Order until the day I die.' "

"I will serve Gruppenführer Joachim Borz, and the

Golden Centurion Order until the day I die." She grimaced.

"Stand." He kicked her clothes in her face. "Get dressed."

Eileen got to her feet and quickly dressed.

The door opened and a large matronly woman entered.

"Greta, take her. Grossman did not want her so now she is ours."

"Thank you, Gruppenführer Borz, you will not regret this. I promise." She groveled and kept her hand over her cheek and her head down as she followed the big woman from the room and deeper into the castle.

CHAPTER 21

COVERED BY A THICK BUSH IN A TRASH HEAP
Sunny had a good view overlooking the Asi
Ghat along the Ganges. It was sunset and he focused his binoculars on a naked man sitting in front of a
fire pit. The flames mesmerized the man. He had been
watching him for the past five days. If it weren't for the
rats and other vermin that scurried all around him, he
would've been captivated by the sky's spectacular twi-
lights of blues, reds, and violets.

It had been a thirteen-hour sleep on the Gulf Air flight
from Manila to the Indira Gandhi International Airport
in New Delhi. He had passed through India many times
and wasn't surprised to see that it hadn't changed much.
The air smelled of curry, burnt everything, clove cigarette smoke, and cow dung. Being homeless from the
filthy streets of Los Angeles, he felt right at home. From
the airport he took an air-conditioned bus to the center
of town.

Next he prowled the back stalls of Delhi until he
found a gun dealer. He bought a Smith & Wesson snub-

nosed .38 knockoff and fifty bullets. He also picked up a nice Pakistani stiletto with an ebony handle.

Then he found a sporting goods store and bought a sleeping bag and a backpack. He outfitted the kit with everything he could think of, a pair of binoculars, ready-to-eat food, and some basic first-aid items. The store's owner was only too happy to rent Sunny a Suzuki motorcycle for a month, paid in advance with American hundred-dollar bills.

As a matter of fact everything was paid in cash and the owner drew a detailed map for Sunny on how to get to Varanasi. It was southeast of New Delhi. The proprietor said Sunny would probably have to stop overnight in Agra before reaching his destination. He gave Sunny a sly grin. "But there are many prostitutes there to keep you warm at night."

The city streets were nuts, but the 200 cc bike responded fairly well and soon Sunny was out in the winding hills and mountains. As in the Philippines, Sunny was struck by the wild and beautiful nature of the land. What a pity it was that he was there because of what had gone before. Instead of some exciting mystic Eastern journey, he was there to uncover the roots of unholy black magic and hopefully end his association with Nathan Happa.

As with the cities, black plastic, lath, cardboard, and tin seemed to be the primary building materials used in the countryside, that and the tires to hold down the flimsy roofs. It was a dirt-poor country; still, it seemed as if most of the weak structures were topped with state-of-the-art satellite antennas.

He arrived in Varanasi, then rode a few miles out of the city, taking a deep turn into the jungle. Slowly following animal trails, he carefully hid the bike in the undergrowth and test-fired his weapon. It worked fine. He donned his backpack and hiked out of the jungle, catching the first bus back to the city.

Varanasi, Divine Light, the city of the Lord Shiva,

was estimated at somewhere between two and three million inhabitants. And every one of them seemed to be on the street at the same time. They were on foot and anything else that rolled, or didn't. It was a sea of Indian people swarming and seething to an ebb and flow just trying to pass one another.

And it was unbelievably, almost painfully loud.

Mixed into the human zoo were cows and water buffaloes wandering freely among the streets and stalls.

Claustrophobic, Sunny had to get out of there. He jumped onto an empty rickshaw and held up a twenty-dollar bill and the post office box address. "You know this place?"

The driver nodded.

"Well then this is yours if you get me the hell outta here and quick!"

How the man did it looked impossible but it seemed as if in no time he had pedaled them to the less crowded side streets. The man spoke broken English and seemed to go on automatic narration, probably wanting to justify his overpaid fare. He called out major temples and their ashrams as they rode past street after street of endless ancient Indian architecture. He pointed out the "ghats," or crematory grounds.

Varanasi, also called Benares, was where Hindus hoped to die. To have your ashes scattered in the Ganges after burning on the west bank ghats meant the soul did not have to endure more reincarnations.

They stopped near a procession carrying several bodies wrapped in yellows and reds on bamboo litters.

"*Ram nam sach hai!*" they chanted.

"God is truth." The driver interpreted. "We near the House of the Dying," he said through cracked and black-stained teeth.

They wound up in front of the Central Hindu College, just a stone's throw from the sacred Ganges River. He paid the rickshaw driver, who offered to sell him some hash. Sunny politely turned down the offer and made his way toward the post office the driver had pointed out.

There were other white people who were on foot and carrying backpacks. He aroused no particular suspicious or hostile looks—another white foreigner looking for spiritual enlightenment. He bopped around and took in the lay of the area.

After a while he sauntered past the post office. Yep, it was the same post office that Osoy's letters were postmarked from. He wandered around the post office until he saw the box number behind the counter. His first thought was to set up surveillance on the box, but that would be almost impossible. He always sucked at static surveillance. He was just too damn tall. An idea hit him.

He bought the biggest envelope he could find and put a few rupees in it. He then sealed it and wrote the box numbers in big, bold letters. He placed the postage, then dropped it in the mailbox and left the building.

Sunny would discreetly watch the post office in the daytime and find somewhere to sleep at night. Up the street he could almost see a direct line to the river and was drawn to the smoke coming from it.

Along the west bank were stone steps and platforms leading into the Ganges. This particular spot looked to be a minor ghat compared to other major setups along the river. Stacks and piles of wood, sandalwood as his driver had pointed out, were either waiting to be sold or being stacked for a cremation.

The man looked like a genuine Aghori. But that was hard to tell at first glance. There were countless thousands of "holy men" who roamed India ready and willing to dispense the wisdom of a con man in search of an easy mark. This one remained where he was and carried a human skull for a bowl. It was a good sign.

There was a bend in the river that overlooked the town. A small tributary emptied into the Ganges. A forest of trash covered the bend. Things were looking good. He had nothing to lose and if he could figure out the habits of these people, he might be able to have an edge next time Happa showed.

There were plenty of people willing to talk for a few rupees. Sunny knew the trail was hot when someone mentioned the "white Aghori" with reverence. Further investigation, and more rupees, and Sunny was almost certain it was Happa. The name Baba Ero came up several times also.

The mention of the white Aghori also made some people angry and frightened. One snack vendor didn't need any prompting or money to tell his story. His accent was thick so it was hard to piece together the whole tale.

The white Aghori and Baba Ero came to Varanasi five short years ago. Then people started to disappear but the more people inquired, the more people went missing, but with the disappearances came much money and prosperity. The people still disappeared, but those left behind were consoled by anonymous gifts of washing machines, sewing machines, and home entertainment systems.

The man's eyes began to mist. "I tell you this for true. My own son, but nine years old, was one of the first to disappear, then, my wife for asking of his whereabouts. Suddenly there was an opening in the street vendor guild and here I am. If I ask any more questions, I too will be gone. Then who will take care of my six remaining children?"

"And how did they vanish?"

"I will not say!" He stopped himself from saying any further. "You have tricked me. I have said too much. You must go."

Sunny didn't need to be told twice.

That was five days ago. Nothing had turned up at the post office during the day, but watching the Baba Ero was an education in death. From his concealment he could also see a little into the town.

He couldn't guess the age of the thin man covered in gray by the ashes of the dead. Quietly asking around, he learned the man's name was Baba Ero, and yes, he was an Aghori. He stayed in the same ghat that the white Aghori once stayed.

The man had made his own spot on the grounds in front of a fire pit. He kept it lit by using the wood from the cremation pits. His entire substance came from what people would put in his skull bowl.

During various times of the evening men and women would stop by and drop something into his bowl, then chat, have him do a quick divining session, and leave. Other times holy men types came and went also. They always bowed to him first.

At night he would drink whiskey, smoke hash, and either go bonkers or do religious rituals. It was hard to tell which was which.

In the morning he would bathe in the icy river and go through prayer and yoga rituals for most of the morning. Sunny could see Baba Ero's lips move, but he could not hear the words he spoke when he did his water ablutions.

The second morning Baba Ero spotted a body floating in the river. He swam out to it and pulled it onto the shore. He closely inspected it, smelled it, then went back to his pit and got a knife. Coming back to the body, he made a cut in the throat, then smelled it. A look of disgust crossed his face, then he dragged the body back into the river until the river current took it away. He continued with his hour-long ritual in the icy water. He might have been cold, but at least he was clean.

Sunny scratched at his growing beard and wondered about calling the watch off and just getting a hotel room *with* a bath. He wondered about his own wisdom in using a disease-infested trash heap as a surveillance base. Something would have to break soon, or he'd just scrub the recon before he dropped dead from something like the plague.

A group of men entering the ghat with a cartful of sandalwood caught Sunny's attention. In a matter of moments they had built a funeral pyre. Then a large group of men, women, and children began gathering near the pyre. Someone placed a bottle of Jack Daniel's, bananas, and a guava into the Baba Ero's bowl. Sunny felt his stomach stir; he was almost out of food. Baba Ero seemed oblivious to everyone as he sat cross-legged with his eyes closed.

Sunset turned into a wash of purples and reds. A long procession came carrying a body completely wrapped in red linen. Other holy men supervised and orchestrated an elaborate to-do by attending the body with flowers and chants.

Baba Ero opened his eyes and began to stir. He opened the bottle of whiskey and took a long drink, then leisurely ate the fruits all while watching the cremation activities. When the ceremony looked to be nearing a climax, he got up and walked over to the corpse.

Oblivious and heedless of anyone around, he unwrapped the linen and stood over the face.

Sunny could see that it was the face of a young woman.

Baba Ero leaned over and removed the simple shell necklace that she wore. He put it on. Getting close to her face he whispered into her ear, then kissed her. It wasn't a quick kiss, but a long and passionate one.

Sunny suddenly wasn't hungry any longer.

Baba Ero walked away and the body was lifted onto the pyre.

From his fire pit he then took a burning torch, circled the pyre several times, then lit the sandalwood. Baba Ero sat crossed-legged in front of the roaring flames and chanted weird noises.

The small gathering began to sing, but Sunny wasn't sure if it was singing; he wasn't sure of anything. He had never witnessed anything like it.

The heat was at its apex and the pyre collapsed, the body falling to the center. There was a hissing pop. And as if on cue, Baba Ero got to his feet and three other men began using wood to clear a path to the body.

With a deft movement Baba Ero pulled out a handful

of the brain. He jumped from the fire and tossed the brain matter from hand to hand until it was cool. Then he ate it.

That night Baba Ero could be heard for miles as he made strange howling noises. Sunny could hardly sleep and found himself itching, scratching, and slapping at real and imagined tormentors. Whether or not if anything happened he vowed he would terminate the watch the next morning.

That morning Baba Ero was going through his usual rituals when a well-dressed man walked onto the grounds. Baba Ero stopped what he was doing and rushed to him. He fell at the man's feet and kissed them.

Sunny studied the man from head to toe. He held a stack of letters in his hand. At the top was one big letter with oversized writing. An ebony-skinned boy held a red umbrella over the man to shade him from the sun.

The man put his hand on Baba Ero's head and kept it there as he bent over and whispered into his ear. Baba Ero shook uncontrollably until the man slapped him and rebuked him, then left.

Sunny was on the streets and waiting for the man with the big envelope and his umbrella bearer. He recalled every technique he'd been taught for a big guy to conduct a foot surveillance, but nowhere did his trainers explain how a white Gulliver could attain stealth among dark-skinned Lilliputians. Sunny used cows, busses, huge movie billboards, and anything else he could to keep the red umbrella in sight without being seen himself. He felt that at any moment he was going to be jumped by Happa's people.

From what he observed, the man was immensely popular. He made what seemed a million stops at shops and stores. The stores' owners all happily dropped coins and notes into the umbrella bearer's purple-and-red sack. They would sometimes give the man fruits to eat or something to drink. He never shared anything with the umbrella bearer. No one acted as if the boy even existed.

Even though they looked like happy and cheerful scenes, Sunny knew a shakedown when he saw one; but that was no concern of his.

It was well into the night before Sunny saw the man finally stopped in front of a light blue two-story building. A little door cut into the entryway opened and several people came rushing out. A stool was placed for him to sit on.

Sunny took refuge in a spice store that had heaps of different-colored spices piled on rattan mats and wooden bowls. Sunny could see the man resting under an umbrella that the kid still held over him.

He was given something to drink and the little umbrella bearer passed the almost full sack to a beefy servant wearing a Sikh turban. Closing his eyes, the man nodded and was swamped by people on the street waiting for a chance to consult with him. Sunny was reminded of the line of people in the Philippines waiting to meet with Osoy.

Discreetly inquiring of the spice store's owner, he learned that the man's name was Kina Baba. He was one of the Varanasi magicians. The man whispered many other things that Sunny did not understand and knew better than to ask any more questions.

He stood in front of Kina Baba's small home, which was next to a smaller ashram, which was next to a giant temple. Across the street was an open market. Behind that were ramshackle hovels, but a few had a second story. Those were worth investigating. But before he set up another surveillance spot he would get something to eat, then find a place to clean up. Worst case he would bathe in the Ganges to get the grime off. From a trash heap to rattrap, there was nothing like moving up in life.

SUNNY WOKE UP COUGHING. DAZED AND BLEARY-EYED, he'd forgotten how strong the mixtures of smells in the Indian air could be. He rolled over and picked up his binoculars. Slowly opening the frayed and colorless curtain, he focused on the temple's entrance.

He had been there for three days. The first hour of the watch proved fruitful. There were times of the day when the temple doors were left open and other times when the beefy Sikh acted as a door guard. Then only the select could now enter the temple.

A Citroën pulled up to the entrance and three men in suits got out.

One man leaned close to the Sikh, whispered something into his ear. The guard made a subtle motion on the table in front of him. The man made another and the guard stepped aside to let them pass.

"Damn," grumbled Sunny. "What was that all about?"

He'd been in the room for three days. The rubble and street dirt were lined with ramshackle brothels made mostly from plywood and chicken wire. A fly-infested, open-air market selling fruits, vegetables, and piles of curry and other spices was on the other side of the street.

By acting the foolish tourist, Sunny had been able to get close to the entrance of the temple before the guard pointed his AK-47 at him and shook his head. Looking around confused, he decided his best option was to stake out the comings and goings of the temple members before the guard chambered a round.

He'd have to crack the code, or move before someone started getting curious about a white foreigner staying in a second-story whorehouse without using its girls.

The temple was popular. Hundreds would arrive, stay five or six hours, then the place would empty. If he was going to make a try at getting in somehow, then he figured he would have to blend in with the crowd as an awestruck foreign devotee and try to slip in that way.

A tall man shuffling up the dusty street caught Sunny's attention. The ocher robes could not hide his white skin. He carried a half skull in one hand.

It was the bald-headed bodyguard that nailed it. He was dressed in a short-sleeved white shirt, black tie, black pants, and black shoes.

"Nathan Happa," Sunny gasped. Zooming in closer revealed a gray pallor on Nathan's skin. His hair was matted and he had painted his face with the high-caste ocher color the Hindu people wore. A few feet behind him the skinhead marched in dark sunglasses.

Sunny didn't realize that he had been gripping the binoculars so tight until he tried to refocus them as Happa reached the giant guard.

The guard jumped to his feet and prostrated himself in front of Nathan. Sunny watched as Happa drew a triangle in the sand with his bare foot. The guard rose to his knees and, without looking up, used his finger to draw an inverted triangle over the top of Happa's.

Stepping around the guard, Happa entered the temple while the guard obliterated the marks in the dirt.

Watching the act, Sunny didn't realize that he had been holding his breath. Happa *was* an Aghori, and from what he had just witnessed, a high-ranking one at that. Kina Baba had to be Happa's guru.

"Now what?"

He'd traveled halfway around the world in search of a man who had tried to kill him, and for what?

A primal emotion began to gnaw at his stomach. He could continue playing the game using spy craft methods and eventually unravel Happa's activities or go charging over there and put some lead into Happa.

"How do you kill a sorcerer?" He already knew. Sunny checked his gun for good operation, loaded five shots, and put the remaining bullets into his pocket.

Walking up the blazing hot and dusty street it felt as if he was in some sort of Indian Western movie. The Sikh guard looked lost in his own thoughts, sitting back in his plastic chair under the bright, frying sun. He looked up at Sunny's approach. The pistol whip caught him across the temple and he went flying over backward, out cold.

Sunny barged into the place ready to fire on anything that moved. Instead of a dark cavern like Osoy's, he found bright, whitewashed rooms with very surprised people.

Happa was engaged in some kind of prayer ritual.

"Nathan Happa! Hey, motherfucker," Sunny called out. "Where's my gun?"

The neo-Nazi stepped in front of Happa and fumbled for the gun underneath his shirt, but got his hand caught in his tie. Sunny fired his gun point-blank at the man, hitting him twice in the chest. He flew back, toppling Happa and scattering everyone into a hysterical panic.

Sunny then aimed for Happa, but Happa ducked behind a terrified woman, then into the crowd.

Happa was out a side door like a shot, with Sunny hot on his trail.

Sunny followed, heedless of the panic he'd caused. He chased Happa through a maze of yard-wide back alleys and through merchant's stalls, toppling merchandise and firing when he thought he had a target.

Nathan was fast, real fast. His long legs were outdistancing him from Sunny like those of a long-distance runner. A little farther and he would lose his quarry. Sunny gave it his all, refusing to slow down.

When Sunny was sure Happa was about to lose him, he abruptly tripped and Sunny saw his chance to get off another shot. He stopped, settled down, and took a careful aim at Happa. For one brief, triumphant moment he saw the look of pure terror on Happa's face when he realized that he was dead in Sunny's gunsight. The first shot was a miss fire. The second shot was rushed and the bullet pinged off the mud walls.

Happa got up and kept running.

Sunny stopped for a second where Happa fell. There was no blood but a small blue-and-black sack lay where Happa had fallen. He scooped it up and looked around. Happa was gone.

A white Toyota truck screeched to a stop and three white men armed with M-16s jumped from it. They were dressed just like the neo-Nazi he had shot.

Sunny rolled behind a flimsy fence. He'd really over-played his hand, missed killing Happa, and turned himself into some nutty white guy with a crappy gun about to get chased by heavily armed crazies with killing him on their minds. It was time to clear out of India before his description was posted throughout the country. "Next time, Nathan Happa. Next time."

He got up and sprinted back the way he had come. Now he was the one on the run, hounded by Happa's goons. They were easy to spot; they were all white. They stood out just as much as he did.

No matter where he ran they were still just behind him. Bullets whistled, snapped, and zipped around him. They were shooting, heedless of the innocent by-standers. Evading on instinct and adrenaline, he had time to think how it reminded him of when he was young living in Los Angeles on a busy Saturday night. He tried losing them in a railway station but once again it was his size that betrayed him.

There seemed to be no eluding the men and his snub-nosed pistol was useless. He ran until he found himself on a bridge spanning the river. From the other side of the bridge he could hear sirens. Things weren't looking good. There seemed to be only one way out.

Legs pumping and knees driving high, he cleared the bridge railing and jumped into the river. Hitting the water hard, he held his breath and swam with the current in the icy water, coming up for an instant to catch his breath after he was certain he was far enough down-stream. He cursed Nathan Happa and his own stupidity for winding up in a river again. But at least no one was after him, yet.

THE MOTORCYCLE WAS STILL IN ITS PLACE AND SUNNY was back on the road to Delhi. It was a brutal twenty-hour ride running full throttle like the devil was on his tail. He ditched the motorcycle in the airport parking lot and headed for the ticket counters to catch the first jet out of the country.

He bought a one-way first-class ticket to Bangkok and was waved through customs without a word or second look. From there he would change IDs again and make it back to New York. He'd missed a chance of taking out Nathan Happa, but he sure as hell made sure that Happa knew he needed to watch his back more carefully.

After takeoff, when the plane leveled out he stepped into the restroom. Sunny carefully opened the sack he took from Happa. There was a tin of hash and other powders of a dubious nature. He flushed the hash and white powder that looked and smelled like cocaine. He kept the tins for fingerprints.

He was about to discard a wadded up foil of gum, but opened it instead. Inside was a micro CD about a quarter inch in diameter. What kind of machine could read it? Who could read it?

Closer inspection revealed that rather than reflect light it sort of *glowed*. Whatever it was, it had the qualities of something from another planet. "Why did Happa choose the skull over something like this?" It was beyond Sunny. Maybe he was too stoned to figure out what to grab. That, or the skull bowl had a significance of its own. Whatever his choice, one thing was for sure; the sucker could run.

Sunny felt a fleeting sense of satisfaction when he remembered the fear Nathan Happa had on his face in his gunsight. Whoever and whatever he was, he was afraid of dying like everyone else.

CHAPTER 22

"Y OU ARE A WORKER AT THE CENTURION CASTLE."
Greta, the head maid, intoned to Eileen the
rules to stay alive as she walked. The first thing
she said was that any servant found outside of their station or the servants' quarters without authorization
would be killed on the spot, no questions asked. She
stopped, turned around, and boxed Eileen's ears for em-
phasis. "We have lost workers this way. Understand?"

Eileen nodded and rubbed her ears. She understood
all right; the Centurion Castle was just like being
back home, beatings included, only the Green Hornet
wouldn't be around to help.

All the other rules followed—not speaking, not seeing anything, not hearing, an endless list that made her
feel as if she was back at Camp X, with the exception
that death was the penalty for infractions.

After listening to the woman Eileen followed her from
the castle through a forest trail to a long one-story concrete building. Eileen found herself in a tunnel-like room.
Thick iron screens covered the windows. An armed
guard sat reading a newspaper next to the door. People
slept in cement stalls that were stacked three high. Greta

pointed to an empty space between two stalls. "You sleep there. If someone dies or is taken away, you can put your name on the list for a cot and a blanket. Don't worry," she said, grinning through broken teeth, "you will get one *eventually*, if you live long enough."

Greta laughed out loud at her own joke. "You eat with everyone else in the morning. Now go to sleep."

Eileen fell into a heap in the cold cement stall, grateful that she was still breathing and had her skin intact. She curled into a ball and put her head on her arm. The fireplaces on either side of the building across the room roared but could not compete with the snoring, coughing, and wheezing all around. They did, however, bring her a few warm breezes once in a while. It was the most that she could hope for at that moment.

Laying on musty hay, she took stock of her situation. Everything had gone to hell. There was no way to contact home base. She was now a prisoner in a strange German castle. Her extended family was undoubtedly starving and dying in a slave labor camp somewhere. She had no idea how close she was to her mission objective. After all her training, it was not looking too good— she never considered that failure could be an option. *The Green Hornet would never find himself in a situation like this.* Then again, he had never tried to take on the Nazis.

Through it all there was a bright side; the mission was shot, but instead of being a caged prisoner, tortured, or set up against one of the embankments and shot as a spy, she was now just a slave. She hoped that slaves ate better than inmates.

Up until then she had never really thought of herself as being a spy; a subversive agent bent on doing as much damage as she could before escaping or being caught. But with her grandmother dead and her family incarcerated she wanted to get back at the Nazis somehow. She had to be innovative and daring, even though she was not much more than a chambermaid. She wanted to make Hitler pay for the things that they had done to her family.

Eileen quickly discovered that the Centurion Castle was much more than an ancient stone-walled fortress. Similar to Camp X, it had several surrounding outlying buildings on its vast holdings. But it was the areas beneath the castle where the real workings existed. Cellblocks, storerooms, living quarters, and more created a vast underground web. But she hadn't known that when she first started her work there.

Her indoctrination from Greta was short and simple: You work or you are dead. "You don't see anything. You don't hear anything. Keep your mouth shut! For your reward you get to eat, but not too much."

Anything missing and the entire group she was assigned to could be severely punished and tortured by Otto Dick until the culprit was discovered and executed in front of the serving staff. Anytime his jangling keys could be heard trouble always followed.

She could relate to all that. It was just another version of all the crap she had been through in her life. A servant's life was just a step above the slaves—she'd been there before. Slaves were never allowed in the main castle except for the purpose of work or the entertainment of the guests.

The cleaning habit she was given was the traditional black maid's uniform with a white apron. She wore a colored band on her arm to designate the areas that she was allowed to be in. The black shoes that she wore were about four sizes too large so she used rags to stuff in the toes.

She could play her part, but for how long? Eileen was trained in spycraft, home and her parents had taught her to be invisible and take it. She was just a part of the castle, like the walls and furniture. Like the livestock they were there to serve and nothing else, then die or be slaughtered. To speak without being spoken to meant an instant beating by the overseers, brutal and harsh.

Making mental notes, one by one, she quickly put together the matrix of the castle's hierarchy. At the top was Baron Konrad von Richter. Medium height, silver hair, and aristocratic, he seemed to be the one everyone toadied to, and quickly, too. His even smile could grow cold in an instant with deadly consequences. Below him was his political adjutant, SS Gruppenführer Joachim Borz. Tall, blond, muscled, and mean. Her first introduction to him taught her that he was one to treat like a rattlesnake. A backhand slash from his riding crop sent many servants sprawling for the least infraction. Below him was Oberführer Lukas Keller. Slight, slim, and bespectacled like a librarian, he ran the day-to-day goings of the castle. He was a bureaucrat. Literally rounding out the cast was SS Rottenführer Otto Dick. A short bald man, Dick weighed at least three hundred pounds. He was vain but a mess. He used three men to fit him in his custom-made SS uniform. Even in his uniform he looked a mess and usually was covered in the remains of his food, or blood. He also was the head enforcer and turnkey, his keys always clinked and jangled when he walked.

The servants seemed to have their own hierarchy also. The servants' wing was divided into several units. They were kept together in different groups. The competition for the best jobs was fierce, even deadly. Eileen understood the things that they did to keep the Centurion Castle going just to stay alive. Staying alive was the always the first priority.

Eileen worked eighteen-hour days. Drudgery, dirt, and filth filled those days. She was white but not *pure* Aryan. So she was nothing, like the décor, she was just there to keep the master race happy. She would work, eat her meager food, wash when she could, then fall asleep in her stall for a few hours and start all over again.

For an isolated castle in the forest it was an up and running concern twenty-four hours a day. Trucks, cars, and vans came and went at all hours. Deliveries could be food, prisoners, furniture, art, animals, and more came during the day. At night dark things seemed to creep and lurk everywhere. She stayed with her group wherever she went.

Her first job was as a chambermaid. There were no breaks but the work was not always backbreaking. Once accustomed to the routines, there were even times when she could get to clean a room by herself. During those times she would look through the personal effects of the visitor. Most were members of the Nazi Party; several had low party numbers. Some were academics. Others were archaeologists or doctors. There were even some who brought strange items that Sybil had explained could be used for a ritual purpose.

A fly on the wall, she began to piece together the inner workings of the Centurion Castle. One wing of the castle was given to expeditions and archaeological endeavors. It seemed as if a team of travelers was always either coming or going. Rooms of different materials were piled high with ropes, picks, climbing gear, and sleeping bags. Eileen made a mental note of the places that held any sort of weapons. There was no telling when they would be useful.

Furtively listening to the conversations, she learned that there were many groups associated with the castle, some were called the Vril, the Luminous Light, the Teutonic Order, and others, even some from the Golden Dawn, the English ones Sybil had spoken of.

Each group had its own space or wing in the castle. It was a certainty that they were all fraternally associated, but what was the real name of their group? The one thing that they all had in common was that they walked around as if they were masters of the world. They all had an arrogant air about them as they conversed. The war was going well and they all acted as if *they* were the reason behind all the Nazis' good fortune.

These men were not just card-carrying Nazis; they seemed to owe an allegiance to something else, something not spoken of in public. Whatever it was it was very secretive. As a chambermaid, she couldn't think of a better position to be in to gain access to the inner workings of the castle.

Small and unimposing, Eileen worked with a fifty-person crew. As in basic training she quickly avoided being caught at the front or rear of the group, but always stayed in the middle. In view, she would become as motionless as the several empty suits of armor that lined many halls. When the conversations between the castle patrons seemed worth listening to she always found a knight's armor or something handy and nearby to shine.

One evening while her crew gathered in the general assembly area Dick came rushing in, then ordered her service crew to move to another corridor. From the hall Eileen saw a bizarre parade of transvestites, prostitutes, young boys, and even animals as they passed her. The next morning she cleaned up the disgusting remains of an orgy.

A morning came when Otto Dick ordered everyone together in the great hall at the base of the grand staircase. Baron Richter stood at the top of the stairs. Borz and Keller stood just behind him. He looked like a kid on his birthday.

"I want your full attention," the baron said. "We have a very, *very* important visitor arriving. From now until he departs we will be at our best. I will tolerate no infractions."

From top to bottom the castle was made ready for arrival of this very important guest. The servants and slaves were pushed, cajoled, and beaten for three days straight. When they were done the ancient castle gleamed from top to bottom and Eileen could barely stand.

Preparations included the arrival of a full orchestra, vans and vans of flowers, and a menagerie of exotic animals.

One cold, dreary morning the entire staff stood assembled in front of the castle. Nazi flags fluttered in the breeze. The flowers and flowing gold, red, black, and white banners did little to brighten the day.

Exhausted, Eileen could barely keep her eyes open.

Several black Mercedes suddenly came thundering into the courtyard. Eileen was instantly awake. Dust stirred up from the cars filled the area and made some cough. Otto eyed and marked those who did cough in his little black book.

The baron stood at the front of the main entrance. He looked splendid in his official red and black silk uniform, just what kind of uniform, Eileen didn't know. Everyone else wore the black SS uniform topped with the silver death's-head on their hats.

There was an excitement in the air that also caught Eileen's spirit. Who was the great evil man who had caused such a stir?

One by one Nazis emerged from the cars and threw Nazi salutes. Smiles, handshakes, boisterous greetings, and good cheer circulated among them. Finally the man of the moment stepped from a car. Things quickly became formal.

Eileen knew the man from the Camp X Nazi hierarchy recognition pictures. It was Rudolf Hess, Deputy Führer of the Third Reich. He wore a black suit. With him were some men dressed in a very strange manner. Peering closer, Eileen saw that they wore what looked to be snakeskin.

The baron and Hess embraced like long-lost brothers. Eileen couldn't hear all that was being said but gathered that his arrival was the beginning of some sort of celebration. She knew the German holidays and wondered what they were celebrating. The baron, Hess, and the rest of the party went inside, leaving the snakeskin men and some of the serving staff outside.

The snakeskin men began to unload several suitcases and containers, pushing away the castle's servants when they tried to help.

"You and they are *contaminants*," one man said to Otto. "You will only show us to our master's quarters. If we have need of you, we will call."

Otto, not used to being snubbed by outsiders, began to angrily push and kick everyone back into the castle.

As Eileen passed one of the snakeskin men she was astonished to see that he wore rattlesnake—she had caught countless hundreds but never once thought that they could be skinned and used as clothing. She involuntarily hissed and he grabbed her wrist and looked at her. His eyes were bloodshot and full of hate and suspicion.

Eileen was instinctively ready to attack the viper. She was ready to go for his throat when Otto snapped at Eileen.

"Do not let me catch you communicating with these men!" He pulled her out of the snakeman's grasp and pushed her toward her work group.

The day was filled with grand events. Eileen found herself coming and going everywhere to do every sort of task or chore. That evening she actually found herself in Hess's bedroom. She was summoned to the room and brought a bucket and mop. Hess had just left to some meeting. Once in Hess's inner chambers a snakeskin man led her to the bedroom. A huge pool of blood was on the floor in the center of the room.

"Clean it. The floor will shine or you will be cleaning up your own blood too."

She bowed her head and shivered like a beaten dog as she looked at the blood.

"What do you want?"

"My lord, it will take many trips to fill my bucket and flush the bloody water down the sink in the bathroom."

"You have less than one hour. Now get to work." He turned and left.

Eileen took a deep breath and got to work. She turned on the bath faucet and went back to work. Most of it was off the floor in no time and flushed down the sink. Making sure that no one was watching she quickly took off her clothes and jumped into the tub.

For what amounted to five short minutes she used the soap she brought to scrub away weeks of the grime and filth that she had to endure. Rinsed and dry from the clean towels she'd been given, she dressed in her dirty clothes but felt new again; ready to take on some very

weird and dangerous psychos. She dried off everything
in the bathroom and steeled herself to go to work. It
was time to have a closer inspection of the room Hess
slept in.

On one side of the room was a big panel of the sun
and on the opposite side was the moon. The sun was
made of pure gold. A man's face was at its center. Eileen
judged that it was the Superman as God. He looked out
at the world with the same kind of arrogant look she
had seen on the masters of the castle. Swastikas on rays
of light emanated from the god. She had to admit that it
was a beautiful work of art.

The rolling-moon panel was made of pure silver. The
face of the moon was the Superwoman as Goddess. She
looked with adoration across the room at the sun.

The sun's planets were strategically placed on poles
around the room. They had incredibly intricate zodiac
carvings made out of copper and precious stones were
strategically embedded throughout the carvings.

Huge magnets hung from Hess's massive bed. A writing stand made from bones was next to the bed. A bone-
connected shaft had a single candle still burning next
to a chair. The chair was made out of bones but the seat
coverings—there were hairs on the coverings—were
made out of what appeared to be human skin. The
bones were probably human.

There were some papers on the desk. She stepped
closer, her heart pounding, and bent over to scrutinize
them. They were astrological charts, very similar to the
ones Sybil had shown her, except that these were spotted
with blood.

"*Achtung!* What are you doing?"

Eileen jumped out of her shoes and fell on the floor.

"Were you going to *touch* something of the master's?" The man was over her, holding her wet hair. He
held a double dagger over his head, ready to strike. They
looked like fangs.

"No, please, I, I saw the blood on that paper. I
thought I splashed it there. I was going to clean it. I'm

sorry." She cowered but was ready to fight back the moment he even moved. She got a quick idea and mimicked the adoring look on the moon goddess.

He looked surprised, then his grip on her hair relaxed. He stood up and walked over to where she was cleaning. "No, you did not. Put your shoes on and finish."

She worked like the devil was on her shoulder, which he quite literally was. When she was done the snakeskin man inspected her work.

"Contaminant, go back to where you come from."

She couldn't get away quick enough.

Her crew was outside the dining room, waiting for a bell, to be called upon by Greta for anything the waiters couldn't do. She headed to a spot where she knew she could hear the conversation in the dining hall. The trouble was that everyone else knew about it too. She had to shoulder her way past everyone else just to find a good listening post.

Hess was speaking. His voice was high, almost strangled. "We have *taken* our *Lebensraum*. We have established our superiority to the world. This could not have happened without direction from this Order, *our* Order, The Freemasonic Order of the Golden Centurion. Gentlemen, I raise a toast to our finest magus, Adolf Hitler."

There was a moment of silence while they drank.

"Before we continue with the jubilee, business. I have read your reports on Project Styx. It looks very promising. I have brought with me a scientific team that will report on your progress and needs. You shall proceed on schedule. I would like to observe some of the methods and techniques that have been developed.

"That said I would like to let you religious cryptologists know that I have brought with me a code that we have paid 100 million American dollars for, and the riddle is *still* not solved. I expect you to have an answer for me in less than sixty days or you will be the first to experience its power when it *is* solved. Which brings me to my next question, Herr Doktor Grossman?"

"Yes, Herr Hess."

"Tell me, why have I not read any further developments of the genetic disintegrator? If this is a success, it may well be the war-winning weapon."

"Herr Hess, if I may speak." Lukas Keller stood at attention and interjected, "Project Styx as you know, consumes massive amounts of energy. While we have enough subjects we do not have sufficient power to increase our experiments. We will need a generator of a much larger size if we are to continue with both programs in addition to providing the electrical usage to keep the castle functioning. I had Gruppenführer Borz send you the information in a *Mikrat* last week."

"I did not receive it. I was in Berlin last week. It is probably still following me. As of now the material disintegrator is part of the Styx project. Lukas, you will make an enlarged report and deliver it to me by the end of today."

"Yes, mein Herr!" Keller clicked his heels.

Eileen's ears perked right up. She heard it right. The microdot! It existed and they were using it. Not only that, she had picked up on three more secret projects that London didn't know about, Styx, the genetic disintegrator, and some strange code.

She was elated and now thanked whatever fortune had landed her there. Knowing Keller had Borz use a microdot, she could now focus on putting together the means to get at it.

She remembered the fatherly way the president had looked at her. It all played out again in her mind but the missing pieces were now in place. He had known what she was going for and the confidence that she could do it. This is what she had volunteered for. This was what she had come for. It was all suddenly clear and she was up for the task. She would crack the secrets of the castle, then get the hell out of there!

Now if there was only a way to get ahold of it all at once she could clear out and go home to tell Roosevelt all about it. Plans began to form in her mind.

She had her mark. She would just have to butter up ol' Keller and Borz somehow. What she didn't know was that her chance would come sooner than she expected.

The night of the jubilee, the snakeskin men locked everyone but the Order in their cells. Rudolf Hess and his entourage had arrived with great fanfare but were gone the next morning. Only Eileen and her crew caught a glimpse of Hess fleeing the castle. His name was never mentioned again after that night.

CHAPTER 23

**1655 THURSDAY / 18 MARCH 2004
NEW YORK CITY**

THE MARK HAD BEEN MADE AND COUNTERMARKED. This time it was Sunny's turn to be contacted. The rush-hour crowd was thick. Hand on his P99 .40 caliber in his coat, he was ready to double tap anyone besides Frank Delgado who tried to make a connection with him.

In a rush, people bumped and shuffled against each other as they made their way home. Sunny just sort of flowed with the tide. Floating. Waiting.

"Sunny, don't turn around and just keep walking," came a familiar voice in his left ear. "Man, just what in the *Sam hill* have you been doing?"

"Why?"

"It's on all the international crime hot sheets. Someone with your description; a big white guy, is suddenly the prime suspect in at least two acts of international terrorism. We got an Interpol alert to keep an eye out for someone with your exact description."

"Really? Where were these acts committed?"

"The Philippines and India. They suspect the killings were done with neo-Nazi overtones."

"Man, word sure does travel fast these days."

"You mind telling me about what's going on? The name Sunny Vicam is surfacing in places it shouldn't be. Did you know that Iblas Osoy was a CIA informant? Some of his tips were crucial to the war on terrorism. Not only that, Interpol's named one of your legends as a prime suspect in the disappearance of Melton. To cap it all off, there's an FBI hot report to keep an eye out for *you* and bring you in for questioning. I wouldn't be surprised if there's a private bounty on you."

"Great! Just what I need; to be wanted in my own country." Until that moment he hadn't really realized that most of the people at Osoy's party probably didn't even have anything to do with his black magic dealings. Remembering the pampering by the beautiful Filipina women of Visaya, he felt a serious pang of remorse for his gruesome act. Only now could he understand the terror he must have created shooting off his gun among the Indian people in Varanasi.

A big, berserk white guy shooting up people in an Indian temple sure wouldn't sit well with anybody but the neo-Nazis. Yep, there wasn't anything smooth or subtle about his methods. At present if there was a bad guy in this mess, he was it. Trying to do the right thing came with a big price tag. "Well, are you still with me then, or what?"

"Sunny, I want you to know that I got the drop on you. I have flankers and buffers in the crowd, so just keep walking."

His eyes darted about. *Where are they?* "So it's like that then? Frank, if you don't make the 'no go' signal and back off, in just three seconds, this is gonna get real messy and you're my first target. One." Sunny gripped his pistol to make the first move but Delgado spoke before he got to two.

"No. Stop it, Sunny. It's not like that at all. I got my people here to cover us in case we get ambushed. Right now I'd advise you to stay low-profile. Sunny, I'm on *your* side. You're not the bad guy. Relax your hand and keep moving." Delgado changed his tone. "So, besides your high profile trip, what'd you find? You never e-mailed me anything."

"I was too *busy* to try to get computer access." Sunny took deep breaths trying to slow his heart. It would've really bothered him to have had to kill Frank. He had to put trust somewhere. He passed Delgado a manila envelope. "Here. Inside is the sack he carried with him when I tried to kill him in India. I don't know what most of it is. I dumped what I knew to be dope. But what's left, like the lip balm, might have some of his DNA in it." He held out the foiled micro CD. "This is something out of this world, I just don't know which one."

Delgado pocketed it. "Sunny, I got to tell you something. You got no home."

"What?"

"Your house blew up yesterday. It was a total loss."

"*What?*"

"Julian Leek, your property caretaker, gave a call to your cutout, who called me. I called Julian and he said that it was a gas line explosion, but he said that it was *very* suspicious. I had him call your insurance, then told him to stay away from the whole thing. Your dojo is undisturbed for the moment, but under *their* watch. I don't have even a secretary to spare for countersurveillance. So, Sunny, do you mind telling me what's going on and who the fuck *they* are?"

Sunny was still so stunned that it was all he could do to keep moving. He'd lost Corey and his money, now a seven hundred and fifty thousand dollar investment was gone up in smoke. Happa didn't waste any time striking back. "Did anything happen to my boat?"

"I don't know anything about it. But it's my bet it's sunk, burned, or stolen."

Sunny was very glad that he'd intercepted Pan or he too would be missing.

"What're your plans? What were you thinking?"

"Well, I thought it was a good idea at the time that if I did Happa, everything would just go away. Man, every step I take is just that much deeper in shit, and I still don't have many more answers than when I started."

They were coming to the subway exit. It was time to break off, then reestablish contact at a later time.

Delgado said, "Right now I would advise you to go to ground. With all the chains you've rattled I'm sure there's a big price on your head. Go to wherever your safe house is and let me cover some of your bases." He passed Sunny a pager. "I'll flash you when I get better intell."

"So you don't think I'm crazy?"

Delgado was gone.

Sunny looked at the pager Delgado gave him. He had to assume a number of things. He had to assume it was clean and without a locator beacon. He had to assume that Delgado really had his back. Mostly he had to assume that he was doing the right thing.

THE STORAGE UNITS LOOKED DESERTED. SUNNY WALKED to the unit he had rented. The lock was still secure and hadn't been tampered with. He opened the lock and raised the door. The BMW motorcycle looked safe and secure. Inspecting it minutely, no bugs or locator beacons were attached. That didn't mean that he was tail free. That was why the bike. He jumped on it, fired it up, and became an uncatchable blur on the freeway.

0730 FRIDAY / 19 MARCH
THE FINE ESTATE / VIRGINIA

At first glance nothing looked different. On closer inspection he spotted the hardware. Security cameras were cleverly hidden. He suspected that there were ground sensors and other unobtrusive measures located at key points around the mansion. He rode a half hour past the estate and parked the bike in a storage shed.

The black Lexus came to a stop in front of an IHOP

restaurant. The driver moved over to the passenger side and Sunny slid behind the wheel in seconds. In ten seconds the low-slung car was moving at 130 miles per hour headed north along I-95. They were the only ones on the road.

Sunny looked over at his sheet-white passenger. "Any changes?"

"A, a few," Jim Lambert choked.

Sunny checked the rearview mirror, then backed off the pedal to a crawl at ninety.

"Losing tails?" Lambert guessed.

"No. Just blowing off steam. So fill me in."

"We stayed in a lockdown mode like you said. The security team is right at home, professional all the way."

Sunny pulled off the highway onto a side road, hit the brakes, and cut the engine. There was no one else on the rural road. "You know anything about guns?"

Lambert looked a little confused.

"You ever shoot a gun?"

"I shot a .22 rifle once."

"Right. Get out. I want to show you something."

They got out of the car and Sunny led Lambert a short way into the woods.

Sunny pulled out his pistol.

Lambert looked confused and scared.

"See," Sunny said as he held out the pistol. "This is a Smith & Wesson SW99." He dropped the magazine. "It fires a .40-caliber bullet. It takes eight rounds in the magazine and one in the chamber." He slapped the magazine back in and smiled. "Here's what I like about this particular gun." He gave it a short rack and depressed the trigger halfway. "See, it's ready to rock." He pointed it at a tree and fired.

Lambert's startle and shock at the noise were genuine. He jumped back with his hands in the air. "Mr. Vicam, why are we here? I've done nothing against you."

Sunny handed the gun butt first toward Lambert. Lambert shook his head.

"Take it! It's hot and ready to fire."

Lambert could see that the deadly look in Sunny's eyes wasn't to be trifled with. He lowered his hands and reluctantly took the weapon as Sunny took a few steps back.

Sunny waited forever for Lambert to do nothing. "Now point it at the tree and fire."

Lambert went through a million gyrations, then jerked the trigger and closed his eyes at the same time. He missed the tree completely.

Sunny tried not to laugh, but couldn't help himself. Lambert looked as if he was scared shitless.

"Come on, that tree ain't but ten or so paces away, about the distance between you and me. Do it again. You missed. You aren't gonna hurt that big ol' oak tree. But this time keep your eyes open and squeeze, don't jerk the trigger."

Breathing hard and still fumbling, Lambert pulled the trigger. The oak tree spit splinters.

"Good! You did it. You got five rounds left. Now point it at me."

Lambert looked astonished.

"Do it. Point the fucking thing at me!" Sunny thumbed his chest.

Lambert leveled the gun at Sunny's chest. The barrel shook.

"Now, Jim, you got the drop on me. If you're working for the other side, this is the time to end it. If they find out that you had a chance to wax me and didn't, then it will be your ass. If I find out that you might, or have double-crossed me, I will kill you, Jim. So go ahead, pull the trigger."

Lambert looked helplessly around. He looked lost. Tears began to stream down his face. Sunny was five paces away. Lambert shook his head. "Look, Sunny, I'm not on their side, no. I swear." He offered the gun back, butt first.

Sunny let out a sigh, then showed Lambert the five-shot miniature .22 Magnum revolver he was holding concealed in his palm. It was cocked. "I'm dead on accurate with this up to ten paces." He took back the gun and decocked the firing pin. He holstered it and put a reassuring hand on the very shaken young man's shoulder. "I'm sorry I had to do that, but right now the hate and killing is on and I gotta know who I can trust with my life and who I'll die for. You were there at the beginning so I gotta trust that you'll be there with me all the way."

Lambert walked unsteadily toward the car and leaned against the hood. He took deep breaths then looked up at Sunny. He looked pissed off. "Sunny, I may not be like you in physical strength and courage. And I have never pointed a weapon of *any* kind at *any* living thing, but I know what is going on and I know I can help." He held out his shaky hand. "I may get scared as hell and cry like a baby sometimes, but I won't run out on Sally or you."

Sunny shook his hand. He felt like hugging him, but didn't. "Come on. Let's get back in the car."

Once on the road Sunny tried to relax the still shaken lawyer. "So, Jim, tell me how you came to get hooked up with a rich old lady like Sally."

Jim took a deep breath, sighed, and said, "A debt of honor."

"Do you care to elaborate?"

"No. That's all I'm going to tell you."

"We are just our deepest secrets anyway." Sunny smiled to himself. He'd shaken the young lawyer, and that was the best way to get his attention. But Lambert still stood his ground. Things were looking up.

The first thing Sunny did when he got to the estate was to get a situation report from Vito—it had been as quiet as a cemetery. Happa hadn't traced things to the Virginia estate, not yet.

The next thing he did was explain to Pan what he had done. "Have you been following the news?"

"No. I don't watch television, but I hear things." Pan had a look of near disbelief on his face. "Sensei, it is true? Osoy is really dead?"

"I don't think that he'll be bothering any one any time, ever." *It was a good killing, buddy.*

A world of relief washed over Pan.

"I saw your family, too. They looked good and still don't believe you're alive. Can you believe it? You can go home anytime."

Pan's eyes were still a wonder. "I call or mail them?"

"You can do anything that you want. Just make sure you don't use anything that can be connected to me, or here in any way. So, Pan, why don't you just go home?"

Pan looked confused as if he didn't understand the question. "Why, sensei, I not go until this over. I tell you true I'm in this all the way. It is my word."

Sunny had to leave the room. Even though Nathan Happa had brought death and destruction to his life, he also brought something new to Sunny—friendship and loyalty. It had taken over three decades, but he finally made some real friends. But it was a toss-up if it was worth all he was going through just to make friends.

Delgado's pager suddenly went off.

**1015 SATURDAY / 20 MARCH 2004
NEW YORK / MANHATTAN ISLAND**

Sunny was tired and cramped from the long motorcycle ride from Virginia. He followed Delgado to a bench that was near the ferry that left for the Statue of Liberty. Delgado sat on the bench and uncharacteristically lit a cigarette. The bench didn't look much more comfortable than his motorcycle seat

"Frank, I didn't know that you smoked." Sunny sat, uncomfortable at being so exposed. He felt like a target. He automatically scanned the environment and ticked off where he'd shoot if he were pulling a sniper trigger.

"I used to, still do sometimes especially when I get stressed, like right now." Delgado took a few deep drags, then coughed and choked on the last one. Held the cigarette in front of his face like a bug. "Shit don't calm my nerves like they used to." He dropped it and stubbed it out with his shoe.

"Maybe you should try meditation."

"Sunny, you got some serious problems."

"Yeah? This I have to hear from you?"

"You know, there are people who for everything they touch turns to gold."

"The Midas touch."

"Right. You got the Shit touch."

"Is this a truth from God?"

"It's pretty close. But if you're willing to play the game with me, things could change."

"Yeah? So what's the deal?" It was odd sitting across from Delgado. It was social, intimate, and almost friendly. There were a lot of personal questions he had for Frank Delgado. Number one was his real name. But this particular intimacy wasn't for those kinds of questions.

"There are government contracts that are done that just go nebulous. Millions, billions are awarded, and after a few years no one ever sees what becomes of them."

"Like Reagan's Star Wars program."

"Right. Research contracts. Sixty billion dollars up in smoke; *someone* got rich. But these research contracts don't always turn up dry. There's this one group in the E Systems of Raytheon."

"Wait. What's E Systems?"

"It's a branch that deals with encrypted communications. Its main client is the Department of Defense."

"Then they are really connected."

"They have ground, subsurface, airborne, and satellite systems that are literally out of this world."

"So what's this got to do with me?"

"I'm not finished talking."

"Sorry."

"All this stuff is open-source material. Anyone can look it up on the Web. But what isn't publicized is that there's a section within E Systems that has developed a technology that is almost unbelievable."

"How do you know this stuff?"

"I have a good contact at the NSA and NRO. When I showed him the micro CD you gave me he just about had a heart attack. I'm serious, he had to sit down or he would've fallen down."

"Wow! So what is the thing?"

"Microbio pixels. Think of one tiny disc being filled with a trillion floating magnetized microdots. Each microdot is its own CD capable of recording and holding the same amount of information as a standard CD. Theoretically that micro CD could hold all the information in the Library of Congress and have enough left over to record every movie and television show that's ever been made."

"You got to be kidding!"

"No. I wish I was."

"So how do you read it? What kind of system does it play on?"

"Ah, now you've hit it. You can only read it on a special reader recorder. Let's get back to my heart attack friend. The E System program that made this thing is under the auspices of the NSA. My contact told me that only two readers in the world exist. I am told that each micro CD is handled with more security than that's given to plutonium. Here it is; that disc you got from Nathan Happa is a bootleg copy. Someone, somehow, stole the program."

"What?"

"Yeah. You freaked out the NSA. They'll do anything to get their hands on you or Happa. Anything."

"So why don't you turn me over to them?" Sunny slipped his hand behind his back and gripped the butt of his gun."

"Cut it out." Delgado looked annoyed. "You made them a counter offer."

"I did?" He relaxed his grip on the gun.

"Now put your hands back on your lap like a good boy and quit being so trigger-happy."

"Okay, now what? You're my boss again?"

"That's right. I said that I was acting as your handler. Rather than be turning yourself in, you will, for a price, go and recover the system and neutralize the principals."

"How much?"

Delgado kept quiet.

"I asked you a question."

Delgado smiled. "A million five. I get a 15 percent finder's fee."

Sunny didn't blink. "No. Three million, tax exempt and you get seven percent of the net."

Delgado's jaw dropped. "What?"

"That's right. Not only that, I want any required backup and a legitimate contingency rescue package." Deep inside he'd known he was onto something, but suddenly he realized just how big it was. It wasn't the money that he cared about; it was the support the NSA gave when they weren't nickel-and-diming an operation to death. Now he had wheels on his vehicle and it could really roll!

"You're asking a lot. A whole lot."

"I know a little about government contracts, too. They assign most of them to suckers like me who work on the cheap. There's nothing like underestimating the cost and overestimating value on those babies. It looks like I'm the one who's holding the marble bag and I'm going to make the most of it. Tell them it's a take-it-or-leave-it proposition. No negotiating." Even though he knew what he demanded was totally outrageous, Sally's money kept him afloat and put him in an even greater negotiating position. "Yeah, you'll get your 7 percent and be my operations command. It's that or nothing."

"All right. I'll take the counteroffer to them, but I'll only do it for 10 percent. You'll have a director of operations twenty-four/seven."

"Yeah, all right." He could breathe a little easier for the first time since he could remember. The prospect of not only financial solvency, but having "backup" made him feel like the journey was finally paying off.

They shook hands. Now it was time to lay all of the cards on the table.

Sunny told Frank the whole story. "I need help," he concluded. "I'm going after a guy who's part of something mystical, the Golden Century. I *still* don't know who those people are. Frank, who are they? Are they real, or am I just nuts?"

"Sunny, I met you when you were coming out of the Colombian drug war."

"Escaping is a better description. Yeah, so?"

"So think about what you were in back then. Other than the players, who here in this country can tell you the first thing about the whole stinking secret culture we have established over there in the 'drug war'? Not even the president knows the whole story. But you and I both know the names and places of the players on both sides of the fence. You tell me who's dirtier, us or them? You know the scene better than I do."

Oh yeah, Sunny knew it well. There were volumes of nasty secret material that spanned over fifty years of the dealings with South American drug politics. He tried flexing his left hand. Sure he knew it; well enough to stay the fuck away.

"See, there's no question that these kinds of people can exist. What they believe in, how they operate, what they are up to, *who* they are, that all remains to be uncovered, for 3 million dollars. You got to get close, Sunny. You got to infiltrate the inner circle before we can get those answers."

"Wait a second, aren't those the *same* crap lines you sold me in Palestine?"

Delgado shrugged his shoulders. "True, but what you discover may not be what we're after. I'll give you an example.

"One of the team just came to me with a problem he says he can't handle. Like you did, he worked himself into a terrorist cell. He had actually befriended his mark. I warned him about doing that, hoping he wouldn't turn up the unexpected. His mark opened up and said that his secret desire is really to be a suicide bomber. He's just waiting to be called." Frank threw his hands up. "So what the fuck is up with that? There are people behind his thinking. They are the ones who helped put those thoughts into his head. They are the ones behind the curtain we're trying to get at. *Those* are the people I'm after. Hell, you ate with them and probably killed some of them. You tell me, are *they* real?

"Sunny, you're not nuts, as a matter of fact you are closer to them than you know."

Sunny nodded.

"The micro CD won't be out to the consumer for another twenty years."

"Yeah? So what's my problem?"

"Sunny, if Happa has the connections to utilize top secret communications, then whoever he's connected to is on the inside on *our* side, a mole. Some of the good guys have turned bad."

"I see. We got to watch our backs. So what was on the CD?"

"It's an agenda at some sort of meeting. There's even a location and time for the meeting. The rest was encoded. The NSA can't read it."

"Where is it?"

"Somewhere in the Caribbean. I'll have more info for you later."

Sunny watched the boats come and go. The good life; he was about to put his life on the line for the NSA, but if he lived through it, then the good life might be his.

CHAPTER 24

UNRELIABLE AS IT WAS, SERVANT GOSSIP WAS STILL one of the best sources of information. Every once in a while different crews came together to meet a demand. There were even times when they shared the common area. When there were no guards close by they would talk and pass gossip back and forth. She already knew how filthy her masters were, so Eileen would quickly, but quietly sidle near the biggest talker of the other crews and listen. The talk was interesting.

Usually the talk was shop-centered, carpenters and builders talking about the goings-on of current projects and such; Eileen learned more about the layout of the castle. From the cooks she figured out the delivery schedules. She listened to every word that was spoken by anyone to figure out how to get into a place, but more, importantly, how to get out. Her favorite, and the most ghastly people to listen to were the sex slaves. They were also the most pitied and despised of the workers.

A very effeminate young man named Hans once spoke of Borz. He liked the heaviest of women, the bigger the better. He mentioned a female's name and everyone became quiet. Greta prodded him some more, playing to his vanity until he told what had happened to the big woman. Borz was a sadist; he liked to beat his sex victims to death. Unless they were under the personal protection of a castle member, they were fair game.

Eileen didn't want to be prey for anyone. She remembered her trainers saying that sometimes going to the most obvious open source, even if it was deadly, could be one's best protection.

The next morning her room cart was heavy with trash and filth. It amazed her that with all the wild Aryan superiority ideas they had, they were pigs when it came to cleanliness. Reaching the waste receptacles near the massive incinerator, she was about to leave her cart when something from the ordinary stood out. A stack of neatly placed folders was sticking out from under one of the trash carts.

She picked up the slim folders. Looking them over she realized that she was reading the statistics of the results of the experiment called Styx. The documents spoke of "successful units" and "foul units." Whatever it was it was an ongoing project. It was the project Rudolf Hess had personally come to see. Her heart jumped when she saw the signature on the bottom of the page—Rudolf Hess.

She knew that it would make a big stir if she could radio the information back to London. It wouldn't be that difficult to get out of the castle to hide the material somewhere in the forest. But what if it was a plant? And exactly what did the information pertain to? Could it be a test of her loyalty? Her first priority was survival.

It was do or die. Papers in hand she marched straight into the office of Gruppenführer Joachim Borz and placed the papers on his desk. She took two steps back from the desk and threw a perfect Nazi salute. "Heil Hitler!"

Borz looked startled for a moment. "Don't do that!" He picked up the papers, and said, "Leave."

Eileen almost reached the door.

"Wait."

She stood still, looking at the wood floor on which she had spent three days to get a mirror finish.

"Do you know what these papers are?" Borz asked.

Eileen jumped right back into her cowering role. Knowing what she did, getting into the role needed very little practice. She wrung her hands together and answered sheepishly. "I'm not a very good reader, your lordship." She could recall almost everything contained in the papers. But what the statistics were for she'd yet to uncover.

"Look at me." He held her chin high with his riding crop. "Where did you get these papers?"

"They, they were under a bag that was for waste incineration."

"I see. Good work. Does anyone else know about this? Have you talked to anyone else about this?"

"No, Herr Borz."

"You will not speak of this to anyone. Anyone. Understand?"

Eileen looked back at the floor and nodded. She felt the crop gliding across her breasts and behind.

"You are still too small, and too skinny. How old are you?"

"Thirty, Herr Borz."

"And far *too* old. You look sixty. But I've seen you work and you actually do get your work done. I will be watching you. I think that I will have Keller move you to a new crew, one I personally task."

She felt a sharp sting on her butt.

"Now get back to work."

The following day Eileen was given over to another crew with an entire wing of the castle to work in. The crew was cold toward her at first, but she already knew the ropes. They were protected so they had their own arrogance; they *belonged* to Gruppenführer Borz. She had to laugh to herself at their silly ways; everyone was a servant-slave, how could they think themselves above anyone? She didn't care what they thought of her after she ate real pork and potatoes for one meal, then slept on a real cot in a smaller, warmer building. Hell, they *were* better in lifestyle anyway. She figured it would only be a matter of time until they accepted her. Maybe she would also learn to look down on the rest of the help. She would do whatever it took until she had her hands on a microdot.

She worked as if her life depended on it. When Borz asked for anything, she made sure that she was always first to deliver it.

Hess had left and suddenly more trucks filled with supplies started arriving. Still there was no sign of a *Mikrat*.

She could almost read Borz's mind and his needs and perversions. She started to add to his intelligence files, filling him in on who came and went from the castle. Slowly, she was becoming indispensable to him. His dependence on her meant living just a bit longer.

One evening Borz called her into his office. She was expecting to have to fill him in on some more sordid details of the habits of some of the guests. She knocked on his door.

"Come in."

He was drunk as usual. In front of him was a gold plate piled high with cocaine. He drank bourbon freely from a crystal decanter. "Ah, Ingrid. How are you? Are you happy here?"

"Yes, Herr Borz." What the hell did he care?

"You lie, but that is fine. You are a good worker. I will allow you one question from time to time. Do you have any now?"

"Yes, mein Herr, I am just curious about the people here. They do not seem to all be Nazis. Who are they?"

"No?" He feigned surprise, then grinned. "We are *not* the Nazis or the SS. We started them. We control them. Our homeland is a place called Hyperborea. It is buried deep within the earth." He could see the confused look in Eileen's eyes. "Oh yes, this is true, and

Hitler is our finest creation. We hold SS ranks only for looks."

"And who are *you*?" What nonsense was he speaking?

"Come here," he ordered.

Eileen obeyed.

"Closer."

She came as close as she dared.

"I said *one* question." He quickly backhanded her, but it was weak and had no sting. "That was two."

Eileen could see the drugged fever in his eyes. The things Sybil had told her were true. Thoughts and ideas began to form, but they were useless if she couldn't relay them to London. Her lost radio was just a memory.

"I have had the information you brought me investigated. Your family is in Dachau."

"Dachau?" Eileen's heart pumped wildly. What did he know about her family and her cousin? Did he know that she was playing a role? "I don't know, mein Herr. The vans, they came and I ran." She was unarmed. She used her cowering to look for a weapon and a way out. But he seemed oblivious to her presence.

"To me and the new world order." He lifted the decanter and toasted himself. "And even to you, *if* you stay alive." He sneered, then smiled. There was nothing warm behind it.

She looked at him as if he held her life in his hands. "Just to live. It's all I hope for." There was no lie to her words.

A feral smile came over his drugged face. His eyes became sharp and focused. "Then, if I help you, you must help me."

"Help you, mein Herr? How? I am nothing." Borz had only pretended to be drugged. He was testing her. She was ready for the bait to be offered.

Borz propped his boots on the big table. "My administration of this castle and land requires that I deal with all classes of people. You are a good worker and you have demonstrated an ability to deliver accurate information. Now, for your next job I need you to keep that information between us. You will see things that others would be put to death for, but I need competent workers. That is why you now work on my own personal crew.

"In return for your silence, you will live as well, even better than you could ever hope for. I will try to locate your family in the camp. If I can find them, perhaps I might make their accommodations and living conditions better, too." He dropped his feet back on the floor and grabbed her, then slapped her. "But that is only if you keep your mouth shut!"

"Yes, Herr Borz, I will do whatever you say if you can help my family." Eileen looked tearfully at him. He hadn't fooled her for a moment; he would only feed her lies. His grip hurt.

He snorted.

Eileen shuddered when she caught his gaze sexually sizing her up again.

He put his boots back on the table. "You need to put on more weight. You look like some of the medical patients you will be dealing with."

"Sir? I am not a nurse." She found herself on the floor staring up at his bloodshot eyes.

"You are here to *serve*." He stood over her and glared at her. "You will know this. I *will* find your family, and if you refuse to do what is expected of you, I will make them pay for it." He snarled, "You have been given preferential treatment because I find you useful, but you cross me one more time, and you will find yourself as one of the patients. Do you understand?"

That Eileen believed. Through his stupor, he was still pulling strings on the puppet in front of him. She couldn't help but think she was missing a good opportunity to kill him. True, she'd made no real discoveries, yet, but just killing him would be helping mankind.

It would only be a matter of time before he would discover that there were two Ingrids, one was in the labor camp and the other was she.

"I will let you in on a secret. What is happening to the world is not just German domination by the Nazis."

"Do you mean the Axis powers?" She slowly got to her feet.

"No. Those that seek total world domination." He caught himself and dismissed what he had said. "What am I doing speaking to someone such as you? You know nothing of the world." He gulped down his bourbon. "Go now. Go and serve."

Eileen felt pretty good. Not only was she existing inside the enemy's lair, she was thriving. She had gained the confidence of someone close to the microdot. She was ready to penetrate the secret of secrets in his world and get the hell out of there. His world?

She had no idea what was going on outside the castle grounds. As far as she knew the world was at war and the Nazis were winning. But gossip wouldn't keep her from pursuing her mission.

WITHOUT A GUIDE EILEEN WOULD HAVE BEEN LOST IN the maze of halls and rooms. She came to a series of lockers. The halls were well lit and the locker doors were wide and high. They looked something like meat locker doors.

A woman named Greta led her inside one of the lockers. Eileen could hear an electric humming and whispering sound. At first she wasn't sure what she was seeing.

Stacked four high on metal gurneys lay forty naked people. At first she thought that they were dead, but two technicians were taking random vital readings and making notations on charts.

Greta pointed out several tubes that were attached to the men and women on the metal slabs. In particular the large colostomy tube and the bladder tube. Eileen's job was to change the offal bag and urine bottles for fresh ones.

It was filthy work but Eileen performed her duties

with the same, almost robotlike efficiency as the technicians. She knew better than to ask questions about what was going on. Any questions and she knew she could wind up on one of the empty slabs.

Once she was on her own, she surreptitiously read some of the charts and was astounded by what she could decipher. If some of the dates read right, there were some people who had been here unconscious since 1901. *What is going on here?*

The number of *patients* didn't always remain the same. Some came and went in days. Only a core of thirty "old heads" seemed to remain constant.

From that time on "unit maintenance detail" was added to her duties.

It took a long time to get the "good" jobs, or be singled out for special jobs. There were snide remarks behind her back sometimes as she passed a few stalls. How was it that she was getting the good jobs already? Only the sexually compliant got the best jobs and she wasn't as fat as she should've been.

She took her place in line and picked up her mop and bucket. She followed the crew to a huge building.

An older woman named Eva walked close behind her and whispered in her ear. "Our guard is named Adolph. He is a drunk. He could care less about guarding us because we have nowhere to go; we get locked in overnight. He just wants to drink and be left alone. You follow and do what everyone else does."

They came to a set of guarded double doors. The guard opened the door, let everyone pass through, then closed the solid doors with a thud. It was the biggest library Eileen had ever seen.

Adolph walked to the library director's office. He said nothing as he pulled out a bottle of vodka and set up his drinking station in an overstuffed chair. Wound up the record player and put on an opera record, sat back in the chair and started drinking. He was already half-drunk and now was drinking himself into a stupor. Soon he was snoring. Someone pulled the door shut.

As soon as the door closed, the workers looked relieved. Locked in the library with the supervision drunk and asleep, a worker was put to watch if Adolph stirred and became alert. Everyone rushed to get the work done, then went to his or her sleeping spot. No one would bother them until morning.

Instead of sleeping Eileen began wandering the aisles looking through the books. Most of them were written in German, or were German translations of other books. There was the Edda, books by Paracelsus, Goethe, *The Method* by Archimedes. It went on and on. Many were rare and ancient manuscripts. A long scroll was laid out on a long table. Notes laying on the table written in German revealed the writing to be Jewish text. Eileen was stunned at the openness in displaying all the arcane and secret material. Who were these people to have access to such extraordinary materials?

It appeared that most of the books all dealt with either mythology or magic. It was disconcerting to pick up some books that were filled with ghastly and gruesome pictures of ritual murder.

A shadow under massive double doors caught her eye. Someone was walking around in a room that adjoined the library. She slowly tried to turn the black knob. It was locked. From the sounds a lively discussion was going on just beyond the door.

She knelt to the floor and tried to see beneath the crack in the door. She put her ear as close to the door space as she could and listened.

"It cannot be done! I will not allow it," a voice said. It sounded a lot like Lukas Keller. "You are stepping over natural bounds that no man has the right to cross!"

"You have no say in the matter. Secret Chief Hess has given us full sanction to proceed. We have all the material we require. The generators are here and are being installed. We will stop wasting our time on a single experiment. How much more power do you need to do, say, fifty experiments at the same time, and do we have it?"

The voice belonged to Borz.

"Then, gentlemen, we will expand our experiments. I do not have to tell you that if this is successful, we will be unstoppable at any level."

The sonorous tone had to be the baron's.

She looked around and saw an iron ladder on the third floor, which seemed to lead to a trapdoor. She turned out the lights and crept to the third floor. Climbing the short ladder, she was surprised to see that the trapdoor was unlocked.

Ever so slowly she lifted the door and climbed into the crawl space. Things scurried and squeaked. The vermin didn't bother her—it was their domain. Vents ran in a few different directions. She immediately saw the potential for further spying.

A dim light was cast across open wood beam trusses. The light came from a vent where the discussion was being held. She crept along a sturdy beam until she was inches away from the light source. The air shaft ran for hundreds of yards in several directions. She was small enough to slip through the narrow opening and slide along the shaft until she came to a grille through which the speakers could be seen.

From the air vent she counted twenty men or so of different ages. She saw the baron, Borz, and Keller sitting at the front of the room. They were engaged in a classroom kind of discussion. A chalkboard was full of diagrams and strange symbols.

She could clearly hear and see all that went below her. In moments she picked up the night's topic, Aryan supremacy. It was a mishmash of race superiority, race propaganda, and mythology. It wasn't much different than the stuff her father had said; but these people acted and sounded as if they were the high priests of hate.

Eileen took a more comfortable position on the wide wooden beam that ran down the center of the shaft and listened to the lectures, making mental notes.

They were the children of the black sun in the Taurus star system. The black sun emitted dark matter in an infinite beam of light. "There is an equal amount of dark matter in light matter," the baron lectured. "Dark matter cannot be seen because the light matter outshines it. Matter and antimatter meet at the zero point. In its final essence the black sun will always dominate." The baron then made his point.

"Like dark matter, we of the Golden Centurion are behind all things, the Thules, the Nazis, and other secret groups," the baron said. "We control. Without our practices the Hitler cannot exist. We are the protectors of the bloodline of the dark matter. It is our design and destiny to control all light matter. The purer the blood of Aryan man the stronger the black sun in him shines, the stronger the metaphysical forces he controls."

Eileen had a hard time believing Sybil's descriptions of the Nazi secret society, but now it seemed as if she had found exactly what she was looking for. She continued to listen with the ear of a trained spy.

In the hours that followed she learned that they believed themselves to be great and glorious. As speakers came and went, the general theme always returned to the "Golden Order."

The baron stood, and said, "The Order."

"The Order comes before God, country, family, and friends," was how one person stood up and stated it.

They held a deadly contempt for anything not of the society's order. Before the night was over they had declared a racial hatred of anyone not of the bloodline. But the big highlight was when the subject of the Jews arose. Then they became positively rabid.

Rather than listen to the rest of the dreck and dross she decided to strike out and see where the shafts led. While some might've tried to get out of the claustrophobic shaft, Eileen found the chance to finally be alone refreshing. All that she had to do was remember where she was in the air ducts and not get lost.

The electronic sounds were familiar so she continued to creep forward. The closer she got the more excited she became. Finally she was over the grille.

She wanted to shout with excitement and had to cover her mouth with her hand. Radio operators sat at five stations relaying and receiving messages. After she settled down she scanned the room and the electronic radios comparing the Nazi equipment to what she was familiar with. If she could only gain access to that room for just ten minutes. Like most of the other grilles steel bars were set over the openings. Any cutting of the bars would leave obvious marks; besides which, she had no access to saws.

What she couldn't quite figure out was how it was related to the layout of the castle. It was time to get back to the library.

She was totally exhausted and almost falling over when it was time to leave the library. She took her place in line, ready to leave.

Eva hissed, "Where were you, girl?"

"I'm sorry. I fell asleep in a closet and didn't hear the call until now."

"And you are filthy. Where have you been?"

"This place is not the cleanest. I was cleaning."

"You will bring too much attention to us. You bring attention and others will be watching us more close." She put her bony hand on her shoulder and dug in with her claws. "In this place we want to draw *no* attention from anyone. Do you understand?"

"No attention, yes." Eva was right; she would draw no attention to her crew, none at all.

CHAPTER 25

2310 MONDAY / 22 MARCH 2004
NEW YORK CITY

THEY SAT AT A BOOTH OF A HOTEL RESTAURANT, Sunny, Delgado, and a guy in a dark suit. He was from the NSA. Sunny knew his type well. He was a bean counter. He opened a briefcase on his lap and pulled out a folder. He opened it and frowned in a businesslike manner.

"Do you know Kyle March?" His black horn-rimmed glasses continually slipped down his nose.

"The CIA guy? Briefly, only long enough to break his jaw." Sunny smiled as he remembered. "It was the briefest debrief I've ever been to."

The bean counter shifted nervously in his seat and pushed his glasses back to the bridge of his nose. "Do you know the whereabouts of Mr. Charles Talon, also known as Ricky Talon?"

"He's in New York somewhere."

"Do you know *exactly* where?"

"Nope." Sunny folded his arms across his chest and cradled the gun under his jacket. He propped his steel-tipped boot on the table edge and felt like putting it in the bean counter's chest. "Lookit. I didn't come here to discuss old business. You called me, remember?" He had to trust that Delgado hadn't brought him to the meeting just to set him up. The idea that he could wind up in a straitjacket in a certain VA clinic wasn't very appealing to him.

"Mr. Vicam, I must legally ask you these questions for record of contract. We cannot engage a known felon."

Sunny burst out laughing, upsetting Delgado's coffee onto his shirt. "I'm sorry, Frank, but are you sure we're talking to the right people?"

Delgado just turned beet-red and grabbed a napkin to try to clean up the mess.

Sunny grinned. He had finally gotten a rise out of him.

The bean counter bristled. "Mr. Vicam, may I continue? We cannot discuss contract matters until you have answered these questions."

"Oh yes, then please do continue."

"Do you have any knowledge of the whereabouts of Kyle March?"

"Nope."

"Did you have anything to do with the disappearance of Kyle March?"

"No. I don't know anything about it, but I'll gladly piss on his grave if you ever find out where it's at." His left hand suddenly felt better than it had for years. "And that's for your record."

The NSA bean counter made marks in his folder and dropped it into his briefcase and pulled out another folder. "Mr. Vicam, we cannot pay what you asked."

"What can you pay?"

"Only the original terms."

Sunny was quiet for a few moments, then took a quick short breath. He felt like breaking things up a little. "Then, Mr. NSA Bean Counter, you can go fuck yourself." He saw the pipsqueak turn white. "Frank, I thought that you might be my friend, but you can go fuck yourself too." He stood away from the table.

He walked out the door and into the hotel lobby. Three men appeared at the entrance.

Sunny loved it. He could deal with these guys and he was in the right mood to do it. "Oh yeah? Do you government-employed goons think that you can keep me here? You are supposed to be the *good* guys."

One of the men smiled a little sick smile and stepped aside.

Sunny was back on the street before Delgado caught up with him. "Sunny, I swear to God, I'm going to put a bullet in your ass if you don't stop!"

Sunny slowed down, then stopped near a street musician playing "Mr. Magic" on a saxophone. He played smooth, clear, and mellow.

"Sunny, you are such an *idiot*," Delgado hissed. "I have no idea how you survive in the field. The man just put his first card out on the table. You don't just get up and walk away like that on the *first* card."

"I don't? I think it's me that's holding all the cards."

"Exactly!" Delgado jumped at his own word—he was used to keeping his cool. "You didn't even deal me in. Now, you turn your ass around and go back in there and lay out an apology. Man, you've always been a terrible card player."

"No, I'm not. See, Frank, I can bluff too. I'm not always a bull in a china shop." He tossed a fin in the saxophone player's case and started walking back to the meeting, tapping a man sitting at the bus stop as he passed. "Come on."

The man stood up and turned around. It was Jim Lambert.

For the next hour Sunny, Jim, and Frank played the NSA bean counter as well as the street musician played his sax, except that they had more cash by the time the last note was played.

A deal was struck and signed. Beaten, but still a bean counter, the suit got up and left with his black briefcase. Jim followed a few moments later.

It was only Sunny and Frank.

"I've got to give you credit for that. Your lawyer's good, real good. Where'd he come from?"

"Classified."

"Asshole. We are on the same team now."

"I'm sorry. You're right. After this I want you to get with him and take a long drive out to the safe house I got set up." Sunny chuckled. "Just wait until you see it. Pan Jhandi is my man there." Sunny settled back into his chair—the hard part was over. "So what's the deal?"

"Okay, here it is. NSA intel has it figured this way. There's a resort being built in the Caribbean islands. The island is called Sprite Cay and it belongs to Nicaragua. Construction was started in 1995 and won't be finished until 2005. The construction company is part of a British corporation called the Golden Day Group."

"And Happa?"

"The records show that his jet left India and went back to Zurich. When it landed the pilot put in a flight plan for the island. The plane will cross American airspace there in three days on its way to Sprite Cay."

"And my mission?"

"Recon."

"Oh sure. Not that again."

"It never changes. You document the proof of a micro CD machine."

"What does it look like? You got pictures?"

"They only provided me with a general description." Sunny started laughing again. "Man, nothing ever changes."

"Right, but this time the NSA is providing the transportation there and back. Wait until you see what's arranged."

"All the backup I need?"

"That's what they tell me. They are assembling a secret strike force to take down the group. They will wait for your signal."

"So who's the Golden Day Group?"

"I got everything I'm going to tell you from my NSA contact. What I'm gonna tell you is classified so high it is almost one of those secrets where you die after you hear it." Delgado smiled a little bit. He fumbled in his pocket and took out a dime and tossed it to Sunny. "What if I tell you that I can turn that for you a trillion times?"

Sunny smiled and tossed it back. "I'd say that I'm in. How are you going to turn it?"

Delgado chuckled. "Only those invited into the Golden Day Group get to find out."

"So who are they?"

"They're three years old. You can look them up on the Internet. Like other investment cartels, such as the Carlyle Group, they just turn money." Delgado squinted his eyes trying to remember the details, then simplify them for Sunny. "They have a published rate of return of 30 percent. Now if you look at their board of directors you will see the most senior executives listed. But the NSA got the list of who directs the directors, and we saw an amazing thing."

"Yeah?"

"They were world actors who go to war against one another. They meet in the strangest of places, Calcutta, Sierra Leone, Nepal, anywhere there's strife; it makes for great camouflage. They go there to turn a buck on almost any deal in the world."

"Political integrity takes a second seat to graft."

Delgado rubbed his forehead. "The richest and most politically connected people in the world are on board with the Golden Day Group. You get what you want, even your own private island. This is a very cozy deal. They can tap in to the Middle East through all sorts of buffers and suck out all they want. The diamonds in Sierra Leone? Billion-dollar reconstruction deals in reemerging countries that they destroyed in the first place, oil, drugs, guns, it's all theirs."

"Wait," Sunny interrupted. "What Americans belong to the group? Is that known?"

"One look at the classified membership and you'll know. But you ask them and they double-talk it away."

"So the rich get richer." Sunny had seen the writing

on the wall—it took muscle and killing to hold it all together.

"You're telling me. The NSA believes that the Golden Day Group, with all its questionable dealings has clearly stepped over the line. But you tell me who is going to try to take them on, if not us. If they did steal the plans for the micro CD and build a reproducer, then Sprite Cay could be just the place where they have one."

"And Nathan Happa?"

"My bet is that he'll be at the Grand Jubilee."

"What?"

"The Golden Day Group does not have annual stockholder meetings; it has a Grand Jubilee."

Sunny felt his body freeze. He remembered how helpless he felt when he became immobilized by Happa's poison. Someone had wanted to take him to a jubilee, but Happa refused. He suddenly had the desire to jump on the first boat to Sprite Cay and meet Happa with a bullet as he landed. "How do I get there? What's my cover? I'm ready to go."

"Slow down, Sunny. One step at a time." Delgado could feel the heat off Sunny's body. "Cool off. Do some of that Zen stuff."

Sunny wasn't clear about a few things. "So is the Golden Day Group inner circle some black magicians?"

"No, not quite. I don't think so. But I think that you're right about the religious bent. With Happa I would speculate that whatever rituals the inner circle uses won't be symbolic. They'll be literal sacrifices. And there's a good chance that other members of the group are not aware of how involved these rituals are. They probably aren't invited to them."

"Well, I'll make sure to make it. Look, if I can find the reproducer and get the video and camera shots, do I blow it too?"

"No. The NSA was specific on that. Just get as many detailed pictures as possible and relay them back via an encrypted data burst. They will also provide the equipment you'll use."

"So after I do this thing. Can I kill Happa?" He owed Happa for many things.

"Once you send the shots you're to get the hell outta there, but if your man gets in the way of your retreat, nobody's going to say anything."

CHAPTER 26

**2230 / WEDNESDAY / 2 APRIL 1941
CENTURION CASTLE / GERMANY**

ILEEN HAD SPENT ENOUGH TIME IN CAPTIVITY TO assume that London had written her off. But she still had a mission to complete, a damned good one too, if she could only get the evidence. She had promised the president that she would retrieve evidence and she intended to do so. She hadn't yet cracked the microdot process lab, the most secret of secrets. But she had made progress. She was a recognized face in most places and usually went unchallenged. She was "Borz's bitch."

She still felt that Borz was a good choice to work for. It was a toss-up as to who was the vilest and most perverted, he or the other monsters in the castle. These were more than just war criminals; they were serial killers, crazy, perverted maniacs. In their minds they could do no wrong. No. To them the real truth was that they were delivering evil to a grateful world. But for Sybil she would not have had a clue as to what these people were all about. One way or another the evil had to be stopped. She had little hope of ever making a difference when an event happened that inspired her but triggered even more mad acts.

One night the Centurion Castle began to shake. Everyone was roused from where they were. The guards left their posts to see what was happening. In moments everyone was in the courtyard and looking to the north.

The sky was brilliant with light far away.

"Turn off all the lights! Turn them off this instant!" the baron cried out from the courtyard. "Now! Fast! Take cover, everyone."

Lights out; Eileen saw this as a chance to disappear. It could have been her chance to escape but instead she headed where duty led.

The door to the restricted wing was unlocked and unguarded. She could barely see but for candles lit in alcoves. She moved as quietly as she could. If the microdot room was close, she could take the processor and be out of there in minutes. It would be all over.

Following the hallway, she came to a locked door. It was simple work to unlock it. She went into the room and locked the door behind her. It was empty. The lights suddenly came back on and she almost jumped out of her skin. She heard yells to cut them off again, but before they did she saw something written on a slate board that intrigued her. It was a formula or code of some sort. Could it have been the one Rudolf Hess spoke of?

It took a few moments, but it started to come to her. She knew what it meant. It wasn't a literal code; it was a frequency. A document lay on top of a skull. She picked up the paper and compared it to what was on the board. The codes weren't quite right. She made a couple of corrections and stood back to look at the work. Like a person with perfect musical pitch, Eileen played the noises she knew so well in her head until she was skimming along the rhythm the code on the board made. Suddenly she felt like all the lights had been cut out, then she woke up on her back. Only seconds had passed and the lights were still on. She got up and wiped away the drool from her mouth.

"Oh my God," she gasped. Was that a seizure that she just had? And did it come from the kinds of noise the code made? If whatever code was on the board could be generated over the airwaves, it would be an ultimate weapon, unstoppable. She was dumbfounded. Enemy soldiers would just fall over. They could be dead if there was enough power generated into the frequency.

Without hesitation she grabbed the soft cloth hanging on a peg and vigorously erased the chalk until no trace of the writing could be seen. She heard the sound of a key in the lock behind her. She grabbed the paper and raced across the room to another door and tried the lock. It opened. She was out of the room and heard someone cry out.

"*Mein Gott!*"

Someone came running after her.

She went from door to door, hallway to hallway, only steps ahead of her pursuer before she was able to get through heavy wooded double doors and slam down the beam across them. She looked for an exit. There were none. There were no air ducts either. She was trapped. The voice on the other side of the room called for help and soon there was a concerted effort to batter the doors down.

A quick look around the room revealed that it was the same kind of icons that Rudolf Hess had brought with him, the sun and the moon, but these were affixed to the walls—it was a Thule temple, but a very small one.

The pounding on the doors grew louder as the door began to heave in and out. The lights suddenly went out. With nowhere to go an idea struck her when the lights went out again. She ran to the door quickly raised the wooden beam before they struck at the door again and got out of the way.

The doors came flying in, rebounded off the thick stone walls, and crashed into the guards rushing in. The whole effect caused confusion and pain among the stumbling guards. Eileen used the situation and the hair's gap between her and the door to slip out and get away.

On the way back to her quarters she heard the unmistakable droning sounds of high-flying Allied bombers heading west and to home after their raid. How she wished that she were on one of those planes. After hiding the paper she found her crew just as her name was being called. She was in luck and hadn't been missed. It was some hours later before all the lights came back on.

In the days after the British bombing of Germany the baron almost went mad with rage. All work stopped. The Centurion Castle and all its possessions were torn apart. The servants could only guess at the reason for the new lunacy.

Everyone was brutally questioned as to their whereabouts during the bombing. Eileen made it through a few questions before she was dismissed as being an imbecile. She walked past Otto Dick, who smacked his sap against a wall just waiting for his chance to use it on a lying suspect.

Whatever they had been looking for was gone and so were a few people who couldn't explain where they had been the previous night. Word came down that everyone was now suspect and punishments would be more severe until the culprit was captured. But other than general gossip no one knew what had been taken.

Eileen was secure in knowing that she was too minor to be considered a threat so she continued working with her crew, breaking away to do errands for Borz, or go exploring on her own. But her quest for the microdot continued to prove fruitless. She started considering the significance of the code that she'd memorized. Perhaps it would be wiser to forget about the primary mission—what was in her head was the key to an incredible weapon that could be used against the Nazis. The microdot or the code, she would have to make up her mind when it was time to leave, and soon. In the meantime she would collect all the intelligence she could on the Thules and their bizarre beliefs and hope to contact London somehow.

She'd grown tired of listening to the quasi-scientific,

pseudomystical, and total bull sessions in the lecture halls. The Thules took everything they said as truth. They believed that they owned destiny and all power. She finally caught a glimpse of the "powers" that they spoke of.

Gruppenführer Joachim Borz stood next to Eileen. The room was freezing. She wore a sanitary mask. Everyone else wore masks so all Eileen could see was other eyes. No one made eye contact. She wore a worn woolen coat but still shivered uncontrollably.

A swinging door opened and Grossman, the Nazi doctor, nodded at Borz. Borz bent over Eileen. His eyes were clear and sharp. He grabbed her behind her neck and squeezed hard. "You will follow orders. Do what your technician tells you. At no time will you stop. If you stop, you will die. Do you understand?" He let go of her, turned on his heel, and left the room.

Eileen followed the rest into a long blue tiled room. The lights were bright and harsh. She was in an operating room of some kind. Ten unconscious people lay strapped to metal operating tables held down by huge leather bindings. There were five men and five women. Each peson had three attendants dressed in gray scrubs and what looked like a doctor in white. On steel carts next to each table lay assorted wicked-looking scalpels and assorted saws, even a saw bolt cutters.

Tubes and electric cables ran to each of the bodies. The tubes snaked up the walls and across the ceiling and ran to large glass vats filled with a glowing green liquid. Next to them were big empty glass jars. The green tube ran from the green vats and clear tubes ran from the clear jars. Electric cables ran across the floor and connected to huge transformers.

It looked as if whatever was going on had been happening for a while.

The entire scene looked exactly like something out of the Frankenstein movie that she saw at the Avalon in Toronto. But this looked ten times bigger. She slowly scanned the room.

A long window ran the length of the room just behind the metal gurneys. Engineers manned consoles. She
saw the baron, Keller, and Borz behind a glass wall con-
versing to others through microphones. Grossman sat
above everyone else and moved like an orchestra con-
ductor.

Eileen could only watch and marvel at the strange
happenings. Generators whined and vats looked about
to boil over. A hanging green tube with a huge needle
was shoved into the left jugular vein of each body and a
clear tube was shoved into the right.

Her ears hurt and she was having trouble focusing
through the voltage fluctuations in the room.

"Now!" Grossman's voice commanded over a loud-
speaker.

Switches were thrown and blood began pumping out
of the first body from the clear tube. It gushed into the
clear container. The green liquid pumped out of the vat
and replaced the blood. The bodies began to have massive seizures, then abruptly went still.

In that instant, the three attendants and the doctors
went to work. They cut and sawed, then used the bolt
cutters to separate the head from the body. Dark red
blood flowed from the steel tables and onto the floor.

"Remove the carcass!" Grossman ordered.

Eileen followed her team pushing the carts. Dark
green goo began to ooze from the headless bodies. One
body after another was unstrapped and rolled into the
body cart.

"Help me roll the body onto the cart!" the cart man
yelled at Eileen.

She rolled the body from the metal slab onto the cart.
She caught a glimpse of a technician using a red-hot bar
to cauterize the oozing ends of the neck.

"Come, girl!" the cart man hissed.

Eileen was in too much shock to do anything else but
follow him out of the room.

She raced next to him as they banged through the
double doors and tipped over the cart in front of a large

oven just outside the castle walls. The body fell into a large container next to a huge incinerator.

Eileen tried to catch her breath, but vomited. Through her nausea she saw the way out—the gate she had gone through was open and unguarded. Apparently even the guards were forbidden to observe this work.

"You cannot stop now, girlie," the man said. "Come on, or I will report you to Borz!"

Her feet wouldn't move. Her mind couldn't deal with what she had just seen and done. One thing was for sure; she didn't want to go back into the horror chamber.

The man pushed her. "Fool! If you don't get your butt back in there, then we are both dead." He pointed at the headless body and blood pooling on the bottom of the rusted container. "What is left of them will all burn within the hour and no trace will ever exist, except for their heads. Do you want to end up like that?"

She weakly shook her head.

"Then let's go!"

Again and again, ten times they reentered the room and rolled out a headless corpse to be incinerated. The first few times she thought she would pass out. By the fifth time she was working up a sweat in the frozen room. Just what in the hell was going on? Still, no guards could be seen outside the castle walls.

The heads were now suspended from cables. The attendants were now engaged in connecting the heads to the monitoring machines.

The blue-tiled floors were slick with blood and gore.

"Time!" Grossman cried out.

Immediately the generators began to wind down. The ten heads were then lowered into huge jars and rolled from the operating room. It was over. Doors were open and a warm breeze began to filter in.

A mop was thrust into Eileen's hands.

"Clean!"

No one removed his or her sanitary mask. Eileen wondered if they did it for health reasons or to remain anonymous. What had just happened? She tried to use an analytical approach to what had just happened, but she couldn't. She wanted to scream. She wanted to drop the mop and run, but to where? It was a castle of horrors!

Dr. Grossman walked into the operating room, inspected some of the machinery and liquid levels left on the vats, and made checks in the folder he carried. He stopped in front of Eileen and brushed her aside to read the pressure on a nitrogen bottle.

Eileen saw the title page on his report: STYX.

For days after that Eileen woke up screaming, but screams in the night rarely brought any attention. She had to get out of there or she would go crazy. It wasn't a matter of spycraft anymore. The mission be damned! She didn't want to participate in any more Styx experiments. She had reached her limit. The thoughts of having to be around all the abominations for one second longer were too much. She wanted out and was inspired to take more chances. She was driven by the desire to escape. There was still no microdot, but at least she had the genetic disintegrator code to bring back. *Take what you can and go!*

She did a lot more exploration from the library air duct access. She tried every door she passed to see if it was unlocked or what was behind it, profusely apologetic and acting as if she had made a mistake on entering if there was someone in the room at the time. She quickly learned that unless there was a diversion, she would probably be caught in a matter of hours.

There was only one wing that she could not gain access to. She was sure that was where the radio room was located. It was guarded at all times.

One evening Borz had asked her to get a carton of cocaine. He was almost convulsing. "You stay there until it is in your hands, then bring it directly to me. You tell him that I said this is urgent!" He took a swing at Eileen but missed. He used Dr. Grossman as his supplier. Dr. Grossman's pharmacy was inside the Secure Area.

"I am on my way, my lord!" She raced through the castle waving her arms and acting frantic.

Grossman was not impressed. "You will wait one hour."

Saying that she had another errand to run for Borz she slipped into the shadows for a preciously short time. From the basic layout of the wing it looked like the opposite end from where the medical building was. That would mean that the air duct was connected somewhere. Carefully listening at each door, she made her way toward what she believed to be the radio room. She heard footsteps and voices so she ducked into the first unlocked door.

The room was bare but there was another door that was locked. It was simple to pick the lock with the pen she had lifted from Borz. She slipped in through the door and locked it behind her. There was a faint green glow coming from the black wooden cabinets that lined all the walls. When she opened one of the cabinets she had to cover her mouth to keep from crying out.

From the floor to the twenty-foot-high ceiling were heads in glass jars. There were all types and kinds of heads. It took intense focus, but Eileen read the labels on the front of each one. They described in detail what kind of head was in the jar, Jew, Korean, black, and where the current information folder was located.

Eileen estimated that there were at least a thousand heads stored in the room. A low light kept them all visible and there was an empty cart to move the heads around. It was as creepy as things could get.

There were no voices on the other side of the door so she felt that it was safe to leave. As she stood next to one of the jars something very strange was happening. Looking closer at the head in the jar it seemed as if it moved, or was that from the bubbles in the jar? She looked closer. The eyes suddenly opened.

Eileen couldn't breathe. That couldn't be real. She backed away and the eyes followed her movement.

She didn't wait for the coast to be clear but ran from the room and out of the wing at a full sprint.

She reached the pharmacy just as Grossman came to the counter with a small red package in his hands. She took the package and ran all the way back to Borz.

"Come here." There was desperation in his voice. He quickly and efficiently cut open the box and dipped a spoon into the box. He had a hypodermic syringe ready and waiting. He added a clear liquid to the cocaine and drew the cocaine up the needle. He was feverish and nervous.

Borz stood up and dropped his pants, heedless of modesty, and injected himself in the leg. He fell back into the chair and, with his eyes closed, began to hum. Eileen recognized the tune—it was the German national anthem.

"Do you know what we are doing here, *meinchen?*"

"No, Herr Borz."

"You must think that we are animals." His pants were still around his ankles. His legs were so white they looked like porcelain.

"I think nothing, Herr Borz."

"Come here." The slap did not catch her by surprise. "Don't you play servant games with me! Ask your question."

She rubbed her sore cheek. "Herr Borz, the operation, I have never seen anything like it. What was that all about?"

"We live and die, yes? But what if we did not have to die. What if death is just a stepping-stone? What if death was only one stop in a longer journey, a gateway to other dimensions? What if we could circumvent the death process? What if we could control what goes on the other side? What if we could come *back?*"

"Impossible." She couldn't help herself.

"Impossible? Impossible you say? You saw them back there. Some of the more successful experiments have been moved to the adjoining room." Borz smiled. "We have brought people back hours after their bodies have expired." He saw the shock in Eileen's eyes. "Yes, that is right. There are those of the Order who believe that only magic incantations will deliver our souls back into the present.

"Magic? Phaw! It is *science* that will bring about this event." Borz was on a roll now, forgetting that he was speaking with a mere servant. "There are those who believe that the Nazis are after world domination. No. It is not. The Freemasonic Order of the Golden Centurion will gain total *universal* domination."

Eileen shivered. He was mad. Worse, everyone in the castle was crazy. In that short span of time she realized that the war was just another tool of their madness.

Borz looked at her, feeling his naked body, rubbing his flaccid penis. "Think about it. When I am done with this body I will be able to replace it with a new, white, hard, leaner one. Adolf Hitler, do you not see how he stands defiant to our enemy's bullets and bombs? He *knows*. He knows that if anything happens, the Order will preserve his soul and put him in a new vessel.

"Material power, who would want that trifle when the power to conquer other dimensions is in our grasp?" Borz looked at Eileen and suddenly changed, awakened from his drugged ranting. "Oh what would someone like you understand? You are too low on the ladder. You are here to serve. How could you know about what is required to take these people over to the other side and back? It takes control of diet, strict discipline. Did you know that the ones being fed beer and opium tend to make the experience last the longest? Ah, why am I talking to a stupid girl? Hess understands."

Eileen bowed her head as if she had been hurt by Borz's insult. He pulled up her chin.

"Ah, *meinchen,* but I need you here. There is a piece of business I want you to help me attend to."

"Anything, mein Herr."

"Those papers you brought me, do you remember them?"

"Yes, my lord."

"There is a mole here who is stealing our secrets. I have found him and now I will kill him. You are the only one I trust to carry this out."

Eileen knew better than to ask any questions—speak only when spoken to.

"It will happen soon, so be ready when I call on you." He caressed her hair. "When your time is over I may put you into a pure Aryan body. Would you like that?" He let her go, pulled up his pants, and headed out of the room.

Alone, Eileen sat in a chair and began to sob. She didn't want to but couldn't help it. How could this happen? What other atrocities were being practiced in this castle of horrors? These people weren't just criminals, they were heretics! She had to get out of there. She had to admit that she was turning into a rotten spy.

All she wanted was to escape before she wound up on one of the cold steel operating tables.

CHAPTER 27

**0300 WEDNESDAY / 31 MARCH 2004
NEW YORK CITY HARBOR**

OKAY, WHERE IS IT?"SUNNY ASKED.

Delgado smiled. "You don't see it?"

"Man, don't play games with me."

Delgado reached into his pants pocket and pulled out a small device that looked an awful lot like an iPod and pressed a button on it.

In the bay Sunny saw movement just below the water. There was no wake, but he got the impression that *something* was in the water. From the dock where he stood the water boiled and hissed, then a huge, gray apparition rose in front of him. He gasped and jumped back.

"Your transport's here." Delgado laughed.

Sunny was awed. A creation right out of a Jules Verne novel had just appeared in front of him. It was about fifteen feet high, fifty feet long and thirty feet wide. Calling it a boat somehow didn't fit because it didn't look like a boat. It looked more like a long, angular pyramid.

"What is this thing?"

"Like I said, 'Your transport.' "

"Ah, screw off. You know what I mean."

"I know. What you're looking at is a test model that's

being looked at and tested by an NSA-related agency. It's called a submersible skimmer. Lockheed's made three of them. This particular one is 'in the shop.' It's not expected back online for two more weeks."

"So that's how long I got to do this thing."

"One week." Delgado handed the remote device to Sunny. "It works a lot like a car remote. Let me show you a few things on it."

Delgado went on to explain the finer nuances of how the doors opened on the vessel.

"Is this thing remote?"

"It can be, but it's so new you have a driver. But the project manager tells me that other than insertion and extraction points, you'll have little contact with him. Ready to have a look at her?"

"Sure. What's her name?"

"It has no name, just a number. You get the boat and the driver for one week. Please don't break it."

They went aboard and Sunny stepped into something that looked like the interior of a small C-17. It was space-age composite material. Delgado pointed out a video screen and a CD library.

"Put in the first one and it will walk you through how things operate." Delgado pointed to a door. "This thing is almost fully automated, but I insisted that you have a pilot. They said okay but the door to the wheelhouse stays sealed the entire time. You will hear your pilot but never see him. He has his own quarters and can separate from the rest of the craft in case there's an emergency."

"What?"

"Look. It's their clause, or no deal. You going to bitch?"

"No."

"Then let me finish. The second CD is your mission specifics. The moment you start it, it will totally erase in ten hours. It will cover the SATCOM system, camera system, your armaments; all that stuff. Make sure you have take it out of the machine because it will burn up just like the ones in *Mission: Impossible*."

"And if I have questions?"

"It's interactive."

"But you know the kinds of questions I ask."

"Well, you're out of luck there."

They covered a few ground rules—they both knew that Sunny called the shots.

THE SEAS WERE ALMOST SMOOTH. HE SAT IN THE FOR-
ward conning chair and looked out over the ocean. It was a strange sensation. He knew that they were moving, and fast. But when he looked aft there was no wake. It just didn't seem right. There also was no bow to cut through the water. The craft sort of moved on the water like a water bug. But, however it propelled itself, it was one of the most pleasant sea rides he'd ever experienced.

The hull of the ship had once been almost black as they left the Miami Harbor in the black night, but now it was an almost turquoise. Any passing ship or plane would never notice it. Sunny wondered how many billions went into the development of the craft.

"Mr. White," the intercom called. It was the nameless pilot of the boat.

"Yes?" White was the name the NSA assigned to him.

"We're coming upon some satellite runs in a few minutes and we have to be submerged for a bit. I want to test out a few things. Mind going below?"

"Not at all." He knew where the crew quarters were. Sunny stowed the conning seat back into its locker, then climbed below and closed the hatch, checking for a visual seal and CLOSED light on the hatch before going aft.

The up and down movement of the craft was smooth and soothing. The crew quarters could hold twenty men, a Humvee, and a trailer, or other combinations of men and cargo. The skimmer held exercise equipment like the Total Gym, Bowflex, and other portable, stowable, and highly effective exercise machines. Sunny started to work out. It was good to get his muscles toned and pumped. Clever levers and latches revealed other things like bunks, a weapons safe, and rations. It even had a sizable head and shower.

"Mr. White. You may follow our progress on the flat screen."

Sunny was hungry. The galley was fully stocked with frozen, microwaveable food.

They had another fifteen hours before reaching Sprite Cay. Sunny went over the CD library full of information that had been gathered on the Golden Day Group, its holdings, stockholders, and directors.

There was nothing on Nathan Happa. It seemed he had the ability to erase himself almost at will. It was just a hunch that Happa was at the cay at all, but it was the only one that he had going.

He was tired. He could continue studying, or sleep and study later. It was no contest.

0420

Sprite Cay belonged to Nicaragua, who leased the island to the Golden Day Group for ninety-nine years. It had formerly been the stronghold of such celebrated pirates such as Calico Jack Rackham and the Fox Pirate. Today it was a self-sustained private island.

A luxury sailing vessel was anchored about a half mile from the cay. Boats ferried passengers and supplies to and from the ship. Several salt barges were tied to anchors near the salt ponds. Radio transmissions from the ship to the barges and the cay said that they had to pull up anchor sooner than expected because a tropical storm was on the way. The pilot verified the same thing on his radar. It was about three days away.

Sunny knew that he could penetrate Sprite Cay. They made many stealthy passes around the key. They mapped the island from an NRO satellite. They took infrared and thermal readings of the small island. They even launched a small, remote spy plane, which revealed a great deal. Then they pulled out three miles and settled just below the surface while Sunny plotted out a plan while studying the imagery of Sprite Cay.

It looked just like what it was; a private company resort. It had luxury accommodations, pristine beaches, recreational activities, and unobtrusive security. People came and went, bathing, sunning on the beach, and water sports seemed to be the main activities. The little spy plane had followed one of the few trucks on the only road that led across the island to a salt refinery on the other side of the almost flat cay.

The airstrip was uncontrolled and had cows wandering the runway. Five private jets were parked on the tarmac. One of them had to be Happa's. The closest estimations he could make was that there were anywhere from five hundred to two thousand people on the island. There was no way to estimate the numbers of people it took to operate the place.

The Grand Jubilee. The people were there to party. Drinking and foolish things were bound to happen. He would look for those kinds of things to move around in unnoticed. But where could the micro CD be processed? Yep, he could penetrate, but what then? *And what if I run into Happa before I get the mission done?*

"When you are ready to make your insertion please give me the coordinates," the pilot said over the intercom speaker.

The almost flat cay was covered with barrier-thick vegetation. A previous thermal scan showed a small, dry riverbed, just wide enough for the skimmer to cut through and get Sunny to just yards away from a small, natural cave.

Sunny explored the cave. It was dank and earthy; he liked it. Further exploration revealed a man-sized hole that broke through the limestone and out into a scrub area. A short foray with night vision goggles and he found the road connecting the salt flats to the resort. It was perfect!

He went back to the skimmer and unloaded his supplies.

"Unless you give me an emergency signal I'll be back here in six days," the pilot said. "If you're not here, I can't wait. Good luck."

Sunny jumped onto land and backed away. The skimmer was gone. Sunny had six days to accomplish his mission, then kill Nathan Happa.

CHAPTER 28

**2015 / FRIDAY / 4 APRIL 1941
CENTURION CASTLE / GERMANY**

SHE PASSED THE DECANTER TO LUKAS KELLER. THE Styx project and the microdot were a wash as far as Eileen was concerned. She had the Thule code and that would have to do. There was little time to waste. Her escape had to be solid. There was only one way that she knew to cover her trail. She had to pray that Sybil would get the transmission or she was doomed. Getting out meant taking chances beyond all that she had done before. Taking chances? She couldn't wait to get out of the nuthouse!

"Well?"

"Herr Keller, do not drink the whiskey."

"Why not?"

"It is poisoned."

Keller looked at the goblet. "How do you know this?"

"I was the one who was ordered to put the poison in it."

"Who ordered you to do it, was it Borz?"

"Yes, my lord."

Keller eyed her suspiciously. "You are his mouse. And just why should I believe you?"

Eileen tried to make herself as pitiful-looking as possible. "He's taken a like to smaller women," she lied. "I, I have seen what he does to his women," she sniveled.

"And what do you want from me?"

"Sanctuary."

"You will need it after he discovers your betrayal," Keller chortled. "Why does he want me dead?"

"He believes that you are a mole. He thinks that you have stolen an important document."

Keller acted as if he'd been slapped. "*Me* the mole? I am the one who has the most to lose if this war takes a bad turn." He walked about his room thinking and speaking to himself. "This is bad. I will have to have proof to bring before the council." He looked at Eileen. "I may have need of you later as a witness, so I will give you a place to hide, if only for a short while. I am the communications officer and run a wing that is off-limits to everyone, including Borz. You will come with me."

The closet might have been small, damp, and dark, but it was just a few doors down from the radio transmission room. She knew that she was dead the moment Keller confronted Borz and prayed that it did not happen until after she got into the radio room. Being so isolated she was able to concentrate on how to code a simple but important message.

She waited until she heard the last radio tuner go silent, then she picked the lock and crept into the radio room. Having seen the setup from the air vent, she knew exactly where she was going. She powered up the transmitter and immediately began to pulse and ping the frequency transmitter.

LONDON

Sybil Leek sat listening to the noise in her headset. Everyone else had written off Number 26 as a lost agent. The mission was over—the plane she was in never came back. Sybil was handed a termination slip and assigned to another time spot. But she knew better and kept searching the airwaves. She heard the pulsing noises that only one person in the world would know how to do.

She wrote letters on her yellow notepad. Ten minutes later she was done, then she transcribed the code. The message read:

> *GREEN HORNET SENDS. CAN ONLY SEND ONCE. PROJECT EXISTS. NO SAMPLE. HAVE URGENT REQUEST. IMPERATIVE YOU BOMB THE FOLLOWING LOCATION AT EXACTLY 2130 TOMORROW. WILL MAKE OWN PASSAGE HOME. HESS IS THE KEY TO THE GAME. STOP. END. 26.*

Sybil noted the target location then ripped the translation from the pad and ran toward Ian's cottage. "She's alive!"

2130
NORTHERN GERMANY

The vibrations from the bombs landing close to the Centurion Castle shook the walls. Huge slabs of concrete cracked. People began to panic. The lights went off and on. It was time to leave.

Heedless of the danger from falling debris, she raced to the radio room and saw that there were no guards. The radio door was open and the room was empty.

Eileen raced to a radio operator's desk and began frantically tapping the keyer, sending out a coded message on the first open frequency she dialed. Done, she threw down the headset and raced from the place.

Several times she almost tripped from the incredible bomb blasts. Running down the tunnel, she felt like she was on a dragon as the tunnel began to buckle. She made it to the kitchen and climbed behind a tall freezer, then wedged herself on her back under the massive machine. If the thing moved even an inch in her direction from a bomb blast, she would be trapped.

She felt around and a panicky sensation gripped her. The Thule code wasn't there! What would she do now? She started to back out from beneath the freezer when she discovered a folded paper was stuck to the back of her hand. "Oh, thank God!"

Back in the kitchen she looked at the code once more and memorized it. It wasn't correct, but she knew where the changes went.

"You!"

Eileen froze. It was Gruppenführer Joachim Borz.

"What do you have there? You traitorous bitch! How could you do that? I was like your father." He covered the space between them in a second and prepared to backhand Eileen.

His hand came down and Eileen stepped into him and ducked as it swooped over her head. She used his momentum and pushed him to the floor, kneeing him in the groin at the same time. He gripped his testicles and screamed in pain.

"You sure were!" she yelled in English. "And I always wanted to do that to him." She took the paper she held and ripped it to shreds, then dropped the remains into a cooking fire. "So much for your 200-million-dollar code." If she'd had a weapon, she would have taken the time to kill him, but the sounds of the bombs were fading and she was losing her opportunity to get away.

The woods were dark and quiet, echoing every move and every step that she made. What did she think she was doing? But she had to get out of that madness. If the bombing destroyed even 90 percent of what was there, it would not be enough. Better to wipe it out completely. She hoped that Sybil received her last transmission, because it probably was just that if she were caught again.

She had to get back and tell all that she knew. But who would even listen to such an outlandish tale? Yes, there was one man who said he personally wanted to hear the tale. The president. He would listen. And he would do something about it.

The howling began. The sounds came from a far ridge in the direction that she was headed. She couldn't turn around.

"Oh no, not again!" *I'm not going to make it.* "I should've killed Borz."

There was nothing left to do but run. "I can make it. I know I can."

But before she even got one step a net dropped on her. The more that she fought to get out the worse she became entangled. Finally, she quit struggling.

"Little one, I see that you have survived the castle," a rough voice said.

It was Vincent, the huntsman. Eileen was not sure whether to be relieved or afraid.

"Will you run if I remove the net?"

"No."

He took off the net but held it ready to throw again if he had to.

There was nothing that Eileen could do but plead her case. "Vincent, I need help." She went on to describe the evilness that existed in the castle. She finished by saying, "I think you had better make up your mind quickly, the wolves are getting closer."

Vincent scratched his beard and nodded. "We go this way. I know where we can go. You hold on to my belt."

The moon was dark and Eileen was effectively blind,

so she closed her eyes tight and held on to Vincent. Soon the sounds of the wolves began to fade and Eileen felt a little safer. They came into a small house in a clearing. Vincent signaled for Eileen to be silent. They entered and Vincent closed the door and locked it. The lights came on. She was standing in front of a seated Borz.

"The game is over, *spy bitch!*" He spoke in perfect English. "I knew it was you from the start," he lied.

Vincent took Eileen's wrists and tied them behind her back. She looked at him with hurt in her eyes. He sneered at her. "You are not one of *us*. You do not know *anything!*"

"Leave us," Borz commanded.

Vincent gave a short bow and left.

"Do not try and escape," Borz said. A guard behind him held a pistol pointed at her heart. "He will fire the moment you try something, anything." He tried to get up but grabbed his scrotum and sank back in the chair. "I would have crawled to hell to get you."

There was nothing Eileen could do. No one was coming to her rescue. It was the end of the line. She tried to put her wrists on her hip but it was too awkward. "I ain't talkin', copper."

Borz gave her a feral smile. "Oh yes you will, you see, we actually *do* have ways of making you talk. And we develop new methods every day. You, my dear, will tell us everything that you know. You will be the subject of a new experiment. So save all your American wit; you are going to need it before we are done."

LONDON

Sybil had the message decrypted. It read:

> *GREEN HORNET SENDS. BOMBS FALLIING.*
> *ESCAPING. IF CONTACT LOST HESS IS*
> *PRIME TARGET. STOP. END. 26*

It was the last message ever received from Number 26.

CHAPTER 29

2325 FRIDAY / 2 APRIL 2004
SPRITE CAY / CARIBBEAN ISLANDS

THINGS WENT ALONG A LOT SMOOTHER THAN HE had expected. He remotely planted optical sensors from the skimmer and had great visual surveillance. There had to be at least three or four thousand people running around. They were rich and bizarre. They had their own sets of rules, hedonism being rule number one. The security seemed to exist as medics as the Golden Day Group investors indulged to excess of everything from drugs to sex and naked beach volleyball. It was a modern-day Rome in all its sleazy glory.

For all the man Sunny thought he was and his worldly ways, watching what was going on was a voyeuristic experience that went way beyond pornography; it was creepy. What did sick orgies have to do with the Golden Century and the micro CD? Now he understood why one of Happa's perverts wanted him there as a sex zombie.

"Well, whatever's going on, I sure won't find out sitting here." It was time to get moving.

There were plenty of clothes left over from parties on the small beach to put together a convincing outfit.

Wearing minimum clothing, just enough to hide his P99 pistol, he strolled rather freely—just more meat. He kept away from anyone or anything that might even remotely pass as a security measure. Eventually he had the area reconnoitered.

Breaking into one suite, he went through the room and its contents. The phone book had a listing of many services, including a whole sex listing. It was prominently noted on the cover that the fine for rape was one hundred dollars. This was no Disney resort.

The security turned a blind eye to everything but the No Entry zones in the Board Members' Quarters and at the salt flats. Entry into those areas then would be his prime objectives, but he first wanted to find some trace of Nathan Happa; he couldn't help it.

Sunny was able to melt into the crowds as they moved from one gala event to the next. They were the most pampered people Sunny had ever seen. What could he ever know about that kind of lifestyle? If Happa were there, he sure wouldn't be among a bunch of Golden Day Group investors playing volleyball in the buff. Sunny would make his next move to the other side of the island.

Three strands of barbed wire surrounded the No Admittance area in the salt flats. There were no ground sensors or cameras, only one guy on a quad came around and he could be heard from a long way off. The security still looked lax, but that could have been by design.

One hour of watching proved that the salt flat workers weren't working salt. Sunny recognized the white bales that were being embedded in the salt barges—cocaine. The salt exports were a front. Sprite Cay was a transshipment point for drugs, a lot of drugs if what they moved was a typical day. The Golden Day Group was sure diversified. He knew that documenting the scene with the digital camera would be useless—the NSA didn't want to hear about drugs. He took the shots anyway.

There were several long one-story buildings near a power plant. He crept along a low sand dune until he was near a building. Some of the security lights were out. Sunny felt for the picklock set in his survival vest.

The building was old. All the lights were out but Sunny could see well enough with his NVGs and infrared flashlight. Linoleum tiles lay loose on the floor. There was a musty smell to everything. He would've thought that it was abandoned but a light from the middle of the building drew him near.

The room was clean and scrubbed. It looked like some sort of medical room. A security camera was on the far wall. It was focused on a hospital bed in the middle of the room.

Sunny circled the room just out of camera range. A woman was strapped to a metal hospital bed. She was attached to several monitoring machines. Who was she? He got as close as he dared and looked at her. At first he thought that she was younger, but she wasn't. How old she was he couldn't begin to guess. She slowly opened her eyes and looked at him.

"Help me," she wheezed. "They are going to kill me. I am an American."

Sunny didn't understand what was going on but she looked so helpless that he had to do something.

SPRITE CAY CAVE

The convulsions came first, later the sweating. The woman was going through some very heavy withdrawals. Sunny had seen junkies and winos go through the same thing in alleyways of LA. She started screaming things Sunny couldn't understand. He gagged her to keep her quiet.

Sunny gave serious thought to returning the old woman back to where he got her before she died on him. There must've already been an alert when the security camera went blank. They probably went insane trying to figure out how the old woman got out of her bindings. He felt that he had made a big mistake but he couldn't help it—it was wrong to do that to an old woman. He would just have to wait until she either kicked whatever she was on or died. "I should've just left you," he whispered to her shaking form.

He knew that he'd royally screwed up when the island suddenly became infested with security teams on quads, motorcycles, and horses. The woman was important for some reason. All Sunny could do was lie low with her inside the cave. If the search for her went on much longer, he would never get his mission completed.

SUNNY WATCHED THE OLD WOMAN STIR. HER BREATHING seemed even and her pulse was strong.

She opened her eyes and looked around the cave. With effort she sat up. She looked as if she was trying to shake the fog she had been in. Focusing, she finally rested her suspicious eyes on Sunny.

"Hello," Sunny said with a weak smile.

The old woman licked her lips and he held out a water canteen. She took the canteen and, though parched, slowly drank while she kept Sunny in view.

"Who are you?" he asked.

She put down the water and tried to form a sentence but stopped, then croaked, "Who are you?"

"I'm the guy who brought you out of your sleep."

"You speak English well," she said.

"I should. I'm an American."

The woman smiled. "Sure you are. You rescued me from the Nazis, right?"

"What Nazis? There are no more Nazis."

The woman looked confused. She held up her hand. "Wait." She stopped paying attention to Sunny and looked at her hand. She ran her left hand up her right arm as if it wasn't really real. She felt her face all over. "Hey, do you have a mirror?"

"Yeah, a rescue mirror, right here in my survival

vest." Sunny unzipped the pocket and unwound the line wrapped around the mirror, then passed it to the old woman.

The woman took it and, seeing her face, froze in horror. "What have they done to me?" she gasped, then looked up at Sunny. "What have you done to me?" she shrieked.

Sunny was on her in a flash. He cupped her mouth. "Shut up, lady! They hear you and we got trouble, understand?"

He held her until she quieted down and just trembled. He let go of her and scooted back to his corner and sat down, watching as she sobbed quietly. "Lady, I didn't do *anything* to you. I got you away from some really creepy people. I'm one of the good guys. You've been going through some heavy withdrawals."

She looked at him through narrow eyes.

"If you're one of the good guys, then what year is this?"

"Two thousand four."

"Oh my God." Studying the mirror, she kept touching her face, not believing what she saw.

Sunny kept quiet and waited an eternity before she spoke, mostly to herself.

"Sixty-three years. How is it possible? I was a young woman back then. This is not possible."

"Ma'am?"

The woman eyed him for a long time. "If it's 2004, who won the war?"

"We did."

"Who's *we*?"

"The Americans, the Allies."

The woman once again got lost in wonder. She got up slowly and touched some of the modern gear Sunny had. "You got a name?"

"Sunny Vicam."

"Mr. Sunny Vicam. It's not a matter of your trusting me. This is the other way around. Tell me how you got me here, and start from the beginning. Don't leave anything out."

"It's a long story."

"Are we going somewhere?"

Like a confessor, Eileen listened to his story.

When he was done telling it, Sunny was awed by the magnitude and daring of what he had actually accomplished. His determination had brought him to a place that belonged to a people that controlled quadrillions of money and world power but were cracked and warped as they came.

The old woman smiled at him. "Sunny, my name is, is Number 26, and the last time I remember anything was in 1942. I was twenty-three then. I was on a secret mission."

Now it was Sunny's turn to be shocked. "You got to be kidding! It's impossible!"

"I only wish it was. The Golden Centurions, at least that's what they called themselves, kept me in a drugged suspended animation for at least sixty-two years."

Sunny was speechless. The Golden Centurions, the Golden Day Group, was it possible that they were the same people? "Okay, Number 26, you tell me your story, as much as you feel you want to trust me with."

When she was done it was all Sunny could do to hold a grip on reality and not let go. Only his compassion for the woman kept him anchored. Time had been stopped for her. She had been a zombie, never to know love or have her own children. *What must she be feeling?* Sunny said, "Do you think you can eat?"

"Honey, I could eat a horse!"

Sunny opened an MRE and heated it up.

Eileen was totally thrilled with the way it worked.

Soon they were like old friends, both with a million and one questions.

"Well, Eileen, what do we do now?"

"What are the options?"

"Like you, I've got my own mission to do, but I think I've blown it by getting you. I don't think I can make it out of this place anymore without being spotted. But we have enough stores to stay here for at least a week, then we can leave."

"You think that's our only option?"

"You got any better ones?"

"I could go back and do the ritual."

"What ritual?"

She explained that a tall man with platinum hair had recently revived her.

"Nathan Happa!" Sunny suddenly felt his heart booming in his chest.

"Is that his name?" She found herself flashing back to what he had said. " 'You will be the ritual offering.' He said, 'I will use the ritual to go into your soul. I will find the Styx code and bring it back, but you will not.' "

She almost passed out again remembering how his eyes suddenly glowed red. " 'No,' he said. 'It can't be! You are a *virgin*.' "

Sunny almost fell over.

Eileen shook her head. "Then he went into joyous passion figuring how much dark power he would be gaining by sacrificing an eighty-five-year-old virgin. 'I may rape you after you die, or before you die, or *while* you die.' I couldn't move and could only see him from the sides of my eyes. 'I know,' he said. 'I will just let the spirit take me away and let it happen naturally.' "

"That damned freak!"

"Sunny, I didn't know who he was. I didn't know that I was like *this* when he said it. He wanted the same thing they've wanted for over sixty-two years."

"And what is that?"

Eileen smiled. "Oh no, you won't get that out of me this easy. I still don't know who *you* really are, not yet. This could all be a trick, but for what has happened to my body."

"Number 26, I know about his sacrifices. So when will it happen?"

"I don't know. That's why I have to get back."

"What are you, crazy? I got you out of there. You can't go back."

"Do you think that I can get back my life from the bastards that stole it from me?"

"If we get out of here, you'll have some years left. If you go back, they're going to kill you for sure, and it's gonna be *nasty*."

"Look. So I die. I die. What else do I have to live for, and for how long? Right now I can go back there and blow whatever hocus-pocus bullshit this Nathan Happa has in mind. You can get on with your mission."

"And just how are you going to do that, Number 26?"

"Sunny, I may be old in body, but you have to understand that I'm *still* twenty-three in my mind. In the scheme of things I've just been trained in how to sabotage an operation and I have nothing to lose. No fear."

"But look at your body. You're *old*."

Eileen scowled and huffed at him. "When I was a kid everyone said that I was too *small*, *a girl*, and I used that against them to beat them. Now I'm *old* and *small*, and still a *girl*. To me that says I'm three times as powerful now!"

"All right! Yeah, screw it. What the hell, I'm with you. What can I do?"

"Do? You can back me up and be ready to make a quick exit for us when the time comes."

"It happens I know the drug that Happa uses on his victims, and I got the antidote. So, let me tell you a few of the things that I know about him."

CHAPTER 30

0730 SATURDAY / 3 APRIL 2004
SPRITE CAY / CARIBBEAN ISLANDS

GOLDEN DAY SECURITY FOUND EILEEN WANDER-
ing in a dried-out riverbed. Naked and dirty, she
mumbled incoherently. She was brought to the
board of directors' quarters and the jubilee suddenly got
serious.

Now there was a menacing force. Towels were thrown
at the stoned investors, who were ordered to their rooms.

At midnight ninety-eight select doors opened and one
man walked to the temple. Only one door of the investors was knocked on. That man was extended an in-
vitation to join the Grand Jubilee. The person either
accepted or declined. If he accepted a hood was put over
his head and he was led from the room. Those whose
doors were not knocked on had to remain in their rooms
under the threat of death if they left.

2330

Sunny scooted over the limestone walls. The wind had
picked up significantly. It was a warm, hot wind, but he

could feel cold breezes every so often. The cruise ship and any other ships near Sprite Cay had pulled up anchor and beat it to the north. Feeder bands of angry storm clouds blotted out the moon and began dropping sheets of rain.

The noise of the building storm provided great cover for Sunny as he moved onto the board of directors' grounds. He hid behind an old cannon. He could see hooded people being led to a churchlike building. A door blew open across the yard and Sunny saw a huge bank of computers before the door was slammed shut. *Bingo!* He would wait until everyone was in the church, then make a move on the computer room.

2430

The hoods were removed and the clothes came off. There was not much space in the room for ninety-nine people. These were the inner circle of the Golden Day Group. They shared the most secret and sacred bonds of the group. Most of the people were in their later years. A few were younger. Everyone was dressed in long, hooded, black robes but two, the white-robed initiate and the purple-robed demon of the Order.

A full-faced, ten-foot-wide sun made out of gold was on one side of the room and a five-foot-wide silver moon was on the other. A green marble altar was at the end of the room and the group was gathered at the other. A crystal knife lay on top of the altar. A few candles lit the sanctuary. The wind howled outside and the rain pounded down on the roof.

The man in the purple robe faced the group. "I am the lodge demon. You who are the select are here to bear witness to the power of the dark matter. We are children of the Black Sun. We serve that which is not light. Tonight one here will return to the Number One and one shall replace him. He shall become our Golden Centurion and the Golden One Hundred will remain. The blood will remain pure."

He turned to a gold tabernacle on the altar and pulled out a large copper bowl. It was encrusted with diamonds. A black velvet cloth covered the top of the bowl. He turned back to the men and put the bowl on an onyx stand. "But for our initiate, you will all line up in any order. It is time for Number One to choose the lodge sacrifice, our Golden Centurion."

0100

Sunny raced across the compound and began banging on the computer room door. The storm was pummeling Sprite Cay. "Let me in!"

The door opened a crack and Sunny was in. Two men stood at the same time. Sunny double-tapped the bigger man with his silenced pistol. He threw the little geeky-looking nerd against the wall and jammed the pistol right between his eyes. Taking a quick scan around the room, he saw that they were the only ones there. Still pinning the geek to the wall with his gun, he kicked the door shut. "Unless you're ready to die, you got three seconds to answer, where's that micro CD processor? One, two . . ."

0115

They had gone through seventy-six men. The seventy-seventh man followed the same pattern. He opened his hand but in it was a black marble. Audible gasps of relief could be heard from the men behind him.

The man looked at the black marble, shocked beyond belief. He trembled and handed it to the lodge demon.

The demon guided the Golden Centurion to the altar. "Priest, come forward."

Everyone moved aside as a tall, thin man made his

way to the altar. He led a small figure who was covered by a green shawl.

"Your witness to tonight's Grand Jubilee is a testimony to those who serve the Vril. But before the Dark Crossover is made there is an issue to resolve that has been before us for over sixty-five years. Tonight we recover our most powerful weapon."

The man in the white robe stopped at the head of the altar. He dropped his robe. It was Nathan Happa. He pulled off the green shawl the person next to him wore. Eileen was beneath it. She was painted yellow. Her eyes stared vacantly at nothing as she was laid atop the altar.

Happa climbed on top of Eileen. He raised his knife and moved it menacingly over her. He was taking his time, enjoying the prospect and orgasmic power that was just moments away. He was ready.

Blade point high in the air, he was at the peak of the ritual.

Just before he plunged the knife Eileen's eyes became focused and clear. She grabbed Nathan Happa's wrist.

"Here's what I think of your bugaboo voodoo."

Nathan was astonished at her sudden animation. This wasn't supposed to happen!

Eileen drove the stiletto deep into Happa's stomach.

All he could do was gurgle and fall over on her.

Eileen pushed him off, then stood up on the altar and spit on him. "Sunny!"

Sunny was beside her, machine gun at the ready.

The coven stood in total shock. No one moved— Sunny had the drop on them. It was time to call in the cavalry. He pressed the NSA Alert Monitor. In the nanosecond it took to press the button the video he shot of the micro CD processor was relayed directly from the camera to a satellite relay and downloaded into an NSA Cray computer. Sunny's mission was done.

Eileen picked up Happa's bloodstained green robe and put it on. She looked up at Sunny. "Shoot!"

The noise from Sunny's machine gun sent everyone

running from the room and out into the howling storm. Several people lay dead or wounded on the floor.

Sunny grabbed Eileen around the waist and high-tailed it out of there too. She was nothing to carry.

They were out in the middle of a tempest. People were running everywhere. Once again he was the bad guy. But it didn't matter this time. He set Eileen on the backseat of a golf cart and quickly showed her how the weapon worked. It only took a second.

"Got it," Eileen said. "Let's get out of here."

"Right."

When he stepped on the gas pedal, the cart lurched forward, making Sunny laugh. Here he was in the middle of another dicey situation, but this time he was plodding away in a *golf cart*.

He almost jumped out of his skin when the machine gun fired behind him. Looking around he saw Eileen blow out the windshield of a truck coming up fast behind them. The truck careened violently to the left and ran head-on into a palm tree. Sunny almost lost control of the cart.

"I can run faster than this!"

"You just keep driving. I'll keep shooting," Eileen said calmly.

Sunny saw that she was grinning widely. She was loving the danger. He couldn't blame her.

They were about to reach the beach but something was wrong. Where was the cavalry? Where were the boats and planes? Where was the invasion? A bad feeling started growing in his gut.

They got to the beach and headed toward the water. Big waves broke on the coral reef. There was no rescue coming. The only thing coming for them was more dark clouds on the horizon.

"Eileen, I think I've been set up." He should've been angry, raging, but instead he chuckled—it was the third time he'd been sold out by his own side. They were about to be taken and his main concern was looking bad in front of a World War II secret agent. "What do you think we should do?"

"Do? Honey, I don't know what you are going to do, but if they think that they can take me again, I'm going to die first; and I'm going to take as many with me as I can!" She got next to the cart and laid the machine gun on the backseat for support. She smiled through the pouring rain. "Well, at least a Nazi sub ain't after us!"

Sunny loved her spirit. He pulled out his pistol and crouched beside her.

The spotlight cut through the storm and pinned them, but the light came from the ocean.

"Come aboard, Mr. White."

It was the skimmer!

Sunny grabbed Eileen. "We're outta here!"

They were aboard the skimmer in seconds and moving out to sea before anyone on Sprite Cay even knew that they were gone.

Once aboard and all the hatches had been dogged down Sunny dropped two berths from the wall for him and Eileen. They fell on them exhausted.

Sunny came to and looked at Eileen, who was up and walking around, still carrying the machine gun.

"This really is 2004?"

"I told you that already."

"And you really are one of the good guys?"

"I told you that too."

"Then you saved my life."

"You could say that too."

She took a deep sigh and held out her hand. "I'm Number 26, Eileen Weiss."

Sunny shook her hand.

"So who drives this thing?"

"I don't know." He pointed toward a sealed forward hatch. "He drives it from there."

"Well, I want to see him. Can you talk to him?"

"Yeah, like this." He reached over and pushed an intercom button. "Hey, pilot?"

"Yes, sir."

"Thanks for coming to our rescue."

"Who are you, honey?"

"Mr. White, is that a *woman's* voice?"

"It sure is," Eileen answered. "And if you don't open that hatch so I can thank you, face-to-face, then I'm gonna blow it off."

"Mr. White, who is she? And is she serious?"

"Have a look for yourself." Sunny saw the remote cabin camera move toward Eileen, who was pointing her weapon at the forward hatch.

"Mr. White, you know what you signed for." There was desperation in his voice.

"I know what I signed for, not her."

In a few moments the forward hatch wheel turned and the hatch opened.

Eileen lowered her gun. "What's your name? Where ya from, China?"

"I'm Korean-American, ma'am. My name is Kim."

"And what name do you call this boat?"

"It doesn't have one, ma'am."

Sunny got off his berth and walked up to the pilot. "Why did you stay for us when the NSA didn't."

Kim turned red. "Mr. Delgado told me that he'd kill me if I didn't return with you. I believed *him*."

"I see." At that moment Sunny knew he had a trusted friend.

Eileen climbed close to Kim. "Kim, your name's not Kim with me, it's Kato, and this boat is now called the *Black Beauty*. Where are we going, Sunny?"

"Home."

"Home? Sunny, you don't know how good that sounds right now."

EPILOGUE

IT WAS A COLD BUT BRIGHT MORNING IN MANHATTAN. Sunny and Frank sat on the benches that looked toward the Statue of Liberty.

"You got the old lady stashed away?"

"I do." Eileen and Sally hit it off like old friends. "And thanks for making the Black Beauty come to our aid."

"I had to. You were my investment. Did you kill Happa?"

"Hard to say, but the last time I saw him he had a knife sticking out of his belly. So what happened back there?"

"It was a shell game and we both got played like peas."

"What do you mean?"

"The information you sent was technology that they *never* had."

"What?"

"That's right. That's why they couldn't give us any hard specifics on what you were after. The Golden Day Group has pioneered the technology from God knows where, and we were after it. Check that, *someone* on our side saw the opportunity to get at it. We were the pawns that they used. That's why there was no backup or extraction for you. There's no money for us but what we already got. Right now secret diplomatic channels are being pumped. I got privy to some of what went on. It's said that you killed many of their members and I can't help but feel that the Golden Day Group wants heads to roll for that. Unfortunately, they have the connections to do it. They want the old woman back and you dead. I'm in the shit because I was on the contract. We both have to go real deep cover."

All that Sunny wanted to do was break things. It was the second time he'd been betrayed. "Do you have any good news?"

"I might have a name behind the whole deal. I think you'd be interested."

"Yeah?"

"It might be the same person who did you in South America."

Now Sunny wanted to pull out his guns and shoot things. "So what's the deal? Are we in this together?"

"Sunny, we are in this together whether I like it or not."

"Who has our backs?"

Delgado watched as a ferry left for the Lady in the Harbor. "Remember when I told you about your Shit touch?"

"Sure."

"You've started a secret intelligence house war that rivals anything that's ever been. Who knows where this will end."

"So now what?"

"So now get ready for war. It's going to be a fireball."

ABOUT THE AUTHOR

Michael Salazar was an Air Force combat search and rescue loadmaster for twenty-three years. The Meritorious Service Medal, Aerial Achievement Medal, Humanitarian Service Medal, and the Kuwait Liberation Medal are among his many decorations. He lives with his wife and children in Florida.